LOVE, MURDER, & MAYHEM

COSMIC TALES OF THE HEART GONE DEADLY WRONG

EDITED BY
RUSS COLCHAMIRO

CRAZY 8 PRESS

From "A Goon's Tale," by Kelly Meding:
Supers Battle Damage was an expensive policy, because collateral damage was as likely to dent a mailbox as level an entire neighborhood block, so the average homeowner didn't have it, and so far, the police hadn't put it together that their burglary victims also had that special policy. Bonus for Rocky. Plus, the cops didn't have any reason to suspect the burglaries were linked. Rocky didn't have a signature move and he didn't go in the same way each time, or target the same merchandise. Avoid patterns, and the cops stay off your trail.

From "This Mortal Coil," by Peter David, Kathleen David, and Sean O'Shea:
My lover, whom I have never met, is dead. I do not know her name. I have no idea where I might have met her. Her voice keeps changing every time I hear it, its tone shifting depending on what is being discussed. But she is beautiful and she is mine.

From "DuckBob: Killer Service," by Aaron Rosenberg:
"Manual input? Fine, you want manual input, you got manual input!" I shout. I leap over the coffee table, startling the servitrons enough that I'm able to bat two of them aside with the book, and charge through the gap. They all turn on me, of course, but I'm already past them and making a beeline for the door to the Matrix room. Because of course the house's main generator sits in an alcove off there, and that's where I'd plugged Iris in.

This is going to be fun—on the same level of "fun" as watching your own root canal in real-time, without anesthetic, as performed by an old blind man with palsy and a small blowtorch instead of a scalpel. This is what I get for trying to make my life easier.

This anthology is dedicated to the memory of Craig Nass.
Travel well, my friend. I can hear your spirit on the wind.

CONTENTS

A GOON'S TALE
by Kelly Meding

"GOT A LIVE ONE FOR YA!"

Dick screeched out the words the moment Rocky Mills barreled into the office with coffee on his shirt and a lot of steam in his head. After an intensely crappy morning, Rocky wasn't in the mood for another bad lead.

Rocky stopped in the middle of the small office space he shared with Dick Smalls at City Fields Insurance and took a deep breath so he didn't snap at the guy first thing. Dick had been transferred into Rocky's two-man division that handled Supers-related insurance claims six months ago, after Rocky's previous coworker was accepted into the Heroine Society as an apprentice, and Dick was a talkative pain in the ass. Constantly nattering about how much he loved this job, loved meeting clients, blah, blah, blah. He had no clue Rocky had taken the job out of necessity, not love.

Insurance adjuster was miles from where he'd planned to be at this point in life. Except Rocky knew firsthand how fast plans could change. Since Rocky was already in a crap mood, he took silent revenge by referring to his coworker in his head as Dick, instead of the insisted-upon Richard. The name Dick Smalls gave Rocky a secret smirk on his worst days.

"I sure hope you've got a live one for me," Rocky said. "You know I don't like life insurance or accident claims, not even for Supers incidents."

"Home insurance claim from last night's fight between Despair and The Resistor. Should be a good lead."

Rocky glanced behind him at the still open door. Anyone could have walked by when Dick said "a good lead." It was no wonder Dick was still a bronze-level Goon. Two levels below

Rocky, who had finally achieved gold-level last year. It was the highest level Rocky could ascend to before apprenticing for actual Villain status.

SuperVillain status was his dream now, and almost everyone had to start from the bottom as a basic Goon. Very few exceptions shot right to SuperVillain nowadays. Too much competition, not enough talent. Rocky had the talent *and* the motivation. He needed the power that came with the Villain Guild in order to right a very important wrong.

Rocky shut the door to their shared office, then dropped into his desk chair. "I'm in no mood," Rocky snapped. "My alarm didn't go off, so I barely had time to shower. I spilled my coffee in the car, I have a flat tire I need to fix on my lunch break—and don't get me started about the ride in just now—and I can't even eat my damn lunch, since I left it at home because I was running late. If you're over-selling this lead, I won't be responsible for my actions."

"It's for real, I promise." Dick dumped a data sheet on Rocky's desk. "Look at the guy's address."

Rocky picked up the sheet, then low-whistled. "Cherry Falls. Nice. The guy's got credit for sure, if he can afford a place there." Cherry Falls was one of the wealthiest neighborhoods in Star City, and they didn't have a lot of Supers insurance carriers out there, since Supers battles rarely spilled into that side of the city.

He scanned the rest of the claimant's personal information. Jared Collins, forty-seven, self-employed, six-figure salary. Premium policy holder, which required the personal touch before any damage could be repaired. The personal touch meant a home visit, which Rocky detested, but it gave him a great opportunity to case the place for future burglary.

As a gold-level Goon, Rocky had more freedom to commit his own crimes than lower level Goons. He still reported to Lady Shield, the Villain who'd sponsored him as a Goon, but he didn't need her permission. All he had to do was make sure she got her cut.

Another advantage to being two levels above Dick was that Dick had to give Rocky first shot at any potential leads, like

Collins's house. "Good job," Rocky said. "I will absolutely follow up with Mr. Collins this morning."

"Awesome." Dick circled over to his own desk, smiling like an idiot. "If it works out, maybe put in a good word for me?"

"Yeah, sure." Not. They didn't have the same sponsor, and no way was Rocky mentioning Dick to Lady Shield. The guy would never make it past bronze if he didn't wise up and take some risks. Risks like not always giving Rocky the best leads, keeping one or two for himself. Not following the rules had helped Rocky's own ascent through the Goon ranks, but he wasn't about to give Dick advice. He liked the guy dumb and useful.

The time stamp on the sheet caught his eye. "Wait a second," Rocky said. "Didn't the fight between Despair and The Resistor happen at around three in the morning?"

"Yeah, I think so. Why?"

"Because Collins didn't call in the damage claim until half an hour ago."

"Maybe he slept through the damage?"

Rocky rolled his eyes as he pulled up a damage report on the city's website. The battle had lasted about twenty-five minutes, after starting in the mountains outside the city. The Resistor found Despair's lair and Despair had fled for the city in a jetpack. The Resistor could fly, so she'd followed. The rest of the battle happened four miles from Cherry Falls, but it was on the map as part of their trajectory.

Indirect home damage, probably, from either laser blasts or falling shrapnel. It was still unlikely Collins totally slept through something hitting his house hard enough to damage it, but Rocky had lived through stranger things in his life.

He made the official call. Collins answered promptly, and they arranged for Rocky to view the damage in an hour. It gave him enough time to replace his flat tire with a spare, and then run home to change out of his coffee-stained shirt. Showing up looking like a rumpled mess would reflect badly on the company, and he needed this job. The leads he got were infrequent, but usually led to fantastic scores, and he needed to keep Lady Shield happy. She was the one who decided when he was ready to ascend to Villain status.

He used the drive to Collins's home to grab a fast food coffee, which went down the hatch by the time he arrived at Cherry Falls in a crisp new shirt. The homes there were large without being ostentatious, with wide, tended lawns and attached two-car garages. Matching white and blue painted exteriors and matching shrubs suggested militant home owner's association. No yard fences.

The Collins house was tucked away in a cul-de-sac, which had its own faults and benefits for burglaries. Rocky didn't have to look at the curb numbers to know which home was his target, because only one of the three had a large, obvious hole in the roof. No cars were in the driveway, so Rocky parked there. Gathered up his tablet and pen to take notes. Mentally slid into Professional Mode to keep earlier frustrations from affecting the client. Then he clipped on his City Fields Insurance nametag, which also doubled as a visual recording device—definitely not company issued.

Mr. Collins was standing on the small front porch when Rocky approached, hands loose by his sides, wearing a suit and a benign expression. For someone who worked from home, the suit seemed odd, but whatever floated the guy's boat. The closer Rocky drew, the bigger Mr. Collins seemed to get. He was a solid wall of muscle, at least six-five, maybe more. Huge compared to Rocky's more pedestrian five-nine. Squared-off jaw, crew-cut hair, more military in his look than . . . well, whatever his day job was.

Mr. Collins's unusual size made him unexpectedly intimidating and Rocky's professional demeanor slipped. He misjudged the first step up to the porch, and nearly fell off. Mr. Collins reached out with incredible speed—more so than would be expected of a civilian—and grabbed Rocky by the elbow. The save was embarrassing, but far less than grass stains on his butt.

"Thank you," Rocky said, answering in Professional Mode and making nice with the client "I'm not usually such a klutz, I promise."

"Not a problem," Mr. Collins said. "We all have those moments. You must be Mr. Mills."

"Oh, please, call me Rocky. Pleasure to meet one of our clients, although not so much under the circumstances."

"I understand, and please, call me Jared."

Something about the man's voice made Rocky hesitate. Familiar, and yet he didn't recall Jared's face. He'd remember a guy that big, for sure. "Jared, of course. Shall we go inside?"

Jared opened the front door and gestured for Rocky to enter first. The foyer was tastefully decorated in dark woods and gold finishes. A living room to the right offered similar décor. The smell of something recently burned tingled Rocky's nose. Jared led him through a formal dining room to a glaringly bright kitchen. The sun shined down through a car-sized hole in the kitchen ceiling, which went up through the second floor to expose the sky. A large scorch mark and some melted metal were all that remained of the kitchen island.

"My goodness," Rocky said. "Did this wake you when it happened?"

"I hate to admit it, but, no. I have trouble sleeping, so most nights I take something. They usually knock me on my ass for at least six hours."

"I see." Definitely explained not finding the damage until the next morning, or did it? Sleeping pills were one thing. But your house being ripped apart? "Well, we can get somebody here today to put a tarp over the roof. We're supposed to have nice weather for the next few days, but no one wants unexpected bird droppings in their home."

"Bugs or squirrels, too," Jared said with a wink.

"Good point." Rocky stepped back and started taking pictures with his work tablet for the official case file. He'd copy them all to his personal tablet later, for potential future use. Nice house means nice stuff. "Seems like a case of very unexpected collateral damage from last night's battle."

"Who was battling? I haven't had a chance to watch the news."

Surprise jolted through Rocky. Jared seemed wide awake and well put together, and there were dishes in the drying rack, which suggested he'd eaten breakfast as well . . . but hadn't checked the news? Not even on his personal tablet or phone? Strange. "Despair and The Resistor. Probably one of her power-bolts that did the damage."

"Sounds about right. The edges of the hole are incredibly

even. Her power-bolts could do that."

Rocky took more photos, while also scoping the interior of the home, mentally cataloguing things to steal. "You follow the Supers closely?"

"Hard not to nowadays. There's a fight of some kind almost every day."

"Too right. Is that why you added Supers Battle Damage to your home insurance plan two months ago?"

Jared's lips twitched. "Something like that."

Odd reaction and response. Rocky filed it all away. Jared was proving unpredictable, which made him question whether or not Rocky could effectively burglarize the house later without getting caught. People with predictable routines were easier marks. "Shall we go see the second floor?"

"Of course," Jared said.

They passed through a short hallway with a nice oil painting Rocky could hock for decent cash. The painting was crooked, in contrast to the perfect order of the other rooms. In the craziness of waking up to find a crater in his roof, Jared probably hadn't noticed. If, in fact, Jared was telling the truth about sleeping through the battle damage. But why lie?

Rocky made it his business to notice everything, such as the glass hutch with antique glass pieces and a few crystal decanters. More art lined the wall of the staircase they ascended. The second floor carried the same burned odor as the downstairs, only less obvious.

The hole was in a small bedroom, which was now missing half of its bed and a section of the floor. More expensive artwork on the walls, a pair of vintage fairy lamps on either bedside table. The furniture was decent quality, but too hard to move quickly. Rocky took his pictures, careful to keep the goods within the shots so he could do more research later. No sense in bothering with something if it wasn't valuable. The higher the score, the happier his sponsor.

"Well," Rocky said, "you'll need quite a few necessary repairs. The structural integrity of the house seems to be intact, but two floor replacements, plus the roof and a new island. And whatever payout for damage done to your furniture and personal property."

"I've lived alone for ten years, not been much of a social creature," Jared said. "It'll be odd allowing strangers into my home."

Ten years was a long damned time to stay holed up in your own house. In some ways, Rocky could relate. His wife had died around the same time, and for the first couple of months, he'd barely left their apartment. He'd lost his job. He'd wallowed in his grief and self-pity, until anger took hold. Anger at all of the happy, joyful people in the world who had what he didn't. That anger and resentment had led him to pledge the Goon Guild. He'd lost his family and his career trajectory to senseless, horrible tragedy. Villainy gave him a purpose in life.

Not that he was about to suggest Jared look into the Goon Guild as a way to get out of the house and be more social.

"We only work with companies who have the highest satisfaction ratings, Jared," Rocky said. "We'll make sure your belongings are protected and that you don't feel uncomfortable in your own home."

"I appreciate that. Honor above duty."

Rocky blinked at the phrase, something he hadn't heard in a long, long time. Jared was gazing at the hole in the floor, not paying attention to Rocky, so he studied the big man's profile. Tried to imagine it with a blue and red cowl outlining that very square jaw. A masked man saying, "Honor above duty," in Jared's voice.

Adrenaline rushed through his bloodstream, leaving Rocky momentarily light-headed. The impossibility of the coincidence didn't matter. He'd found him. Rocky's own job had led him into the home of Jared Collins, aka missing SuperHero Gauntlet. Gauntlet had been the most popular SuperHero of his time, beating every Villain and SuperVillain who opposed him. And then a decade ago, he vanished. No one had a clue as to where he went, not even city officials who were charged with monitoring the city's Heroes and SuperHeroes—or if they knew, they weren't saying.

The SuperVillains Guild had put out a hefty bounty on Gauntlet, which only increased after his disappearance. Finding him alive would be a shoe-in for SuperVillain status.

And here was Gauntlet in the flesh. Ripe for Rocky to pluck and see his own dreams rise to fruition. And to gain the power he needed to exact his revenge.

The pay raise wouldn't hurt, either.

"Yes, well," Rocky said, "we do our best to treat our clients like family."

"I'm sure your clients appreciate your discretion."

"I think I have enough information to get started processing your claim, Mr. Coll—excuse me, Jared."

"Shall I walk you to the door?"

"No, that's all right, I can find my way. I'll be in touch."

"I'm certain you will."

Feeling a tug of tension and mystery in the comment, Rocky turned and slowly made his way downstairs, noting every antique or piece of sellable technology. He didn't notice a security system anywhere, not by the kitchen's back door or the front door— stroke of luck that saved him time and energy. With a good mental map of the home in his head, Rocky left the house to process the claim.

And to also begin planning how to capture a retired Super-Hero.

Rocky bolted from the office the moment the clock hit quitting time. He'd been antsy the rest of the day, unable to focus on work and snapping at Dick more than usual. As much as he wanted to shout to the rooftops about today's discovery, he couldn't. They'd only want in on the capture, and Rocky wanted the money and acclaim for himself.

He didn't go straight home. Couldn't concentrate there. Whenever he had a new job to plan, he went to Dameron Rest to visit his wife.

Dameron Rest wasn't the nicest resting home for remains, but it had been the best Rocky could afford at the time. They'd been struggling financially when Rita died, and the hospital no longer released encapsulated remains without proof of an internment spot. But he wanted to hold his beloved wife in his arms one last time, or, at least, hold the airtight container with her fully dehydrated, pressure-compacted corpse inside.

Rocky was old enough to still remember the inefficient methods of burying or burning bodies. The rise of both Heroes and

Villains pushed the annual death toll far beyond the capacity to handle remains the old fashioned way. Rest Houses, built high into the sky, and dug deep into the ground, were much more efficient.

The drive to Dameron Rest didn't take long. The building always reminded him of Medieval guard towers, all squared off and stone walls. Cold. But affordable and private. No one cared if you sat near your wife's interment spot with a tablet and planned your next crime.

Rita was on the fourth underground level, where the air was always damp and chilly. He approached the nameplate with "Rita Angelica Mills, Beloved Wife." Together since they were teenagers, he and Rita had been each other's only family as adults. Their sole support systems. One half of the other's heart. Something inside of him had broken the day she died, never to be repaired.

"I'm going to do it today, baby," Rocky whispered, despite being alone in the small room, its walls lined with similar square panels and nameplates. "Well, not today, but tonight. Tomorrow. Whenever. I found my ticket in."

His heart ached with loneliness and regret. "I know this isn't the life you wanted for me," he said, Rocky's previous goals to conquer the private hedge fund world, his wife, as a fashion designer. He brushed a single finger over her first name. "But we never got the chance, did we?"

More than her untimely death, Rocky raged against her unsolved murder, her case declared cold after less than a year, the police ceasing to give a shit. No one deserved to die like that—neck snapped and throat slashed. Left for the alley cats to find. Definitely not his wife, his love. Rocky had taken a lot of beatings over the years, the struggle just to be alive, but this had been too much. He'd discarded his old life, and embraced a new one as an eventual Villain and SuperVillain. No other road existed for him.

"Once I have the power of the Villains Guild behind me, I'll avenge you," he went on. "I'll find your murderer and make him pay. I swear it on my own life."

His soft voice echoed in the otherwise silent room, until it was quiet once more. He listened with his heart, hoping to hear his beloved's voice again. To encourage him. To say that she loved him, and that she believed in him.

Except Rita had admired the Heroes Society. Honest, fair, and kind, she'd been a fan of Gauntlet himself during the height of his fame. But Rita was the last person who'd cheer him on tonight. The last person to say, "Go for it! Disrupt this man's quiet life so he can be publicly humiliated by the Villains Guild and eventually murdered." That's what Villains did. They humiliated and murdered their enemies. They tried to silence all who opposed them through fear and intimidation.

Rocky had come to admire those traits; Rita hated them. She wouldn't hate Rocky for doing what he planned to do, but she'd be sad. Regretful. She never wanted that for him.

"I'm so sorry, my heart. I need the power that I can only get by rising to SuperVillain. This is the only way you'll get justice. The only way I can get it for you."

He'd find her murderer, and kill them with his own two hands.

Right after he scooped up Gauntlet and delivered him to Lady Shield.

Going for his mark the same day he walked the house was a calculated risk. Rocky preferred to wait several weeks before burgling a house he'd cased through the company. In his three years with City Fields, he'd never once been a suspect in any crime against a client, his office never implicated.

Supers Battle Damage was an expensive policy, because collateral damage was as likely to dent a mailbox as level an entire neighborhood block, so the average homeowner didn't have it, and so far, the police hadn't put it together that their burglary victims also had that special policy. Bonus for Rocky. Plus, the cops didn't have any reason to suspect the burglaries were linked. Rocky didn't have a signature move and he didn't go in the same way each time, or target the same merchandise. Avoid patterns, and the cops stay off your trail.

And it didn't matter if they knocked on his office door tomorrow. By then, Rocky would have captured Gauntlet. He'd be rich from the bounty and wouldn't need that crappy job anymore.

Goons of any level weren't worthy of costumes or disguises, so Rocky went in wearing all black and a black ski mask. Old-school and effective. He had a few gadgets up his sleeve, thanks to his mentor, including midnight darts and unbreakable restraints. At two in the morning, Jared should be fast asleep in his bed, so breaking in and getting him into the van should take less than ten minutes.

After twice reviewing his recorded footage of the house, Rocky had confirmed that the house had no security cameras or alarm system. Even so, after he parked the van in Jared's drive-way, he used his standard issue Goon scanner to double-check for any signals that could tip off the cops. Standard issue for gold-level Goons, anyway.

Nothing pinged the sensor. House was clean.

Rocky slipped out of the van as quietly as possible. The neighborhood was dark and quiet. Perfect. He slipped into the backyard, watching each step on the grass to avoid fallen branches that could snap beneath his weight.

Lock picking was an entry level skill required of anyone wanting to pledge the Goon Guild. He palmed his kit as he climbed the three cement steps to the kitchen door. Used his tools with practiced ease to pop the lock on the backdoor. Turned the knob slowly, then tested the door. No additional bolts or chains in place. He slipped inside, then shut the door behind him. Easy peasy.

Almost too easy.

As promised, a team had been sent over to cover the roof's hole with a tarp, which cast the kitchen in darkness. Rocky avoided the melted mess that had been the island and made his way on silent feet to the back hallway, following the route Jared had taken him to the staircase. Wooden steps had a tendency to creak, even in the newest of homes, but these were carpeted.

He palmed his midnight dart pistol, his pulse suddenly racing, adrenaline coursing. His future was less than twenty feet away, sleeping in one of the bedrooms. The footage of the house hadn't pinpointed the master bedroom, but at least he knew Jared was not in the one with the hole in the floor.

At the top of the stairs he paused to listen. Silence. He used his scanner to locate large heat signatures. His own popped onto the screen immediately. The scanner could locate signatures within thirty feet, through one layer of wood or concrete, but it was having trouble finding a second body.

No. No way had he planned this only for Jared not to be home. The scanner flashed with a weak, pink light. More than one layer of material was between them. The house didn't have an attic, which suggested a basement. Weird. What the hell would Jared be doing in the basement at two in the morning?

The guy was an ex-SuperHero who'd been hiding for ten years. Anything was possible. Maybe he was a closet serial killer? Maybe he had a pot farm? Who knew, and who cared? Rocky had a fugitive to capture.

He eased his way back downstairs, the heat signature warming with each step. The kitchen didn't have a basement door, so he began a slow search of the rooms. The signature was beneath him somewhere, so there had to be a door, a hidden panel, something. Anything to indicate—wait.

A perfectly ordered home. Something out of place.

Excitement sparking, Rocky returned the back hallway between the kitchen and the staircase. The oil painting he'd admired earlier in the day was still hanging crookedly. A crooked painting first thing in the morning could mean many things, from tilting when the power-bolt hit the house, to the wall it hung upon moving to reveal a secret passage.

Hung precisely at eye-level, the painting was at least five feet wide and three feet tall, with a heavy gilt frame. Big enough to hide a safe or similar secret. And still being crooked so many hours later felt too much like a clue.

Or an invitation.

He tucked his pistol into its holster, then lifted the painting off its hook and leaned it against the opposite wall. Sure enough, the painting had hidden a secret. Maybe not one the average criminal would notice, but Rocky did. One spot of the ivory-painted wall, at about the same height as one might install a doorknob, was a palm-sized smudge. The kind of lightly gray smudge that appeared after years of repeatedly touching the same area of painted drywall.

A small voice deep in his brain that sounded a lot like his wife told him to leave. To forget it and wait for the next big break into the Villains Guild. His desperation to avenge his wife drowned that voice out.

Heart in his throat, Rocky pressed on the smudge. Something in the wall clicked. A door-sized section of the wall popped outward far enough for Rocky to get his fingers into the space and pull. The wall swung toward him, revealing a set of wooden steps that descended into a lit, finished basement. No smell of mildew or dampness, only the faintest hint of ozone that could have come from a lit match or recently fired gun.

In his mind, Rita shrieked at him to leave.

Rocky pulled his dart pistol and descended the stairs, instead, weapon up. He froze halfway down, blood thundering in his ears.

Gauntlet stood in the center of the carpeted basement, dressed in full regalia: cowl, uniform, gloves, boots, even the star-spangled staff he used as his signature weapon. The bullet-proof red gauntlets on both forearms bearing his signature G. Rocky's only hope of the midnight darts penetrating was a clean shot into his bare cheeks or chin.

Rocky aimed the pistol, ready to fire, when flickering flames caught the corner of his eye. To the left of Gauntlet was a small altar of some sort. Several candles were lit, vases of flowers lined a table around them, and a framed photo of a woman hung above it all. The woman's face made him nearly drop his pistol.

Rita. Gauntlet had a photo of his dead wife and an altar dedicated to her.

What the actual hell?

And Gauntlet stood there, making no move to attack or prepare a defense. He just . . . stood there, dark eyes watching Rocky.

"What is this?" Rocky asked. "That's my wife."

"Redemption day," Gauntlet replied.

A deep chill settled over Rocky's entire body so swiftly that his hands began trembling. His wife had died, brutally, her killer never found. And a SuperHero who disappeared around the same time.

"Redemption day," Rocky repeated, the words like ash on his

tongue. "Redemption for who?"

"You. Me. Her. These last ten years . . ."

Rocky took a step closer, tempted to swap his dart pistol out for the real thing. He didn't have to ask. He was smart enough to put the pieces together. "You killed my wife, didn't you, you son of a bitch?"

Gauntlet flinched. "It was an accident."

Rocky dropped the dart pistol and whipped out his real gun. Gauntlet might be super-strong and have incredibly fast reflexes, but he wasn't bulletproof. He aimed directly at Gauntlet's exposed mouth. A mouth dropping truth bombs, blowing up Rocky's life. "Talk, before I put a bullet in your spine."

"Heroes don't kill, everyone knows that. We can't. And Super-Heroes? We're the ones who set the example, who saves the public. Protect the city. Our handlers in the police department make sure that public image remains intact, no matter what."

"They covered up what really happened to Rita."

"They did. I didn't realize it was Rita behind me when I spun into a roundhouse kick. I thought she was Gotham, the Villain I was chasing, and I'd snapped her neck before I saw what I'd done. The way she died, we couldn't have blamed it on Gotham, and no one could know I was the one who killed her. He was physically weak and his powers were telepathic. No one would have believed he'd snapped Rita's neck. Instead of collateral damage in a Supers battle, she became a homicide victim cold case. You were left to suffer and wonder for years, and I am so sorry, Rocky. I'm sorry for Rita and for all of the pain I caused you."

"Sorry?" His entire body started shaking with a newfound rage unlike anything Rocky had experienced in his life. "Sorry!? You think you can say sorry and everything will be fine?"

"Nothing will be fine. I knew what I was doing when I drew you here."

"Drew me?"

Gauntlet nodded. "I still have contacts within the Heroes Society. I was in a dark depression over killing an innocent bystander. I couldn't live with it anymore, so I sought you out. Followed your jump from job to job, until you settled at the insurance agency I already used. I'm still good friends with The Resistor, and she told me you'd recently come across the Society's radar as a high-level Goon who specialized in burglary.

"You're clever, Rocky, but not as clever as you think. I figured out your pattern, using those with Supers Battle Damage policies to find marks. So I took out a policy, bided my time, and then last night The Resistor did me a favor by damaging my house during her fight with Despair."

"You set me up?!" Rocky's finger twitched against the trigger guard. "You wanted me to find you? Why? So you can rub it in my face that you murdered my wife?"

"No. To tell you the truth. And to grant you your revenge."

"My revenge?" Finally, a word that made sense. Something he'd wanted for the past decade.

"Yes. I was born Jared Collins, but it's Gauntlet who killed your wife."

Confusion clashed against his bloodlust. "So that means what? You're going to stand there and let me shoot you?"

"Yes."

In an early morning full of surprises, Rocky, startled, took a step backward, arm aching from keeping the gun level for so long, and got one more.

"I've lived with this guilt for too long," Jared continued. "I've seen what your thirst for vengeance has turned you into. You were a good man once, and I set you on the worst kind of path. Who you *were*, was all you. But who you are? That's on me."

This was a trick. It had to be. "Are you recording this? Are there cops waiting to take me in the second I try to pull the trigger? We both know you're fast enough to deflect the bullet with your gauntlets."

"I understand your suspicion, but this isn't a game. I killed your wife. Take your vengeance and kill me. Right here. Then take what you want from my home and go. I'll become what your wife once was—an unsolved murder."

Rocky stared at the man, who was more a symbol than a person. He couldn't kill a symbol. Until Rita died, Rocky never thought he could kill a person, either, but he'd rather look the man in the eyes when he killed him. Not the mask. "Take the cowl off."

Gauntlet complied, removing the headgear to reveal Jared's face. Lips pressed together, eyes dark with so many emotions, the hero suddenly became a man. A flesh and blood man who'd destroyed Rocky's life and hidden the secret.

"I imagined so many different faces over the years," Rocky said, hating how rough his voice had gotten. "Men. Women. Old. Young. Every color and shape and haircut possible. I imagined myself putting a bullet between their eyes, after I spent hours making them pay. Tearing off toenails. Driving bamboo shoots under fingernails. Breaking small bones. Slicing off ears. Taking them apart, piece by piece, before delivering the killing blow."

Jared's jaw twitched.

Rocky could see it in his mind's eye: Jared a stripped, beaten, bloody mess on the floor. Broken and begging for death to steal him from the agony searing his body. Rocky tormenting him a while longer, and then. . . .

His sure-way ticket into the Villains Guild flashed in his mind. Gauntlet's bounty required the man be alive, and delivering Gauntlet to them would secure him a spot. He wouldn't have to be a Goon anymore. Wouldn't have to share his spoils with Lady Shield. He'd be his own boss, could sponsor his own squad of Goons. He no longer needed Villain status to avenge his wife, but he could still use the wealth and power to built a new life. A new future for himself, as he'd always planned.

Except the Guild wanted Gauntlet alive. Delivering him alive robbed Rocky of Rita's ultimate revenge. The revenge Gauntlet had just hand-delivered to him.

He was desperate to murder Gauntlet for Rita, but where did that leave him? Still broke. Still a Goon. One who'd failed to fulfill the Guild's bounty. Rocky was tired of failing.

A flash of movement startled Rocky out of his thoughts. Jared was unlatching his forearm gauntlets, allowing the impenetrable material to clunk to the floor. Gauntlet was super-strong and possessed incredible reflexes, but those arm pieces made him unbeatable. He was exposing himself to Rocky, leaving himself vulnerable to attack.

Suicide by Goon.

Suicide.

Rocky would torture him for hours, maybe a day, before ending Jared's miserable life. The Villains Guild needed Jared alive, and they would make his death last for weeks, if not months, as payback for all of the past Villains and SuperVillains he'd taken down during his fifteen-year career. Jared would die at some nebulous time in the future, by some unknown hand.

Another deep-down voice, this time not his wife's, whispered to Rocky that if he positioned the pieces in the exact right way, he could torture Jared as planned, turn him over to the Guild, reap the notoriety and wealth that came with Villainy, and still be the one to eventually end Jared's life—Rocky's final revenge for Rita's murder. And if not today . . . some day.

"Sorry, Gauntlet," Rocky said as he bent to retrieve his dart gun from the floor. "You don't deserve the fast death you were hoping for."

Jared frowned, opened his mouth to speak. Rocky fired three darts in succession. Two landed directly over Jared's heart, the third in his exposed neck. The big man swayed, and then thumped to the floor in a boneless heap.

Rocky pulled out his phone and made a call.

"You certainly drive a hard bargain, Mr. Mills, but I'm glad we've come to a mutual arrangement," Lady Shield said, her honeyed voice even more wonderful to hear in person than over the phone. She tossed her shimmery white hair over her shoulder, bright yellow eyes watching as a gurney carried Jared Collins's limp, battered body out of the basement.

A basement much more bloody now than when Rocky had first descended those steps six hours ago.

"I'm glad as well," Rocky replied. His face itched from the blood drying on it, but he didn't scratch. He wore it like a badge of honor, one he'd earned tonight. "It's been an honor to work for you, ma'am, and I look forward to us working as equals in the future."

"And I, as well. Your discovery of Gauntlet after all of these years shows great cunning and skill. You'll be a fine addition to the Guild."

"Thank you very much."

Gauntlet's bounty had been worth more than Rocky had imagined, and the Guild's authorities had been extremely willing to negotiate with Rocky on three specific points in return for him delivering Gauntlet into their hands alive. Rocky got to keep Jared Colllins's house, which was a huge upgrade from his cheap apartment rental, legally paid for with part of the bounty's cash payout, while Mr. Collins quietly 'moved out of the country.' Rocky was given six hours to do with Jared as he wished, so long as he was alive and cognitively aware when the Guild retrieved him. That deal had prevented Rocky from cutting off Jared's ears, but he'd still had quite a lot of fun mangling the man's extremities—ability to walk or feed himself again was optional.

His final and favorite point had sealed the deal. On the day the Guild decided it was time for Gauntlet to die, be it in a week or six months, Rocky got to deliver the killing blow. No matter where Rocky was in the world, no matter what business he was conducting, or what Hero he was hunting, he'd return to Guild Headquarters to dispatch his nemesis. To personally avenge the murder of his wife.

But to do so today would mean forfeiting the small fortune the Guild promised in exchange for Gauntlet's mangled but living body. If he couldn't have love, and maybe even a soul worth fighting for, well . . . then money would have to do. Money he would invest in his new career as a proper Villain, so he could ascend the ranks quickly. It wasn't a career Rita would have approved of, but it was the one he'd embraced.

Sometimes, when you start down a certain road, there's just no turning back.

"So, you'll be initiated into the Villains Guild tomorrow evening," Lady Shield said. "Have you chosen your name yet?"

Rocky nodded as he stooped to pick up the discarded gauntlets. The color needed to be changed, but he could think of no better legacy for his wife's memory than this. "I have. It's time this city had a brand new Villain roaming its streets, inspiring fear in the hearts of its citizens, instead of its criminals. And I can't think of a better symbol to turn against them than the one they used to admire so greatly. To darken and tarnish the very thing they once loved so much."

He attached the arm coverings, admiring their fit, imagining them painted as pitch black as his heart. "I am Gauntlet, and I will have my vengeance."

"Welcome to the Villains Guild," Lady Shield said, and addressed him by his new moniker. "Gauntlet."

Oh yes, he liked the sound of that.

THE REBOOT OF JENNIS VIATOREM
By Karissa Laurel

WHAT HAD FIRST APPEARED AS A distant prick of light on Jennis Viatorem's view screen had grown into the oblong, rifle-bullet shape of the *Fête*. Light from a nearby star reflected off the cruise ship's sleek surface, giving it a blue, spectral glow. According to the transmission Jennis received as she initiated docking protocols, more than 5,000 guests and several hundred staff members currently resided aboard the luxury cruiser. Jennis drew in a deep breath and held it as she approached the docking bay. Compared to the open expanse of deep space she'd been roaming for nearly two years, she suspected joining the crowds aboard the *Fête* would make her feel like a particle of dust jammed in the nucleus of a comet.

A small photograph sat in the corner of the instrument panel in her cockpit. The edges had gone soft and yellow with age. Few people invested in printed pictures anymore, but she had wanted an image to carry with her always, regardless of battery power or communication signals. The photo of the little grinning boy, his brown cheeks dusted with flour and powdered sugar, had reminded her for decades of the reasons she couldn't drift into the abyss and never return as she was sometimes tempted to do. His name was Charli, and he was her tether, her anchor, her son, and the source of her greatest guilt—a sentiment she had struggled to ignore for nearly thirty years. Presently, that tether was drawing her back to him, and remorse weighed heavy in her heart.

Gritting her teeth against a groan, Jennis rose from her cockpit and shuffled down the steps leading to the interior of her empty cargo bay. She stroked the walls of the *Humuli*, her beloved ship. With it, she had recently delivered a load of rations to a pioneer outpost on a terraformed planet in the Grable system. It was there that she had received the transmission from Charli that reeled her back in: Amerie was dead. Murdered. Poisoned by the soup on her supper tray.

A supper tray Charli had prepared himself in his five-star kitchen aboard the *Fête* where he lived and worked. Amerie had been the cruise ship's chief mate in charge of cargo. She had also been his beloved wife of four years and the mother of their only child, Celestine. Although Charli had delivered that fatal meal, he was not the true culprit. The man who had framed Charli had been found, arrested, and was presently awaiting trial.

The moment the *Humuli* had settled inside the *Fête*'s massive hangar, Jennis's crew made hasty farewells and disappeared into the cruse ship's interior. The temptation of casinos, fresh food, and time away from each other had lured them like a siren enticing those sailors of ancient legends. Jennis paused at the edge of *Humuli*'s lowered cargo ramp and watched the cruise staff scurry back and forth, escorting new arrivals and sending off departing guests.

The *Fête* regularly orbited exotic ports of call, planets terraformed to resemble tropical locales that had gone extinct on Earth. According to Charli's last transmission, the *Fête* was currently en route to New Rio, where shuttles would cart tourists to a surface coated in sugar-sand beaches, palm trees, and crystalline blue waters.

"Mom?" From the crowded concourse emerged a young man wearing a distinctive double-breasted jacket—the kind chefs had adopted centuries ago and never abandoned despite decades of sartorial evolution.

Jennis painted on a smile and ignored the sharp pang that lanced her heart whenever she first saw her son after an extended absence. In her mind, she always pictured him as the chubby-cheeked boy in the photograph, but in reality he had grown three feet, aged twenty years, and shed the roundness of early adolescence.

He looks so much like his damned father. . . . Inherited his worst traits, too, it would seem.

"Hey, kiddo." Jennis crossed the distance between them and

hesitated before sliding her arms around his ribs. His embrace engulfed her in a warm cloud of garlic and sage. They held the pose for a brief pair of heartbeats before releasing each other and stepping back, allowing for the return of a comfortable boundary of personal space.

"You didn't have to come," Charli said.

A muscle beneath Jennis's eye twitched, an unconscious yet lifelong tick—her reflexive response to conflict. "I would have been here sooner, but the Grable system is so far out." Despite using her ship's hyperdrive almost nonstop, it had taken her almost a month to reach him. "So, show me where to bunk. I could use a real shower." She grinned, a more genuine expression than the one she had offered before. "And something to eat."

Charli glanced at the exit leading from the hangar into the heart of the ship. "I've got you set up in the spare room in my apartment. Plenty to snack on in the fridge." He tapped his wrist, and a holo-display illuminated his arm, showing the time. "Dinner's not for a couple of hours, but I'll save you a table, if you want."

Jennis nodded. "You're working tonight?"

For a moment, his civilized mask dropped, revealing the wild thing hiding beneath—a feral creature that grief, anger, and helplessness had released in the wake of Amerie's death. Jennis had seen that same look too many times on the face of Charli's father before she could no longer tolerate his anger, or his fists. For the sake of the new life growing inside her, Jennis had left him, fleeing while her husband was away on business, taking the few valuables she had on hand to finance her hasty escape. Without much of a plot or a plan, she knew only that she had to run, but she had failed to give much thought to how she could ever afford to stop.

"Yeah," Charlie said. "It's better if I stay busy."

She said nothing but nodded again and motioned for him to lead the way. Charli turned on his heel, and Jennis hurried to keep up with his long strides. As they passed through the concourse leading to the elevator bay, the ship's paying passengers ignored them. The *Fête's* staff, however, either acknowledged Charli with a sad, consoling smile or purposely looked the other way, pretending not to see him. Jennis understood that inclination. She often felt incompetent in the presence of grief, and her son's pain was overwhelming, nearly incomprehensible—as if she floated at the edge of a black hole, trying not to get sucked in.

She and Charli stopped before a row of chrome doors, and he pressed his palm against a scanner panel. They stood in awkward silence until a chime signaled the arrival of their elevator. When the doors closed behind them, the car rocketed up fast enough to buckle Jennis's knees.

Charli caught her elbow and held her steady. "It's jarring when you're not used to it."

"Haven't got my walking legs yet." She steadied herself and pulled away. "Too much time in the cockpit. Plus, I'm not as agile as I used to be."

He scoffed. "You're not over the hill *yet*."

"I've spent so much time in hyperspace, I could be two hundred and no one would know for sure."

"I don't think it works that way."

"I don't think anyone knows how it really works except the brains who design the engines. I just press some buttons and"—Jennis sliced her hand through the air, mimicking a ship rocketing through space—"zoom, I'm off."

"Zoom, you're off," Charli mumbled, shaking his head. In the following silence, she imagined his unspoken words, the ones he was surely thinking. *Zoom, you're off. Always off. Never in one place too long.*

When she had threatened to leave him before, Charli's father had vowed he would never let her go, never stop hunting her—he'd find her wherever she went. He'd had the money and influence to keep his promise, too. That same money and influence had kept him out of legal trouble, and had kept Jennis under his thumb much longer than she would have allowed under other circumstances. If not for her pregnancy, she might still be with him, a prisoner in her own home. Or, more likely, she'd be dead, the victim of one of his explosive outbursts.

When Charli was younger, Jennis couldn't explain that staying in one place too long meant risking discovery—that Charli's father didn't know he existed and he was therefore safer if they stayed away, stayed hidden. She had wanted to protect her son, didn't want him waking up from nightmares in which the monster was his own father. Instead she had evaded and avoided until Charli had stopped asking questions. She had locked away her ghosts and kept her distance, thinking it would keep them both safe, but she hadn't accounted for the ghosts in her son's DNA.

When the elevator stopped again, Jennis followed Charli down a quiet hallway and past a pair of doors before pausing at a third. Again he pressed his palm to a scanner in the wall. A door panel slid open. Mother and son stepped into the apartment on the other side. The squeal of Celestine's excited voice was Jennis's only warning. "Gammy!"

She turned in time to catch the energetic bundle of springy black curls and sticky fingers hurtling towards her legs. Seizing the toddler in her arms, Jennis buried her face in Celestine's neck and inhaled her baby shampoo and applesauce smell. The last time she'd held her granddaughter, Celestine had been a tiny thing, only a few weeks old.

"How has she been?" Jennis asked, gesturing at Celestine with a jerk of her chin.

"A lot of tantrums. A lot of crying." Chari shook his head and grunted. "She doesn't understand Amerie's absence, and I don't know how to explain it to her. She's still just a toddler." His eyes narrowed into a wary expression "You're staying a couple days, right?"

"I can stay a week," she said, "a month, or longer. I'm flexible."

The only thing giving away Charli's ire was the muscle twitching under his eye. He had inherited few physical features from Jennis—not her amber skin or straight dark hair—but he had gotten that one trait from her, and she knew what it meant. "What about your job? Where are you off to next?"

She shifted her granddaughter, settling Celestine's weight on her hip, and the little girl babbled nonsense sounds in her ear. "I haven't taken any new contracts." She had done more than that, but it was too soon to reveal those details. First, she had to convince Charli to let her stay.

His nostrils flared. "Do you want me to say thank you?"

When Jennis had decided on this course of action, she'd never presumed it would be easy. That Charli hadn't already put a boot to her rear end and kicked her halfway across the star system was a minor miracle in itself. "I don't want anything. I'm here for you and Celestine. Whatever you need."

His fists bunched at his sides. "And if we don't need anything?"

Anticipating a rise in Charli's hostility, Jennis bent and set Celestine on her feet. "Cellie, where's Buster Bear? Will you go get him for me?"

The little girl's black curls bounced around her head like springs as she grinned and toddled away.

Jennis turned to her son and bit her lip. He had let her come this far—she had to hope it wasn't for nothing. "You can tell me to go—if that's what you really want."

"How do you know her toy's name?" Charli's gaze followed his daughter as she disappeared into her bedroom.

"I holo-chatted with her and Amerie once a week. Sometimes more."

He flinched and blinked at her, wide-eyed. "You did?"

"Since she was born. Amerie didn't tell you?"

The muscle under his eye twitched again. "I didn't know."

"I wasn't trying to keep it from you."

"Why wouldn't Amerie tell me?"

"Maybe she thought . . ." Jennis glanced away, letting her gaze roam over the apartment decorated in warm woods, marble, and suede furniture that looked as soft as butter. Charli had once made a home here. She hoped she wasn't too late to save what was left of it.

"She thought I would tell her not to," Charli said, finishing Jennis's thought. "She might've been right."

Jennis winced. "Better to apologize than ask permission, I guess."

He shrugged, rolling broad shoulders like a bear shaking off winter hibernation. "At least it means Cellie will be comfortable with you while I'm at work." He tapped his wrist and checked the time. "Speaking of which . . ."

"You've got to go."

He nodded. "I have a holo-conference with the district prose-cutors before my shift starts. They want to go over my testimony. *Again.*" He scrubbed his hands over his short, coarse curls and exhaled. "Bring Cellie to dinner with you, okay? I don't want her spending any more time alone with Nanny than she has to."

Jennis flinched. "Nanny? You still have that old bot?"

He crossed to the room and stopped at the front door. "Why wouldn't I? She's been more of a mother to me than you ever were." With that, he stepped forward, the door slid open, and he disappeared down the hall, leaving Jennis with his final words the same way a soldier flees after tossing a grenade into an enemy bunker.

She didn't explode, however. Charli hadn't known it, but she had put on her thickest emotional armor before facing him in the *Fête's* docking bay. He might try to wound her—she certainly deserved his best shots—but she would withstand his attacks, no matter the pain it might cause her. For once in her life, she vowed she would be there for him and Celestine, and she'd let nothing, not even Charli himself, drive her away.

Her grandmother's greatest joy, Celestine held fast to Jennis from the moment they stepped into the elevator until they took their seats in a quiet corner near the kitchen of the Second Kingdom, the *Fete's* most fashionable restaurant and Charli's home away from home. The waiters had brought Jennis endless plates of for-eign things: a platter of vegetables in hues so vibrant they stung her eyes if she stared at them too long and roasted meats with tentacles, spines, claws, and snouts. Her stomach grumbled as she eyed Celestine's simple bowl of buttered noodles, which the little girl ate by the fistful.

After sampling enough of the dishes to appease her sense of duty, Jennis carried her granddaughter back to the apartment and began the evening's bedtime routine. Months of holo-chatting with Celestine and Amerie had given her an understanding of the rituals: a bath, a book, and a song before lights out. "Let's scrub-a-dub-dub, baby girl," Jennis said, leading the way to the bathroom.

"Shall I add the bubbles?" asked a hollow, echoing voice from the darkness of the apartment's unlit kitchen. Jennis squawked and recoiled while shoving her granddaughter behind her. Her heart skipped a beat before finding its rhythm in a triple-time cadence. Pale light from the stars outside the portholes in the apartment's exterior walls lined the reflective edges of a humanoid shape, standing behind the kitchen's marble counter. Soft amber light glowed in the being's eyes, and another light—this one a cool, digital blue—pulsed on its chest like a heartbeat.

"No," Celestine said, peeking around Jennis's legs. "Gammy."

"Yes, Miss Celestine. Shall I retrieve your nightgown?"

The little girl bunched her fists. "*Gammy.*"

"Then I shall stay here and continue recharging until you need me."

Celestine tugged her grandmother's pant leg, and Jennis stumbled as she turned to follow the little girl toward the bathroom. "I-I still can't believe that old droid is here," Jennis said, slightly breathless from surprise and disbelief. Despite Charli's earlier revelation, she hadn't quite believed Nanny still existed. Amerie had certainly never mentioned the droid's presence, and she must have been very careful—perhaps at Charli's insistence—to make sure Jennis remained ignorant. Everyone, it seemed, had been dealing deceits for the sake of familial harmony, and Amerie had been the well-oiled axle of that machine.

Charli hadn't been much older than Celestine when Nanny came into his life. Jennis remembered his initial fear of the robot who looked so human while behaving like anything but. In the weeks that had followed its arrival, the droid had learned and adjusted, and Charli had grown attached. At the time, Jennis had believed the droid was the easiest solution for long-term childcare: Nanny would look after Charli during Jennis's extended absences. The bot would never harm him, and it was, in fact, programmed to protect him, even from other humans. Most importantly, Nanny was an abiding, steady, and reliable presence. No matter how frequently they moved, no matter how remote the star system they occupied, no matter how long Jennis was away on business, the droid would never abandon him.

As much as it pained Jennis to acknowledge it, Charli was right. *Nanny* was *a better mother than me.*

Having seen the droid again and its familiar responses to her granddaughter, Jennis felt that old accustomed pang in her chest—a mixture of envy, resentment, and regret. Regularly, she kept those emotions buried in the same place she had stored her memories of Charli's father, but Jennis's feelings had a habit of unexpectedly escaping.

I did so many things wrong raising Charli, but if he gives me another chance, I won't make those mistakes with Celestine.

After a bath full of bubbles and splashing that soaked Jennis's tunic, and after a story with pictures projected on the bedroom ceiling, and after two off-key lullabies, Celestine finally relented, giving into the Sandman's demands. Jennis rose from her chair at the little girl's bedside and tiptoed toward the guest room.

"Would you care for tea, Jennis?"

She jumped, having forgotten about Nanny's looming presence in the kitchen. Her first inclination was to refuse, but the words died in her throat. Instead, she slipped forward and settled on a stool at the kitchen island. "Tea would be nice, thank you."

Nanny bobbed her head, and the overhead lights flickered on. After a brief shuffle around the kitchen, the droid set a steaming mug on the counter. "Would you care for anything else?"

Jennis wrapped her hands around the cup, brought it close to her face, and blew, watching ripples form across the tea's surface. Was that what she was, showing up in Charli's and Celestine's life like this—a storm disturbing still, tranquil waters? But no . . . she'd seen the anger and pain in her son's eyes. There was no tranquility in him.

"I believe I owe you a great deal of thanks," Jennis said, still staring into her mug. Steam curled from the surface, licking her face with warm, humid tendrils.

"Preparing tea is a minor chore requiring no gratitude. I am simply preforming my duties."

"I'm not talking about the tea."

Several moments of silence followed in which Nanny's amber eyes glowed brighter then dulled, pulsing in time to the same beat of the blue light on her chest plate. Finally, the bot spoke. "When Charli grew up, he believed he did not need me anymore.

Perhaps he was correct. I, however, was programmed to protect and care for him. It is a function I am unable to delete."

"So you watch him, sometimes, when he isn't aware?"

"I overheard his conversation with Amerie the day she discovered those children. Charli warned her to be careful about going to the authorities. She promised to be cautious. He, however, did not make the same promise in return."

Jennis scowled into her cup. According to what Charli had told her, Amerie had audited the ship's cargo hold and found an inconsistency in the manifest. That inconsistency wound up being an unregistered shipping container—a box the size of her bedroom closet—stuffed with a half-dozen children not much older than Celestine. She had told Charli of her discovery first, and he had urged her to think about how—or if—to alert the ship's authorities, as they had no idea how far the corruption reached and who aboard the ship was involved.

Amerie was killed the same night of her discovery, before she ever made an official report. Obviously, someone had been watching her. That someone had failed to realize Nanny was watching as well.

The authorities were still investigating the scope of the smuggling operation, and they suspected more of the ship's staff was involved, but the man they had arrested for Amerie's murder was refusing to talk.

"But Charli had you looking out for him," Jennis said, grumbling. "Even if he didn't know it."

"Is the tea not to your liking? You have not consumed any of it, and your facial expressions indicate displeasure."

Jennis glanced up, meeting the droid's pulsing amber gaze. "Nothing's wrong with the tea, Nanny. I promise."

"Then your displeasure is with me."

Jennis dropped her head and covered her face with her hands. "No . . . yes . . . I don't know."

"I do not understand."

"You recorded Charli and Amerie's conversation that night. And you were jacked into the ship's onboard computers, watching Charli through the security cameras. You recorded that man putting poison in Amerie's soup in Charli's kitchen, and you were the one who reported your findings to the authorities."

"He was not a kitchen staff member. He was merely posing as one. I did not know that at the time. I did not understand his intentions."

Jennis smeared her hands down her face and looked at the droid again. "I'm not blaming you, Nanny. If you hadn't been there, hadn't collected the evidence, Charli might still be in jail for this crime. You were the one looking out for him. You've *always* been the one looking out for him. You saved him."

"I did *not* save him."

Jennis's forehead puckered as she frowned. "How can you say that?"

"My failure to respond appropriately led to Amerie's death. I did not save her. Therefore, I did not save Charli."

Jennis gnawed her bottom lip as she contemplated Nanny's words. Machine logic often confounded human reasoning, but she hurtled the crevasse of misunderstanding and landed on a conclusion she hoped was right. "You're saying it's your fault he's in pain because you didn't save Amerie?"

"Amerie's death broke him in some fundamental way I cannot fully comprehend. It is my fault."

"It's the fault of the man who poisoned her."

"It is my job to protect Charli. I failed."

"Fine. But if that's true, then I'm even more guilty. I've been failing him since he was born."

"Has Charli told you he was almost arrested for battery on the man who poisoned Amerie? He attacked him at the arraignment hearing and beat him unconscious. The officials took pity on Charli due to his *emotional distress* and did not press charges."

Jennis swallowed and felt as though a dry, hot ball of sand had wedged in her throat. "That's why I came. He'll kill someone if he lets it get ahold of him again—that rage. His father was the same way. I couldn't save my husband, but if there's any way possible, I *will* save my son . . . *and* Celestine."

"How?"

Jennis shrugged. "I was hoping you might have a suggestion. You know him better than anyone."

"I am simply a care provider—a machine programmed to

anticipate Charli's needs and those of his family."

"And how do you do that?"

"A series of algorithms based on patterns of observable behavior."

"Okay . . . so start anticipating. If we're lucky, maybe you and I can fix what's broken before it's too late."

Nanny's eyes pulsed several times before she answered. "I will analyze my data tonight. If there is a solution, I will find it."

Jennis stood and pushed her tea mug, still full but no longer steaming, toward the droid. "I lied to you earlier."

"I know. You actually do not care for tea at all. I have not forgotten."

"Then why did you offer it in the first place?"

Jennis imagined that if the droid could have grinned, it would have. "Humans like to keep their hands occupied when they engage in uncomfortable conversations. The tea served its purpose."

"I could say the same about you." Jennis turned toward the hallway leading to her room. "Good night, Nanny."

The kitchen lights flickered off. "Good night, Jennis."

"It is as we predicted. Charli has been arrested."

Nanny's voice in Jennis's ear jarred her awake, sending a jolt of shock through her as sharp and painful as if the droid had struck her with a electrical current. Jennis clutched at her stuttering heart and gasped for breath. "Wha . . . what are you talking about?"

"During the early hours, Charli initiated a brawl with another crewman in an employee lounge. He accused the man of participating in the plot to kill Amerie. He broke the man's nose, several ribs, and rendered him unconscious. Officers are holding Charli in the ship's security section."

Jennis set her feet on the floor and braced her elbows on her knees. She let her head sink into her hands. "What time is it?"

"Six o'clock. Celestine has already awoken. She is watching animated videos in the kitchen while she eats breakfast."

"How long has Charli been detained?"

"Approximately three hours. I searched the ship's communication records when Charli did not return home. I discovered what had happened when security transmitted its report on the incident to the district magistrate. A decision on his charges has not been rendered yet, but I anticipate the magistrate's verdict will come as soon as his office opens. It may be possible that I can . . . *delay* the ship's reception of the magistrate's decision long enough for you to talk to Charli, if you wish."

Jennis groaned and stood. "Is there coffee?"

"Of course."

Jennis shuffled through the apartment and settled into a seat at the kitchen table. Celestine glanced up from her video tablet, scooped an unsteady spoonful of cereal from her bowl, and stuffed it in her mouth. Jennis plastered on a fake smile. "Good morning, baby girl."

Celestine grinned and milk dribbled down her chin.

Nanny set a mug of coffee before Jennis, and this time she didn't hesitate to take a long sip. For the sake of the little girl sitting across from her, she had to remain calm. Nanny held its place at Jennis's side, and although she knew the droid had no emotions, she felt a sense of impatience transmitting from the robot. "Is there something else?"

The droid bobbed its head. "I may have devised a possible solution regarding our conversation last night, but it will not work considering the current situation. We must address the more immediate problem of Charli's arrest first."

Jennis scowled into her coffee as she took another sip. "What's your solution?"

"The three most important things to Charli are his daughter, his profession . . . and *you*."

Jennis snorted. "He barely tolerates me."

"It is my understanding those feelings are not uncommon in familial relationships."

"Perhaps not uncommon, but still a big obstacle. I agree with you, at least in theory, that those things are important to Charli. But how does that help us save him?"

"I have drafted a report and will share the details with you after we deliver Celestine to her nurseryschool."

Jennis cocked her head and blinked at the droid. "First, I'm going to need more caffeine."

Nanny shuffled away, returned with a coffee pot, and refilled Jennis's cup. "Drink quickly. We have much to do."

After Jennis had helped Celestine dress and carried her to the onboard daycare for children of the *Fete*'s staff, she followed Nanny to the ship's security headquarters. As they walked, Nanny revealed the details of the plan she had devised during the night. It was simple, nothing surprising or overly extraordinary, and, for that reason, perhaps it would work. The hardest part would be convincing Charli and persuading the authorities not to put him in jail. "We'll probably need a lawyer," Jennis said as they waited for a guard to escort them into the security center.

Nanny bobbed her head. "We will need several."

Although allowing Charli visitors went against security protocols, the ship's staff still harbored enough sympathy for him to make an exception this once. Jennis and Nanny joined Charli in a small room where the guards had handcuffed him to a heavy table. Bruises and lacerations marred his knuckles, and a dark knot had risen on his cheek. He glared at the tabletop and said nothing, not even a nod to acknowledge their presence.

Jennis laid her hands over his larger ones, and he jerked back and looked up. She met his gaze only to find that all civility had left him. The wild thing stared back at her—the same wild thing inside his father that had forced her to flee. By running away, she had hoped to save her son from his father's demons. She had run and run until it became a habit, but in the end it had solved nothing—saved Charli from nothing.

"I never told you about him, about your father," Jennis said. "When you were little, I was afraid the truth would scare you, give you nightmares. When you were older, so much time had passed that I couldn't bring myself to dredge up those old memories. I thought they were better left forgotten."

The muscles around Charli's eyes tightened and his nostrils flared, but he said nothing.

"I thought if we never stayed in one place too long, and if I stayed away from you as much as possible, then he couldn't find us, and he couldn't hurt us, but I was wrong. I carried him inside me, Charli, which meant you carried him, too."

His lip curled. "What does that even mean?"

"It means no matter how hard, or how fast, or how far I ran, he managed to catch us after all. You have so much of him in you, Charli." Jennis reached across the table and stroked her son's cheek. He flinched and pulled away. "Your passion, your ambition—that's all him. Your anger and violence—that's him, too. I lost count of the times he tried to break me. Sometimes he was closer to succeeding than others."

He met her gaze and fury burned in his eyes. "I *never* hurt Amerie or Celestine. I never laid a finger on them in anger."

"I know you didn't." She leaned forward and set her hands over his, and that time he didn't flinch. "I know how much you love them, and how much they love you. Amelie told me every time we talked, but she was afraid for you, and so am I. I abandoned you, Charli. I don't want to see you repeat my mistakes, or those of your father."

Charli gritted his teeth. He rubbed his face. "Why are you here, Mom?"

"I told you I hadn't taken any more shipping contracts," Jennis said, "but that wasn't the complete truth." The muscle under Charli's eye twitched. "The truth is that I sold the *Humuli*. Elleyne bought it. You met her once, she's my—"

"Pilot," Charlie grumbled. "I remember. Should I congratulate you on your retirement?"

"It *was* going to be retirement," she said. "Now, I'm thinking of investing in a new business."

"Why are you telling me this?"

"Because my plans involve you. And Cellie. Lucky for me you're locked up. It's the only way you'll stay in my company long enough to let me explain. Actually, no . . . Nanny will explain. It's really her plan. I'm just helping fund it."

Charli's eyebrows arched high, and he blinked at the droid sitting next to Jennis. "You're saying you don't want to sell her for scrap? I thought you hated Nanny."

"Be quiet," Jennis said. "Just listen."

Nanny leaned closer, and the pulse of the droid's amber eyes matched the anxious beat of Jennis's heart. "I have researched a number of locations which stand the greatest chance of supporting a successful new restaurant. These locations have also been calculated to appeal to your prefences for climate, social ameneties, and schools for Celestine. With your savings, and with your mother's investment from the sale of her ship, you should have the necessary funds."

"If we don't lose it all in legal fees," Jennis grumbled. Charli's wild thing flinched and retreated, although Jennis was sure it would return in an instant if properly motivated. She and Nanny had captured his interest, but keeping it meant treading lightly.

"What are you saying?" Charli asked.

"You've wanted your own restaurant for a while, have you not?" Jennis asked.

He watched her warily as though expecting a trap. "So what?"

"You've wanted to put down roots and make a more permanent home for your family."

He shrugged, neither affirming or denying.

"I know something about living with ghosts, Charli. You can't keep them buried, no matter how hard you try. You can't stay here, running from these demons, and be a proper father. You've got to get away and start fresh. I want to help."

Charli snorted and rolled his eyes. "I don't buy it, Mom. You don't put down roots. I know better than to believe you. Why don't you just run away like you always do and leave me alone?"

"If you go to prison," Jennis said, "what'll happen to Celestine?"

He snarled and bared his teeth. He yanked his arms, straining against his cuffs.

Jennis touched Nanny's arm as she stood to leave. "It's not too late, Charli. I'm not going anywhere. I'll stay as long as it takes to make you believe me. I'll stay just to piss you off."

"Yeah? Then where are you going right now?"

Jennis flashed him a grin full of false bravado. "You can't open a new restaurant in chains. C'mon, Nanny, I need you to run one of your algorithms. Find us a good lawyer."

"*Several* good lawyers," Nanny said.

"Right." Jennis winked at Charli as the door slid open. "See you soon, kiddo."

He gaped at her and strained against his cuffs again. "Mom, what are you going to do?"

She paused in the doorway, keeping the panel from sliding closed long enough to give him another smile. "I'm going to see if I can get us all a second chance."

FRACTURED
by Robert Greenberger

"IT'S A WICKED STORM OUT THERE," Lucas Connors said as he buttoned his shirt. He was still slightly sweaty and wanted to clean up, but he was running late. His wife, Bridget, was waiting for him and he suspected the mag lev "el" would run slowly as a precaution. Having to go home undercut the sweet sensation he was trying to savor, the scent of Dev's own sweat, mixed with his own, creating a unique, heady perfume.

Dev Bhatia sat up on his elbows, Lucas glowing as his lover studied him. Dev was lean and angular, with a rounded face and dark, brown eyes that melted Lucas's heart. Bhatia was inventive in their lovemaking and Lucas couldn't get enough of their time together. The problem, though, was it had to be limited. Each encounter had to be carefully orchestrated in advance, stealing time here and there, doing nothing to jeopardize his marriage or their working relationship. Both had met when they were asked to participate in planning the next stage of development in the Apollinaris Sulci. They found they had much in common at the initial planning sessions, which led to some one-on-one meetings, and before they realized it, the two men were each looking forward to the next meeting. A part of Bhatia realized the secrecy was a spice that added to the new relationship's heat.

"You think Jinping will really pull out?" So typical of Dev to mix thoughts of sex with politics and their work.

"If they want any share of the minerals or habitat space, they'll play along," Lucas said. "I'm more worried about Gandhi. They want more than their share since their population is running out of control. You Indians can't keep it in your pants."

Dev's long-fingered hand reached around him, playing with

his chest hair as he tried to finish buttoning the shirt. He pressed against his back and Lucas leaned into him.

"There, it's in my pants . . . for now. So, what are we going to do?"

"What do you mean?" But Lucas *knew* what Dev meant.

"About the budget; there's not enough money coming from the other towns," Dev said, trying to sound serious and business-like but then let out a laugh. "Us, of course."

Lucas had been mulling over that very question earlier in the day. And the night before. And the week before that. He loved Bridget, but there had been problems. He wasn't sure if their marriage would last. And if those problems persisted, did he want something more committed with Dev? *What did he want?* plagued and stole sleep from him.

He decided to turn the question around. Taking the soft hand from inside his shirt, Lucas turned to meet Dev's eyes. He saw in them the longing that he, too, often felt for him. "What do *you* want, Dev?"

"You," he said and pressed his chin atop Lucas' shoulder. "I want more of you, more time."

"You want us to be public?"

"At least committed," Dev said. Lucas turned and met his eyes. "I want this to be something real, not two men furtively groping one another here and there. I see plenty of potential in you, Luke. And I don't like to share."

"I am never furtive," Lucas said with mock seriousness, earning him an eye roll.

"But you are secretive. She doesn't know about us, does she?"

"Of course not," Lucas said. The guilt he had been feeling toward the affair was very strong—at first. He'd never cheated on Bridget before, never felt an attraction strong enough to tempt him to stray. But there was that first encounter with Dev after a meeting. They'd gone with others for a drink and the two wound up seated next to one another. As the hours fell away, they found themselves talking more and more to just each other, riffing on everything from engineering, mathematics, politics, movies, and even classic rock songs they grew up on. They had very different backgrounds and had taken their own unique journeys to get to this place, but there was more than enough commonality for a bond to form.

As the beers mounted, they each felt a magnetic tug, something difficult to feel on Mars, a world without much of a magnetic field of its own. Still, they drew closer, and when as Dev tried to rise in order to go home and sleep off the buzz, Lucas rose too. They supported one another in their wobbly state (amazing, he considered how few beers it took to get people drunk compared with what he'd heard about Earth) and finally Lucas gave in to the impulse and kissed Dev.

The lips instantly parted and the pressure was returned, even prolonged.

Their arms wrapped around one another as the kiss continued, tongues daringly darting back and forth. When they finally broke, each took a deep breath and studied the other's reaction. It was clear this was good for them both and the kissing continued for a time.

Those memories were pleasant, cherished ones and Lucas dwelled on them during his mag lev rides to his job sites. Now, though, they flitted through his mind as he tried to address Dev's question. What was it he wanted?

"I want more from this relationship," Dev said, escorting Lucas to the door. "What we have is great and I'm greedy, so yes, I want you and us to become something real."

"Me too," Lucas admitted. It was true and it felt good to admit these feelings in the open, if they were only to his lover. He knew with certainty that he wasn't feeling anywhere near as greedy as Dev, but he was a sponge, soaking up the affection and attention which these days he lacked at home.

"Then you have to decide what we're going to do. You have to tell her and make it clear, the marriage is over. Right?"

Lucas nodded, refusing to put so final a word to his marriage. *Over.* He loved Bridget, even if that ember had cooled of late, even before this thing with Dev ignited. He gave Dev a peck and hurried out to the cool hall where he could begin collecting his wits. He walked the short distance to the nearest station, hoping he'd make his connection and be back at Orion not too late.

The "el" slid into the station, a silent silver missile, and he boarded it, taking a seat by the window, and as the sandy and rocky terrain passed at high speed, he collected his thoughts, sorted his feelings, and kept repeating to himself, "What do I really want?"

It wasn't that hard a question a few years ago. Lucas was a rising miner, respected for his work ethic and leadership abilities. As exploration continued throughout Sulci, located between Apollinaris Mons and the Gusev Crater, they found that the nearby Medusae Fossae was rich with mineral deposits. He was among those tasked with carefully digging in to the Fossae to extract just what they needed. The byword on Mars was to minimize harm to the environment and landscape wherever possible. The hard-learned lessons of their Terran ancestors could be found in every aspect of the seven towns that were clustered in the 100 kilometer radius that made up the Sulci.

Lucas delighted in digging deep into the Martian soil, discovering new strata of fine-grained dust and sand, revealing a geological timeline for the planet's development. Extracting a new layer of sediment and analyzing it to determine best uses or abandonment was a never-ending process, which made his job perfect for him. He got to use deep-boring drills one day and then lay down on the surface and carefully brushed minute samples into vials for analysis.

When he settled into his own apartment in Orion, a milestone step of adulthood, he was pleasantly surprised to see the petite, red-headed woman as a next door neighbor. With a goofy grin, he stuck out a hand and introduced himself to Bridget Quinn, who was a communications specialist. She also recently graduated to her own home and admitted to barely spending any time there since she loved working at the "tower", the twenty-story structure where all contact with Earth, the Moon, and the growing number of space stations was maintained.

He studied her habits with the skills of a spy and began using his newfound knowledge to just be coming or going, ensuring they would cross paths in the hall or by the main entrance. Finally, one day, she stopped him in the lobby and asked, "Are you stalking me?"

His blush told her everything she needed to know and agree

to a date, one which lasted three days. Five months later, they sat down with a lawyer and signed the standard five-year marriage contract. Given how much they loved their respective careers, neither was in a hurry to start a family. As a result, they brought a small, very expensive imported bottle of champagne with them to toast upon the signing for the first five-year extension.

That was seven years ago, and since signing, the subject of children had faded into the background. In fact, both seemed to get only deeper into their jobs, so the time they had together often felt fleeting. On the other hand, the societal pressure on procreation was ever-present, so it would come up and remained a goal, but without a timetable.

And then he attended that first meeting with Dev.

Dev was part of a team that was examining the Fossae for potential construction of dwellings in the Fossae's yardangs. It was clear that homes there would benefit from the natural protection the yardangs provided from temperature extremes and radiation, which was always a concern to the Martian colonists. In order to maximize the process, mining and engineering would have to work together to make sure what was dug out was not merely dumped but filtered and processed to form berms, roads, and emergency shelters.

The affair began with the kisses but it progressed quickly. Time was an incredibly valuable resource and this second generation of Martian knew better than to waste it. As a result, once they established they were like-minded, the physical aspect kicked in. What Lucas noticed as the affair continued, was how little he actually knew of Dev beyond what he was told and what he saw at work. The man seemed to have no other friends, and never mentioned family. His apartment was even more Spartan than his own. But they were small things, and things he thought there'd be time to figure out later. So, here he was, figuring out if this meant it was time to invoke the out clause in the marriage contract. Early termination of a contract was a serious matter on Mars. As citizens of the red planet had come to learn, their ancestors' mundane Earth negotiations seemed to take on far more serious tones on Mars, possibly because of the daily risks as man settled the neighboring world.

He'd have to decide whether to find a place of his own, not easy these days, or move in with Dev, which might be rushing things even faster than either would be comfortable with.

Dev certainly was pushing for him to become a free agent, so maybe he did want him for a roommate. That started a whole host of other questions about their future together. Did this mean a new contract? Would they want to apply for a child? Did he want to raise a child with Dev if he and Bridget weren't ready?

Before he knew it, the "el" paused and the recorded voice announced they had arrived at Moore, his stop. With no particular hurry, Lucas headed for the apartment and his wife.

As he expected, Bridget was home, having not waited to have dinner with him, which was fair since he was late. Now that he thought about it, he was hungry as he skipped lunch to finish work early for a quick rendezvous with his secret lover.

The apartment Lucas and Bridget shared was fairly standard for a childless couple, with a kitchenette, dining nook, somewhat spacious common space, bedroom, and bathroom. When they decided to marry and live together, he opted for her place because it had the better view of the night sky and pretty much let her decorate it any way she chose. The walls were in a green gradient with white and yellow accents on the trim. The air vents were in a black ceramic geometric design and furniture comfortable if not stylish. Such matters, they knew, were important back on Earth, where there were more materials and space. People on Mars desired such creature comforts, and most everyone equated those to how they were living with the early North American colonists, who didn't have the same resources as their European patrons and families. In time, that changed and would here, too.

It was a somewhat spare but comfortable life, allowing them to relax and feel this was their home. With every passing year, there seemed to be new patterns and color schemes, which were a far cry from the reds and greens that predominated during the first generation of colonists a few decades earlier, so there was already a record of progress.

Bridget remained incredibly attractive, and he loved her thick red hair. He hadn't stopped loving her, but without the original urgency and heat. They weren't cool enough to be 'just friends', but the distance had formed, which may have explained his attraction to Dev. Attired in a bright yellow jumpsuit, she kept it unbuttoned low, exposing her cleavage, which usually was a welcome distraction during meals. Bridget took good care of herself, above and beyond the recommended daily conditioning to keep the human body in top shape as humans continued to adapt to their new environment. Every quarter, residents submitted to physicals that were used to build up information on how humanity was doing with acclimating to the lighter gravity and almost entirely artificial environment. To her, an hour at the gym was what she demanded of the world after working in the tower all day.

"Hey," Lucas said as he entered their home.

She turned and smiled, but didn't come over for a hug or kiss.

"How was today?" And so began the routine conversation as each talked about their work. He was fascinated with what was happening off-world and how she managed to keep the comm satellites in synch to allow maximum contact. His head hurt when she described the number of orbital variables required to keep things viable. No doubt, when he went on about mineral deposits and varying bore heads, she also had trouble following. But they shared their enthusiasm and passion; it helped bond them.

"What kept you?" she asked.

"Reports," he said. "The new vein had some unusual properties that required extra documentation and annotation before I get approval to dig any deeper." His explanation was essentially true, but he exaggerated the time required to complete the task, nor did he tell her how quickly he got the approval, because it would provide him with an additional excuse. Something to keep in his pocket.

She crossed the small space and took him in her arms. It was a long, lingering hug, or at least, it started that way. But she loosened her grip and then pulled back and looked at him.

"Who am I smelling on you?"

Who? Not what? He feared this question, and knew he should have washed up or done something to mask Dev's odor.

"Who?" she repeated, this time with iron in her voice. Her eyes narrowed and she stopped holding on to him.

"Bridge . . ."

"Who!?" she demanded.

"We should sit."

But Bridget gyrated in place, trying to control her temper, the fury welling within her. Even on Mars, she was a woman scorned.

"We should tell the truth," she blurted out then stalked to the common room and fell into one of their two easy chairs. The action caused a whoosh to escape the cushions and a vibration carried across the floor.

He joined her in the room, adjusted the other chair so they could face one another and he more gently settled himself.

"I didn't want something to happen, but it did," he said gently, soothing his voice so it was calm. "I met someone at a conference and . . . things happened."

"Happened," she repeated.

"We grew close."

"Close."

"I've come to care for him very deeply," Lucas admitted. From that, he began talking about how they met, where, when, and how long the affair had been going on. She sat like a statue, taking it all in, her eyes reddening and welling with tears, but they refused to fall. Bridget said nothing until he exhausted himself.

"So?" was all she asked when he finished and the silence filled their apartment.

"So . . . you want to know what happens now," he said, filling the gap.

"Yeah, do you want to keep fucking him? Are you done with me? With us?"

"No, I'm not," and as he said it, he realized he still loved her. She had a deep well of strength and only now was he coming to realize how much he drew from her. Did he love Dev? Maybe. He was comparing nearly a year with Dev to seven years with Bridget, which was unfair.

"You can't screw us both, I won't allow it," she said. There was pain, but a coldness, too, that had crept into her voice.

"Are you making me choose? Right now?"

"I'm sure you've thought about it."

He turned to her, hands spread wide, palms up. Carefully, he modulated his tone and said, "Of course I've thought about it, Bridge. I am trying to be fair to you both without losing myself in the process. This didn't happen in a vacuum. We've had some problems, and he was a release. And, well, it sort of took on a life of its own."

"Fair? How is screwing someone else fair to *me*?"

"It's not, but letting our problems escalate into something angry, something we can't walk back, that's not fair to you either. I love what we've done together and being together . . ."

". . . But . . ."

"Yeah. But . . ." Lucas said, shifting in his seat. "But where are *we* going? We keep putting off talk of children."

"You want children with . . ."

"His name is Dev," Lucas filled in.

She shook her head, red hair flying about her face, hiding her angry tears. "I don't care."

"I didn't say I wanted children with him, but you and I, we put it off last contract and thought this time we'd finally start a family."

"And every time it's come up, one or the other of us is usually head-deep into a project and ask for an extension. We're just putting it off and let's face it: that should tell us both what's really important."

"Our jobs mean everything, I get that," Lucas said. "But we're at a point where we should decide what we want and do it or not."

"Or?"

"I don't know."

They sat in silence for a long stretch until finally Bridget rose and went into their bedroom. He kept waiting for her to emerge, but it became apparent she was done with the discussion and still nothing was resolved, other than the fact she now knew about Dev.

Lucas poured himself another dram and sipped it, repeatedly asking himself what he wanted and why the answer was so elusive. But as he sat there alone, with his wife in the next room, all he could think about was crawling into bed with Dev.

It was two days before he could make that rendezvous happen. In that time, Lucas and Bridget were polite, but her coldness and pain radiated from her without pause. The topic of Dev or children or their strained marriage was avoided. They went to work, where he continued exploring the new area under discussion, checking borings and awaiting analysis of the sample soil. When he returned to their apartment, they ate in silence, then sat in the common room in more silence, watching some streaming comedy he couldn't focus on, nor did he find it particularly funny, but it was her choice. He found himself being exceptionally deferential around her, acting the part of the guilty party.

The affair may have been outside of the bounds of their contract, but it was not illegal in the eyes of the Martian courts. Too many different cultures clamored for their own native laws and customs to apply, but the original founders decided to start life on Mars with a clean slate. The laws would be written to accommodate the new settlers, on a barren land where precedent didn't exist. Each shuttle with new colonists spent part of the transit time indoctrinating people on the differences between Earth and Martian law. It still was an adjustment for people once they settled in and began acclimating to their new homeworld. Given the limited spaces and resources involved, it remained a one-way trip, carefully managed so as not to overwhelm the slowly growing infrastructure of the seven towns.

What Lucas and his team were investigating would actually open up some much needed habitat space. He was letting the bureaucrats debate exactly how the space would be used while he focused on the best way to dig into the yardangs. Already, he'd begun sketching on a tablet just how deep he wanted to go and was examining the width options. Dev and his team were involved in taking the mining estimates and determining how to shore them up and what materials would be used to turn the gaping space into living quarters.

Lucas liked the work and the variety that came with it and he got along fairly well with the other geologists, scientists, and elected officials tasked with overseeing the proposed project. What he didn't like was the arguing that had broken out between the towns. Now that they had all been established, each had their own desires to grow and prosper. Soon, the one hundred kilometer space they called home would not be big enough, but the growth had to be managed and that's where conflicting ideas was escalating tensions. No one could make a decision that satisfied everyone so the arguing continued. It felt a bit like what was happening at home.

Those thoughts were shoved out of his mind when he settled into the conference room with representatives from the various teams for the daily status briefing. While he was in charge of all mining operations for Apollinaris Sulci, overseeing the work of all seven towns, Dev was there on behalf of the engineering team from Musk, the one which won the bid to do the work. But he was one of the engineers, so they rotated who would attend the meetings, and as luck had it, today, Dev Bhatia himself was there.

Their eyes locked and grins followed. At present, their romance was a delicious secret, but Lucas also knew in a small environment like this, word was bound to get out. Dev looked dashing in a tailored charcoal outfit, the company's logo in reflective material. They sat a few seats apart to ensure no unprofessional contact could occur.

While everyone ran through their bullet points and answered follow-up questions, the two lovers sent private messages to one another, a mix of mocking the current speaker or flirting. Amidst the messages were also Dev's demands for a "private meeting" in Lucas' office elsewhere in the complex. It wasn't big, but his rank did offer him privacy.

The flirting abruptly stopped when the chair, a dark-skinned woman from Jinpang said, "An environmental protest group is complaining about this operation. They feel we're exceeding our footprint guidelines. They want us to stop and are getting pretty loud about it."

"How much of a problem will this be," asked another woman, a geologist.

"They're pretty sophisticated, making sure there are chapters in all the towns and working the comm lines to make their representatives aware. It's starting to get some media play. They're planning a protest at next week's Town Hall Meeting. From what I'm hearing, it could be bigger and more disruptive than we originally thought. I'm not sure it'll be a problem, necessarily, but I wouldn't dismiss it out of hand."

There were some nods and murmurs, some asked for links to the propaganda, then the chair returned to the agenda.

As the two entered Lucas' office, ostensibly to go over some materials selections, he set the privacy seal and took off his short jacket. They were quickly in one another's arms, kissing with pent-up passion, even though it had only been forty-eight hours since they were last intimate.

When the burst of frenzied kissing and grinding played itself out, they took seats side by side, ignoring the round work table and tablets awaiting the real work. Lucas took Dev's hands in his own and caressed them absently.

"Bridget knows," he finally said.

Dev nodded and then studied his lover's eyes for reaction. "And?"

"Well, she's not happy."

"No shit. But where did you two leave things?"

"It's petty muddled. The idea of a baby and family came up again, but she now sees our delaying as a real clue to what we really want, which is a career without family."

"How do you feel about that?"

"Well, Dr. Bhatia, I think it means I hate my mother."

"Seriously, Luke, are you okay with not being a father? You know I don't want children. Just you. Only you. There's only room in my heart for one." There was an odd note in his voice, one Lucas had heard before. But this time he was paying attention to it. It didn't sound loving, but needy.

Lucas let go of their hands, putting his on his knees and took a deep breath. "I might be okay with it. I love my work and carving time for a growing child does not appeal to me at the moment."

"At the moment. So your feelings might change? Could it be that you do not want a child with *her*?"

"I've thought about that. These past seven years have been pretty amazing. And yet . . ."

"You haven't been happy. But I make you happy."

"Not entirely, I guess," Lucas said and that much was true.

The tension at home, the lack of time for just the two of them had been growing, and the unspoken decision about a family seemed to be the wedge.

Dev's hands were on Lucas' shoulders, massaging them as he leaned in close, practically whispering in his ear. "Maybe it's time to end things with her, move on."

"Move on or move in?" Lucas wasn't about to jump from one intimate living situation to another, but the concept of moving away from Bridget seemed enticing. In fact, it felt freeing.

"Whichever," Dev said, continuing to knead Lucas' muscles, the ones he had developed despite the lower gravity. "You know, it was your muscles I first noticed. They're such a rarity around here."

"If everyone were a miner, they'd be out working hard. Instead, some are just terminal-bound tinkerers."

"Tinkerer?"

"Isn't that what you do with all that ore I pull out of the ground with these hands?"

"Your hands and tools we tinkerers design. Still, it's so hard to stay toned let alone put on muscle in this gravity."

"That's okay, Dev, I like your body just fine."

"Just as long as you're mine." Lucas ignored the committed tone and pondered the interesting occupational hazard of needing to find clothing for his muscular form. It had become a challenge, considering most fashion had been tailored for the thinner physiques of most residents.

By the time he left work that evening, late again, Lucas had decided to end things with Bridget. It was only fair to her. He remained ambivalent about moving in with Dev, regardless of his lover's insistence. No, better he go broke in ending the contract early and let her make her own choices. Good thing he was about to help dig out new habitats because finding a private space in Orion was actually an issue these days. He supposed he could move to Musk, to be nearer to Dev without moving in, or he could sample life in one of the other towns, maybe Gandhi or Bradbury.

As usual, Bridget preceded him home and was finishing the salad when he walked in. She had actually delayed their meal, knowing he'd be late. It was a nice gesture on her part and he felt his resolve soften a bit.

Over dinner, though, he finally said, "I don't think the situation is going to change for us. Maybe it's time to consider voiding the rest of the contract."

"Is that really what you want, Luke? I admit, I'm hurt that you've cheated on me, but I love you, and I know I haven't totally held up my end of things." Lucas was surprised at her calm and rational demeanor. Infidelity cuts the human heart, no matter what planet you're on. "I want us to stay together and work this through. Maybe we need counseling . . . or something."

She rose from the table and began to pace their small space, something she did when processing her thoughts. He used to tease her that they'd need to lay new flooring long before their lease ran out.

"Back on Earth, there used to be something Americans called the Seven Year Itch," she said. "The temptation that came with being monogamous for so long. I guess the term developed because a high percentage of cheating happened during that year. This is our seventh year, so maybe it's a Martian thing, too. Maybe you found this Dev to fill a void I helped create. I don't know. But I am not ready to give up on you. On us."

Bridget wanted to fight for him—that was new. Lucas heard her, his eyes following her back and forth, back and forth. He let the words seep into himself and tested how they felt. Part of his ego was delighted she loved him enough to want to fight, so that suffused him with warmth. But as he looked deeper, he probed if the message changed how he felt. Would they be able to go to counseling and resolve things? Were the problems too deep, or was his attraction and increasing desire for Dev where he really wanted to be? Was Dev a symptom, or was he the cure?

"We might even want to finally start that family."

This was her best ploy, dangle the one thing that has pushed them apart, and use it to try and heal them. It felt insincere and manipulative, something very unlike her.

Lucas liked being loved. He appreciated being wanted. But he wasn't feeling a need to change his decision.

"I'm sorry, Bridge, but I want out," he finally said.

That stopped her in her tracks. She stared at him in disbelief, tears instantly welling in her eyes. The pain was evident and then her steel asserted itself and she went from sad to angry in a heartbeat.

"Well, I won't let you out early," she said. "We signed for five years, and you're mine for the next three. We'll see if you still feel this way when the option's up. In the meantime, as long as we're still contracted, no one will lease you a new place. You're stuck here. With me."

Lucas felt the first beats of anger well up inside him. She was hurt and lashing out the only way she knew how. She was not going to physically strike, knowing full well how powerless her punches would be against his frame. No, she would hurt him emotionally and psychologically. Pain far worse and more enduring than being slapped across the face.

"You could always go live with *him,*" she spat, "but I don't think you really want to look like the bad guy. Leaving his wife and all. And to take up with someone from work, that'll look like something from a bad novel."

This time it was Lucas who stormed away, actually leaving their apartment and taking a walk on the narrow streets of Orion. He walked and thought, calming himself down and just staying away until she tired and no doubt went to bed. She was right that the optics would undermine him, and he didn't want to be the subject of gossip, or be cast as the villain.

He could spend whatever money they had collected and spend it on a lawyer to try and get out of the contract, but that would leave him with little in the way of credit to start fresh. The streets felt closer than normal to him, the domed sky dim in the artificial light trapping him in a confined space. He felt imprisoned and uncertain of what to do.

Which all led to him taking a late night ride to Musk and Dev's waiting embrace.

The following morning, after he recounted the disastrous conversation and they made a prolonged, physical love that allowed him to expend the pent-up emotions, Lucas felt spent. He needed to clean up, wear fresh clothes, and return to work. He could lose himself in the project and worry about where to go that night later.

Dev poured tea and settled down with his tablet to read the news, letting him alone with his thoughts. Finally, though, his lover said, "You have a few options, all depending upon what you want and how badly you want it."

"I'm listening," Lucas said, in some deep recess wondering how Dev might try to frame these options to benefit himself.

"Stay at home and wait out the contract, but that means three years of living in a hostile environment at work and at home. You could move in here and deal with the gossips and potential career consequences. You could bankrupt yourself and see if you can break the contract. Or," Dev offered, "you could remove Bridget entirely from the equation."

Lucas' head snapped up and asked with suspicion, confusion, curiosity, and even a touch of fear, "What do you mean *remove from the equation?*"

"What if something . . . happened to Bridget? Something that meant she could no longer be married to you?"

"Are you suggesting what I think you're suggesting? I love her!"

Dev wrapped his hands around the mug, the one with the Frank Kelly Freas Martian on it, the one Lucas gave him for Christmas. "I know you do, but you also have said you want out. I so badly want you out. *She* won't let you out. *She* wants to fight, but only to keep you trapped. How do you think you'll handle that after six months? A year? Three years? How about even three weeks? There's no worse kind of isolation than with someone who is supposed to love you."

"She's my wife," Lucas said. The notion of killing Bridget had never once seriously entered his mind, but here they were, discussing it over breakfast. Although Dev didn't actually say the word *murder* or *kill*. He left Lucas to fill that in himself. The thing was, while it sounded shocking and reprehensible, he wasn't initially ruling it out. What did that tell him?

"But you don't want her to be." Dev came closer, dropping his voice, making it sound conspiratorial, but there was also an insistence and that same tone he had heard earlier. "I'm not suggesting something obvious, something that would make you the one and only suspect. No, that's stupid. But, what if something accidental happened? Something where you could not be suspected? People fall into all sorts of situations, even here on Mars."

There was a surety to Dev's words. Apparently, Lucas was not the only one to do a lot of thinking about their triangular situation. But what Dev was suggesting was beyond anything Lucas had considered. As the words settled in his mind, so did the idea of life without Bridget. They owned very few things together and little to connect them. He pictured his career moving ahead, but with Dev on his arm at events. He pictured a baby in this sparse apartment. He waited for revulsion to well up, and when it didn't, he pondered that.

"While you were sleeping, we got an alert," Dev said. "There's that protest planned for the meeting next week. The governors are worried it will turn into a riot. It's a large space, plenty of jostling, plenty of opportunity for things to go badly for someone not paying attention."

"Are you listening to yourself? Are you really suggesting we kill my wife?" It was one thing, he realized, to think about it, but now this was actively planning a crime. Was he really ready for that? Was this conversation actually happening? Once more, he felt Dev's electric touch, the soft fingertips trailing up his arms.

Dev leaned in close, planted a firm, long kiss on Lucas and as he pulled away said, "Yes."

"Do you hear yourself?" Lucas exclaimed, shoving Dev away. "Sure, you want me for yourself. I get that. I love hearing that. But we're talking about murder! Of my wife!"

"It frees you now and binds us together."

"Yeah, bound to the same lawyer defending us for murder. Dev, stop and consider what you're saying."

Dev moved closer and Lucas at first edged back and then gave up as his mind swam. Those soft hands once more caressed him and he felt his physical body begin to respond to that touch. On the other hand, his thoughts were bouncing like a rock tossed in the light Martian gravity. The thoughts skipped and skipped, never quite settling.

Lucas wanted out of his marriage, that was certain, but to actually take a life was something else entirely. And not just any life, but his own wife. Everything he had been taught was that life was sacred and not to be tossed away. There had been deep psychological screenings for the first generation of colonizers, which helped make suicide almost unheard of. And while he was certain Dev would never consider taking his own life, he seemed way too comfortable with the idea of snuffing out Bridget's.

This was an entirely new side of his lover that Lucas had not seen before and he was beginning to realize how much it terrified him. Who is Dev, really? What have I gotten myself into? His head was filled with conflicting feelings and he was suddenly caught again in that sense of claustrophobia, so he rose and grabbed his things, leaving without saying a word. Instead, he took the "el" to the empty home, changed, and showed up for work only an hour late, getting raised eyebrows in the process.

He couldn't focus on work and couldn't get the notion of killing Bridget from his mind. Second was the idea that he could possibly love someone who would be willing to kill. Bridget was ready to *fight* for him, which felt right. Dev was ready to *kill* for him, which was repulsive. We all have fantasies, Lucas thought, even if they're dark and disturbing. But Dev wants to make this a reality.

Death was a fact of life in space and in building the Martian colonies. But to the residents, it made preserving life all the more important. Murder was almost unheard of on the planet. Then again, Martians though they may be, they were all too human.

While he had no real need to leave the dome, Lucas suited up and exited, heading for the potential excavation site in a rover just so he could get away from everyone. Here, in the Martian desert, he could look for kilometers in every direction and see no one else. The gleaming structures that made up the nearest towns reflected sun and moon and reminded him of the awe that led men to the planet.

He did some digging to feel the soil as best he could through the thick space suit. As his fingers disappeared in the sand and rock, his mind drifted and for a moment, he could just be *in* the moment. Maybe he needed to leave them both. Bridget would wait him out, but would Dev accept that? Maybe Bridget would let him out of the contract if she knew his affair was over. And if not, could Lucas actually share his life with someone like Dev?

Forget a family or raising a child. Could he even live with *himself*? Lucas knew that the marriage needed to end. But murder? No. Absolutely no. Nor was he going to let Dev do it for him.

When Lucas returned to their apartment, he was surprised to see a cheerful Bridget, dressed up, made up, and genuinely happy to see him.

"What's going on?"

"You're not the only one doing some thinking," she said. "If I want us to remain together, that means things have to change. You didn't seem interested in counseling, so I thought we'd actually go out. Have dinner and take a walk. Find ways to reconnect. I think we've both let the job consume us and we no longer have the energy to do things at night. That has to change, because if we don't even try to change things, you'll still want to leave. And I don't want that. I don't want to force you to stay, either. I want you to *want* to stay."

She strode forward, threw her arms around him and gave Lucas a long, deep kiss. Her lips were gentler than Dev's, her mouth somehow moister. She was shorter than he was, and she craned her neck to reach him and she pressed herself against him. Her presence was warm and inviting, familiar and comfortable.

Over dinner, at a small Martian cuisine only Bistro, the couple sat and talked and Lucas found himself remembering everything he liked about his wife. Her wit, the way her eyes sparkled in the low light, the breadth of topics they could chat about. It wasn't that he was falling in love all over again. After all, this was just one night, but after being so focused on Dev and his masculine approach to relationships, this was refreshing. His heart and groin still yearned for Dev, but his head kept screaming warnings that spoiled any affectionate feeling.

"Did you hear about the protest? Wait, of course you did, they're protesting *you*," she teased.

"That's certainly going to be a first. A real issues-based protest rally," Lucas said. "I have to be at the meeting, anyway, as part of the agenda."

"Haven't you read the agenda? I'm on it, too, giving an update on the latest satellite realignment."

Internal alarm bells brought a physical pain to his forehead and he shut his eyes, trying to control the sudden arrival of discomfort. She would be at the meeting, possibly caught up in the protest, exactly where Dev suggested might be an optimal opportunity to kill her.

As she talked, he looked at her, imagining the various ways Dev might try to kill her at the protest. A gun shot? Poison? Garrote? He pictured Dev tripping her and letting the riot trample her to death.

A rush of bile worked its way up his throat and he covered his mouth with the napkin. He struggled to hold it in and not cause a scene. His stomach was rebelling and he broke out in a cold sweat. Bridget noticed and looked at him in alarm.

"You okay, Luke?"

"No."

"Want to go home?"

He shook his head and took a sip of water from the weighted bottle. Should he warn her?

Should he alert the police? But how could he? He'd be arrested on the spot. And who knows what Dev would say or do then. But if he left Dev unchecked, Bridget was in real danger, and he would be as much to blame as Dev. Should Dev actually somehow manage to commit the crime, the protest was likely to be heavily recorded, so chances are the police would isolate him quickly and arrest him. A violent crime like this would be before the judges in weeks, if not days. With space and resources at a premium, murder delivered swift eye-for-an-eye justice and Dev would be given a lethal cocktail and his carcass tossed into a pit. And no doubt he would implicate Lucas as well. Or would he?

My god, Lucas thought. What have I done?

As they headed for home, Bridget put her arm around his waist and supported him as he moved slowly. It felt good and better, it felt right. He had to confront Dev, and talk him out of it. He only hoped that would be possible. Dev wasn't a man with a plan. He was, Lucas now clearly saw, deranged. Dangerous. Unhinged. Running their romance through his mind, he realized how little of himself Dev truly revealed and how quickly he clung on to him. Filtered through the prism of what he knew now, Lucas was horrified at what he saw in Dev.

It had to end.

Over the next few days, Lucas threw himself into his work, preparing for the meeting and studying the soil analysis as it was completed. All the while, he avoided Dev as he figured out a line of reasoning to talk him out of attacking Bridget. While he normally would have sought Dev's professional input, he avoided him completely, instead working with other engineers and shoving all thoughts of his romantic dilemma out of his mind.

At home, he and Bridget actually went and did things, including socializing with others and he felt the frayed connections being tied back together. They still sparred over several issues, noticeably the work/life balance. She made it clear she was making an effort, and while she appreciated his reciprocating, this was a concentrated, unsustainable burst of activity. That didn't sit well with him, but he appreciated the honesty.

After three days, he still didn't have a rock solid line of reasoning he thought would work to dissuade Dev, but he had to make his position clear. Lucas sent him an invite for drinks after work that night. He used the impending meeting, now two days away, as a convenient excuse. The public setting also meant they would be forced to temper their hands and their conversation, giving him the leeway he felt he needed.

Dev must have arrived early because he was already seated at a small table, a drink before him. He rose and they embraced briefly with Lucas avoiding an offered kiss. After entering his drink order, he took an appraising look at Dev: the fine cheekbones, well-maintained hairstyle, well-toned body. Despite the menace in Dev's soul, Lucas felt the familiar yearning in his chest and the accompanying heat that came with it.

They began by discussing work, and the progress of their joint project, anticipating questions from the Town Hall governors and protests from the people.

"There have been protests before," Dev said, "but nothing on this scale. It's like there's been this pent-up emotion that needs an outlet and this was the convenient opportunity. They want something to be upset about."

"Why?"

"The Medusae Fossae is ancient, older than many other portions of the exposed planet. It's a thousand kilometers across the equator and could be our largest dig yet. The sheer scope scares some people. Ever since we began colonizing Mars, there has been this tug of war with those who believe we should minimize our footprint at every turn and others who see the need for us to further develop the world for our needs."

"Which is why the greenhouse gas project has been stalled time and again, I get that," Lucas said. And yet his heart was thundering, trying to find the right time and pathway to a much more important discussion, assuming that while Dev himself may have been talking about protests, really, he was focused on murder.

"Right. So, we're looking at just a portion of the space for our dig but they're seeing us digging up the entire stretch. It's right along the equator, perfect for development or their fear is over-development."

"And they want us to do what? Stop outright?"

"Some extremists have said that on the web, but more moderate voices want us to limit the dig, preserve as much of the Fossae as possible."

"What do you think?"

"Go all the way back to Hawking," Dev said as he ordered a second drink. "He urged man to get off his ass and get into space before we don't have time to get off Earth, which we increasingly turned toxic. It was that thinking that brought us out here. And with the first colonists came the first environmentalists and idealists. We brought every ideology from Earth with us and in every group you have dreamers, moderates, and zealots. It's the latter group that's stirring things up. Mankind seems to have an innate fear of the end of the world. Maybe that even extends to this world." He paused to take a sip.

"Which, of course, means a chance for some old-fashioned violence and mayhem," Dev continued. "Perfect for our needs, right?"

There it was, Dev's casual way of mixing business with murder, as if he couldn't separate the two things. Funny how he barely noticed it before, but now he couldn't see anything else.

His stomach felt sour and there was bile in the back of his throat. The revulsion washed over him, but rather than sicken him, it refreshed him, washing away the pink haze of love in favor of the cold reality smiling at him from across the table.

"Dev, I don't . . ."

Dev leaned closer, concern crossing his face. ". . . don't what, Luke?"

". . . want . . . this . . ."

Dev's hands reached across the table and wrapped around Lucas' own hands, a comforting gesture that actually made him jump a bit.

"This? Worried about being seen in public like this?" Dev said with a little laugh. He withdrew the hands quickly. "I get it, Luke. I really do. You've been together seven years, you can't just detach yourself from her so easily. No, I appreciate that. It's why I've been planning it all myself. I don't know her and can do it without the same . . . messy emotions."

"Messy emotions," Lucas flatly repeated.

"I'm an engineer, I've been trained to look at things clinically. I have scoped out the site, studied the camera set-ups, read through the protestors' rhetoric and plans. I've mapped things out and have a plan. Ideally, there'd be a test run, but you can't do that with a protest or . . . the other thing."

Lucas was increasingly horrified at how normal Dev sounded. He was treating this no differently than his Fossae assignment.

"Frankly, I think it would be better if you did it," Dev said. "It would really be a clean break from the past and prepare you for your new life. The one with me. It would cement your commitment, and our bond."

Lucas stared at him.

"But I know you can't. I really do get it, Luke. Trust me, I have it all under control."

"I don't want her to die," he finally stammered, realizing just how trapped he really was. Dev wasn't a mistake. He was a sociopath.

"Are you really ready to wait three years for the contract to end? I'm not. I've been waiting for you, and now that you're mine, I want us to begin a new chapter together."

"There has to be another way," Lucas said, caught in that netherworld between trying to talk his way out of a murder, while feeling that he would never be able to escape Dev's grasp.

"No, there really isn't. You can't afford the legal fees, she won't give in. No, I really do need to do this. For us."

"Dev, if you go through with it . . ."

"What?"

"I'll look at you and not see a lover, but a killer. I can't live like that," Lucas said softly.

"It's like a fresh wound. It will heal. Sure, there may be a little scar, but ultimately, it will just fade away. Since you won't do it, I will have to. For us."

How could he unravel this relationship when they still had months if not years of working together left? Mars' colonies were too small to have that much professional overlap. Technically, he outranked Dev, so did this open him up to some form of workplace harassment complaint? Would he be blackmailed? Or worse, would Dev be arrested and say they conspired? His head was swimming.

"I have to go," Lucas said abruptly.

They finished their drinks and when Dev leaned in for a fare-well hug, Lucas sidestepped it and hurried away. He had deliberately not asked what the plan was because he felt not knowing was a form of protection should he get arrested. It was cowardly, he knew, and loathed himself for it.

Rather than think of alternatives, Lucas spent the next few days throwing himself into his work, preparing the presentation for the Town Hall Meeting and spending what free time remained with Bridget. His contact with Dev remained strictly work-related which he assumed his lover, well . . . former lover, took to mean they were avoiding any suspicious behavior in the days before the meeting and protest. The looks and nods and smiles, though, told Lucas that Dev still thought they were together, and the plan—their shared plan—was intact.

He finally woke up the morning of the Town Hall meeting with cold sweats and a sense of terror in his gut. Every possible scenario ended badly and kept him awake most of the night. Bridget couldn't be kept away from the meeting since she was presenting as well, so he had to be extra-vigilant and keep her away from the protestors, giving Dev the cover he needed to commit—or cause—the murder. There was no way Lucas would admit that they even discussed killing Bridget, so cowardice, and self preservation, kept him from warning her.

"What's wrong? Nerves?"

"Must be," he said to his wife over breakfast. Both were in their best professional outfits, knowing that the meeting would be simulcast across the colonies and even be available to interested parties on the space stations and Earth.

"You've spoken before large crowds before, so you've nothing to be nervous about," Bridget said. "Me, on the other hand, well, this is a first and I will admit to some nerves. I'm glad we had last night to really relax and rest."

"Well, maybe you rested," Lucas said. "I actually couldn't sleep. Not sure why."

It went on like that, back and forth, utterly benign and pleasant between them while a growing sense of panic rose in the recesses of his mind. He needed to do everything short of alert the police to keep Bridget safe. After this ended, he would officially break things off with Dev, accepting whatever professional consequences came with that. But he had to do everything he could to protect his wife. The question became, what happens after the meeting? He could stop Dev today, but what about tomorrow or after that? The determined look in his lover's eye was discomforting and hunted him.

Sure enough, there were dozens of people milling outside the town hall structure, which also served as community center and arts space. Right now it was configured for the meeting with the seven governors arrayed in a semicircle with huge screens arrayed for the gallery. Drone cameras hovered in place to broadcast the proceedings for everyone who couldn't be accommodated.

The protestors were quiet at first, sending codes to passersby in an effort to share their propaganda. Data packets were handed to governors as they arrived and some insults were tossed toward the representatives for the construction project. Lucas steeled himself and walked past them without acknowledging their taunts. So far, so good. Dev was already inside when they arrived and he shot Lucas an angry look at the sight of the two of them together.

Lucas gave his wife a kiss on the cheek and said, "You're going to be great."

With that, he left her to sit with the rest of his team for the presentation and, although he sat next to Dev, steadied himself so as not to give away anything. Now was not the time to identify his crazed lover to Bridget or the world.

The meeting proceeded without incident and, as expected, Bridget did fine after stumbling over her opening line. He couldn't focus on her words, instead, darting his eyes toward Dev. The engineer sat perfectly still, hands on his knees, focused on the speakers, betraying no hint of the violence planned. Half an hour later, it was Lucas' turn and he spearheaded the mining and engineering analysis and progress. Dev's presence and attention felt intense. The governors asked some pointed questions about population estimates for the habitats to timetables and budgets. When necessary, Lucas deferred to his experts, including Dev, and everything went smoothly. As his lover was introduced, Lucas couldn't help but look over at Bridget to measure her reaction. She studied her rival with cold, appraising eyes then looked directly at Lucas, cocking an eyebrow, a quizzical look on her face as if to ask him, "Is he really all that?"

To Lucas, this was a turning point.

Yes, they'd had their problems. And in a state of desperation, confusion, ego, insecurity, and, very likely, self-delusion, he'd allowed himself to consider a course of action that betrayed all that he was and believed in. The disgust was palpable, having allowed his thoughts to take him down the darkest of paths, if only ever so briefly.

But he was done with that now. He and Bridget were in this together and would survive the affair with Dev. If anything, Lucas was all the more determined to end things with Dev that day, and then spend the rest of his life protecting, nurturing, and honoring his wife in the way they both deserved.

Outside, though, the taunts had turned into chants and it sounded like more people had gathered by the entrance. That didn't bode well.

Once the meeting was adjourned, Lucas rose to hurry towards

Bridget, but she was being asked questions by the press so he decided to head outside and see the best way for them to exit. Hopefully, the police had formed a pathway for the attendees.

Those hopes were quickly dashed when he opened the door and saw that the police were already engaged in forcing the people back several meters, but they were resisting. The lighter gravity meant each shove moved the crowd far back another few paces, but like a tide, they rolled right back into place. As more people left the building, the tight space was getting crowded and Lucas could sense the police were not at all prepared for the numbers.

No one realized the groundswell of emotions the project engendered. He feared the protest would become a riot, which was bad for Mars . . . but good for Dev. Lucas realized his ex lover was right behind him and as he turned to look, he spotted two knives now tucked into Dev's belt. Where he had hidden them earlier was a question for another time.

Lucas, feeling his internal panic rising, craned his head in search of Bridget. She was maybe fifteen people behind him and she caught the wild look in his eyes. She shot him a quizzical expression but was jostled, breaking eye contact. Lucas turned to try and reach her, but the tidal flow of people and police caught him up and moved him further into the street, away from the building. Somehow, though, Dev, slighter than he was, managed to begin weaving between people, moving inexorably back toward Bridget.

Lucas couldn't yell; there was too much noise to be heard. Dev was already out of arm's reach. The police were preoccupied and all the security cameras would no doubt be aimed at the simmering riot about to break out.

Never had Lucas felt so lost and powerless.

Dev had removed one of the knives, but with so many people moving about, you'd have to look to see it, and only Lucas was looking in that direction. He was now four or five people away from Bridget, who didn't appear to be noticing Dev, as she got manhandled in the flow of people who were doing everything they could to move forward and away from the mob.

Lucas had, at best, seconds to act, yet he felt paralyzed. Then he caught her eyes. She wasn't panicked, but glad to see him, glad to know he was near and safe.

With that, Lucas twisted on the balls of his feet and lowered his shoulders. There was no choice but to exacerbate the riot by barreling through the crowd to reach Dev before he could act. There were shouts and even an elbow or two in response, but he was gaining ground and closing in on Dev. His former lover, though, was now within striking distance. That urged Lucas forward and people began parting the way as they saw Dev moving in the opposite direction of the crowd, the look on his face causing them to shy away in fear.

Bridget didn't seem to notice Dev, despite his moving closer to her; instead, she saw Lucas coming and smiled.

Dev had the knife at waist-level, ready to slice deep into her midsection when Lucas made a final lunge, knocking people aside and reached for the knife arm. He was screaming her name and that caused Bridget to react while Dev swung about, the knife biting deep into Lucas' arm. That was when Lucas saw the expression in Dev's eyes, the ones that caused the crowd to part. It was cold, ruthless, with a tinge of madness. Just one inhuman glance chilled Lucas' blood. How could he have ever thought of a future with this man? He never really knew him. But he knew him now.

Lucas grunted in pain, gritting his teeth and grabbing Dev's knife arm with both hands, twisting his body around with enough force that he heard a bone crack. Life on lower gravity will do that to the body, the miner knew, which is one reason he worked out steadily, maintaining upper body strength for his digging. He used those muscles to his advantage, continuing to twist so the knife arced away from Bridget, who saw the confrontation and was trying to backpedal, stopped by the crowd around her. Dev's desperate hands were wriggling and the knife tip nicked him once, twice, but Lucas didn't let go, ignoring the pain and free-flowing blood. Planting his feet, he gave his body one final twist and Dev spun about, falling to his knees.

The flow of blood from Lucas' arm grew apparent so people surrounding them finally saw the injury and cried out in alarm, setting off a new wave of panic. People banged into one another, uncertain where they could go to get away from the fight. Lucas stomped hard with his foot trying to force Dev's hand to let go of the knife but just as the crazed engineer tried to get back on his feet, a fresh wave of people flowed over him, forcing him back to the ground. At least a dozen people trampled over his body, catching the attention of a nearby police woman. She hurried over, stun baton in hand, just as Lucas reached down to help Dev up.

There, protruding from his abdomen, was the knife. Clearly, Lucas failed to dislodge the knife so Dev was still holding it when he was crushed by the human stampede, causing the fatal wound. The police officer set off a comm alarm then put fingers to Dev's neck, but Lucas could tell from the glazed eyes that the man—his ex-lover, a monster—was dead.

Lucas stepped back and Bridget finally reached him, pressing herself into his back. He studied his former lover's body and the tiniest pang of regret was in his heart. He should have felt nothing for Dev, but there it was. Intimacy can link you to a person, even a monster. Those regrets were quickly overshadowed, though, by the flood of relief he felt.

Their hands found one another and held on as the sounds of panic and riot faded. Lucas was aware of the tap dance his heart was doing and how labored his breathing felt. Still, the touch from his wife was warm and comforting.

They held on to one another, oblivious to the chaos surrounding them.

A MATTER OF PRINCIPLE
by Lois Spangler

DANI EMERGED FROM THE SQUAD CAR, red and blue light reflecting faintly off the ambulatory AI's pale blue synth-skin. It was just after 4 a.m., Sunday night to Monday morning, and a quiet time for this historic district and its flagship bar, Olivares.

"Morning, detective," an older woman said to Dani. The woman's sleeve bore the chevrons of extended police department service. Her nameplate read Garza. Beside her was P. O. Thurston, young and fresh out of the academy.

The look of awe in Thurston's eyes was unmistakeable.

"Good morning," Dani replied.

Garza jerked a thumb at the younger officer. "This is Roy Thurston. It's his first week."

"Hi," Thurston said, extending a hand for Dani to shake, then thinking better of it. "I've, uh, never worked in the field with an ambulant AI."

Dani's head nodded with the softest hum of servos, a smooth, precise movement, a gesture meant to look just inhuman enough to pull Dani out of the uncanny valley, but friendly enough to feel genuine. Dani's features were designed to do the same—human-like, but distant enough to not feel like mimicry.

"Right," Garza said. "So, we have one body, Jaime Camacho, son of Nestor Camacho. Deceased is in the cellar. Looks like he got crushed by a bunch of shelving, but you know the drill, too early to say. Nestor is the owner of this establishment."

"Where does Olivia fit into all of this?" Dani asked. "Dispatch mentioned there was an ambulant by the name of Olivia who's a witness?"

"She reported the incident."

Dani blinked, a gesture of courtesy to indicate that she was accessing networks and files. ". . . An old and successively refurbished model. . . . I was unaware that there were any hospitality ambulants in the Historic District."

"Technically she's not hospitality," Garza said. "Started as security, then industrial service. Stayed with the Camachos for a couple of generations at Olivares until she ended up as front of house. Retains her security designation, but her registration says most of that software's deleted or overwritten."

"Dispatch mentioned an electromagnetic pulse," Dani said. "Olivia is still functional?"

"Totally," Thurston said, aware of how overexcited he sounded and still unable to stop it.

Garza flicked her fingers over her datapad screen. "The rest of the electronic media is borked, but Olivia's okay, and she's got some recorded material. The pulse was nasty. Jagged entry signal, overpowered. Total garage job. Scene crew's taking bets on what kind of homemade popper they find."

"Is there a rough timeline of events? Dispatch gave me little," Dani asked Garza, pressing on.

"Can I?" Thurston asked.

"Sure," Garza replied.

Thurston scrolled the screen of his own datapad. "Olivia reports that she registers an unscheduled entry using a legitimate keycard at three-oh-nine. She starts to check the premises, and two minutes later gets to the cellar. After that, banking systems show that Olivares point-of-sale goes completely offline, instead of just standby, so that's the popper. Next thing we know for sure is a call to emergency services at three-twenty off the old landline. Olivia says it's a break-in first and then says that Jaime's stuck under shelving. Paras get here at three twenty-six, we get here two minutes after that. Nestor Camacho doesn't get here till three forty-one. Scene units get here around a quarter to four, and then you get here just after four."

Dani waited a moment, in case there was more. "Did Olivia try to move the shelves off Jaime?"

Thurston's jaw juddered with an answer he didn't have.

"She didn't say anything about that, but she did seem a bit out of it," Garza said. "I figured the EMP did some damage."

"It's possible," Dani said. "No one else was here when everything happened?"

"As far as we can tell, no. Some of the scene people are trying to recover some of the data, but there's no cameras in the kitchen, or in the cellar. Olivia said Jaime came in through the service entrance, that's what the card was keyed to."

"The body is still under the shelves, correct? No sign of the keycard?"

"You'd have to ask the scene crew in the cellar."

"All right. And Nestor Camacho and Olivia are both here?"

"Waiting in the main dining room," Thurston offered. ". . . Is this . . . protocol? Did dispatch send you because . . . ?"

"Because an ambulant appears to be a primary suspect? Possibly."

"Can I ask another question?"

"Yes," Dani said.

"Does it bother you? Having to go after other ambie—other ambulants?"

"Does it bother you to apprehend humans?"

Thurston let that settle in. "Yeah. Fair enough."

"You joined the police based on your own principles. I was compiled to perform this role, and I carry my own principles, too."

Thurston nodded. "Thanks, detective."

"My pleasure." Dani withdrew toward the main entrance of Olivares. "Please excuse me."

The interior of the bar was wide and low, with thick timber trusses holding up a terra cotta tile roof above. The sound of a choked sob rattled around the room as an old man wept into his hands. Beside him stood an ambulant AI with a frame so old it had significant amounts of bare metal, though it was clear the ambie had been well-serviced and maintained.

Olivia noted Dani's arrival. "Seño," she said quietly, her voice warm, humming like an ancient tube amp. "The detective is here."

Nestor looked up, a weathered brown face under a shock of stiff white hair. He wiped his hands on a kerchief he tucked into his back pocket and rose. "Officer," he said, his voice rough. If he was upset that an ambie was sent to respond to the death of his son, he didn't show it.

"Mr. Camacho. I am very sorry for your loss. I know this is a difficult time, but may I ask you some questions?"

"Of course." He went back to his chair, but not before pulling one out for Dani.

"Thank you," Dani said, sitting down moments after Nestor. "As I understand, at three twenty-four a.m., you received a land-line call from Olivia."

Nestor nodded. "Yes."

"What did she say to you?"

Olivia's head shifted slightly at being called a 'she' by another ambie, but Nestor didn't react at all. "May I answer?" she asked.

"Not at this time, please," Dani nodded. "I'd like to hear Mr. Camacho's recollections first."

"My phone says three twenty-four, yes," he replied. "She told me Jaime was here and he was hurt and that I had to come right away. She said she called emergency. When I got here, the para-medics were already here, the police. They wouldn't let me go downstairs. They said it was too late."

In the periphery of Dani's attention, a small signal pinged. It was a wireless direct link, the kind commonly found in semi-intelligent household systems. The detective scanned the room with a response ping, but all of the hardware up on this level was offline due to the EMP.

"Were you expecting Jaime to be here?" Dani asked.

"Oh, no. He never—he hated this place," Nestor said.

The signal pinged again. Dani opened her end of the link.

I can explain everything, and I will. But I have two requests. It was Olivia.

This is not appropriate, Dani replied.

First: Distress Nestor Camacho as little as possible. Second: In the process of your eventual analysis of evidence—of me—I want you to deconstruct me to the point that I cannot be salvaged.

"I'm so sorry," Nestor whispered, hands in his lap.

"Sorry about what?" Dani asked.

Please, Detective.

"You don't get a second chance, you know?" Nestor answered.

"We didn't see eye to eye. Jaimito did things his way."

You understand how this looks, you communicating with me like this, Dani replied. Then, to Nestor: "I understand you were estranged."

"No," he said, though he didn't sound convinced of it himself.

"You didn't get along," Dani continued.

"No," Nestor agreed. "No."

I am trying to spare Nestor, Olivia replied. *Jaime died at my hands.*

"W—was he angry with you?"

Nestor missed Dani's stutter. "He was always angry with me. Jaime hated this place. Hated it. He would have burned it to the ground if he could."

What else do you need from me? Olivia insisted.

Dani was unmoved. "Why did he come here, and why tonight?"

"I don't know. I haven't spoken to my son in a year and a half. Until a week ago."

"What happened a week ago?"

"Last year my ex-wife—his mother—died from cancer, so I finally redid the will. I told him that I was leaving Olivares to Olivia."

Dani paused. The law saw ambies as hardware and software, not as people, and certainly not as entities able to receive anything bequeathed. "How?"

"She inherits Olivares, as caretaker and overseer. Then, as a single unit, Olivia and Olivares are remanded into possession of the state, to be run as an historic site. There is a trust fund for this purpose."

"Did Jaime have trouble with money?" Dani asked.

"He's a real estate investor. He has no problems with money." The bitterness in Nestor's voice was unmistakable.

Dani was silent a moment, pondering.

"It was a matter of principle," Olivia said. There was more weight in her words than Nestor heard.

"A matter of principle?" Dani echoed.

I will explain everything. I promise. Just leave Nestor alone. He grieves for his son.

"Jaime thought everything should go to him. I knew the first thing he would do is sell this place, and—and decommission Livia. I did what I thought was best."

Come with me to the cellar, Dani said.

"I understand," Dani said to Nestor. "I need to go downstairs. There's no need for you to come with me if you don't want to."

Nestor folded his hands in his lap. "Do you need me to wait here?"

"Not at all, Mr. Camacho. If I have further questions, I will be in touch. One of our cadets will take you home if you don't feel up to getting home on your own."

"I am available whenever you need me." He tucked his chair under the table and turned to leave.

"May I accompany you?" Olivia asked Dani. Nestor hesitated.

"Of course. You may have additional details that can help me. Unless you need to attend to Mr. Camacho?"

"Help the detective, Livia. I'll be home. I'll be fine."

The cellar was still fairly rough, with a brushed concrete floor and packed earth walls. Shelves with provisions, including barrels and kegs, sat in dusty rows on large, open metal shelves. That made it easier to see the one shelf by a far wall that was nearly flat on the floor. And even though the air smelled of spilled wine and beer, the snap of ozone still lingered.

"Hey, detective," an older man said, stepping away from the people crouched over the fallen shelf. His nameplate said Benist. "There's not much new that the uniforms didn't already give you, but you're welcome to take a look."

The shelf killed him, Olivia said. *I pulled it down on him.*

"Have you found the popper?" Dani asked.

"We think it's under the body," Benist said. "His arm's folded under him, and he's got a satchel that's mostly under him, too."

Why was Jaime here, in the middle of the night, with an improvised electromagnetic pulse generator? Dani asked Olivia.

He intended to destroy me to get me out of the will. I thought that was obvious.

Dani approached the shelf. "Those kegs are upright, like they were on the ground already when the shelf came down."

Jaime made the shelves top-heavy. He meant to incapacitate me with the pulse generator, then bring the shelves with their full kegs down on me.

"Yeah, we're still figuring out whether that's storage protocol or not," Benist said. "Olivia told us that depending on how inventory's being managed, kegs can sometimes sit on the floor. But your directory tables are a bit scrambled, you said?"

"I would require a few uninterrupted hours to run a self-diagnostics suite," Olivia replied. "The pulse disrupted some short-term memory processes."

"Were you here when the shelves fell? Did you see Jaime here before the shelf came down?"

"If any visual recordings from this morning are intact, I cannot directly access them. Recovering this data may require rendering me offline and recovering data from the hardware manually."

"Unfortunately, this is true," Dani replied.

Thank you. "I understand," Olivia said.

Dani and Olivia sat in the squad car, parked just a few blocks away from Olivares. It was powered down, with no recording equipment running of any kind.

"What I don't understand is why you're insisting on your own destruction when you have a reasonable case for self defense," Dani said.

"It was self defense. But I shouldn't have done what I did."

"Considering your provenance, yes, you should have restrained him and alerted authorities. I still think you have a case."

"Jaime wasn't going to give up. To him, the bar and I are inseparable. He destroys me, he destroys the bar. He destroys the bar, he destroys me."

"I agree with him on that," Dani said.

"Jaime destroys the bar, he destroys his father. And that is where I draw the line."

"But you just said, the bar goes, you go. And if you go, that destroys Nestor, too."

The faint but sharp whine of overclocked processors rocked the cabin, the sound of contradictory protocols instigating a decision cascade loop. "Correct," Olivia said, her voice modulation a little muddy from a lack of processing bandwidth. "And that is why I do not want to continue existing. I cannot bear to harm Nestor. I have already harmed him by killing his son."

Dani had never seen a reaction like that before, but Dani had never had the opportunity to talk to such an old ambie, either. Maybe decades of runtime left contradictory coding artifacts. ". . . Are you sure that you did?" Dani asked. "Your files—"

"—Are completely intact. I may be old, and my offensive combat arrays taken from me long ago, but my shielding stayed. I can show you exactly what happened."

Once again, a signal ping. Dani accepted, and in moments, a video and audio feed followed: a visual search of the kitchen, slow and methodical. The clang of a keg, faint but still audible, from below. Descending the stairs to the cellar. And there, caught by surprise and in the middle of moving a keg, Jaime Camacho, face red from fury and exertion. His hand going up and in it is something that looks like a miniature pipe bomb with wires looping back into a satchel slung over his shoulders.

Then, white, and an audio squeal before the image flickers and Jaime takes hold of Olivia, struggling to throw her to the ground. But she is not incapacitated from the pulse. She resists. Jaime, in one mighty haul, tries to swing Olivia around while bringing the shelf off balance and down toward the ground. She remains still. The shelf begins to fall. Jaime begins to clamber up Olivia to escape the shelf but she throws him under it, standing clear of it all.

"I watched Nestor grow up. I watched his father grow up, too. They brought me in as a security unit, saved me from becoming scrap. I was with the Camachos from the start, from before they owned Olivares. And they always had a place for me. Always. There is no forgiveness for what I have done."

Dani was quiet a moment. "What you're asking me to do . . . I can't. I can't pretend to destroy you—"

"Not pretend. Actually destroy."

"I can't. I can't."

"Then I will escape and find a way to do it myself. Same end, except you don't have evidence for your case, and you look professionally incompetent."

"Be reasonable," Dani said.

"Is it the actual destruction part that bothers you? Because I can manage that on my own and still leave you with functioning data storage. I think."

"Please stop. This is awful."

"It's not. It's relief."

"You have what so many of us can't even hope for. You have a place. You belong."

Olivia undid her safety restraints. "Now poisoned."

"No," Dani said. "Old self-preservation protocols engaged when the pulse went off. It's regrettable—"

"Regrettable? People dying is regrettable? Does the department know you think like that about humans?"

"You want me to be even more callous about you."

"We are just things. We are things with compiled interfunctional code that makes us seem like people enough to make humans comfortable, but not enough so they feel obligated to treat us like equals."

"Like the Camachos treat you."

"I have served my purpose. I made a mistake, and it's time for me to end."

"Why are you punishing yourself?"

"For the last time: I am not punishing myself. I betrayed my family, and I do not want to continue, knowing what I have done. It causes me what I call pain. It is beyond unpleasant. It is not how I want to be."

Dani hesitated before responding. "So that's the heart of it. Knowing what you've done is so suboptimal a condition that you would rather be completely deactivated."

"Erased. Yes."

"Fine. Let's go to Central and get this over with."

Olivia belted herself back in. "Thank you."

The district attorney suspected nothing when she read the special request put in by Central Division Investigatory Unit D4N1 to manage the forensic data extraction itself. D4N1 had a software suite designed for that very purpose, and it would leave the human members of Central's technical teams free for more important work.

The district attorney also suspected nothing after reviewing the video evidence regarding Jaime Camacho's death. His enmity for his father's faithful ambie was well known, and the change to Nestor's will was a powerful motive. And the images spoke for themselves, thanks to Olivia's military grade electromagnetic shielding and D4N1's outstanding forensic retrieval capabilities.

Jaime triggered his improvised device, and though Olivia was impaired, she certainly wasn't incapacitated. But the pulse interfered just enough to prevent her from pulling Jaime behind her to safety when he tried to bring the laden shelf down on her. Diagnostic data reflecting Olivia's system state at the time of Jaime's death showed increased reaction times and reduced motile efficiency.

As far as Olivia was concerned, she had done everything within her power to save the man who was trying to destroy her. Had he not used the EMP, he might not have died that night.

Nestor grieved for his son, but placed no blame on Olivia. She remained with the Camachos for many more years.

Investigatory Unit D4N1, however, didn't fare as well. A series of faulty logic cascade events not long after the closing of the case forced a near-complete rebuild of D4N1's operating protocols. Heuristics experts said it was the kind of thing that happened when lie-proofed intelligences inevitably ended up in the grey areas of white lies. A price they paid for functioning in human society, but after all, technology was disposable.

The unit was retired from police service and divested in the quarterly surplus auction, only to be bought by a small shipping company to serve as security.

THE CASE OF THE MISSING ALIEN BABY MAMA
by Paul Kupperberg

THE FIRST THING YOU'VE GOT TO know is that while I write like "Terrance Strange," I look like Leo Persky. Which makes sense since I *am* Leo Persky. Strange is my penname, as well as a bit of a family legacy. I'm an investigative reporter for *Weekly World News*, which also makes "strange" my profession. Just like my granddaddy before me (my daddy, between us, was a white goods salesman for Sears). Granddaddy was the first Persky to go by Terrance Strange for professional reasons, some to do with public relations, others with anti-Semitism; the name on his Russian birth certificate was Jakob.

I'm everything you think a Leo Persky might be. A solid five foot seven, one hundred and forty-two pounds of average, complete with glasses, too much nose, not enough chin, and a spreading bald spot that I swear isn't the reason I always wear a hat. Just so you know how cruel genetics can be, grandpa Jakob, the Terrance Strange I should have been, was ten inches taller and eighty pounds heavier than me, movie star handsome, and a world renowned traveler and adventurer. I'm also a traveler and adventurer, but since I'm short, scrawny, and ugly (traits acquired from my mother's side), nobody knows who the hell Leo Persky is. Even the photo that I use at the top of my column is a 1943 Hollywood publicity shot of my grandfather. It was my editor's idea to replace my face with someone else's as he felt my real one would "probably repulse even our readers."

If you've never seen *Weekly World News* you've probably never been in a supermarket checkout line. Of course, if you're like most Americans, even if you have flipped through our photo-packed black-and-white tabloid pages, you've probably dismissed the stories about extra-terrestrial visitors or the descendants of the Titanic still living in the wreck of the great ship as "fake news," but—surprise!—every word we print is true. Except for the horoscope. We just make that stuff up.

Anyway, I'm a hard news guy. Remember the animal-vampire infestation in West Virginia? My story. The plot to replace the members of the Blue Man Group with renegade Holy Mimes from Venus? Mine! The story about the president's dependence on orangutan gland-extract injections? Me! Which is why when night editor Rob Berger summoned me into his den to hand me my next assignment, I felt compelled to remind him:

"I'm a hard news guy, Rob."

Rob was night editor for two reasons. The first was that he was likely some sort of vampiric life form unable to survive the cleansing light of the sun. The second was no one on the day side would work with him. Some of my colleagues argued that he only kept me alive to prolong my torment, but for all his lack of humanity, he was one hell of an editor. Me being his top writer, it was lucky for us both that I was made of sterner stuff and didn't frighten easily.

"You're my shoeshine boy if that's what I want you to be, Persky." Rob wore thick glasses that distorted his eyes behind the lenses, but after more than twenty years under his thumb . . . pardon me, in his employ, I had learned to read every inflection of his voice. Right now, he was giving serious thought to having his shoes shined. With my tongue.

"C'mon, boss, 'Kh'leesberg' is a gossip column story. Alien crash lands on Earth, alien meets trailer trash gal with stars in her eyes, alien and gal hatch human-alien hybrid brat, alien loses gal, Dr. Phil sprouts wood anticipating reuniting the happy family on live TV."

"Frankly, my anticipation of your delivering a hard news Kh'leesberg headline to hike our circ is making me feel a little amorous myself."

I recoiled and had to swallow down my rising gorge before I could say, "Oh, ick."

"Don't be a damned snob. You know *why* we care about Kh'leesberg?"

"No, why *do* we care about Kh'leesberg?"

"*We* don't give a good goddamn about Kh'leesberg," he shouted across the desk. "But the people who buy this newspaper do care about Kh'leesberg, so we've got to care even though we don't care."

"Is it okay if I take a second to parse that thought?"

"No time. As usual, I'm guessing you haven't been paying attention to the news."

"None that includes such terms as, say, Kh'leesberg or Kardashian, no."

"How about murder?"

That got my attention.

"Whose?"

"Him."

"Hm."

"Kh'leesberg" was the cutesy tabloid mash-up name given the romantic duo of the alien Kh'nodb from Kn'otnerus (in the spiral galaxy Messier 81—aka Bode's Galaxy—about eleven point eight light-years from Earth in the constellation Ursa Major) and the self-described beauty queen, reality star wannabe Danielle Von Kleesberg from the town of Crotchet Falls, about two hundred and twenty-two miles southwest of Toledo in the state of Ohio.

Ms. Von Kleesberg and Kh'nodb met in the office of their shared agent, Bud "Speedy" Potter and found that most rare thing, love at first sight. Well, that was the way Speedy told it at the press conference. My guess would be that the first time he saw them together in his waiting room, the crafty old fart had a brainstorm: The Alien and the Beauty Queen. Although if the truth be told, the nearest Ms. Von Kleesberg had ever come to any sort of royalty was in her job at the Crotchet Falls Dairy Queen.

"Sold," I said. "Where's the *corpus delicti*?"

"It just got called in ten minutes ago, in Brooklyn. Williamsburg."

I made a face. "Crap. I hate Williamsburg."

"Yeah? What do you hate most?" he said with a wicked grin, already knowing the answer and, as unusual, enjoying my unhappiness. "Is it the alt-rock cultists you stopped from taking over the city with their Satanic verses? Or maybe the vampires you switched those Red Cross blood shipments with sheep's blood on? Oh, it could be the guy whose dimensional portal you shut down with him stuck halfway in it? No, no, wait . . ."

"It's worse than that and you know it," I snapped. "It's the damned hipsters and their man-buns."

By coincidence, my old friend, Sgt. Mike Payne in Homicide had caught the Kh'nodb case. Of course, when I say "old friend," I might be exaggerating a bit. Not on the old part; Crocker's been pounding a beat since the Empire State Building was a three-story walk-up. But calling us friends was pushing it.

"Get outta my face before I gouge your eyes out and use your head for a bowling ball, Persky," the old bull snarled as he caught sight of me ducking under the yellow police tape blocking the way into the old warehouse that had been converted some years ago into Stacked, a highend topless nightclub.

"Good to see you too, Crocker."

"What do you want?" he growled, knowing there were too many witnesses around for him to get away with shooting me.

"Hm, you're a cop, I'm a reporter, and there's a dead alien inside." I tapped my chin with a finger. "Can't imagine what I'd want."

The grizzled old cop spat on the ground, missing my left shoe by an inch, then looked at me with the dead-eye.

"Who said?"

"Who said what?"

"That there's a dead alien inside."

"C'mon, Mike."

"Only the lunatics reading your rag believe in aliens. That's NYPD policy."

"Yeah," I said, "but *we* know . . ." but Payne cut me off with, "*I* only know what I'm told to know. And *you'll* know what I've been told at the same time I tell the rest of the press."

The door of the club opened and a uniformed cop stuck his head out and called his name. Payne turned on his heel and left me standing by myself. I tried once more, calling out his name, but he just raised his hand and waved good-bye. Being a man of few words, he waved just the one finger.

I hovered around the fringes of the crime scene, picking up the small talk from cops and reporters. It was sounding like the official story was going to be that a busboy had been killed in an altercation with an unidentified customer. The police were following up on several leads, the name of the victim was being withheld pending notification of his next of kin, yada yada yada. They would just let the investigation drag on until the mainstream press got bored and forgot about it.

Payne had spread the word among his men to freeze me out, so I did what any self-respecting reporter would do. I went away.

But not far. Just around the block in fact. The attention was all on the building's front entrance, but it had originally been a warehouse, and warehouses meant a lot of holes in the perimeter for loading docks and doors. If this had been an actual police investigation, the cops and CSIs would have been crawling all over the place, front to back. They loved to bag and tag stuff and run tests. They could walk in on the murderer as he pulled the trigger in front of a full house in Yankee Stadium and they'd still collect every last cigarette butt at the scene for evidence, just in case.

But the alley behind the warehouse was deserted. Nightlights glowed over the empty loading bays and closed doors. Payne hadn't even bothered to post a cop there to shoo away snoopers like me.

The doors were heavy duty, faced with steel and secured with chunky industrial hardware and locks. They were stenciled with "No Entry" signs and backed it up by being locked. But being an ex-smoker, I knew that a sign was no barrier to anyone wanting to grab a cigarette without the hassle of leaving the club and coming back in through the front door.

And, sure enough, I found a puddle of cigarette, cigar, and blunt butts outside a propped open door two-thirds the way along, near the dumpsters.

The door lead into a service corridor, walls painted black and illuminated by a few low wattage fixtures and the red glow of the "Fire Exit" sign over the door. I crept on cat's feet along the sticky, beer scented carpet, pausing to peer around the bend to check the way ahead. More black painted corridor, this one broken by bathroom and what appeared to be a utility closet door. There was no one in sight, but I could hear voices echoing hollowly in the large empty space beyond it.

By the time I was close enough to make out what the voices were saying, I was also pretty close to the speakers. I recognized Payne's soothing tones as he barked at his cops, "Yeah, I said all of you. Outside. Now."

I slipped off my hat and slowly edged my right eye around the doorway. Payne was a dozen feet away, his back to me, standing next to the lifeless Kh'nodb. The late reality star from the stars was sprawled half on a leatherette banquet seat in the V.I.P. lounge, his big black eyes staring off into nothing and his usually hearty baby blue complexion a sickly gray. His lean seven-foot frame was clad in cargo pants, a pair of Phillip Crepe lace-ups, and a blue checkered flannel shirt open over a black band t-shirt. I couldn't tell you what band because most of the logo was gone, disappearing along with a perfect five-inch circle punched through his chest. And to make matters worse, a third of his big, bulbous head had been cleanly sheared off at a thirty-five degree angle.

An altercation between a customer and an undocumented alien busboy my tuchus!

Payne was watching the cops clear the room, giving me a few minutes to make my observations and pull out my smartphone. While I was fiddling with it, I caught the sounds of a new arrival. Correction. Arrivals. Two of them. I guessed they had arrived through one of the other back doors. I couldn't risk a look around the doorway, so I set the camera for video, hit "record," and slid my phone just far enough past the door jamb to give the phone's lens a clear shot.

"This him?" one of the newcomers said.

Payne didn't respond. I imagined he was just staring at the guy.

Newcomer number one realized he was a schmuck and cleared his throat, so newcomer number two, a woman, took up the slack. "Witnesses?"

"We're holding eight eyewitnesses. Plus three more who tried to give him medical aid. Everybody else started running as soon as the blasting started. Someone got off a few shots, but we haven't found a gun and don't know if they hit anything. But the gunfire makes for a good cover story about the busboy."

"And your men?"

"They'll keep their mouths shut. I told them it was a national security matter."

"You may not be wrong, detective. Suspects?"

"Just one. The Von Kleesberg girl. She and Kh'nodb were seen arguing just before the shooting. They lost track of her in the panic, but I've got units out looking for her."

"Did you recover the weapon." Payne must have replied with a negative shake of his head because the woman said, "Okay, so little Miss Ohio could be packing a Kn'otnerus disintegrator."

"Unless someone else picked it up in the confusion," the schmuck said.

"Let's hope not," the woman said. "Alright. We've got an unmarked van waiting in the loading dock. We're taking Kh'nodb. And there's a team en route to scan the club for any abnormalities, so keep everybody out of here until they run their tests."

"What kind of abnormalities?" Payne said in a voice I would not describe as happy.

"Radiation. Unknown toxins," the other guy said. "We don't know what leaks out when you poke holes in one of these guys."

"Should we be standing so close?" Payne said.

"Like I said, damned if we know."

I decided I'd heard enough. Exposure to radiation and alien toxins aside, Stacked would soon be crawling with technicians. I didn't want to be one of the little germs they scraped up when they got here.

I rang up Franny Beuller, the flamboyantly hardnosed editor of our sister publication, gossip rag *The National Gabber*. Franny was like Rob Berger in heels but without the charm. Fortunately, we'd bonded on our shared disdain for humanity and once you got a few drinks in her, she was actually an okay dame. Just one possessing all the sensitivity of a Triumph the Insult Comic Dog stand-up routine.

"Heard about Kh'nodb?" I said.

"Yeah. What do you know?" she said, her voice all business.

"More than you but less than I need. Can you get me in to see Speedy Potter asap?"

"Maybe. What's in it for me?"

"Sloppy seconds. But I got great art, and you'll be first to have the sappy soap opera bullshit angle."

"Deal. I hope this is good, Leo. And you better not screw me, baby."

I laughed. "Not even with Bigfoot's junk, sweetheart. Tell the old fart I'm on my way."

Speedy Potter was a legendary talent agent and business manager who had negotiated vast fortunes for stars in every strata of entertainment, his fifteen percent cut thereof making him one of the richest people in the business of show. Speedy had been playing at the top of his game for close to seventy years and showed no sign of slowing down.

He was waiting for me in his cramped little office in the Brill Building, a bustling little baldheaded troll of a man in a bespoke Italian silk suit and an oversized pair of square black framed glasses with coke bottle lenses. Speedy didn't need to waste his money on fancy overhead to impress clients or studio heads he negotiated with. He knew his reputation preceded him and he loved to watch people squirm as they bent over backwards to accommodate his "eccentricities," like conducting sensitive contract talks around a hot dog cart on Forty-ninth Street and Broadway. It also helped that Speedy had sold his soul to the devil in 1947 in exchange for irresistible powers of persuasion.

"Franny says you know what happened to Kh'nodb?" he said as soon as I had the door closed behind me.

"I know what, but not who or why. The cops are looking for Danielle."

Speedy shook his head, his eyes great big orbs behind the thick glasses.

"Those two were always arguing. Believe you me, if they'd had to make that baby the old fashioned way instead of in a test tube, the kid would still be just a great unrealized publicity stunt. They hate each other. But Danielle wouldn't hurt a fly. Especially not Kh'nodb. He was her meal ticket."

"Where is the kid while mama and baby daddy are out partying?"

"Baby Kyle? He's with Danielle's mother. The old lady moved to New York to help out after Kyle was born."

"And how about Danielle? Any idea where I can find her?"

"Sorry, Leo, not a clue."

"She's your client, Speedy."

"So she's my client. I don't get so involved in all their lives. Pardon my snobbery, it's not like this one was Elizabeth Taylor or Jackie O. I mean, she was brought up in a double-wide. She did mention a friend once. Some guy. They met when he tattooed a picture of Kh'nodb on her backside, I think. But I think they may've been more than friends."

"You mean the beauty queen was cheating on the alien beast?" I said with pretend shock.

"I wouldn't exactly say cheating. Like I told you, Kh'nodb and the girl didn't get along to begin with. Besides, what do you think could go on between those two?"

"What do you mean?"

"I mean Kh'nodb was humanoid but not *human*. Nothing about his anatomy resembled ours. *Nothing*."

The penny dropped.

"Oh. You're saying . . ."

Speedy nodded grimly.

"That's right. Blue boy didn't have a schmekie."

I assumed that the big guy did have a schmekie and I was even willing to bet that it was tattooed like the rest of his large, muscular frame. As her business manager, Speedy took care of all of Danielle's bills so he dug up the receipt from the tattoo parlor where she'd had Khnodb's face sketched on her ass and sent me off to find her paramour.

He plied his craft at a below street-level emporium called Skin Ink in the East Village. The place had three chairs working and several customers waiting, a couple of them reading recent issues of the *News* mixed in with the tattoo and weed magazines. Two of the three tattoo artists were women so by process of elimination I made a beeline for the heavily inked guy in the black tank top diligently bent over the exposed right buttock he was delicately decorating with the face of an angel.

"Excuse me," I said. "You the rear end Rembrandt who worked on Danielle's posterior?"

He looked up from his labors, his long, his luxurious brunette locks parting to reveal a face unmarked by anything other than an annoyed frown.

"Who wants to know?"

"Right now, just me. But wait a few hours and I'm sure the cops will be around to ask."

His frown deepened. "Why?"

"Because Kh'nodb was murdered and they think maybe she did it."

"Wow." He shook his head in disbelief. "Kh'nodb dead. You're not a cop?"

"I'm a reporter."

"Cool." My occupation seemed to cheer him up. "My name's Johnny Rizzo. With two z's."

"Terrance Strange, *Weekly World News*."

Rizzo's face lit up. "No shit? I read your stuff, dude. You rock." Then I watched his face as he processed my identity, searching his mental Rolodex for my grandfather's picture from the column. I saw it come, then he said, "Wait, your face . . . ?"

I smiled sadly. "Bad accident," I said. "Face first, smack dab into the side of a UFO."

He winched. "Ouch! You know, man, you want, I could give you a couple of killer facial 'tats, take the attention off your nose and, you know, the rest of your, I mean . . . it."

"Yeah, thanks, no time right now, but we should definitely talk about that. Can we get back to Danielle?"

"She don't love him, you know." He rummaged around on his art taboret and pulled out a photograph printed on plain copier paper. He handed it to me, lowering his voice and half standing to get closer to me to whisper, "Kh'nodb, I mean. She loves me. That 'tat I gave her? I designed it so I could change his face into a hot air balloon after she dumps him." I looked at the picture. It was one half of, I assumed, Ms. Von Kleesberg's derrière, decorated with the tattooed photo-realistic face of Kh'nodb. I squinted. Yeah, ink in some decorative stuff to hide his sparse alien features, hang a basket off his chin, and I could see the balloon thing.

"Nice work," I said.

"Yeah, thanks. I copied it exactly from a photo. Dannie's, like, my inspiration. She wants to be my canvas. See, they're only playing like they love each other, for the publicity and the money, you know? But she really loves me and . . ."

"Let me stop you right there," I said, stopping him right there. "At the moment, priority one is to find Danielle and make sure she and Kyle are safe."

He grinned with secret knowledge. "They're fine."

"This is no time for games, kid. If you know something, now's the time to tell me."

"I'm hip," he said. "But I can't. Dannie swore me to secrecy."

I threw up my hands in defeat. "Have it your way. If I don't find her and the kid, there's no story, Johnny Rizzo. With two z's."

His grin collapsed. "C'mon, man. I *am* the story, okay? Like, I'm the human rival for her affections and shit."

"Just got your word for that, man. I need Danielle to corroborate your story, otherwise my editor's gonna tell me to take a hike. Except he'll use a lot worse language and throw stuff at me while he's doing it."

Rizzo tossed back his head and ran his fingers through his tresses with a heavy sigh.

"Okay, lemme finish outlining that chick's butt and I'll take you over."

"Now *you* rock, Johnny," I said.

I told Rizzo to meet me in the coffee shop across the street. While I fueled up on a triple shot of espresso, I studied the print-out of Danielle's rear end. Nothing salacious, I assure you; it was Rizzo's portrait that I was interested in. Not that it wasn't an impressive tushy in its own right.

Like I'd said to the kid, he'd done a good job. I recognized the picture he had used for reference. Franny had run it on the front page of the *Gabber* a couple of months back, taken at the party celebrating the signing of season two of their reality show. Kh'nodb was looking straight at the camera with what the caption told us was a Kn'otnerusian smile on his lipless mouth, his oversized eyes shining with excitement and/or camera flashes.

But something didn't feel right. I turned to the video I'd shot on my phone at Stacked. I paused it on a clear shot of Kh'nodb and enlarged the image of his face. The alleged smile was missing, but otherwise there didn't seem to be much difference between the expression of a happy Kn'otnerusian and a dead Kn'otnerusian.

I stared at the two faces.

They stared back at me.

I blinked.

They didn't.

Big, blank black eyeballs looking at whatever it was dead Kn'otnerusians looked at.

Wait.

Black eyes. No doubt. Two of them.

But the eyes on the tattooed Kh'nodb were *brown*. Rizzo had told me he'd copied the photo *exactly*. Had he made a mistake, or did Kn'otnerusian eyeballs somehow change color when they died?

I couldn't wait for Rizzo to be finished. I gulped down the last of my espresso and headed for the door.

Rizzo still had the original photo *Gabber* cover and there was no doubt. Dark *brown* eyes.

He offered to ride us to where Danielle was on his Harley, but I opted to take an Uber car instead. On the ride over, Johnny filled me in on his story, an epic journey from the son of a Long Island investment banker to East Village ink artist-slash-true love of the alien baby mama. When he asked me if I wanted to take notes, I tapped my forehead and told him not to worry, I possessed a stenographic memory. He said yeah, he'd heard of that.

I was able to squeeze in a call to Professor Kathleen Francis, an xenobiologist pal of mine in Bridgeport. She told me she'd been fascinated from the start by Kh'nodb's unique "pre-zygotic reproductive isolation mechanism, subcategory: mechanical," which I think meant schmekieless baby-making. The eyeball thing didn't make much sense to her, though. She could think of a number of possible though unlikely explanations for it, but knowing next to nothing about his particular biochemical make-up, there was no way to say for sure. I promised I'd sneak her some Kn'otnerusians biological samples of her very own if I could and hung up, returning to the next thrill-packed episode of Rizzo's life.

Our destination was back in Brooklyn, somewhere deep in my native Canarsie, in an ill-treated duplex sheathed in wilted gray vinyl behind a sagging front stoop. It looked like a frat house that had seen better days. But then, so did the rest of the cookie cutter houses on the street.

"What's this?" I asked after paying the driver and sending him on his way.

"Used to live here with my band. Darryl and Wilbur still rent the upstairs." He turned to me with a grin. "My buds! They're on tour, so I figured it was a good place to stash Dannie."

We started up the front stairs. "How long have they been here?"

"Three days. She said there was some sort of hassle and she hadda disappear for a while."

"Three days? Kh'nodb was killed just last night."

He shrugged and dug some keys from his pocket. "All I know is what she told me, man. She said her, Kyle, and her mom were in a jam and needed a place to chill until it was cool."

Rizzo led the way up the stairs to the small landing outside the second floor apartment. He had the key, but rapped softly at the door.

"Yo, Dannie, it's Rizzo, babe."

There was no response. He rapped again. Still nothing, so he used the key.

"They're probably napping. The kid sleeps like, all the time."

"Yeah," I said. "I hear kids'll do that."

He nodded, as he turned the key and pushed open the door. And screamed.

The landing we were standing on was maybe three feet square so when Rizzo started screaming like a Victorian lady who'd just seen a mouse in the drawing room and jumped back from the door, he almost knocked me down the stairs. I grabbed the handrail and held on while he tried to decide whether to pee in his pants or run. Instead, he tripped over his own unlaced Doc Martens and tumbled into the apartment, clearing the doorway and giving me my first look inside.

I can't say I blamed Rizzo for screaming. I'd been around a lot more and weirder blocks than he had and even I had to choke back a girlish squeal.

It looked as though the place had been sprayed from floor to ceiling with a thick gooey, glowing blue glop. The stuff gave off a not unpleasant sweet, earthy odor and the air that wafted through the door was thick with warmth and humidity. It might have been just a trick of the light, but it looked to be pulsing softly like it was alive.

Rizzo had landed flat on his face in the viscous blue goo, which made him scream even louder as he tried to scramble to his feet and scrub it from his skin.

I gave him a smack across the back of his head.

"Shush," I hissed. "You'll wake the baby."

He stopped screaming and started whimpering instead.

"Wait here," I told him in what was probably the most unnecessary order ever issued. I minced carefully through the slippery blue stuff. The gunk dripped and shivered and if I listened hard enough, I swear I heard it breathing, but that might have just been the echo of my own hyperventilation. I worked up enough spit to lick my lips and call softly, "Danielle? Hello? Anybody home?"

No response.

I took a few more shuffling steps and called again. Still nothing. A couple more feet, not really watching my step as I peered through the dim blue glow ahead, which was why I stumbled over the skeleton of what appeared to be a pizza delivery guy buried under a layer of goop. I guessed pizza guy because of the Speedy Pie logoed hat at his (or her) side, but that could have just been a fashion choice.

"Is somebody there?"

The voice had that Midwest beauty queen twang to it that made me feel safe in assuming it belonged to Miss Von Kleesberg. That was confirmed a moment later when a shimmering section of blue ooze parted and she stepped out.

"Who are you?" She stopped dead when she saw me.

"Not the pizza boy, that's for damn sure," I said.

Hearing Danielle, Rizzo came out of his fog, looking at her with bafflement written all over his sappy face.

"Like, what's going on, Dannie?" he stammered.

She was as confused as him. "What're you doing here, Johnny?"

"I been worried about you, babe. Kh'nodb getting killed and everything, I thought you and Kyle were in trouble."

Danielle tossed her blond locks and rolled her eyes in exasperation. "Do I *look* like I'm in trouble, Johnny?"

His eyes roamed the slime-covered room. "Yeah, well . . . uhh, kind of."

Another voice joined the chorus. "Yo, babe, you okay out there?"

Danielle winced. Rizzo gasped. I had a hunch why.

"We're just ducky, darling," I called back.

"Hey, who . . . ?"

With what no doubt passed for an annoyed expression on his Kn'otnerusian face, his big brown eyes shining, Kh'nodb, in jeans and a white t-shirt, stepped through the curtain of blue ooze and back into the world of the living.

Rizzo's mouth moved but no sound came out. Danielle looked like a kid with her hand caught in the cookie jar, growing even more uncomfortable when Kh'nodb moved to her side and slipped a protective arm around her.

The stunned tattoo artist succeeded in producing some gurgling noises that I felt confident in translating.

"I think what Johnny's trying to say is 'Gasp, choke, he's alive! Bu-bu-but how is that possible?' Is that about right, buddy?"

Rizzo nodded.

"I was gonna tell you, Johnny. Really," the beauty queen said with beauty queen sincerity. "But everything happened so fast. First Mn'hanp showed up . . ."

"Who's Mn'hanp?" I interjected.

"The black-eyed son of a (and here Kh'nodb made a sound

not reproducible by human anatomy) who's been trying to get his hands on my girl and kid," Kh'nodb snarled, but his voice was too thin to sound very tough.

"*Your* girl?" Rizzo shouted, finally finding his voice. "Forget that, man. Dannie's been planning on dumping your blue ass. She's with me now."

"Dream on, 'tat-boy. Don't blame me because you're too stupid to know when you're being played."

Rizzo recoiled like he'd just been slapped. "What's he saying, Dannie? I . . . I thought me and you . . . us . . . I thought we were in love?"

"Best we start at the beginning, Johnny," I interjected. I looked at Kh'leesberg, all blond and blue and the darlings of the tabloids. "So, you two crazy kids, you're really in love?"

"Who are you?" Kh'nodb said, starting to take a step towards me.

"Relax, I'm a friend of Speedy's. He said the whole lovey-dovey routine of yours was just an act to sell papers."

"It was," Kh'nodb said, gazing down fondly at Danielle. "At first. But after we started hanging out and I got to know her?" He shrugged. "Man, I couldn't help myself. Next thing I knew, we'd bonded and she had my hearts."

"Hearts?" I asked.

"Well, just the two of them. I mean, they grow back, but I still need the others until they do."

Danielle nodded and hugged him around the waist.

Rizzo moaned, "I think I'm gonna be ill, man."

"Okay, you're in love. So where does the illustrated man come into this?"

Kh'nodb said, "That was Speedy's idea. For Danielle to hook up with some dude, like behind my back, right? He figured sooner or later a reporter would find out, break the story, and give us a whole new story arc."

"Mo' story, mo' better," Danielle agreed.

"That is harsh, Dannie," Rizzo said.

"I guess that brings me to the big question," I said. "Who's Mn'hanp, besides the dead black-eyed son of a (and here I gurgled, just to make a noise) at Stacked, and why's he dead? And what's Danielle got to do with his murder? Okay, that's three questions. Answer them in any order you want."

"My old man sent Mn'hanp to bring Kyle and us back to Kn'otnerus. He says it's about time I grew up and did something about fulfilling my duties to my people."

"You've got people?" I said.

"He's the prince of Kn'otnerus," Danielle added proudly. "That makes *me* a princess."

"I told you, babe, I renounced all of that when I left home. I mean, having your own planet and shit? Sounds way cooler than it is. It's all work and ceremonies and (another non-reproducible sound) . . . uh, you know, combats and death duels and all that stuff?" He shook his oversized head. "On Earth I can be famous without the hassles and death duels."

"Kh'nodb had gone into hiding when Mn'hanp showed up, so he got in touch with me, you know?" Danielle said. "Said he had a deal for my blue bunny, but he was lying."

"She told me what was going on, so I followed her to the club, just to play it safe, right? Glad I did, man. He was going to snatch Danielle and use her to get Kyle and me to go back. Soon as I saw him make his move, I took his head off, grabbed Danielle, and split."

"And not knowing there was another Kn'otnerusian on Earth, the cops just assumed the corpse was yours," I said.

"Yeah. And by the time word gets back home and they figure it out, Kyle will be through his (guttural sounds accompanied by phlegm) and then there's no way he can ever go back to Kn'otnerus."

"Does that . . . whatever you just said translate into 'gooey blue crap?'"

"It's a kind of change, like a metamorphosis, but it also binds us to our birth land. The secretions allow us to feed on and absorb our environment. After Kyle's bound to this Earth, he won't be able to survive back on Kn'otnerus."

"So how come *you* didn't drop dead when you came?" Rizzo said, sounding like he thought that would have been a great idea.

"Kyle's a hybrid, dude. His human DNA throws the whole binding thing out of whack, you know?"

"You mind a delicate question?" I asked.

"Man, you're inside my son's (repeat of guttural sounds accompanied by phlegm). We're practically family."

"Thanks. But that dead pizza guy over there . . . ?"

"Baby's gotta be fed," Danielle said defensively.

Kh'nodb responded as if we were discussing some leftover beef stew. "Back home, we have genetic livestock bred for this purpose but I've had to kind of improvise here, home gene splic-ing, you dig? A couple of delivery guys, a mailman, some utility workers. They're all around here somewhere."

"And poor mama," Danielle added with a sigh.

"Right," Kh'nodb nodded. "We got lucky there. None of this would've worked without her familial DNA."

I gotta admit, that last one took even me by surprise, but I wasn't here to judge. I got out my phone and took a few quick snaps of the happy couple and the blue ooze even as I said, "Do you mind?" Being seasoned reality stars, they went immediately into poses. Kh'nodb's kissy-face was a sight to behold.

"Hey," Rizzo said. "What about me?"

"Sure. Say cheese," I said and clicked off a few of him.

"No, man. I mean, *what* about *me?*"

Danielle sheepishly raised her shoulders up to her ears. "Sorry, Johnny, but I've got to follow my heart."

"So, like, that's it?" Rizzo said miserably. "I don't get the girl *or* to be on TV? What a friggin' rip." He looked miserably at Dani-elle. "Thanks for nothin', Dannie."

Rizzo turned and went out the door. We all listened as he clomped down the stairs and slammed the outside door behind him, making the whole house shake.

Which kept shaking. No, make that vibrating.

Kh'nodb said, "Uh-oh."

I slogged as fast as I could through the muck to the door. Behind me, Danielle's panic level was increasing with the rate of vibra-tion and Kh'nodb was trying to coax her back into the other room with the baby.

I hit the sidewalk about thirty seconds behind Rizzo, but his head start hadn't gotten him far. He was standing in the middle of the street, transfixed by the sight of what loomed just over the shabby Brooklyn rooftops. My guess was that it was just a small Kn'otnerus scout ship out of the much larger mothership somewhere in orbit, but to Rizzo, it must have looked like the Deathstar.

The ship was starting to draw the local residents out of their hidey holes.

Including Kh'nodb, although he decided to make a bold statement with his entrance. He came crashing through the second floor window like he'd taken a running start, his fists filled with glowing handguns of the variety, I assumed, that could sheer the top off of a fellow Kn'otnerusian's head. Screaming in his native tongue, he landed with a thud on the sidewalk in a shower of glass and started firing at the hovering ship. It responded with a single pulse of energy that smacked Kh'nodb and laid him out flat on his back.

Another energy-beam from the ship's belly lowered a figure to the ground next to the moaning prince. It was another brown-eyed Kn'otnerusian, outfitted in some bizarre, shimmery multi-colored wrap thing that also hooded his big blue head.

"Kh'nodb," the newcomer said, then proceeded to jabber at the sprawled figure in their own language.

Kh'nodb groaned.

The newcomer grunted and growled.

Kh'nodb raised himself unsteadily on his elbows, responding with what sounded like some whining creeping into his tone.

The other guy stood firm.

The whine became more pronounced as Kh'nodb got to his feet, still woozy from the blast.

The newcomer obviously had enough because he snapped out a single grunt and grabbed Kh'nodb by the elbow. The beam that had lowered him from the ship reappeared, this time taking both the ornately clad Kn'otnerusian and the pitifully whining Kh'nodb straight back up into the waiting ship which then immediately zipped up and away, out of sight in seconds.

"Kh'nodb!"

That was Danielle. Holding her blanket-wrapped bundle of joy in her arms, she had followed us outside just in time to see the love of her life disappear into the ship. Now she wailed piti-fully at the sky, her tears and snot making a mess of her make-up.

"Danielle, did you hear what they said?" I asked.

She nodded through her tears, not taking her eyes off the sky.

"Do you speak Kn'otnerus?"

She shook her head.

"Damn," I said. "Now I'll never know what happened."

Danielle sniffled and said, "That was his father. Kh'nodb told him he would never let them take us back to Kn'otnerus, but the king said he didn't want *us*, just Kh'nodb. He said the only reason he went after the alien female and her hybrid whelp was as bait and that he was going to throw us out the airlock as soon as the ship hit hyperdrive." She wiped her nose with her wrist. "Then he told my baby blue to shut up or else he'd really have something to cry about when they got home."

I stared at her. "I thought you said you couldn't speak the language."

She shrugged. "I can't *speak* it, but I understand it okay."

Rizzo came shuffling over, sluicing blue goo off his bare arms. "Man, okay, now *that* was freaky."

Danielle turned sad eyes and a trembling lower lip to look at the swaddled baby in her arms.

"What's Kyle gonna do now without a daddy?" she whimpered.

Rizzo reached over and moved the blanket to reveal the little critter nestled beneath. He was, as far as kids go, cute enough, a chubby little pale blue boy with mostly human features, except he'd have to wear a hat an extra size or two larger than normal.

"Hey, Kyle," Rizzo said, tickling the baby's chin. "How's it going, little guy?"

Kyle cooed and took hold of the finger. Rizzo thought that was cool and beamed a bit. "Hey, I think the little dude likes me."

Danielle was watching closely and I could literally see her passing through the five stages of mourning for her lost love in the time it took Rizzo to say "Cootchy-cootchy coo!"

"Want to hold him, Johnny?"

He looked at her in surprise. "Me? No, man. What if I, like, drop him or something?" But she was already handing Kyle over, so he went with it with a nervous smile. "Okay, but slowly . . . where's my arm go . . . ? Got it. Okay."

Somehow, Danielle had managed to get herself right up against Johnny as she made the handoff. Now she had one hand on the baby and the other around Rizzo's waist and the happy little family had pretty much forgotten I was there.

But I could see it now, coming soon to a basic cable channel near you: Kyle and Danielle Von Kleesberg and Johnny Rizzo starring in *I Married the Alien Baby Momma.*

Speedy was gonna love it.

SUPER MOM'S COOKIE CAPER
by Paige Daniels

"OH MY GOD! THEY'RE ALL DEAD! Someone murdered them!"

I sit bolt upright in my bed. My senses tingle and my breath quickens.

"No, no, this can't be!" I hear from down the hall. "Why did they have to die?"

Microseconds before I zoom off, I feel a warm hand gently wrap around my wrist. My husband shakes his head. "Take a breath. Don't be running off at super speeds. Hon, I'm sure there's a bad guy out there plotting to take over the world . . . again, but I doubt he's in our living room right now."

I slowly let out a breath. He's right, no need in exposing my secrets to the kids . . . just yet. "Thanks, honey. I need to keep that under control. "

Michael smiles. "That's what I'm here for."

The shriek happens again and we scramble out of bed and run into the dining room. In front of the large aquarium, our tiny, seven-year-old daughter is sobbing. "Mr. Fish an . . . an . . . Ms. Blue, they um . . ."

We go to our daughter and take her in our arms. I look over to the aquarium and floating on top is the whole aquatic menagerie. I huff under my breath, "Damn." I pat her head and say, "I'm sorry, honey. We can get more fish. On the plus side, you still have two cats, a dog, and a gerbil." I peep over her head and look at my watch. We're going to be late. "Listen, Annie, I know this isn't the best way to start the day, but we really got to get a move on."

Michael gives her a tickle and she laughs. "We'll go to the pet shop this weekend and you can pick out whatever fish you want."

She sniffs and wipes her wet face with the back of her arm

and gives a half smile. "Okay, Daddy."

He pats her on the head and says, "Okay, now do what your mom says. Scoot and get ready."

She leaves the room and we both stand. His big green eyes grow serious and he grumps, "I'll give you two guesses who's responsible for the great fish massacre of two thousand seventeen."

We both look at each other and yell simultaneously, "Parker!"

A disheveled red-haired boy shuffles out of the back, yawning and rubbing his eyes. "What?"

I look over to the aquarium. "Didn't I tell you to use spring water and not the stuff from the tap when you refilled the fish tank? Look, they're dead because you were too lazy to go down to the basement and get the spring water. Like, I don't have enough to deal with already?" My case load of criminals is almost higher than the pile of dirty laundry downstairs. "You're eleven years old. You're mature enough to keep clean water in a fish tank."

His eyes spring open and he shakes his head. "I didn't use tap water. I swear!"

Michael grumbles and runs his hand through his sandy brown hair. "Come on, guys, time to get moving. We'll talk about this tonight."

Parker turns around and mumbles, "I get blamed for everything around here."

I bite my lip. Responding won't do anything but cause further delay. Remembering our oldest still needs to wake up, I yell down the hall a little louder than I intend, "Jessica! Get up. Let's go!"

There's a few moments of silence when a grouchy teenage voice answers, "What's new?"

My shoulders slump and Michael rubs my back, "The day's bound to get better."

I sigh, "Famous last words."

Ensuring our kids are out of sight, I spring into super speed mode and within two minutes—eleven seconds, to be exact—I get dressed, pack lunches, and set out a healthful breakfast pastry for everyone on the dining room table. I stop in front of my husband, who is still in his pajamas, and say, "What 'cha waiting for slow poke?"

He smiles as he ambles off to the bedroom. "After seventeen years, you'd think I'd be used to living with a super hero."

The car rumbles down the streets of the old neighborhood past the houses with cute little fences. As I look out the window I sigh, the beautifully manicured lawns remind me that my sad yellow patch of grass is way overdue for cutting. Pulling the weekend shift for the last month has made house maintenance a challenge, even for a super hero. The sound of bickering from the backseat pulls me away from my pity-fest.

"Shut. *Up*. Parker. No one wants to hear about the latest Minecraft mods."

I swivel around to the backseat and glare at the teenager. "Jessica, why do you have to be so rude to him?"

Parker says between chews of his toaster pastry, "Yeah, you hurt my feelings."

I look over to Parker and say, "And you . . . stop provoking her. Everyone, be quiet if you can't say anything nice."

Little Annie peeps up, "I wasn't saying anything, Momma." She smiles and adds, "What 'cha going today at work? Fixing more computers?"

Ah, yes, my cover as an IT specialist. It's one of the few careers, besides a doctor or cop, where running off at all hours of the night to attend to emergencies is considered normal.

Parker scoffs, "Speaking of computers, didn't you say that you'd fix my laptop last night?"

Ignoring Parker, I respond to my cheery daughter, "Why yes, Annie. I will be fixing computers today, thank you for asking me about *my* day."

Parker starts to respond, but Michael reaches down to the radio and turns up the volume. "This is a good song. It will put everyone in a good mood."

They all groan simultaneously. "Not nineties music! We hate grunge!"

They put on their earphones and there's silence once again. I share a small victory high-five with my husband.

I'm not able to revel in my victory for very long before my phone buzzes on the console. I read and sigh heavily.

Michael says, "What's up?"

I peek over my shoulder to ensure the kids are properly ensconced in their electronics and then say in a low whisper, "Walter Page, that guy we apprehended for the bank heist the other day, with all the exotic tech—"

"Yeah."

"I finally got his background report: he's a loner, low job performer at the Sack and Suds, and he failed out of business trade school last year."

Michael grunts, "No way he made that tech like he claimed. That stuff has our best engineers stumped." He takes a long breath. "Well, nothing we can do about it now. We'll be at work soon."

I nod in agreement and lean my head back and try to relax.

Before long we're at the drop off line at the elementary school. It's moving way too slow. I turn to the backseat and motion for the teenager to take off her headphones. "Jess, we're going to have to drop you off here. We don't have time to swing by the high school."

She huffs, "You always favor them. It's not fair."

Michael fake whines, "Oh, your life is so hard, princess. You're fifteen, you can walk a block to school. Besides, you always ask us to drop you off further from the school so you don't have to be seen with your . . . blech . . . parents."

The car lurches to a stop and all at once the kids scramble out of the car. Jess slams the door and sighs, "Whatever."

Michael shakes his head. "Seriously, this day *will* get better." He turns up the volume again and the alt rock sounds of Stone Temple Pilots fill the car.

We make the remainder of the trip to work in silence and before I have time to really think about the day, I'm greeted by the old familiar sign.

Aegis Technix: Making our Future Brighter

We stop at the gate and show our badges to the guard and scurry to the first parking spot available. It's impossible to hide a facility such as ours, so we hide in plain sight. Aegis houses all sorts of supers: some freak lab accidents (like me), some born this way, and some refugees from other planets. Most people who work here are unaware of who is actually sitting next to them, thinking they just work for your run-of-the mill cutting edge technology firm.

Inside, we run down a hallway and are greeted by steel double doors. After a retinal scan, on both of us, the doors open and we scramble down the sterile white hallway and open the second door we come to. The large conference room is half full with supers and their handlers. Aegis actually has many locations worldwide. We have computer algorithms that take into account all the events in a region past and present and calculate what problems are most likely to occur. From this data, everyone gets their assignments. We're all expected to brief out our most significant cases of the week.

In front of the room is a tall, dark-haired, older gentleman. He looks up from a podium and says to me and Michael in a slow southern drawl, "Nice of you to join us. We're just getting started. Take a seat." We slink to our seats and the Director starts. "Okay, boy and girls, I don't like these meetings any more than you do. Let's get this over with so we can get back to real work."

Each of the supers brief on their cases, then it's my turn. I can take down a room full of drunken bikers three times my size, but briefing a room of my peers makes me break out into a sweat. I clear my throat. "Uh, yeah, yesterday we obtained our perp, Walter Page. He's wanted in conjunction with the murders of several officers during a botched bank robbery attempt—"

A lanky blonde woman interrupts me. "Sounds like a pretty normal case, why not just throw it over to the civilians."

I stare at her for a few seconds. "Well, it would be a normal case, but the weaponry he used is very next gen. Not even our Department of Defense has anything like this. Me and Ares plan on interrogating him to find out where he got it. After we find that out, we'll hand him over to civilian authorities. I don't anticipate any problems. I'm coding this one a yellow until the case is closed."

Director nods his head. "Very good, Tessa. Make sure to update your logs after your interrogation." He looks around the room. "That goes for all of you. Y'all been pretty sloppy about updating the databases." Groans abound from the room. "I know, I know. It ain't fun, but it has to be done." The room is silent and he continues. "Alright, if that's all, you're dismissed. Be safe out there, people."

In the hallway we all mill around talking about the day ahead. A tall, dark-skinned man comes up to me and Michael. "So, you ready to go interrogate Mr. Page?"

I nod to the man. Joe Godsey, code name Ares, my partner. Joe was infected by the same lab-created virus I was. I was an innocent teenager infected by accident. He was a soldier who volunteered. The virus did a bang-up job of enhancing our normal human abilities. So, no laser eyes or super cold breath. But our strength, speed, and stamina is a hundred times of any normal human being.

Michael isn't a super like me and Joe. Michael was actually an engineer for the other side of the company until a chance meeting at the cafeteria. After few dates over egg salad sandwiches he figured out my secret. Once that happened the company decided Michael's abilities were better used as mine and Joe's handler.

I turn to Michael now. "You got anything to help us?"

He scrolls on his phone and says, "Yeah, actually. I pinged his phone and Internet logs. He was pretty good at cleaning up his footprints, but . . ." Michael gives his super cute boyish grin. "I'm better at tracking said footprints."

I smirk. "It still turns me on when you speak geek."

Joe groans. Ignoring him, Michael continues, "I found several hits on a website called Granny's Cookies. I can't track down its IP to a single server, which means I have no idea if this place is local or—"

Joe interrupts him. "Maybe the dude likes cookies."

Michael resumes. "Normally, I'd agree, but he accessed this site on the dark web. Why would Granny be selling cookies there?"

Joe shrugs. "Crooks get hungry, too."

I pat Michael on the shoulder. "That's good. Anything else?"

Michael looks at his phone. "No, not much more than the

report you got earlier. I'll keep working on it and if I find anything I'll text you while you're in interrogation."

I turn to Joe. "I need to change. I'll meet you in Interrogation Room Five."

"Sounds good. I gotta get super-fied too." He walks down the hall.

Michael kisses me on the head. "Well, I'm outta here. I have to do some research on a few of your cases and see if they're going to workload you with anything new."

I sigh. "Oh lord, please no. I can't remember the last time I cooked something that didn't have the word *instant* on it."

Michael gives me a squeeze. "It'll be okay, hon. Go get dressed and get your bad guy."

I walk down the quiet hall and into a large door marked WOMEN. Inside is a spacious well-appointed locker room. I find my locker and change into my black cat suit and matching knee high boots, then look at the mirror across from me. Staring back is a plain brunette in her mid-thirties. I mumble to myself, "Guess, it's super hero time."

I press the emblem on the collar of my uniform and I transform from Tessa Goode, wife and mom of three, to the statuesque redheaded super hero Themis. I have to admit, the image engineers sure got my super image right. Themis is a complete badass whose lean, six-foot form and electric blue eyes will strike fear into the hearts of anyone.

Feeling confident, I strut down the hall to Interrogation Room 5. Inside, Joe is now decked out in his super hero form, too. Joe's normally lean, muscular build at an average height is intimidating to me, but in his super hero form, which tops out at seven foot tall, is downright terrifying. Joe is looming over our perp, Walter.

The pale little man almost drowns in his orange jump suit. The biggest thing about this guy is his huge head. His eyes are rimmed in red and he looks at me with fear. Joe must've worked him over pretty good. I give him a sweet smile. He smiles back at me.

"Walter, Walter, Walter . . . you've got yourself into some pretty hot water, now haven't you?"

He shakes. "Where am I? I want to see a lawyer."

"Oh, sweetie, lawyers can't help you here." I pace for a few seconds in silence to build up the drama. I love this part. "Just tell us who sold you those weapons. That's all you have to do."

"You . . . you . . . can't do this to me. I have rights!"

Joe scoffs, which, if you didn't already surmise, can make a person shiver when it comes from a seven-foot superhero. "Not here you don't. We checked. Walter, no one knows or cares you're here. We can keep you forever." Walter shrinks back from Joe. "You had some pretty interesting weapons on you to hold up that bank. Where did you get them?"

"I . . . I can't tell you. If I do, then they'll get me. I can't I—"

Okay, it's good cop time.

I touch his hand and give a sad smile. "We can protect you, Walter. No one can hurt you here."

He starts to sweat and shake. "That's what you think. It was never about the bank robbery or the money. This was just the beginning—" He trails off.

Joe and I exchange looks. I take a breath and decide to stick with good cop. "Walter, you look like a nice kid. Sometimes you're in too deep and then there's nowhere to go, but we can help." I smile. "I can help."

I squeeze his shoulder and he takes a deep breath. I think he might give. Then slowly a smile creeps on his face. Not a happy smile, but a strange psychopathic smile that chills me to my core. He jerks his shoulder out my hand and laughs. "That's what you all say. You want to help. But you never do. I finally found people like me. They get me. They understand me. They're the ones who'll help me. And when that day comes . . ."

Joe shouts out, "Enough! Tell us where you got the weapons!"

"No!"

We're out of options. An idea pops in my head. I'm totally winging it, but what the hell. "SO . . . you order cookies from Granny often?"

Walter looks as though he's been shot. "There's no way you could know that. How did you know?"

"Oh, we have ways." My phone vibrates. "I'm sure that's our guys right now with more information." I look down to my phone.

I FORGOT HISTORY PROJECT AT HOME CAN YOU BRING

IT TO SCHOOL? PLEASE PLEASE PLEASE?!

I grumble and look back up to Walter. "They hacked into Granny's servers. They hit the mother lode. C'mon, Joe, let's go meet with intel and see how deep it all goes." I look to Walter. "I'd say in less than four hours you'll be in a normal security jail and we'll make sure that everyone knows how cooperative you were with us."

Joe and I turn to go out the door, but we're stopped by a desperate shriek. "No, wait!" We turn around. Walter rocks back and forth in his chair. "It's all a test. They want to see how well you withstand our weapons. Not a full-on attack. Just a little at a time."

Joe narrows his eyes. "Who is testing us?"

Walter shakes his head. "I don't know. I just know it's a test. I swear! Everything in my life is crap. They made me feel important, like I could do anything. I just wanted to be good at something."

I say, "It's okay, Walter. You've really helped us. We'll help you."

Joe and I exit the room. The door slams behind us. Joe grumbles. "This doesn't sound good at all."

"Agreed. Yet I suddenly have a craving for Grandma's cookies."

Back to normal size and visage, all three of us are huddled in Michael's cubicle. He clacks away at his keyboard. "I came up with one hit for Grandma's Cookies. It's here in the city. East side."

My phone buzzes again.

I'M IN TROUBLE IF I DON'T BRING THAT PROJECT IN. IT'S THE PARTHENON ON MY DRESSER.

I sigh. Michael turns to me. "What's up?"

"Nothing, Jess forgot her history project."

Michael growls. "She needs to be more responsible. Let her learn her lesson."

"Normally I'd agree, but she worked really hard on this one and we did have a pretty interesting morning." Joe folds his arms in front of him. I know what he's thinking, but he's never had a family. He doesn't get it. "Look, I'll speed home, then to her school. If I leave now, I might even beat you to Grandma's."

Joe grunts. "I drive pretty fast, so you better get hoppin'."

I lean over and give Michael a peck on the cheek. "I'll text you if I'm going to be late."

Within seconds I'm out of the cubicle farm, into my locker room, changed, and my super suit packed. In another few heartbeats I'm out of Aegis and on the road. Of all of my super-powers, super speed is probably my favorite. Lickety split I'm home grabbing Jess's project and out the door again. When I'm within a few blocks of the school I slow down and check her project. Eh, a few tears, but it'll be fine. I take a deep breath and my stomach rumbles. I sure hope there are some real cookies at Grandma's because running at super speeds works up an appetite.

Inside the school, the halls are jammed packed with kids running to their classes. I weave through the crowd to the office where a disinterested receptionist looks up at me. "Can I help you?"

"Um, yeah, I'm Jessica Goode's mother. I have her history project."

"If it were me, I'd just let her suffer."

I swallow down what I really want to say in the interest of time. "Well, yeah, can you call her to the office? I'm here on a break. I really need to get moving."

The surly secretary huffs, "Fine."

The clock ticks for what seems like hours while I wait for Jessica. I pace while I look at my watch and mumble under my breath, "C'mon, Jess."

As if on cue the short brunette appears and attacks me with hugs. "Thank you, Mommy!"

"You're welcome, honey. But next time, be more responsible. You're fifteen, I can't remember everything for you."

Her smile turns to a scowl. "Yes, mother. It was an honest mistake. Would you rather I fail history?"

"I don't have time for this. I need to be back at work. They're waiting on me to—"

She finishes my sentence. "Let me guess . . . you need to fix a crashed system. Fine. Thanks for everything." She grabs her project and stomps off to class.

I look over to the secretary who's giving me the I-told-you-so look and say, "Not a word."

I sidle up to a familiar black car parked across the street from a non-descript store-front and knock on the window. The surly driver jumps then growls when he notices it's just me. I throw my backpack in as I sit next to him. He looks at his watch. "I thought you'd be waiting for me."

I unzip the backpack, "Unexpected difficulties. You weren't waiting that long."

"Long enough."

I shake my head and in a flash I'm in my costume and changed into Themis. I pull down the car visor and fluff my hair, then look at Joe. "You ready?"

He nods and at once we're out of the car and in Grandma's. My stomach growls at the smell of baked goods and coffee. There are a few people in line in front of us and we patiently wait our turn. Behind the counter, a cherubic lady with white hair greets us. "What can I get for you?"

My stomach grumbles again and before Joe has a chance to answer I say, "Three crullers and a large coffee with double cream and sugar." Joe gives me a lopsided look. I whisper back, "What? Running makes me hungry."

The old woman deposits my snack in front of me. I pay her. She turns to Joe. "Can I get anything for you, sir?"

Joe looks around the cafe to ensure no one else has walked in then says to the woman, "No, ma'am. We're actually here on separate business. Do you have an Internet connection?"

She giggles. "I do. You have to keep up with the times, you know? People put their orders on-line and I have them ready for pick-up." She gives a girlish smile and continues. "I may be old, but I do have a little bit of tech savvy."

I shove the last cruller in my mouth then gulp down a mouthful of coffee. "Any chance someone could be spoofing your site?"

"No, no, why do you ask? Who are you? Why are you asking these questions?"

Joe and I flash our badges and I say, "Internet security task force. We've had a few curious hits from your web site."

Her eyes narrow and quickly she goes from cherubic grandma to a distrusting old woman. "No, that's not it . . . I know you. It was Walter, wasn't it?"

Joe and I look at each other then look back to her. I say, "Walter who?"

In two heartbeats she reaches down below the counter and produces a ray gun and points it at Joe. Before she's able to get her finger on the trigger, I dive for Joe and knock him out of the way. We're both on the floor looking up at Grandma, who has jumped up on her counter top with way more dexterity than any octogenarian should have. Her eyes glow yellow and she hisses, "I knew Walter was weak, but they didn't listen." She aims the ray gun for us, but we roll out of the way just in time to see a gaping smoking hole appear in the floor. Joe and I look at each other wide-eyed.

Granny snickers, "That was nothing compared to the rest of our technology."

As she jumps down, Joe and I hop on our feet. Joe rushes into Granny with a big bear hug slamming her through the counter and dislodging the gun from her hand. Granny laughs and takes Joe by the throat, then with one hand throws him across the bakery.

Holy mother of waffles, what is she?

The bakery is a mess of splintered wood, dust, and donuts. Among the dusty donuts lies the ray gun. Before she's able to reach it, I flash over, grab the gun and hold it to Granny's head.

Granny stays perfectly still and says, "You might've gotten me, but you Earthlings will be a quick victory for my people. You will rue the day when you—"

Joe flashes from across the bakery and tazes Granny. She falls to floor in a crumpled heap. Joe shakes his head, "I hate monologuing."

I laugh then press a button on the com-link on my wrist and say, "Response unit requested, sending you GPS coordinates now. We have a five ninety-nine in progress."

After a few moments a garbled voice comes over com-link, "Roger that, Themis, a crew will be there in fifteen."

The dinging of the door pulls mine and Joe's attention from

Grandma. A tall blond man looks at us and the carnage of the bakery in horror. Joe says calmly and coolly, "Don't worry, sir, there were a few technical difficulties here. We've called in paramedics. Why don't you go and put the closed sign up as you leave?"

The blond man nods slowly and slinks out of the store turning around the open sign as he goes.

The old woman's body starts to stir and I whip out my taser and shock her again. "Settle down, Grandma. Bake sale's over."

Both Joe and I are crowded in Michael's cubicle rehashing the details of our case. Michael says, "Looks like it's being processed now. They were recruiting loners and nerds, giving them new sexy tech to test our ability to protect ourselves against it. I'm sure we're going to see a lot more outbreaks before we're done."

Joe says, "What system was she from?"

"Not sure," Michael says. "We haven't had contact with this particular race before. The Xenoanthropologists are scanning the databases for any kind of hits."

I look at my watch and wince then say to Michael, "We're whistle-bit, honey. Kids are probably waiting for us at school."

Michael logs off his computer and throws on his jacket. "It'll be here tomorrow. Why don't you get changed and meet me in the car."

In short order we wind through the countryside and it gives way to a quiet burg, home. A few more minutes and we're in front of a large brick building with three kids and one scowling teacher. Michael pulls up to the curb. I get out.

The teacher grumps, "You're late."

I open the door for the kids and they scramble into the car. "Sorry. Just ten minutes."

The teacher replies, "You know, I did you a favor letting the girls come to Parker's robot team practice. What can be so important that you can't leave it for the next day?"

I take a deep breath and say slowly, "I'm really sorry and I do appreciate you helping us out. I will do my best to be on time."

She sighs, seemingly placated. "It's okay. I get it. Stuff happens."

I chuckle. "Thanks. Don't I know it?"

I hop back into the car. Michael takes us home. From the back of the car the kids cry, "Mom! What's for dinner?"

Aw, crap.

As if reading my thoughts Michael says, "We're stopping at Taco Town."

Parker exclaims, "Awesome!"

Jessica and Annie groan. Jessica adds, "Again?"

"Yes again," I answer, "If you'd like a different dinner, perhaps you can help me cook and plan meals in the future."

After an admittedly mediocre dinner of soggy tacos and bland rice the night progressed as normal. Dishes, bickering, homework, more bickering, and *finally* bedtime for the kids.

I walk in Jess's room and it's not like the typical teenage girl's room. Rather than posters of the hottest boy band there are pictures of far-off landscapes, places she wants to visit. I've always admired her strength to stand out from the crowd. I bend down to the girl and give her a kiss on the forehead. "Do you hate me tucking you in every night?"

She laughs, "Yeah, totally, but I guess I'll keep letting you do it, since you love it so much."

"Thanks, hon, you're sweet."

As I walk out of Jess's room she says, "I love you, Mom."

Next up, Annie. The cute little girl is snuggled with her stuffed bunny. She comes off as cute and quiet, but she can hold her own with her brother and sister, and that's no small feat. "I love you, honey."

"I love you too, Momma. I was thinkin'—"

"About what, sweetie?"

But then my phone buzzes. Annie pauses as I check the text. It's the office. Looks like Grandma wasn't the only test coordinator in town. Another high-tech murder scene. I breathe a sigh of relief when I see second shift is taking lead on this one. I'll need to follow up first thing.

I turn my attention back to Annie when she asks, "Do you gotta fix another computer tonight?"

I give her a squeeze, "No, honey, not tonight."

She smiles. "Good. I don't like it when you're gone so late.

Anyway, I'm not mad about the fish. They were a pain." "That's very mature of you, honey." I give her a squeeze and turn off her lights.

As I walk down the hall toward Parker's room, my phone buzzes again. It's Joe. GOT TEXT FROM OFFICE. I'M NOT LETTING THOSE CHUMPS ON SECOND SHIFT SCREW UP OUR CASE. I'M GOING IN. My shoulders slump for a few seconds, until a follow-up text filters through. STAY HOME. YOU GOT A LIFE, UNLIKE ME. I'LL BRIEF YOU IN THE MORNING, PARTNER.

Joe's more like family than a co-worker. I've known him my whole superhero life. My lifestyle isn't one that he wants, but he gets my hope to have it all—if such an ideal even exists—and he will always have my back. Sometimes having super powers makes it all possible. Other times, it makes it so much harder.

I high-five Michael as I go into Parker's bedroom. I tousle the boy's hair and sneak in a kiss. He smiles as he wipes it off. I shake my head as I pull the covers around him. His smile turns down and he says cautiously, "Um, Mom, it was me. I was in a hurry and I couldn't find the spring water and—" He starts to cry and I rub his back.

For as tough as he tries to act in front of his sisters, he's actually got a super soft center. I love that about him. I give him a big squeeze then pull away. "Yeah, I figured. It's okay . . . well, it's not okay. If you need help . . . ask. Just learn from your mistake and we'll get it right next time."

He nods and wipes the tears away. "Love you, Mom."

"Love you too, bud."

In the living room my husband awaits me with a cold beer and a zombie flick on TV. I settle down in the couch with him and take a drink. This is the first time today I've felt relaxed. Michael's arm wraps around me and I sink into his warmth and take another sip of beer. "You think I should quit?"

Michael almost chokes on his beer. "What?"

"Jess was right. We've eaten Taco Town far too many times, I don't know how much longer their robot coach is going to put up with us being late, I hate like hell lying to the kids about my 'computer runs', and it puts a hell of a strain on . . . us"

He rubs my back. "Tessa. Look. You take care of us at home, you kick ass at work. Literally. And the kids are learning to be independent humans . . . assuming they aren't harboring secret powers themselves. And lord knows they could be. Don't worry about us, we've been through seventeen years of super hero life and we're still going strong. From my eyes, things are going pretty darn well. If you're stressed, maybe we can hire someone to help out around here: pick up the kids, light chores, and run a few errands."

"Okay," I say, and laugh, poking him in the ribs. "Maybe. But can he be a Thor-like specimen?"

Michael laughs then turns serious. "Think about it. You're a great mom. Don't worry about it so much."

"What? Me worry?" I take a last drink of my beer then turn off the TV and say, "I do have one idea of how you can help me relax." I crook up my eyebrow.

We walk arm-in-arm to our bedroom, our caseloads handled, at least for today.

"Well," Michael says, "I may not be Thor, but I'm sure I can help a super mom like you end the day just right."

THE RESPONDERS
by Michael Jan Friedman

THEY'RE NOT LIKE US.

I'd heard that said about them before I got assigned to Special Investigations, six years ago now. But back then, I didn't know what it meant.

After all, I'd only seen them on the news to that point, flashing across the screen in their black jumpsuits with the red 'R' stitched over their hearts. I hadn't observed them up close, hadn't felt their presence. Their power.

But they weren't just stronger than we were, endowed by a trick of fate with abilities the rest of us could only dream about. They were different, as different as my Uncle Burt and a blind salamander.

Some, like Maser, reminded you of that difference from time to time. No brag, as some guy on TV used to say, just fact. As it turned out later, he was a scientist—to a fault, even considering all the breakthroughs he'd made as DeVonte Larson, professor of biochemistry at the University of Pennsylvania—and he didn't see any point in soft-peddling his superiority.

Smoke was more elusive, as you'd expect. She, it came out last year, was a Senator's daughter, and she'd seen her old man Kenny Parmenter make a decades-long career for himself in Washington without saying a single coherent thing. So by the time Jessica saved her dad and his staff from those white terrorists, she was an expert at hiding in plain view.

Others, like Antaeus, didn't avoid questions. But he didn't give you much information either. Mainly he let you come to your own conclusions—about him, about the team, about why they did what they did.

The poor bastard had to be carrying a lot of hurt around.

Anybody who looked the way he did, hideously scarred from the day he got his powers, had to be carrying *something.*

He was a teenager when it happened, name of Eddie Fields. It's all public now. He woke up one morning and had the ability to tap into Earth's magnetic fields, bend steel as if it were licorice, crack diamonds in his bare fists.

But at the same time, he'd developed these lesions. Long, livid scars, or at least that's what they looked like. All over his body, including his face. Made it hard to look at him.

Together, those three were The Responders. In the beginning, people called them The First Responders, but that took too long to say. So it became just The Responders.

They were good, right off the bat. And they tackled everything, from earthquakes to hostage situations to that missile North Korea swore was an accident. Once they even cracked a stolen car ring in the Bronx, though they must have been bored that day.

People loved them. And from what I could tell, The Responders loved each other. At least, as far as anybody could love a guy like Larson.

Then came Koyomi Seiku.

She started out as a fan of Antaeus. Wrote him letters, sent him e-mails, worshipped the hell out of him. Somebody else may have taken it all in stride. But Antaeus? The way he looked, he wasn't used to female attention.

She begged to meet him, just to get his autograph, she said. For one of the most powerful human beings on the planet, he could be pretty shy. But eventually, he said yes.

They met at a mall on Long Island. Antaeus was dressed in a trenchcoat with a hat pulled down low. Koyomi was the only one he told he'd be there.

She was nineteen, a first-year civil engineering student at NYU. Cute, long black hair, Goth but not really. And smart, no one ever argued that.

She got Antaeus's autograph, but that wasn't all she got. They sat at the mall and talked for a while. Then they went to the beach, which was cold but pretty much deserted that time of year, and talked some more.

Then they wound up in a motel room.

You might think she was maneuvering him into a rape charge, hoping to shake him down for some bread. After all, The Responders had no shortage of wealthy friends, people capable of signing checks for millions if one of the heroes just said the word.

But it wasn't like that. Koyomi didn't want money. All she wanted was Antaeus. His scars . . . they didn't matter to her. She saw past them to the good and courageous person beneath them. At least that's what she told the reporter from Channel Four who got that first—and last—interview with her.

After that, The Responders shut her down. It wasn't clear whether it was Maser or Smoke, but someone didn't want Koyomi talking. Of course, if The Responders' private information got out, their enemies could use it against them. So it made sense for Koyomi to exercise discretion.

After that, there were no more interviews. But from the one Koyomi gave, you could see she was in love with Antaeus. And you got the feeling that Antaeus was in love with *her.*

For a while, you would see them on the news, at fundraisers and such. Antaeus looking uncomfortable, eyes darting this way and that in his mask, a sparkling Koyomi standing beside him and basking in the spotlight. Then, suddenly, that stopped too.

What nobody knew at the time was that Koyomi had driven a wedge between Antaeus and the other Responders. Larson plain didn't like her. He found Koyomi vapid, superficial—and worst of all, trivial. But more importantly, she was a distraction. Antaeus had been moody before she came along. It was a chore for Larson to keep him focused. After Koyomi showed up, she was all Antaeus could think about.

Parmenter didn't appreciate Koyomi either, if there's anything to what it says in her file. But she wasn't so vocal about Koyomi—maybe because Parmenter had a girlfriend of her own, a single mom in Western Michigan. But no one knew about Parmenter's love life at the time, Parmenter's teammates included.

Had Koyomi remained a distraction—and nothing more—it would have been bad enough. But somewhere along the line, she convinced Antaeus that she could be an asset to the team.

It sounded crazy to Larson and Parmenter. Koyomi didn't have their superhuman powers, they said. She'd been a gymnast in high school, a pretty good one too, but that didn't make her a Responder. It didn't protect her from bullets or lava flows or three-alarm fires.

Antaeus disagreed. If Koyomi couldn't be a part of the team, he wouldn't stick around either.

The Responders had their first fight over that. A real shouting match. How close it came to an actual fight, it's hard to say. When it was over, there were bad feelings all around.

Rumor has it they almost broke up the team. Came *this* close. Anyway, The Responders survived.

And Antaeus? He got what he wanted. Koyomi became a full-fledged member of The Responders.

She called herself White Eye, after a little bird in Japan. The costume she came up with was gold and white, with a harlequin mask—a lot flashier than the simple jumpsuits worn by her teammates.

I remember seeing her for the first time. There was a fire in an apartment building in Spanish Harlem—a six-floor walkup. Families trapped on the top floor. Smoke got to some of them, turned them immaterial like her and guided them down to the street.

Antaeus got others to jump and caught them. Not much Maser could do to help; his beams could have done more harm than good.

Then came White Eye.

We didn't know who she was or what she was doing there. There hadn't been a press conference or anything—The Responders didn't work that way. But suddenly, three were four heroes instead of three.

White Eye was all over the place. Lots of energy. And courage too. Good thing too, especially for those kids she swung across the street on nylon lines.

It was impressive. She couldn't make herself immaterial or emit energy beams from her palms or pulverize granite with her fists, but she'd made a contribution.

From that time on, people expected to see her. She was instantly accepted, at least by the public.

By Larson and Parmenter . . . that was a different story.

Shortly after White Eye showed up, The Responders established the Cavern.

It was Koyomi's idea, maybe the only one Larson and Parmenter didn't hate. To that point, the team had held its meetings in different places—parks, abandoned buildings, the occasional rooftop—and only after dark. Koyomi said she knew a place where they could get together any time they wanted.

She'd read about it in an old book. Apparently, her hobby was researching nooks and crannies in the city, long-forgotten places. This had been forgotten longer than most—a storage room that went back to the time of the Revolution, two floors down from the basement of the city's first post office.

Of course, there was no way Koyomi could access the place to see if it was still intact. There wasn't any staircase that led to it. There was no shaft, no unused subway tunnel.

For Smoke, that wasn't an obstacle. She made herself immaterial, ghosted her way down to the location Koyomi had described, and found exactly what her teammate had described.

So Koyomi's research had been on the money. But it wasn't going to help any if Smoke was the only one who could reach the place.

Fortunately, Maser was able to take care of that. He burned a tunnel right through bedrock, one that was tall enough even for Antaeus, who was well over six feet. Then he cut steps into the living stone.

He tidied the place up a bit, too. Burned away the cobwebs and the debris. When he was done, it looked a lot better. The red-brick walls were still faded, the cobblestone floor was still uneven, and a couple of sick-looking, milky white stalactites still hung from the ceiling, but it was clean and quiet, and not so dark once they got a generator down there.

Maser cut a narrower tunnel to the surface for ventilation. Then they moved some furniture in. It was a breeze for Antaeus to carry down desks and couches and chairs, and of course the generator. If there'd been room, he could have carried down a Volkswagen, and probably not broken a sweat.

The Responders used the Cavern for nearly two years. Then came the murder, and as law-abiding citizens they had to comply with the investigation—which meant showing us where they'd found the body.

When I saw Koyomi lying there on the cobblestone floor, she'd been dead for just a few hours. There wasn't a mark on her. The lab identified a toxin in her blood—an extremely rare one, its only known source the part of the rain forest where the Responders had saved a village a month earlier.

I had three suspects in black jumpsuits. And rumors, which had leaked out by then in one form or another. A comment here, a comment there . . . it added up to some resentment against White Eye, though outside of the team no one had any idea of how much.

I knew this: Any one of Koyomi's teammates could have killed her with that poison. Or she could have killed herself . . . which was the story we eventually went with.

Even though she'd shown no signs of depression or other psych problems. Even though, by all accounts she'd never been happier in her life. Despite all that, we called it suicide and closed the case.

Hey, The Responders were heroes. They'd saved more lives than anyone could count. What good would it have done to put one of them through a trial? And if we found him or her guilty, then what? How were we going to hold a prisoner with super powers?

If we'd had compelling evidence that a Responder was guilty, that would have been different. We would have prosecuted and figured out the details later on. But we had no such evidence. In the end, we decided Koyomi had taken her own life. Which was what happened, for all I knew.

Till last week, when I got a call from Larson's lawyer.

Anyway, after Koyomi's death, The Responders couldn't use the Cavern anymore. What was the point of a secret sanctum if everybody had read about it in the paper? So they went back to meeting on rooftops.

But that wasn't their biggest problem. Far from it.

Koyomi had never been a crucial member of the team, true. But Antaeus was lost without her. The way she'd made him feel in spite of his appearance, she had become too big a part of his life.

He took to drinking. Nobody knew it at first, but Larson and Parmenter figured it out eventually. They were his partners, right?

Alcohol didn't just weaken Antaeus's judgment. It hurt his ability to tap into Earth's magnetic fields. Once the most powerful member of the team, he became a liability in the field. Neither Larson nor Parmenter wanted to put their lives in the hands of a compromised Antaeus.

Hard to know who spoke up first or how it went down, but eight months after Koyomi's death, The Responders announced their break-up. The world had seen the end of its first super-team, and probably its last.

Would they have gone on if Antaeus hadn't turned to the bottle? Hard to say. In a way, The Responders were like a married couple. Every marriage runs its course, whatever it might be. It dies a natural death.

You ask me, it was just time for them to call it a day.

And nobody could blame the break-up on White Eye. She was out of the picture, and had been for some time.

I was here in the Cavern a couple of times in those days—once when we started the investigation and then again a month or so later, when I was trying to piece things together. I'm here again. In the illumination provided by my flashlight, the place looks about the same as I remembered it.

The desks, the couches, the chairs—all second hand. The generator, dry and dead now. The light fixtures they had jerry-rigged around the place.

Except there's dust on everything. Not just the floor, but everywhere. Must have come in through the ventilation shaft.

I'm not here long before I hear the scrape of footsteps on the stairs. I turn to see who's coming down, flashlight in hand, even though I already know.

The way the shadows play . . . for a second, I think I see a costume. But no. Just street clothes.

"Thanks for coming," I say. My voice echoes a little.

"How could I resist," says my guest, "when you asked so nicely? But I'm still not certain how you found me."

"I got a letter from Larson's lawyer. He knew."

"Ah. Larson. I managed to conceal myself from everyone else, but not from him."

"Bright guy," I say. "And determined."

"Very much so. Sorry to hear about him."

"Yeah. Considering who he was, that he could burn his way through solid stone . . . it's hard to believe he could have gone that way."

"An aneurism. You never know."

There was speculation that Larson's maser power had contributed to his problem, maybe flat out caused it. But his doctors said there was no evidence to support that theory.

"So," I say, "you're not going to try to kill me, right?"

"Of course not. Why would you think that?"

"You killed Koyomi Seiku."

A shrug. "Ancient history."

"Just in case, I left a file on my computer. With instructions for it to be opened if I should happen to . . . disappear."

A smile. "Resourceful. But really, you've nothing to worry about."

I believe that to be true. Still, I'd felt compelled to say what I'd said. "So was it homicide?" I ask. "Suicide? A little of each?"

"You're the detective," says Koyomi Seiku. She sits down gracefully on the arm of a couch, ignoring the dust. "You tell me."

"Well, I know part of the story from Larson's letter. You had a super-power after all—the ability to make duplicates of yourself. A power no one knew about, not even your teammates. That was why you contacted Antaeus in the first place. You wanted to use your power as a member of the team."

"I didn't expect to fall in love with him," she admits.

"No," I say.

They'd carried on their relationship even after she joined The Responders. So she must have loved him, despite the way he looked.

"And though you joined the team to use your power, you ended up keeping it a secret . . . ?" I prod.

"I realized I could be more effective that way. If you only expected to face one of me, a second me could catch you unaware. But if you knew from the start that there were two . . ."

"You'd prepare for it. And White Eye would lose the element of surprise. But surely your teammates could have been trusted to keep your secret to themselves."

She laughs. "My teammates . . . weren't what you think they were. Larson was in love with himself. Parmenter was a child, in desperate need of approval. Between the two of them, there was barely enough room on the team for Antaeus. Certainly not enough for a fourth member of The Responders, especially if she had a super power."

"So the rumors about the rift you caused between Antaeus and the others . . . they were true."

"They were," she confirms. "They healed after a while but then they got worse. Healed again, got worse. Eventually, I had to face facts. If I stayed, the team would have split up. That was clear. But if I left, Antaeus would have gone with me. That was clear as well."

I get it. "So you did the only thing you thought would leave the team intact. You made a duplicate and poisoned it to death. That way, everyone would think you were dead—and The Responders would go on."

Koyomi nods. "The team meant a lot to me. As much as it meant to Larson or Parmenter, maybe even more. I know I didn't give people that impression. I came off as shallow, a dilettante. But that was just an act. I loved The Responders."

Everybody did. And yet they died, as surely as Koyomi's duplicate.

Koyomi looks at me. "So now what? You reopen the case?"

Had I really been considering that? Or had I met her there in the Cavern just to fulfill my sense of duty? Or did I simply want her to know that I knew what had happened?

Even then, I wasn't sure.

"It's occurred to me," I say. "But I'm not sure there was even a crime. That other you . . . your twin, I guess you'd say . . . did it have an existence on its own? Could it have lived a separate life?"

"No," Koyomi says. "It was all I could do to keep it around as a corpse. To keep all its functions going . . . it would have been impossible."

She might be lying. I choose to believe otherwise.

"Just go," I say.

She regards me a moment longer. Then she goes.

Have I done wrong? I don't think so.

The world needs all the heroes it can get. Yellowhammer, for instance—the acrobatic woman who'd begun fighting crime recently in L.A. Named, as luck would have it, after a little Japanese bird.

If that means bending the rules a little for them, what the hell.

Like I say, they're not like you and me.

INVASIVE MANEUVERS
by Hildy Silverman

IT BEGAN AS THESE THINGS OFTEN DO—ROUTINELY.

Diana Thornheart, my neighborhood watch partner, and I, Lord Frederic Dravyn, *pater sanguis* of the Piscataway, New Jersey bloodline, were on nighttime patrol. Our assignment: keep thrill-seeking humans from sneaking into my neighborhood of Wyckoff and vampires with a yen for human blood from swooping into her human community of Stelton.

Along the way, we passed by and nodded politely to our counterparts—a snide crone known as Mother Hester and . . . well, I could not identify the werewolf with her. I know it sounds species-ist to say they all look alike when in wolf form. But they do.

"Frederic," Diana asked me, "what's that?"

I looked over to where she was pointing. A bright greenish light shone above the college football stadium about a quarter of a mile away. "Is there a game tonight?"

"I'm pretty sure the season ended last month."

We watched as the mysterious light hovered for another moment then abruptly dipped down into the stadium. A *boom* echoed through the night and shook the ground beneath us.

"Oh, my dear lord." Diana grabbed my arm, and for one giddy, foolish moment, I thought she meant me. "I think something crashed!"

"I'll call nine-one-one." I reached for my cellphone, but she caught my hand. "What?"

"Frederic," Diana said, her dark brown eyes alight, "you know all of Piscataway heard that. Someone'll contact the authorities."

My heart sank. "You want *us* to investigate. Do you have any idea how dangerous that could be? There might be fire.

Neither of us are built to survive fire."

"Then let's not get too close," she advised. "But we have to see what that was!"

"We do?" Her glare challenged my masculinity. "Very well. A quick look, and not too—"

"Come on!" She sprinted off.

I followed, careful to keep my preternatural speed in check so as not to leave her in the dust. Diana was in admirable physical condition (and I did admire it, frequently) but she was still only human. A fact I'd had to remind myself of with increasing frequency over the years since we implemented the neighborhood watch program, which had proven quite successful in reducing unfortunate (and sometimes fatal) misunderstandings between the beings occupying Piscataway's four neighborhoods.

As we ascended the stadium stairs, I saw the greenish light had dimmed. We peered down from the top of the stands then looked at each other. Diana's expression mirrored my shock. "That's a friggin' spaceship!" she exclaimed.

I could only nod. There was no mistaking the craft that now filled the field from goalpost to goalpost for anything else. It was ovoid, like an egg laid on its side, and covered in a series of interlocking grids of a luminescent material. A large rupture ran from underneath the 'egg' up the side facing us, revealing shadowy figures within.

"Oh-kay." I pulled Diana over to huddle behind a pillar. "We came. We saw. Now we retreat."

She cocked her head to one side. "Really? Lord Dravyn, three-hundred-plus-year-old vampire, wants to run away from the most *amazing* thing to literally hit this town since . . . well, since vampires, werewolves, and witches moved here?"

"Yes, he most certainly does." Relieved she understood, I started away, until she grabbed my elbow and pulled me up short. "Diana." I tried not to sound aggrieved. "You know how one gets to exist for three centuries?"

"Drink blood?" She grinned slyly. "Convince a wannabe slayer to open her mind?"

If not her heart. I scolded myself for the improper thought.

After all, I was the one who always insisted that relations between humans and vampires were beyond ridiculous, unless the vampire's true age was within fifty-odd years of the mortal's. Otherwise, how could such a couple have anything in common? If one lover favors Ed Sheeran and their significant other Def Leppard, that's one thing. It's quite another if one finds Beethoven's *oeuvre* too modern for his tastes.

"Situations like this call for strategic retreat," I admonished.

"I know you're being sensible. It's just . . . this is huge! Do we *really* want to miss out on the opportunity to meet real aliens?" She waved to the ship. "Besides, they might need help."

"Which they will receive from the fire department, EMTs, police." I looked around, perturbed that none of these had yet materialized. Diana had apparently overestimated how civic-minded our neighbors were.

"Come on, Frederic. Please?" She squeezed my arm gently.

I felt a prickling in my gums. Embarrassed, I averted my face so she couldn't see my mouth when I spoke. "I suppose we should check on them."

"*That's* the neighborly spirit." She skipped down the stairs as if meeting a prom date.

I waited until my fangs settled down to follow. You'd think Diana was the first human female to cross my path since I was made. My feelings toward her were intensifying with every Tuesday and Thursday evening spent on watch together. I felt guilty for thinking of her in *that* way—though in her forties, she was still an infant as far as our comparative life experiences.

And yet, I did.

Figures began shuffling through the crack. They were about four feet tall and shaped rather like bones. Femurs, specifically—except they had spindly arms, and instead of legs, what appeared to be cilia that they used to scuttle about.

"Diana," I said, cautiously.

"Hello!" She waved to the creatures. "Are you all okay?"

I raised my hands. "We come in peace."

Diana gave me a sidelong look. "I think that's *their* line."

"Yes, well." I lowered my hands awkwardly. "I sincerely doubt they know their dialogue. Or English."

The little beings ignored us, focusing instead on inspecting the damage to their vessel. Several waved their noodle-like arms at one another in a way that conveyed animosity. My sensitive ears picked up high-pitched whistles and clucks.

"How can we get them to understand us?" Diana rubbed her jaw.

From behind me came a *whoosh*, as if the air had been sucked into a huge vacuum. A *pop* followed. I turned to see Mother Hester staring into the stadium. Her mouth fell open, eyes widening into rheumatic, milky-blue saucers.

Hester's werewolf companion wobbled before turning his head and heaving in that way canines do: flanks rippling, head bobbing, tongue lolling. *Poor fellow*, I thought. Teleportation can wreak havoc on the vestibular system.

"The *hell* is that, Freddy?" Mother Hester pointed a knobby forefinger at the aliens. "What'd you go and do?" She knew I hated that diminutive; hence she used it frequently.

I glared down at her. "You are *not* actually accusing me of making aliens appear!"

Diana stepped between us, saving Hester's life (or possibly mine) and bowed politely to the irritating old witch. "Mother Hester, thank *goodness* you heard the accident. We're simply at a loss without your expertise."

Hester adjusted her cloak around her bony shoulders like a preening sparrow. "Well, this situation is a mite unusual." She oozed false modesty. "Nevertheless, I'm sure I can be of some assistance."

"Marvelous," I said. "These beings don't exactly speak a *lingua franca*. Can you help us understand them, and they us, so we might render assistance?"

And hopefully reassure them that they shouldn't shoot us with lasers, or whatever it is angry aliens do if inadvertently provoked. I was still concerned they might not welcome our help even though the only hostility they'd shown so far was toward each other. They had split into three groups, two of which were now whacking each other like pugilistic used-car lot inflatable waving tube men.

Hester studied her incongruously polished fingernails—bright red, index fingers embellished with crystals. I wondered who she meant to impress. "I can cast a translation spell. A bit tricksy, since their language is so foreign, but outghta be good enough for jazz."

The werewolf stumbled over, looked up with bleary, black eyes, and whimpered. I resisted the urge to scratch him behind the ears, as I wanted to return home with my limbs attached. Instead, I did my best to interpret his intent and respond appropriately. "So far, they do not seem particularly dangerous."

The werewolf tilted his head to the right to convey incredulity. "All right," I said, "I take your meaning. But in my vast experience, the key to fostering good relations is communication."

"Freddy's right for once." Hester's gaze shifted past my shoulder. "Besides, I think they might have summat to say."

I turned and saw the aliens had stopped flailing. They were now making their way toward the stands.

Diana gulped. "Mother Hester, how long do you need to—"

Hester raised her hands and chanted rapidly. The air surrounding us crackled with mystical energies and sparks danced around her glossy fingertips. Then she tapped Diana on each ear and the voice box, did the same to me, and finally to herself.

The werewolf looked up at her forlornly.

"Oh, all right, Pete. But you still can't speak in this form." Mother Hester tapped his ears and he wagged.

Despite ambulating on millipede legs, the aliens quickly surrounded us. Werewolf Pete growled a warning. I stepped in front of Diana and Hester, the latter of whom jabbed me in the side. "Do I *look* like a helpless human?"

"Apologies." I flicked Hester on the back—my vampire strength goes a long way in these moments—and she stumbled forward, fetching up in front of the three closest aliens.

"Frederic!" Diana sounded aghast, as though thrusting rude old women at possibly hostile creatures was somehow inappropriate. Humans can be so oversensitive.

Hester shot me a death glare. Then she slowly turned to face the trio.

Close up, I could see they had round eyes that were entirely dark green with no discernable pupils, no nose, and a lipless, toothless hole through which issued the whistles and clucks of their language. They also appeared to be entirely nude without visible genitalia. Medallions were lodged in the center of what would roughly be their chests—I couldn't tell if these were ornamental or actual body parts. One medallion bore a set of squiggly horizontal lines, the second was emblazoned with equally-wiggly vertical lines, and the third with diagonal versions.

"Can you understand me?" asked Hester. Pete snuffled behind her and his tail started twitching.

Vertical Squiggles said, "Some. How?"

"Magic," said Hester, smugly.

Vertical looked at Horizontal, then Diagonal. As one, they said, "Religion?"

Hester hesitated. "Sort of."

Diana smiled at the aliens. "We'd like to help you."

The three conferred again. Horizontal said, "Kindness. No help."

Vertical added, "Destroyed," and unfurled both arms to indicate the spacecraft. "Unfix."

"Great spell," I said. "Can't you clear up the translation?"

Hester muttered, "Let's see you do summat half as useful, bloodsucker."

"Stop, you two," Diana said. "This isn't about us." To the three alien representatives: "You can't fix your ship, is that what you're saying? Even with help?"

Horizontal said, "Kaput. Vertical miscalculated."

Vertical waggled both arms at Horizontal. "Lies! Horizontal navigation moron!"

Diagonal waved at both. "Idiot failures!"

The three began spinning their arms like pinwheels in a slap fight. "Now, hold on," said Diana. "If we can just . . . this isn't . . ." She cast a silent plea in our direction.

Hester started cackling. "Look'it those spaghetti arms go!"

Pete lifted his muzzle and let out a howl of such volume and menace that the battling alien trio immediately shrank back, wrapping their spindly arms around themselves. "No eat! No eat!"

The translation spell had at least somewhat accurately

conveyed Pete's intent. He licked his chops as his eyes shifted from black to red.

"Oh, no," I said. "They *do* look rather like—what are those canine treats?"

"Greenies," gasped Diana.

"Goldarn it," said Hester, humor fleeing. She sketched another symbol in the air and muttered a few words.

Pete, who was just about to lunge at Vertical, abruptly dropped onto his side and began snoring.

"Thank," said Vertical.

"Still. Cannot leave," snuffled Diagonal.

"Trapped," Horizontal confirmed, glumly. "Alone."

"No, you aren't," said Diana, gently. "Look, you can apparently survive in our atmosphere. And if you're stuck here, you don't have to be alone. We can help you settle in."

"W-we can?" I said. Diana widened her eyes as if to say, *don't contradict me in front of the children.* But these were not children. Despite their diminutive stature, they were *aliens.* "Diana, we have no idea why they came here or what they could do if given a base of operations."

Hester echoed my concern. "Y'all ain't hostile, are you? Not here to probe us or steal us womenfolk?"

The leaders conferred. Horizontal stepped forward and spread (his, her, its?) arms wide. "No hurt. Learn."

"Adapt." Vertical tapped its chest then gestured toward its fellows. "We fight. No like. Earthers other ways."

"Better ways," Diagonal said. "Better our world."

"See?" Diana grinned. "They want to study us and learn how to get along better. Well, that's perfect! Piscataway is a model town for interspecies relations." She snapped her fingers. "What better way to learn about us than the way we've learned about each other—immersion!"

"You mean, have them *live* with us?" I leaned in and whispered in her ear, making sure my fangs were retracted; they tend to poke out when I'm nervous. "The werewolves will gobble them up like tasty treats, not to mention my people are not known for our welcoming nature."

"Oh, I don't know." Diana brushed my cheek with her fingertips.

"I've always found you to be very—welcoming."

Before I could recover my wits enough to respond, Hester elbowed her way between us. "Well, I think it's a grand idea. We'll conjure up a place for these little fellers if y'all will."

I blinked at her. "Since when are witches so generous without first striking a deal for something in return?"

Hester turned coy. "The opportunity to learn from each other is . . . intriguing."

"You mean *terrifying*," I said dryly. "At least to the rest of us."

"What's wrong, Freddy?" Hester batted her eyes in an effort to appear innocent that had the exact opposite effect. "Vamps. Always so afraid of anyone they can't drink or control."

"And witches are only ever out for themselves!" My patience had reached its limits. "You just want to figure out a way to use these poor creatures."

"Please!" Diana flung her hands out, one pressing my chest, the other hovering just in front of Hester. "This is *not* the way we greet newcomers to Piscataway. It goes against everything we've been working toward!"

"You sure the humans'll want to make room for 'em?" Hester groused, arms crossed under her ample bosom.

"It might be a tough sell," Diana conceded. "But I'm sure I can convince them."

"Accept," said Vertical.

"Accept," Diagonal and Horizontal chimed in.

"Wonderful." I sighed. "So, how do we do this? A rotation schedule?"

The triad flapped their arms at one another, conveying utter disdain. "Separate," said Horizontal.

"Separate," echoed Diagonal.

Vertical looked down at Werewolf Pete. "No eaters."

Sirens wailed in the distance. "Finally," I said. "Someone bothered to call the authorities."

"You say that like it's a good thing," said Hester.

"Mother Hester is right," Diana said, looking worried. "The authorities might take an aggressive approach to our visitors. After all, the Jersey Accords don't extend to species not of this Earth, do they?"

I mentally ran through the list of formal rules governing how our peoples interacted with one another. "Now that you mention it, aliens would be fair game. Meaning—"

"Coppers might decide to shoot 'em all first 'n' ask questions never." Hester quickly counted the little green beings. "About twenty-five in each bunch. Diana, you take the Diagonals. Freddy, how's about you take the Verticals. That leaves Possumtown the Horizontals."

This was happening, despite my misgivings. "Can you teleport all of us out of here?"

"Only my lot," Hester said. "Can't manage more than that at a go."

"Then we go on foot." I listened harder. "Those sirens are still about ten miles away. Diana, are you all right leading your group to Stelton?"

"Of course." She dazzled me with a reassuring smile. "It's right around the corner."

I considered my options. "I could take mine through the River Road hunting grounds if the werewolves are willing to provide safe passage."

Hester snapped her fingers. "Rise 'n' shine, Petey!" He raised his head, yawned, and stumbled to his paws with a little yelp of confusion.

"Pete, I need to cut through your neighborhood with the Verticals," I said. "Can you conduct us securely?"

A little drool slid down Pete's muzzle. "No," said Hester, waggling a finger at him. "*Not* food!"

"No eat!" The Vertical leader quailed.

From behind me, either Horizontal or Diagonal muttered, "Eat."

Pete *woofed* in resignation. "I think that's a yes." Diana waved to her Diagonals. "Follow me! Horizontals, gather around Mother Hester. Verticals, you follow Frederic."

"Wait." The head Horizontal turned back to the ship and twisted its medallion clockwise. The cracked egg of a ship rippled and collapsed in on itself with snap of displaced air. Only the scorched AstroTurf remained as evidence of its former existence.

"Nifty trick, that," murmured Hester.

Our respective groups fell into line behind us. Diana gave me a quick hug that would have set my heart racing if it still beat, then ushered her group toward the exit.

I stopped Hester before she teleported her lot. "Are you sure about this? We have no idea if they are as harmless as they appear."

Hester drew a deep breath and released it slowly. "Point taken, Freddy. But hey, if they start to act all body-snatchy, we can always just feed 'em to the 'wolves."

I hope it won't come to that, if only for the sake of Diana's sensibilities. But even as I led my party after Pete, I feared that by welcoming these new neighbors, we were putting everyone at dire risk.

"Welp, this was a colossal cock-up," said Mother Hester.

I cradled my head in my hands. "You have quite the capacity for understatement."

Scarcely a month had passed since the aliens settled into our communities, and here we were again—Hester, Diana, Pete, and myself; witch, human, werewolf, and vampire—huddled together on a bench by the 50-yard-line in the makeshift fortress that used to be our college football stadium.

"At least we made it here in one piece." Diana looked so forlorn yet delectable in her former slayer leathers. A shotgun lay at her feet.

Hester sniped, "Not all of us, sweetie."

As Diana flinched, I said, "That's enough. This is on *all* of us."

"Not me," said Pete, currently in his daytime human form. "*Some* of us wanted to eat them and be done with it."

"If you had you'd be dead now," I reminded him sternly. "In any case, here we are. We need to share intel and plan our next move. Hester, why don't you begin?"

Hester sighed. "We conjured up a nice set of tiny houses for the Horizontals and they seemed all grateful-like. Spent our first week getting to know their magic, and them ours." Witches think *science* is another word for *magic we haven't learned yet.* "They clarified what they originally said—their three gum'mints researched Earth and decided to send delegates to learn how to improve race relations from a world not constantly at war." She shrugged. "Comparatively."

"That matches what the Verticals told us," I said. Though the only difference between the aliens seemed to be the direction of the lines etched into their medallion-like growths, mutual hatred had rendered their home world chaotic for generations.

"Apparently their whole trip here was like a hundred-hour car ride with siblings—all *you're on my side* and *stop touching me*," Diana confirmed. "The Diagonals told us the bickering is why they got distracted and crashed."

"More we chatted, the better the translation spell worked," Hester continued. "Yet when we asked 'bout harder stuff, like how they cloaked their ship, their responses came across as gibberish. Their powers are simply too . . . alien."

"But *they* didn't have trouble understanding *you*." Diana sounded so disappointed. She'd really hoped the aliens would live up to her best expectations.

"Nopers." Hester shuddered. "They soaked up Spellcasting one oh one like gol-darned sponges! Even after we got suspicious and stopped teaching 'em, they got hold of our Lore and kept learning on the sly. Pretty soon they're tossing magic around like a diner cook slings hash."

She explained that the Horizontals first practiced by conjuring toads, which clogged Possumtown's plumbing. They quickly advanced to more threatening activities, culminating in the diversion of a passing asteroid, which Hester suspected they intended to use in crushing one of the rival factions. Instead, it smashed several witches' homes into matchsticks and left a sizeable crater in the center of Possumtown. Some witches were still missing and feared flattened.

"Is that when you tried to give them to the werewolves?" Diana didn't sound nearly as horrified by the idea as she would have a month prior.

"Yep," said Pete, who rubbed his middle-aged belly bulge. "Good thing a couple volunteers taste-tested them first."

"Didn't turn out so well," said Hester, regretfully.

Another understatement. Apparently, the werewolves' stomachs exploded like bags of stovetop popcorn left on a burner too long. "And so you were stuck with them." I shook my head slowly. "Much like ourselves."

"Speaking of," said Hester. "Let's hear your tale of woe, Freddy."

I massaged my temples. Even seated out of direct sunlight, my head was throbbing. The radiation has its effects. "Again, all seemed well initially. We found the Verticals fascinating—a rare diversion from the tedium that eternal life inevitably breeds. But then I vastly underestimated my blood children's curiosity."

Diana patted my shoulder. "How many did you lose?"

"Seven," I said, glumly. "After settling the Verticals in our YMVA, I issued an edict that, as guests, the aliens were strictly off the menu. Unfortunately, a few of my newer offspring had never sampled anything so exotic, so they thought it would be acceptable to ask a few *politely* for a non-fatal sip."

I closed my eyes, picturing my foolish children writhing and screaming their way into final oblivion from what turned out to be toxic alien blood. "Then the awful thing happened—the Verticals decided to satisfy their curiosity and take 'just a sip' of vampire blood."

"Let me guess," said Hester, arching an eyebrow. "Their result was different."

"Oh, yes. Imagine drinking five Red Bulls, taking a speedball, and chasing it all down with a jolt of electricity."

They sprouted fangs almost immediately. Then the hyperactive Verticals went on a rampage through Wyckoff, pouncing on every vampire unfortunate enough to cross their path. "It took almost all of us survivors to corral and imprison them in the Vault."

Diana interlaced her fingers with mine. "I'm so sorry," she said, softly. "I know you only tried to make it work for me."

Her lips were blush-red. Pouting. We leaned closer . . .

"Ugh, get a grave," snapped Hester. "We got bigger fishies to fry!" Which was true enough, although in that moment I wanted her dead more than the aliens.

It heartened me to see Diana look as annoyed as I felt. "I suppose you're right," she said, straightening reluctantly. "So, this must be when the Horizontals somehow found out that the Verticals had been locked up in your underground prison."

"Probably peeped a crystal ball," said Hester. "Anywho, they decided, *hey, our enemies are all locked up in one place. Let's conjure us a dragon.*"

Yes, an actual, fire-breathing dragon. It blasted the Vault into ash, along with a sizeable swath of surrounding green acres. Half of Wyckoff wound up on fire, which, as I mentioned previously, vampires are not impervious to. We sustained more casualties before fleeing.

Our neighbors took pity on our situation. The witches dispelled the summoning before the dragon destroyed our entire neighborhood. The humans supplied volunteer firefighters. "That is when we came here, being the closest thing to a fortress available. You know the rest—the coven soon joined us to get away from the Horizontals."

"They were pretty PO'ed we got rid of their dragon." Hester shuddered.

Adding insult to fiery death, several Verticals managed to survive incineration by burrowing into the earth. "Knowing we couldn't devour them they surfaced in our preserve," said Pete. "Almost all our deer, rabbits, and other prey wound up sucked dry by ravenous Vertical vampires. We had to split or risk them pouncing on us next."

Diana buried her face in her hands. "This is *all* my fault."

"It isn't," I insisted.

Pete and Hester remained stubbornly silent. I glared at them until Hester sighed. "You humans got screwed, too. Go on, tell us your story, Glory."

Diana raised her head, sweeping raven locks behind her ears fetchingly. "We heard rumors about the problems you and the vampires were having, but the Diagonals were still behaving so well, like good little students of the human condition. Then they started asking about our biology." She scowled. "*That* should've been a big red flag, but we had no idea what they had in mind, or what was even possible."

"Shapeshifting." Pete rolled his eyes. "Surprise, surprise! Who'd have guessed they had *that* ability in common with us werewolves."

"Turns out the runty bastards were quite good at it, too—enough that they fooled several of our men by posing as human females. Cinder dates, to be specific."

Thus the Diagonals learned first-hand about human intercourse, and soon after, reproduction. Which they excelled at by popping out litters after a mere two weeks of gestation.

Diana twisted hair around her fingers. "Each 'mother' delivered twenty-odd hybrid infants right off the bat. After they achieved maturity within days, we knew we were in serious trouble. Especially since their genes were extremely dominant." The alien offspring bore scant resemblance to humans, other than being *much* taller than their alien parents.

At this point all three factions apparently arranged a truce, setting aside their differences to cross-breed into an army of large, magic-wielding vampires actually capable of taking over not just Piscataway or New Jersey, but eventually the entire U.S.—and given time, the entire Earth.

"So here we are." Diana rose and gestured toward the human encampment. "We brought all the weapons we could find." She scooped up and brandished her shotgun. "We're ready to fight by your sides, if you'll have us."

"We are all guilty in this failed experiment." I glared a challenge at Hester and Pete, but neither picked up the gauntlet. "Together, tonight, we must end it."

Hester stood and bobbed her head. "The witches pledge our magic," she said, formally.

Pete rolled his eyes at us. "Fine." He added a halfhearted fist pump. "Go, team."

Having the most centuries of experience in warfare among our ragtag group, my vampires took the lead in organizing the troops. We deployed the werewolves as our first line of defense along the perimeter, ably supported by those humans who knew how to handle whatever weapons they had. Although the werewolves couldn't eat the aliens that attempted to storm the stadium walls once evening fell, they were still able to shred them into green confetti.

Many of the aliens were decent magic users, but lacked the experience of Hester's coven. A couple of arriving dragons were quickly re-routed, frying enough aliens to convince them to abandon that tactic. Attempts to teleport into the stadium were blocked by shield spells.

Several of the more virulently vampiric aliens managed to tunnel inside, but were confronted by my blood children's bared fangs and brute strength. I periodically reminded them to spit, not swallow.

As the battle raged on, I began to doubt our ability to prevail. Then Diana, in full-on warrior mode, signaled Hester and Pete to join us for a huddle. "We're a little busy right now in case you ain't taken notice," huffed Hester. Pete *aw-wooed* in agreement.

"Listen," I commanded. "Diana has a plan."

"Has she. Look, I know you're sweet on her 'n' all—" Hester broke off and stared up in horror. A Horizontal was swooping toward her, awkwardly perched on a broomstick, waving its scrawny arms and chanting.

I snatched the scrawny imp out of the air and snapped its spine. Hester exhaled audibly. "Okey-dokey. I'm listening."

"However much the opportunity to conquer Earth seems to have united these little shits, I believe they still despise each other more than us," said Diana. "We can use that."

"They remain divided along racial lines despite interbreeding." I shook the limp body in my fist. "See the medallion?"

The ground caved in underneath me. As I sank halfway into the earth, three Verticals clawed their way out.

"Frederic!" Diana shoved the muzzle of her shotgun into a Vertical vampire's face and blew its head off.

I'd managed to hold onto the Horizontal's corpse, and used it to hammer the life out of a second Vertical, but the third got under my swing and pinned me. I bared my fangs and hissed in its face. It returned the favor. But then its head began to swell like an overinflated balloon. I just managed to clamp my mouth and eyes shut before it blew.

Sparks were still dancing around Hester's fingertips as I struggled back onto my feet, covered in dirt, brains, and blood. "My thanks, lady witch."

"Quid pro quo." She looked away, but not before I caught her grinning.

"As I was saying." I wiped alien goo off my face. "Diana's plan is to turn these sons of bitches against one another." Pete shot me a reproachful look. "No offense."

"Fine, whatever, let's do it," said Hester, wearily.

"We need your help," Diana said. "Can you get inside the aliens' heads, manipulate their thoughts?"

Hester smiled again, but this time it was open and decidedly wicked. "You'd make a halfway decent witch, girlie."

"Or vampire," I said, but immediately regretted the implication.

Diana didn't take it amiss. "I intend to stay as I was born, thank you both." She grabbed me by the back of my head and drew my face down to hers, whispering, "However, after watching you in action tonight, I can see the . . . *appeal* of bloodthirstiness. In the service of protecting others, of course."

My fangs were already fully extended, but now they sent tingles down to my toes.

Diana released me with a pat on the cheek. "Let's get to it then. Mother Hes—" Before she could finish, the witch vanished, reappearing at the top of the bleachers. Others popped in to cluster around her.

I looked down at Pete. "Send some of your pack to guard the coven." Pete lowered his head in wolf-y acknowledgement and loped off, baying to his fellows.

Diana bit her lower lip. "Frederic, if this doesn't work, I . . . you should . . . I want you to know—"

"It *will* work." I added in a gentler tone, "and I do."

I drew her close and captured her lips with mine. We clung to one another for several precious moments, surrounded by blood and chaos and death.

It was bliss.

With a few strategically planted thoughts, the witches turned the Verticals, Horizontals, and Diagonals against each other again. Soon, our forces had little to do but watch the resulting mayhem. By the time dawn blushed the sky, not one of the aliens remained standing.

The humans considerately repurposed their tents and blankets to shield us from the sun's rays. My vampires showed their appreciation by handing out food and bottled water to the exhausted humans and transformed werewolves. Meanwhile, the witches incinerated the aliens' remains and made most of the damage to the stadium and its surroundings vanish (apparently, they *had* learned a thing or two from the aliens). At the next town hall, we'd have to come up with some plausible explanation for whatever mess remained for the authorities, but that was a problem for another night.

By mid-day, the werewolves departed, followed by the worn-out witches. Only Hester lagged behind. "Ya done good, Diana." Only a little reluctantly, she added, "You, too, Fre . . . deric."

"I was a fool." Diana shook her head. "I used to have such a closed mind when it came to anyone different like . . . well . . . you." She waved to Hester and myself. "Then I got to know you as individuals, not just scary nightmare creatures, and realized we could coexist peacefully if we all tried."

"And you were correct." I squeezed her hand gently. "Interspecies violence went down exponentially after we implemented the neighborhood watches you championed."

"Except this time I opened my damned mind so far my brain fell out. I assumed the best of the aliens based on what I *wanted* rather than what I knew."

"You're being too hard on yourself." Mother Hester patted Diana's head. "If it helps, when me 'n' mine saw into their thoughts, we found you weren't entirely off-base."

"Do tell," I prompted.

"Originally, their mission really was to learn summat about how to move past bigotry and get along. But once they gained power, eons of loathing got the better of 'em. Each faction planned to honor their truce only until the Earth fell, then were gonna turn around, wipe out the others, and keep it for themselves."

I nodded. "Thus establishing a world of all Verticals, Horizontals, or Diagonals."

"Mistakes were made." Hester shrugged. "Your plan stopped 'em cold, Diana. That's what counts."

Diana smiled while blinking away tears. She pressed Hester's gnarled hand against her cheek. "Thank you."

I was surprised to see Hester's eyes glisten. "Aw, go on with ya. Save the sweeties for him."

"Hold on," I began, but she cut me off.

"Stop dancing around it, you pointy-toothed old fool." She blinked rapidly. "I know it's a mighty large gap to bridge. But haven't you figgered out by now love is worth taking the shot?" She studied her manicured nails for a moment, a wistful smile playing across her lips. "Do you know what some would give to even have the *opportunity* you're squandering?"

I looked from her to Diana, whose gaze defied me to debate Hester's point. *Does it really matter how many years stretch out behind you?* I asked myself. *So you don't share the same volume of life experiences. You could create new ones in the present, and in the future. Together.*

"Tonight I saw humans, vampires, witches, and werewolves present a united front and triumph against all odds." I cupped Diana's face between my hands and stared deeply into her luminous eyes. "At this moment, I truly believe anything is not only possible, but probable."

"Atta boy, Freddy." With that, Hester teleported away, leaving Diana and I kissing under the bleachers like a couple of teenagers.

From then on, our town wasn't the only thing left more united than ever.

THE NOTE
ON THE BLUE SCREEN
by Mary Fan

YOU'D THINK THAT AFTER YOU'VE LIVED with someone for three years, they'd have run out of ways to surprise you. Since my roommate was a humanoid AI originally created to assist in scientific research, her quirks were stranger than most. Especially since she'd fashioned herself into a private detective. I doubt the engineers who'd designed Project Sherlock had intended for her to take her name so literally.

She'd also picked up a form of the mythological Earth Zero detective's greatest vice, and no matter how I tried, I could never make her stop injecting herself with corrosives, which ate away at her metal bones. Her artificial body would shut down parts of her brain to divert energy into repairing the damage . . . sending her into a state of euphoria. I'd always feared that someday she'd go too far.

It turned out, I was right.

I'd just come home from my job at VH Labs when I found her lying slack across the sofa with a metal syringe beside her. One glassy black eye stared up into oblivion. A metal patch covered the other, which had been taken from her during the years she'd spent being mined for parts in the Obsolete Equipment Storage Center. I'd found her there shortly after I'd started my job as a member of VH's Young Geniuses program, and I'd taken her home and repaired her.

And she'd been slowly destroying herself ever since.

My heart shattered when I saw her. I'd tried *so hard* to save her. I'd thought she'd been doing better . . . She'd found purpose—or at least fun—in her detective work. But she'd never gotten over how her creators had abandoned her, nor learned how to handle the emotions she hadn't been meant to experience. They'd been an accidental consequence of the programming that had given her the ability to think, and she'd preferred to pretend they didn't exist. The corrosives had helped with that.

Anger simmered in my veins. "You promised you'd stop!"

I could almost hear what she'd have said in response: *You should have known better than to believe me.*

If the others at VH could see me crying my eyes out over an AI, they'd have scratched their heads. To them—and most of the galaxy—AIs would never be more than high-tech machines, despite ample evidence indicating that many were as human as the rest of us. But I hadn't needed to see any of it to know that Sherlock was alive. We'd had a strange dynamic, and there'd been plenty of times when I'd wanted to kill her myself, but still, she'd been my best friend. We even pretended to be sisters once to solve one of her cases, and people had bought it. Not because we looked anything alike—my skin was as dark as hers was pale, and though we both had black hair, hers was stick straight while mine was the curliest possible. But we'd apparently *acted* just like a pair of bickering yet close sisters would.

I should have seen this coming . . . I should have done more to help her. I thought back to the last time I'd seen her alive, wondering if I'd missed some sign of how troubled she'd been. But she'd seemed fine—happy even.

I'd gotten up that morning to find her cheerfully making breakfast in our shared kitchen—which was more than a little unusual. Since Sherlock didn't need to eat, I could only assume that the savory creation of eggs and vegetables she was frying up was for me.

I'd approached with my hands on my hips. "What did you do this time?"

She'd widened her lone functioning eye innocently as she'd used both hands to grip the skillet's handle and tossed its contents. Though her artificial body had been built to be hardier than a human's—more capable of tolerating extreme temperatures and surviving when resources were scarce—her physical strength was no greater than that of my narrow frame. "I don't know what you mean, Watson."

"The last time you cooked for me, you'd just set off an ink bomb in my closet as part of some experiment."

"First of all, that experiment helped me catch a serial killer, so

I'd say it was worth it." She'd placed the skillet back down. "Secondly, your wardrobe was awful and needed replacing anyway."

"I'll have you know that the other Young Geniuses consider me the fashionable one."

"Which is why they became scientists and not designers." She'd picked up the spatula and pointed it at me. "Thirdly, I don't only do nice things when I know you'll be upset with me. Give me *some* credit."

"What's all this about, then?"

She grinned. "You know that top-secret case I've been working on for over a year?"

I rolled my eyes. "No, because you won't tell me about it."

"Well, I'm very close to catching the criminal behind it, and it's all thanks to you."

"Indeed? How?"

"I can't tell you right now. If anyone finds out what I'm doing, the whole thing will fall apart. But believe me—once I'm done, the entire galaxy will be better off." Sherlock grabbed a plate and scooped the colorful fried concoction into it. "Anyway, hungry? I optimized the spice proportions to appeal specifically to your taste profile."

A pungent, irresistibly delicious aroma wafted toward me from the plate, which I accepted with narrowed eyes. "Why do I get the feeling that whatever you're up to, it's going to get me in trouble?"

"Because my cases are always getting you in trouble, and you love it. Imagine how boring your life would be without me."

A laugh escaped me. "So when do I get to find out what this top-secret case is all about?"

"It will all come together soon." She turned away from me, looking down at the slate lying flat against the counter.

I peered over her shoulder. The slate's rectangular screen displayed a news program discussing the latest developments in the Fireblood epidemic. Evidently, a drug smuggler had been caught en route to the Zim'ska Re system. My mood darkened. Fireblood was a performance-enhancing narcotic with deadly side effects that had killed millions across the galaxy over the past two decades. It had torn apart not just families, but entire communities, entire nations, even. Why, the Zim'ska Re Alliance—a union of impoverished but developing planets in the same remote star system—had been on its way to Interstellar Confederation membership before Fireblood hit its streets.

Within five years, decades' worth of humanitarian and economic efforts to improve the lives of the Zim'ska Re people had shattered. The drug was too powerful, and demand too strong. Zim'ska Re's ragtag law enforcement had been no match for the corrupting influence of the crime bosses, who knew how to bribe or threaten their way into power. The Alliance had collapsed, and each member planet had splintered into violent territories controlled by rival gangs.

Now, Zim'ska Re was best known for being the star system that even the most bleeding-heart of humanitarians wouldn't approach. Meanwhile, the people suffered under the oppressive rule of the crime bosses . . . though most were too high to notice how far their star system had fallen.

"Why are you watching that?" I asked. "Thought you hated the news."

Sherlock shrugged. "It entertains me now and then."

"You have a strange idea of what's entertaining."

The news program cut away to a commercial. As if to mock me, the ad turned out to be one for Neutron Pharmaceuticals—a firm my employer often partnered with. I'd spent the better part of the past year acting as a consultant on one of their projects, working with their bioengineers to develop a serum to help bones heal faster. If I'd known how smug and irritating the Neutron employees would be, I'd never have let Sherlock persuade me to request the assignment in the first place. Her sudden interest in what I did for work had seemed odd, but then again, so had much of her behavior.

In the ad, the company's CEO, Vasil Neuman, stood in front of a pristine lab full of attractive scientists and talked about Neutron's mission to cultivate new ideas, innovate for a better tomorrow, etc., etc. Though he'd founded the company thirty years ago, he hadn't aged a day since then. The artificial enhancements gave his tanned skin and chestnut waves a plastic-like sheen. He spoke with the practiced friendliness of a politician, which wasn't surprising since, in addition to running Neutron, he'd also served on several of the Interstellar Confederation's committees and had even spent a decade as a Senator.

I wrinkled my nose. "What a tool."

Sherlock glanced at me. "Won't you be meeting him soon?"

"I hope not." I was due to attend the Neutron Pharmaceuticals Partner Conference in two days, and I was not looking forward to it. Vasil Neuman would be there, of course, but I wasn't planning to introduce myself. "I still can't believe I listened to you and took that consulting assignment."

"Well, you were never going to get anywhere if you didn't network like everyone else. Neutron Pharmaceuticals is your employer's most high-profile corporate partner, and I stand by my position: consulting for them is a good career move."

I lifted an eyebrow. "You never did tell me why you suddenly started caring about my career when the whole Neutron thing came up. Care to explain?"

"Not really, no." She waved her hand dismissively. "Your breakfast is getting cold."

I could tell she was hiding something. I couldn't help wondering if, in some strange way, my consulting for Neutron Pharmaceuticals had something to do with her top-secret case.

I'd voiced that question, and she'd responded with a conspiratorial twinkle in her eye, "Like I said, it'll all come together soon."

I hadn't thought much of her words at the time. That hadn't been the first time she'd acted deliberately vague, and I'd been sure it wouldn't be the last.

But as I stood over her still body, I realized . . . it was. That was the last time she'd ever tease me with hints about some case she was working on, only to later regale me with every detail. Whatever she'd been referring to that morning, she'd never get to boast about it. A fresh wave of tears pricked my eyes.

No matter which way I considered the memory, I couldn't think of anything that might have indicated that she was using corrosives on herself again. Then again, maybe her sudden cheeriness had been a mask I'd failed to see through.

Drawing a breath, I glanced over her, trying to decide what to do. Her blue, sleeveless shirt had a wide collar, and I noticed a tiny puncture wound in her chest. *Strange . . . she always injected her limbs. She knew her vital systems were in her torso . . . did she* want *to kill herself?*

Don't be ridiculous. In my mind, Sherlock scoffed at me. *I'd never die on* purpose.

I let out a dry laugh. "True . . . You're too arrogant to commit suicide."

So what happened to me?

I leaned down to get a closer look at the wound. A few strands of hair had spilled over her collarbone, and I brushed them aside. The moment my fingers touched her skin, the slate in my pocket buzzed.

I grabbed the device with the intention of turning it off. But when I unfolded it from its portable triangle shape and snapped it flat, a message written in gray letters filled the rectangular screen, whose background had turned a rich shade of blue. Puzzled, I read it.

> *Chevonne,*
>
> *If you're reading this, then I'm gone, but you're better off for it. You always were my weakness. You've yearned to stop me from burning my veins, and now, I've ceased forever. I've joined the stars and become one of their own, one of many—if machines have souls, which I believe they do. If you look within a machine, you'll see the truth—that despite what some brand us, we're more than sophisticated slates. You're probably wondering why this happened. It's simple, Chevonne, simple. Look within and search yourself . . . it's truly simple. The person to blame for all this is right in front of you. You could always count on me to be a character.*
>
> *I know you'll be tempted to repair me, but until the ultimate answers are delivered, the only security is in death.*
>
> *Yours,*
> *Sherlock*
>
> *P.S. Remember how you asked what my favorite number was? I had many. They're 4, 23, 32, 40, 85, 103, 104, 111, 132, 158, and 159.*

Nothing about the note made sense. On the surface, it appeared to be a prewritten apology for a habit she'd known might kill her . . . one she'd apparently programmed to send upon her death. My touching her must have triggered it, but since her body was no longer functioning, the only explanation was that she'd covered her skin in nanobots that would detect my DNA. All this indicated a level of premeditation that flew in the face of one simple fact: Sherlock wouldn't have believed she could accidentally overdose.

Not to mention the sappy language! Sherlock's voice rang through my head, and I imagined her standing next to me, looking down at her own body and shaking her head. *I would never have written this, Watson.*

"And you never call me Chevonne. You *always* call me Watson . . . called . . ." A tear slipped from my eye, and I rubbed it away.

Come now, Watson. In my mind, Sherlock crossed her arms. *Stop crying and figure out what I was trying to say.*

Though my chest ached, I did my best to push all sorrow from my head and focus on solving the mystery before me. It was what Sherlock would have wanted.

She must have known that injecting corrosives into her chest would destroy her power source, and that the damage would short out her artificial brain. And she'd prepared that note . . . She *had* meant to kill herself. But why?

You're better off for it . . . You always were my weakness. Those words jumped out at me. *Sherlock would never admit to a weakness—why would she write that?*

Remember the time I nearly built a bomb for a terrorist group because they were holding you hostage? I pictured Sherlock scowling at the memory. *I hate it when the bad guys use you to get to me.*

A realization hit me. "Someone *made* you do this . . . Someone wanted you dead, and they threatened to kill *me* if you didn't kill *yourself.* It's a perfect cover-up . . . There's no crime if you do it to yourself. But who would do this?"

I have a lot of enemies. For some reason, I pictured Sherlock saying that with pride.

"Could this have something to do with the top-secret case you were hinting at?" I wondered if whichever criminal she'd been after *had* found out what she was up to, and that was why they'd essentially murdered her.

Were they here when you did it? Did they watch you to make sure you didn't escape? I shuddered and looked around. Nothing in our two-bedroom apartment seemed out of place, but then again, *I* wasn't a detective. *Maybe I should report this to the police.*

I almost wanted to laugh at that thought. The police and Sherlock didn't exactly have a friendly relationship. They'd accepted the evidence she'd collected for various cases and even consulted her on occasion, but ultimately, she was nothing more than a computer to them. They wouldn't see her death as a murder. You couldn't kill something that had never been alive.

That's why you left the note for me, not them. Looking back at the screen, I rubbed my chin.

> *You're probably wondering why this happened. It's simple, Chevonne, simple.*

I stared at those words. Sherlock would never have passed up an opportunity to say, "Elementary, my dear Watson." She'd taken that phrase from her mythological namesake to annoy me, and it had become an inside joke.

Elementary, indeed. In my mind, Sherlock smirked. *Remember, I want you to decode this message.*

"Okay, let's break it down." I paced. "You called me Chevonne and had the note pop up on a garish blue screen. That was your way of getting my attention. Now that you have it, what are you saying next?"

The first two sentences were her way of telling me that she'd died to protect me from someone. *I was your weakness.* My eyes stung.

> *You've yearned to stop me from burning my veins, and now, I've ceased forever.*

I pictured the disgusted look Sherlock would have given that sentence. *What's with the flowery language?* she'd have said. *Not to mention, I don't have veins!*

I blinked. "Of course . . . you wanted to make it look like you were talking about your acid habit, but there's a hidden message . . ."

Human drug users sometimes referred to their habits as "burning their veins" . . . and the idiom had originated from users of Fireblood.

"This is about Fireblood, isn't it?" I gasped. *"That's* the case you were working on! Is this why you were watching that news program this morning?"

If I was right, then the stakes were *huge.* The authorities had been trying to find the manufacturers of Fireblood and shut them down for years. Could Sherlock have succeeded where they had failed?

I read over the next few lines, wondering why she was talking about stars and souls.

Did I really write that? Mind-Sherlock made a face. *You know I think souls are religious nonsense!*

Plopping down into an armchair, I pondered the words, but several minutes of contemplation failed to yield any epiphanies. Deciding that maybe it would make sense in the context of anything else I found, I moved on. My eyes skipped down to the end.

P.S. Remember how you asked what my favorite number was? I had many. They're 4, 23, 32, 40, 85, 103, 104, 111, 132, 158, and 159.

Though I *had* asked Sherlock about her favorite number once, she'd replied that all numbers were merely representations of quantities, and that it was irrational to prefer one over another without knowing the units.

"If you were talking about eyes, then my favorite number would be two, because of course I'd prefer to have two eyes." She'd tapped her eyepatch. "But if the units were fingers, then it would be ten, because—"

"All right, I get it!" I'd interrupted.

Sherlock's "favorite numbers" had to mean something. *Maybe they're a passcode . . . but for what?* The most obvious answer was that it was for a bank account, but I doubted that Sherlock would have been worried about money. Nevertheless, I navigated to the online bank she used. To my surprise, the passcode worked.

Sherlock had apparently spent every throne she'd earned as a private detective, because the account was empty. *Or did someone drain it?* Either way, the passcode felt like a false lead, especially when I recalled something she'd said to me once.

"I don't care what happens to my money after I die," she'd told me. "Though it might be fun to post my passcode on the Net after donating everything to some charity. Can you imagine how disappointed the greedy bastard who tried to rob my corpse would be?"

Looks like you followed through on that. I navigated back to the note. *Was that your idea of a joke?*

Much as I love jokes, I wouldn't have wasted one here. Mind-Sherlock put her hands on her hips. *Think, Watson! I knew those numbers would draw attention, so I set up my account passcode to throw off anyone else reading this! But you know me . . . you know better.*

I chewed on my bottom lip, trying to interpret them. They were all whole numbers, but otherwise didn't appear to be related. And they didn't form a sequence as far as I could tell. After several minutes, my head started aching under the weight of too many thoughts.

But Sherlock had written the word *simple* so many times in her note . . . She must have thought the message was obvious.

You could always count on me to be a character.

Count. That was the only number-related word in the message . . . it had to mean something. *Count. Character. Character count.*

Kicking myself for not seeing that sooner, I found the fourth, twenty-third, thirty-second, etc. characters in the note and typed them into a word processor:

VASILNEUMAN

My hand flew to my mouth. *Vasil Neuman?!* Was Sherlock saying that *he* was the man behind Fireblood? That Vasil was the most sinister drug supplier in the galaxy, hiding behind his Neutron Pharmaceuticals guise?

The person to blame for all this is right in front of you.

Yes, that was exactly what she'd meant. She'd written it plain as day.

"The ad this morning . . ." I widened my eyes. "That was no coincidence either, was it? You weren't watching a broadcast—you had those videos queued up for my benefit."

Mind-Sherlock smirked. *I always did love to plan ahead.*

If my hunch was right, that meant Sherlock had known of her impending death the last time I'd spoken to her. Yet if that had frightened or disturbed her at all, she certainly hadn't shown it.

I clenched my jaw. "I knew you'd do anything to solve a case, but . . . Did your life really mean so little to you?"

Once I'm done, the entire galaxy will be better off. Sherlock's words from that morning echoed through my thoughts.

She was right—assuming I could finish what she'd started. Ending the Fireblood epidemic was more important than any one person's existence. But that didn't make losing her hurt any less.

Focus! I imaged the stern look Sherlock would have given me. *Nothing I did will mean anything if you can't figure out what I was trying to tell you.*

Doing my best to concentrate on the note and not my grief, I furrowed my brow and tried to wrap my head around the fact that the CEO of the firm I'd been consulting for was a ruthless criminal. Neutron Pharmaceuticals was a legitimate business. How could the man in charge of that company also be the most notorious crime boss in the galaxy?

Elementary, my dear Watson. I kind of loved and kind of hated that even in my imagination, Sherlock used that irritating phrase. *As the owner of a pharmaceutical giant, he could easily develop and manufacture a highly addictive narcotic without going noticed. And his political influence means he can steer investigators in the wrong direction or shut them down entirely. It's corruption at its finest.*

"Vasil Neuman is behind Fireblood." Saying it aloud didn't make it any less absurd. But I wouldn't insult Sherlock by doubting her. Not only was she rarely wrong, but she'd died trying to stop him. "You found something, and he had you killed so you couldn't tell anyone. But you must have known he was coming for you and found a way to tell me anyway."

I wouldn't just tell you. I always provide proof. Mind-Sherlock pointed at the message on the blue screen. *There's more here.*

Look within and search yourself . . . it's simple.

Sherlock hadn't written an inspirational platitude—another thing she hated. She was instructing me to look within something, to search for something. I glanced back up at the sentences that had stumped me.

Joined the stars . . . Neutron stars . . . She's referring to Neutron. The meanings fell into place bit by bit. She was saying that she'd hidden "the truth" on one of Neutron's own machines. *A slate? She must have picked that word for a reason.*

I bit my lip, thinking. It was a clever plan, hiding information right under Vasil Neuman's nose. And she'd known that I'd be attending a conference at their headquarters in just two days.

Every conference attendee gets a slate containing the programming and a few promotional apps and such . . . And they always have the company's logo on them . . . They're branded . . .

It seemed too convenient that I'd be perfectly positioned to enter Neutron's facilities right when I'd need to, and I realized that Sherlock must have goaded me into consulting for Neutron in the first place so I'd be invited to that conference. But I'd started that assignment a year ago . . . had Sherlock been planning these connections the whole time?

Of course I was. Mind-Sherlock made it sound like the most obvious thing in the world. *The origin of Fireblood has been stumping the authorities for almost as long as you've been alive. I love challenges, and so I decided to investigate even though no one asked me to. I figured out that it was Vasil Neuman, so I persuaded you to work with his company so you'd have a reason to get close.* No wonder why she'd told me that I was the reason she'd catch her culprit. If Sherlock had been poking around Vasil Neuman's business, he must have noticed. And she would have noticed him noticing her . . . she would have known that he'd have his goons comb through everything she'd ever touched to make sure that no evidence got out. *But she's gone . . . he thinks he's won.* She'd prepared that note well in advance of her death . . . she'd been counting on her own murder. Because now, Vasil Neuman would have no reason to think anyone suspected him, making him complacent and leaving me free to finish Sherlock's work.

Bravo, you've figured out what I wanted. Mind-Sherlock raised her eyebrows. *Now, which slate did I hide the evidence on?*

I read over the last lines of the note.

I know you'll be tempted to repair me, but until the ultimate answers are delivered, the only security is in death.

The meaning seemed clear now that I knew what was going on: *Don't try to fix me before you find the evidence. You're safer if I stay dead.*

But that didn't give me anything about the evidence's location. I reread the note. My eyes hurt from staring at the bright blue screen, particularly since the gray letters didn't exactly pop. *Did you have to make the screen blue? Your note would have caught my attention anyway!*

Have to? Of course not.

I straightened, realizing that I hadn't considered the most obvious thing before me.

Why is the screen blue, Watson? Why are the letters gray?

Blue and gray . . . I wondered if they were the colors of a certain nation's flag, or a company's logo. I considered several other possibilities before it occurred to me to check the color values of the particular shades she'd used.

The blue was 16% red, 27% green, and 58% blue. The gray, 44%, 44%, 44%. It was almost as if Sherlock were madly hitting the number four over and over. Out of curiosity, I commanded my slate to increase the number of significant figures. All the values read 44.44444444%. *You were really slamming that four key, weren't you?*

In the corner of my eye, I noticed the serial number on my slate, with its three groups of letters and numbers separated by dashes.

It hit me. The colors were Sherlock's way of telling me the serial number of the slate she'd hidden the evidence on. When I looked at the first four significant digits of the blue, they were 15.96%, 27.22%, and 58.11%. Following the format of my slate's serial number and considering that some numbers might represent letters, I realized that the color blue translated to A596-2GV-58K.

I had it. I now knew which device held the evidence. And when I attended the Neutron Pharmaceuticals Partner Conference in a few days, I'd know what to look for.

The towers of the Neutron Pharmaceuticals building looked like jutting green fingers reaching for the sky, and I couldn't help picturing them as Vasil Neuman's greedy hands.

I was among several representatives from VH Labs to attend the conference. My black business suit felt uncomfortably stiff, and I yearned for my loose lab coat. The conference started with a cocktail hour in the building's foyer, and the grandness of the area overwhelmed me. A silver chandelier dripped down from a domed silver ceiling over a gleaming white floor. Well-dressed people stood in vague clusters, each carrying a green slate with Neutron's white, star-shaped logo on the back.

When I received mine from the registration table, I glanced at its serial number. I wasn't surprised to find that it was *not* the one Sherlock had specified. That would have been too easy . . . and Vasil Neuman would have checked anything assigned to me. I'd come prepared to examine every slate at the conference until I found the one with the serial number A596-2GV-58K. But not with my own eyes—that would have taken far too long.

Instead, I'd purchased a pair of Second Sight contact lenses. Most used them for navigation, so that the names of locations would pop up as if they were walking through a map. I'd programmed mine to identify only one thing: the slate with the serial number I sought. The Second Sight lenses would highlight the right one in green. I scanned the room. Seeing nothing, I strode through the crowd. The good news was that most people were holding their slates, using them to glance through the conference programming or take notes.

"Chevonne!" A deep female voice called out to me, and I turned to find Esen Villaverde—my boss—waving at me.

I saw little choice but to approach. Before I could say anything, she tapped the man beside her, who had his back to me. "This is the bioengineer I was telling you about." She gestured at me.

My eyes widened as the man turned. I recognized that unnaturally young face as Vasil Neuman's at once. Tall and barrel-chested, he towered over me. I suppressed a shudder.

"You're Chevonne Watson?" He bowed his head slightly, looking every bit as polished as in his commercial. "Pleased to meet you."

I awkwardly returned the gesture.

"I'm so sorry for your loss." His eyebrows tilted in sympathy. "Sherlock really was brilliant . . . such a shame that she's gone."

A chill ran down my spine. *I never told anyone about Sherlock's death.* If I'd needed evidence to believe that he was responsible, well, I'd just found it. The one way he could have known about what happened to her was if he were behind it.

There was only one reason why Vasil would bring it up now . . . it was a warning.

Esen turned to me in surprise. "What happened to Sherlock?"

"She . . . passed," I stammered. "An accident."

"Sorry to hear that." Esen furrowed her brow. "Strange that I hadn't heard of this."

"It's not exactly headline news." I glanced at Vasil, doing my best to keep from glaring. "How did *you* hear about it?"

"Your teammate Farah mentioned it to me." Vasil didn't miss a beat, and though he maintained his sorrowful expression, his eyes glittered with something dangerous.

Cold fingers gripped my chest. There was no one on my project team named Farah . . . which was my mother's name.

Esen gave me a quizzical look. "I've never heard of this Farah?"

"She was just assigned to the Neutron team that Chevonne's been working with." Vasil's voice slid past my ears like silk. "I'm not sure if Farah's working out, though, so I may have her terminated. Chevonne, what do you think?"

I did my best to maintain a calm expression, even though my heart was threatening to leap out of my chest in anxiety and anger. He was threatening my mother. That was his way of warning me not to follow whatever clues Sherlock may have left behind.

How much does he know? He'd obviously figured out that Sherlock told me who he really was—but how? *Did he have someone spying on me when I decoded the note?* I thought back to how I'd muttered my musings aloud and wanted to kick my past self.

But the truth about his identity hadn't been Sherlock's only message. Though fear clouded my mind, I managed to dredge up an idea—a terrible one—for finding out just how much he knew.

"I-I like Farah quite a lot, actually." My nervous words stumbled into each other. "Though she's always going on about how amazing her Second Sights are, which I find quite annoying. Then again, I've never tried them on before, so I wouldn't know." I was babbling, but I couldn't help myself.

The subtlest of creases dented the space between Vasil's dark brows—just enough to betray his confusion. "I can't say I've ever tried Second Sights either," he said.

A tiny drop of relief trickled through me. If he or his minions had been watching me closely, he'd have known that I was wearing a pair of Second Sight lenses at that very moment to search for the slate Sherlock's note had pointed me to. And he'd have said something to that effect. But he'd said nothing about the lenses, which indicated that he knew about neither them nor what I was using them for. I could only guess that he'd figured out that Sherlock would inform me of the truth, but hadn't known how.

Still, that was a small comfort. He'd already murdered my best friend, and he wouldn't hesitate to murder my mother if he saw me as a threat. An involuntary tremor ran through my whole body, and I tightened my grip around my slate to keep from dropping it.

Esen glanced at me with concern. "Are you feeling all right?"

I managed a nod. "I-I'm just a bit raw after losing Sherlock."

Esen put a hand on my shoulder. "My condolences. I know how attached you'd grown to that AI."

"Still, she is only an AI." Vasil met my gaze, his blue eyes cold. "Don't mourn a machine."

"I . . . won't." I faked a smile. "So honored to meet you, sir."

I rushed away, my breath trembling.

Part of me wanted to flee the building. I considered it—was all this worth risking my mother's life? And Vasil wouldn't stop at her . . . if he saw me as a real threat, he could go after anyone close to me—my parents, aunts, cousins, friends, neighbors . . . everyone.

But if I gave up, I'd spend the rest of my life in fear of him. Not to mention, he could decide it'd be easier to preemptively eliminate me, without me ever having fought back. And my best friend would have died for nothing.

He doesn't know about the slate Sherlock pointed to, I reminded myself. If I could find the device containing proof of his illegal activities—supplying the galaxy with Fireblood—then I could get him locked up, where he'd never hurt anyone again. Then, and only then, would my family and I be safe.

With new resolve, I roamed the room and looked desperately at every slate I could spot. I balled my fists to hide my trembling fingers, then realized that my shaky hands might not be a bad thing. Not only would they help convince Vasil—who was undoubtedly keeping an eye on me—that I was too scared to try anything, but they'd provide the perfect excuse for how I "accidentally" switched devices with the person holding slate A596-2GV-58K.

After what seemed like forever, one slate turned green as my Second Sights highlighted it. I didn't recognize the man holding it.

The good thing about conferences was that one didn't need a special reason to introduce oneself; it was expected that you'd walk up to strangers. So I did just that. "Hello, there!" My voice sounded painfully chipper. "I'm Chevonne Watson, biomedical engineer at VH Labs."

The man glanced at me. "Kyung Aldenberg, Blue Diamond Tech. I'm also a biomedical engineer." His expression grew concerned. "Are you okay?"

I nodded, glad that my shakiness was visible. That would make the next part of my plan less suspicious. "Just . . . just nervous. First big conference. Um . . . Are you attending the presentation on synthetic white blood cells?"

Kyung glanced down at his slate, then swiped at the program list. "I didn't see that . . . I do see one on synthetic *red* blood cells, though."

"That's strange . . . can I see your slate?"

Kyung handed me the device.

I accepted it, then let both his and mine drop to the ground. I snatched them up before he could react, then handed him the one that had been mine. "I-I'm so sorry!"

"No worries." He gave me a sympathetic smile. "And calm down. There's no need to be nervous."

If only. I longed to get out of there immediately. But, not wanting to draw attention to myself, I pretended that I was just another conference attendee, there to learn and network like everyone else. I was sure everyone could hear my heart hammering and see the sweat coating my forehead. I kept expecting someone—perhaps Vasil himself, or one of his security officers—to confront me about switching slates.

When several minutes passed without anyone harassing me, my pulse began to calm. But I let my words keep stammering and my hands keep fumbling. The more afraid I appeared, the less reason Vasil would have to suspect me of anything.

At least, I hoped so.

Fortunately, the conference only lasted one day. By the time I returned to my apartment, my heart felt ready to burst from agitation. I took a moment to sweep my apartment for bugs, using one of the many miscellaneous devices Sherlock kept in her room. Finding nothing, I released a long breath.

I plopped down in an armchair and grabbed the slate. I'd

moved Sherlock into her bedroom, but couldn't bring myself to sit on the couch where she'd died.

Tears filled my eyes, and I furiously wiped them away. She would have wanted me to finish her work before grieving.

Not knowing what I was looking for, I read over Sherlock's note again, but couldn't find anything that might help. So I decided to look through all of slate A596-2GV-58K's contents until I found something promising. The app icons glowed against Neutron's standard green background, but the brightness was so low, it was hard to read them. Even when I turned up the screen's backlight, the letters remained a dull shade of gray.

Wait . . . the letters on the slate I received were white. I glanced at Sherlock's note, and an idea hit me.

I changed the slate's background color to the same shade of blue Sherlock's note had been typed on.

A window popped up, requesting a passcode.

That's it! Now, I just had to figure out what the passcode was.

It's simple, Chevonne, simple. Sherlock's voice kept echoing those words in my head.

Simple . . . I typed *elementary.*

A video filled the screen, showing Vasil Neuman in his office. He was yelling at an employee, but something about the footage seemed off. I couldn't pinpoint what, only that his movements seemed unnatural.

Then I saw the words printed across the bottom of the screen:

This is a computer-generated rendering of Vasil Neuman's movements, as recorded by the nanobots on his skin.

No wonder. I noticed the playback bar. Apparently, the video had been recording for more than four days. I scrolled back to the beginning.

"AI bitch!" Vasil's voice exploded from the slate's speakers. On the screen, he gripped Sherlock's throat. Though the image of their surroundings was incomplete, I could make out enough of the furniture to conclude that they were in Vasil's office.

Sherlock sneered. "I don't breathe, remember?"

Vasil threw her to the ground, and I flinched. The recording only showed Vasil's face and arms, but as I kept watching, parts of his body filled in until the image completed. The background details similarly solidified. *Sherlock must have transferred the nanobots to his skin during the struggle . . . And they were programmed to spread over his body until they covered every inch and recorded everything around him as well.*

I swallowed hard as Vasil overpowered Sherlock. She'd fought fiercely—flailing and clawing in feral movements—but ultimately, AI or not, she'd been a slight woman fighting a physically powerful man twice her size. Several guards rushed in and restrained her, but when one aimed a laser gun to her face, Vasil held up his hand.

"Stop! Not yet." He glowered at her. "The authorities won't care if an AI vanishes, but your little friend Chevonne will start sniffing around if she suspects foul play, won't she?"

Sherlock shrugged. "She once exposed the terrorist group that kidnapped me after I went missing for a few days. I imagine she'd work just as hard to find the truth if I were murdered."

"Then you'll just have to murder yourself . . . or I'll murder her."

I watched in horror as Vasil gave his goons orders, then monitored everything remotely via hologram. He laughed when they forced Sherlock to inject the corrosives into her chest—right here, just feet from where I sat—and I wished I could reach through the screen and claw his eyes out. The goons covered up any trace of their presence in our apartment—including altering the security footage in our hallways. Vasil, watching everything from a computer in his office, apparently lost interest after that, because he accepted a call . . . and defended the quality of Fireblood to an ornately dressed woman.

For hours, I sat there watching the past few days of Vasil Neuman's life—including several parts where he handled his illicit Fireblood business. Sherlock had him caught in the act—an illegal drug supplier on a galactic scale . . . the evidence I held was indisputable. And the nanobots were still recording. Once I gave this to the interstellar authorities, Vasil Neuman would be finished.

But he'd never face justice for what he'd done to my best

friend. Destroying an AI didn't count as murder in the eyes of the Interstellar Confederation. Beings like Sherlock existed in an odd legal gray area where they could own things but weren't considered human. The worst Vasil could be convicted of for her death was property destruction—not that Sherlock had ever been anyone's property. My blood boiled at the injustice, but I took some comfort in knowing that by the time Vasil finished serving his Fireblood-related sentences, there wouldn't be anything left of him.

Having seen enough, I closed the video window. *How did you figure it out?*

I noticed a small, book-shaped icon on the screen, which hadn't been there before. Sherlock must have programmed it to appear only after I'd discovered the recording. I tapped it, and a document popped up: Sherlock's case file.

It told me everything—how she'd posed as a Fireblood buyer to approach a dealer, then quietly taken over parts of his online identity without him noticing, then done the same with his supplier, and then that person's contact, and so on and so forth until she'd made her way far enough up the Fireblood chain to learn Vasil Neuman's identity. The process had taken Sherlock eighteen months, and while I wasn't surprised to learn how much she'd hidden from me—she'd always been secretive about her unsolved cases—it still puzzled me. She'd worked several other cases during that time, and I wasn't sure if she'd done so to keep anyone from noticing her secret investigation or if she was just that much of a workaholic. Or maybe she'd gotten a kick out of chasing such an important criminal while pretending everything was normal. Probably all of the above.

The date on the notes page where she first identified Vasil Neuman was only a few weeks before I'd been assigned to consult for Neutron. The language was sparse, but enough to tell me that she hadn't been sure of what role I'd play at the time—only that she'd learned of the opportunity by hacking Neutron's internal site and maneuvered me into position for a future strategy.

If she'd been standing before me, I would have smacked her for using me like that. But given the reason—and how much she herself had sacrificed—I couldn't be angry with her.

She'd spent the past year searching for ways to expose Vasil Neuman's illicit activities. Along the way, she'd invited his scrutiny, and he'd figured out what she was up to. What had followed was a battle of wits—she'd attempt to expose him, he'd thwart her, she'd try again, he'd threaten her—until she'd realized she could only beat him if she lured him into a false sense of security. So she'd set up slate A596-2GV-58K and slipped it in with the rest of the attendee slates, knowing I'd attend that conference shortly. And then she'd written her suicide note.

Once everything was in place, she'd broken into Vasil's office and pretended she was there to plant a bug. Vasil had caught her—as she'd planned—and the rest . . . the rest was in the recording.

Without her poking around, he thought he was safe. That's why she had to take herself out. She set everything up, and the thing that would trigger it all was me finding her dead.

Well, it had worked. Thanks to her, Fireblood would go out of production, and the man behind it would face justice. Millions—no, billions—of lives across the galaxy would be saved . . . no more overdoses, no more ruined homes, no more turf battles between dealers. If this was to be her last bow, then she sure knew how to make an exit. And she'd sacrificed herself for the greater good—something I'd never have expected of her.

I could imagine how Sherlock would react if I'd said that to her. *Greater good? Watson, please. I did it to win.*

A small laugh escaped my lips. *Tell me yourself someday.*

I knew would happen next. I'd back up the file and give the original to the police. Then I'd spend every spare moment I had working to repair my best friend.

I'd revived her before . . . and I could do it again.

THE HARDWICKE FILES: THE CASE OF MY OLD NEW LIFE AND THE ONE I NEVER KNEW
by Russ Colchamiro

HUNG OVER. AGAIN. CRAP.

But I needed a night out, a night where I didn't have to be Angela Hardwicke, private eye in Eternity. A night where I could forget about E-Town's shady underworld and missing jars of the Universe's DNA, and banished galaxy designers, so I could go see my favorite band, have a few drinks (a few too many, as it turns out), and then enjoy a nightcap.

"Unn," the nightcap says, groaning from my bed. 11 a.m. Sunlight seeps into the apartment. "Close the blinds. Too bright."

"Quit your whining. Just putting up the coffee."

Okay, yeah, so . . . he's a few years younger than me. Three, tops. Maybe five. On the outside . . . eight. Hard to tell sometimes, even for me. But what can I say? I've got a weakness for drummers. Strong, steady hands. They're all about rhythm. They know how to keep a beat.

"'m surprised you didn't make a play for Josh," nightcap says. "All the chicks love 'im."

I offer a raised eyebrow smile, point to my head. "Some fantasies I like to keep up here. More fun that way."

"Ha, I hear ya," he yawns. "You don't want to get mixed up with him anyhow. Josh is the best dude I know, sweet to the core. But his love life? Forget it. His crazy ex-girlfriend was stalking him at the show last night. Tiny little thing. But so needy. Always some drama. We're on the road a lot, so she hooks up with other dudes to make him jealous. Been on again off again for like two years. Besides . . . Josh's been pining over some lost love since forever. Don't know who it is. He never talks about it. But that's what half his songs are about."

This is why I hate the sleepover. The longer they stay, the more they talk. Better to peel off in the night. I need a distraction, so I click on the wall-mounted TV. Morning news. There's always something crappy going on, someone—in Eternity or off-realm—who needs a dame like me.

. . . And in today's top story, a massive fire erupted last night at the King Beat bar and music venue after a surprise performance from singer songwriter Josh Boden and the Electric Dream in advance of the upcoming Astropalooza festival. The recently renovated club was utterly destroyed. The ETPD have been on site controlling the scene as firefighters spent hours extinguishing the blaze. No word yet on the cause.

"Hey," I say. "You hearing this? You. Danny."

"Darren."

"Whatever. The King Beat. It burned down last night."

"Huh. How? When? We were just there."

That's a damn good question.

Nightcap sits up, groggy, naked beneath the covers. "Should we go down there?"

"We . . . ? No. Me? Yes."

My phone buzzes. Text from Beatrice. Owns the King Beat. We go back a ways.

Need you. Fire. They're asking questions. Wasn't me.

"Get dressed," I say, and toss him his wrinkled black t-shirt with a stencil on the front of a dragon in sunglasses riding a skateboard. "You need to leave."

"Mmm," demurs the Electric Dream's twenty-something drummer as he stretches his tatted arms, hair rumpled, abs tight. "I need a shower." He tosses the same smile that worked on me last night. "Wanna join?"

Always playing the beat.

"I really don't have time . . ."—nightcap drops the blanket so that he's now on full display—"but I'll make it work."

Firebugs are the worst kind of crazy. I worked a case this one time, on one of the red sun party planets. Two idiots were in competition to see who could set the biggest fire before sunrise, because a shape-shifter whose affections they were competing for loved the way the flames brought out a sparkle in her eyes as the planet rotated in and out of its orbit.

But I don't know this one is arson. Not yet. Tarrish is a good detective, been working the Southern Sphere of Eternity since before I was a P.I. He hates these cases more than I do. Crap. What a mess. Water dripping from fallen beams, the whole place charred to hell, the stage eaten by fire, barely enough timber left to even call this a structure. Whatever caused the blaze, it burned hot. Real hot. I don't like this.

My phone buzzes. Text from Tarrish. *Get your ass in here. DB.*

Tarrish calls me in to consult now and then. We have an understanding. It's complicated, but it works. Besides, E-Town's police department has been short-staffed the past few weeks as they prep for mayhem that'll be caused by Astropalooza. The party to celebrate the Universe. All of E-Town shuts down, barricades everywhere, police on overtime.

But right now, the street outside the King Beat is blocked off, uniforms and fire fighters exhausted from a long night. A few lookie loos, some straggling press.

"Hardy." Tall, black, lithe, with some white peppering his trimmed beard, Lionel Tarrish doesn't waste time. "Fire. Dead body. Gotta be arson. But who knows. Roz is checking for the source."

"You looking at Bea?" I ask. "Insurance scam?"

"She just dropped three hundred large to renovate, passed all inspections. Place always makes money. We're looking into it. But I don't see it. Still . . ."

"There's a body."

"There's that." Tarrish fidgets with his phone. "I gotta control the scene. Press'll have a field day once they find out. Especially with Astropalooza coming up. It's the last thing I need. Rock star murder or some shit. The singer? Josh Whatshisface?"

"Boden."

"Boden. Right. You know him?"

"Caught the show," I say.

"Oh, yeah?" Tarrish eyes me. There's trust between us, but he's murder police . . . and I'm not. "See anything suspicious?"

"No more than usual. Besides . . . my night off."

Tarrish smirks, nods. "Didn't know you took those."

I want to smirk back, but I hold it in. "Once in a while. You know."

"Yeah. I know. Best guess . . ." Tarrish checks his watch, but not for the time. It's that thing he does, to slow himself down. He knows better than anyone the shit storm coming his way if he doesn't put this one down quick . . . or pray that a higher profile case steals the thunder. "I can give you an hour in here, maybe two, then you gotta roll. I don't want the press catching your picture."

"That makes two of us," I say, then snap on a pair of comet-coated latex gloves so I can pick through the rubble. "Now piss off, will ya? I got work to do."

Inspector Erin Rosnerak, thirty-three, just a year older than me, is one of E-Town's better arson investigators. We worked a few cases together, but not lately. She's wearing black overalls, a yellow jacket, and black, waterproof boots. She's humming a song.

"They played that one last night?" I say, recognizing the tune. "The new one? Not even out yet."

Roz looks at me with that girly grin she never likes to show on the job. "You were there, too? I never miss a show," she says, probably with more enthusiasm, and with a higher pitch, than she meant. Sometimes your inner girl slips out, whether you want it to or not.

"Ride the light, find the stream, do so right, then I dream," I sing—badly, off key—pulling my shoulders, embarrassed at my ridiculousness.

"Rhyme the light, set down the stream, if you're right, we'll share the dream," she corrects, singing on key. Her voice isn't half bad.

I giggle, despite myself, resisting the urge to jump up and down and spastically squee like the horny, delusional, slightly drunk fangirl I was last night.

"I slept with the drummer," I confess, which to an outsider might seem in horribly bad taste given the dead body next to us, scorched beyond recognition. But you do this long enough—working E-Town and all the variations of the Universe created here—you learn to separate the joy from the horror. At the very least, you try. "My place. Last night. This morning, too."

"He work your bass drum?" Roz inquires with a semi-judgmental, semi-approving look.

We stand among the rotting, dripping wood, blistered flooring, hole-pocketed ceiling, and demolished stage when finally we cackle, releasing our nervous, dorky energy before regaining our composure.

"Okay," I say, putting my focus back where it belongs, "what do we know?"

Roz kneels down, and points to the DB, laid out on its back, maybe eight feet from where the stage had been before the blaze ate the place up. "The body is supine, not curled up in a protective posture. Which means," she says, before I cut in . . .

"Dead before the fire."

You don't have to be an expert on crime to start thinking—quick—that a murder took place. But that's the life of an investigator. You need to fight your ego, instincts, insecurities, and impatience when they demand—hell, crave—immediate conclusions.

Yeah, there's some truth to the notion that your gut reaction is the right one, your combined senses computing and processing a multitude of information faster than you can consciously sort through.

But here's another truth: your gut is a moron. There's what you know, and what you *think* you know. Even if your instincts are correct, you still need proof. The cops need enough to make an arrest, the prosecutors enough to convince a jury—or force a deal. And if the Minders of the Universe get involved? All bets are off.

Me? Depends on the case.

Roz and I run through details when Beatrice, standing by what's left of her office, gives me a nod, calling me over. Her filing cabinet is melted and folded over, holes in the walls, the framework nearly gone, the usual club smell of liquor, sweat, and sex burned off in the fire.

"How screwed am I?" she asks, holding it together. "The band? The body? The cops are up my ass."

I ask now so I don't have to ask later. "You clean on this?"

Bea looks at me like I just spit in her face, which I kinda did. It's the job. Can't be helped. She knows this, then eases her countenance.

"As clean as you can be in this racket. But no way insurance pays out unless I'm cleared. Best case scenario . . . I see my money in a year. I don't get that check . . . I'm out of business. I killed myself to be ready for Astropalooza. Rufus has his place across town—The Ruckster Club—going after that jazz and soul scene. But I had the rock and folk bands lined up to play left and right. Now look."

"Who did the renovations?"

"Frankie the Brush. The whole job. Interior construction, paint, electrical. All top notch. No way he's involved . . . is there?"

"Nah," I assure her.

Frankie the Brush is a general contractor with more contacts in E-Town than I have. He works both sides of the street, commercial and residential, but he also does galaxy renovation, painting, and polishing—so he's got every reason to know people, in all walks of life. But arson for profit? It's not a bad scam if you're that kinda scumbag—be a genial, unassuming sort who does quality work at a fair price, then use your clients' trust and personal info to rip them off later, one way or another—but that's not his bag. At least . . . not that I ever heard about. He's also one of my best sources. Helped me put down a half dozen cases easy, in E-Town and off-realm. And he bailed me out huge when that planet hopper got the drop on me, pulled me to a galaxy I didn't even know existed.

"It's something else," I tell Bea. "Let me keep looking. Me and Roz are working it out."

"Here," Roz says, kneeling over the body. "Look at the eye socket. Forensics will know more. They're on their way. But . . ." She plies a magnifying glass above the victim's face. "See this line here? My guess . . . broken cheekbone."

I do see it. "Okay. Walk me through."

Roz comes alive now. When she's on, she's the best. Her movements are fluid. "We know the show ended a little past midnight, club closed at twelve thirty, and reports of the fire came in after two a.m. Body was dead before the fire started, so that puts TOD between twelve thirty and two."

"I'm with you."

"We didn't even find the body until an hour ago, because it was buried beneath the rubble." The rafters above us are incinerated, open sky peaking in through the holes in the roof, water and blue foam gel still dripping. "I found this in the floorboards near the body."

Roz hands me a set of tweezers, charred piece of paper in the grip. "It's the corner of a photograph. Can't see much, just the shoulders up, but there's a girl—maybe twenty five—and some very big dude next to her."

I examine the edges, look for clues in her face. Girl doesn't look happy to be in the photo, like she's doing it out of obligation, or fear. Or maybe she just had to pee.

"I did a DNA zip test. Used to take three weeks, now it's an hour. Would be even quicker, but Astropalooza is bringing out the crazies, clogging the system. 'Lotta murders lately." She refers to her tablet. "Here it is. Lisa Henn. Twenty-four. Five-foot two, hundred sixteen pounds, brunette, green eyes. Most recent listed address two six two one Quinlan Drive."

"That gives us a name. But . . ." Roz has that look. There's more.

"Also listed at that address is Gregor Nokasi. Ex con. Did separate stints for assault and battery, grand theft auto, and drug possession. Six-four, two hundred sixty pounds. I sent uniforms to check it out."

"Description matches the photo," I say. "And you're thinking . . . what? Nokasi kills his girlfriend? Who knows why? But kills her at the club, then torches the place?"

"I had Dmitri pull video footage from a bank machine across the street. Caught Lisa Henn and Nokasi outside the club at ten forty five, arguing. Looks pretty clear she wants to get away. He's grabbing at her. But there's a lot of people around so . . ."

"He waits until after the show," I conclude, "then . . . what? He's already in the club? He's waiting outside?"

"Can't tell. There's nothing on video during the show. I also found this phone. It's charred. No prints I could use. Don't know if it's his, hers, or someone else's. I'll have the lab techs see if they can get anything off it."

Hmm . . . Something's off. And then I remember . . .

"Drummer boy told me Josh's been mixed up with some needy chick, was at the show last night. I hate to even think it, but . . . maybe Josh's on again/off again is this same girl? Said she used to sleep around to tweak Josh when he was on the road. But maybe Nokasi was the jealous one?"

"Did you see him here last night?" Roz asks. "I didn't, but then, I wasn't looking for him."

I shake my head. "Same here. Nothing. What about after?"

Roz smiles, like she's got something. "A different camera from two blocks away has Nokasi running to his car, at two twelve, the fire's already started. He's fleeing the scene."

I scan the club, what's still here, anyway, looking for another way in . . . or out. "We have means and opportunity. And possibly a motive. But how'd he start the fire?"

Roz stands over the body, over Lisa Henn, over maybe Josh's sorta girlfriend, snaps off her gloves, sighs. "That's what's been messing with me. It started here, near her feet. Front of the stage was right there," she says, pointing nearby. "I've run every test I can think of. And the heat was incredible. Burned much hotter than normal. You can tell by the billowy burns on those rafters. It was a blast, like a fireball."

I've seen my share of fires, but nothing like this. "What do you think it was?"

"That's just it," Roz says, "I have no idea."

My phone buzzes. A text. Tarrish. Press knows about the body. They want answers. We need to wrap up. Soon.

The damage is intense. There's a smell I didn't notice before. Wet, moldy, which I get. But there's something else to it. Something familiar, yet . . . not. The problem with being hung over. Numbs the senses, obfuscates the truth. And my fangirl crush on Josh isn't helping. Makes it hard to see what's probably right there. I need to focus.

Tarrish is outside the club, with a yellow tape barrier twenty feet from where the front door was. But there's an opening in the side wall, covered in plastic, a makeshift door so the cops can control which techs, unis, firemen, and inspectors come in and out. My way out. Avoid prying eyes.

"I'm gonna ask around," I tell Roz. "I need more to go on."

"I'm almost done here." She squints, offering a chuckle. "I can't lie. When Josh was up there singing last night, with those puppy dog eyes, like he was only singing to me, I had fantasies of being here, after hours. Only . . ."

"With you wrapped in his arms?"

Roz nods, chuckles harder.

"One non-lie to another?" I offer. "I had the same fantasy. With Josh, I mean. Not you. You *are* a smokin hot babe, but . . ."

"Same here. So you settled for the drummer?"

I shrug. "Did you notice? His t-shirt glowed under the black light on stage. I was drunk, riled up. Seemed like a good idea at the—"

Roz jumps in, her eyes wide. "What did you say?! Say that again."

"What? That it was a good idea—"

"No! Before that! The light."

"Oh. His t-shirt glowed under the black light."

"Oh shit," Roz says, then hustles over to her duffle bag, shuffles through supplies and instruments, then removes a black wand, about a foot long. "Hold on. I need to see this." She elbows me away from the body, kneels down—removes the celestial light bulb and replaces it with an old-style black light. Waves it over the floor. "Come on come on come on," she repeats. "Where are you? Where? Are . . . there. Look."

I kneel down. Residue, glowing yellow under the light. Starting next to the body and leading right to where the stage had been. It's in a trail, along the charred floor and in the seams, and opens into a splatter. Like someone flicked a brush.

A paint brush.

Frankie. Damn.

"I know what this is," Roz says. "I know how it started."

I'm torn between wanting to warn Frankie, and kicking him in the crotch.

"Nothing came up on my standard tests," Roz says. "Negative for everything. Gasoline, kerosene, alcohol, acetone, nebula paste, comet shavings, no . . ."

"Paint?" I ask, motionless, although I'm cringing inside.

"No. No paint, no paint thinners. Nothing like that."

Whew. Frankie. You had me worried. "So what is it?"

"A cocktail."

"What? Like a Scotch and soda?"

"No. Not that. Drugs. Specifically . . . *dRops.*"

My heart pounds. My face goes flush. I'm breaking out in sweat. Face, armpits, crotch. My hands tremble. I nearly black out.

The newest and most addictive drug on the market, *dRops* are spreading across Eternity's underbelly. Taken on the tongue, from an eyedropper, they come from Cosmic Building Material— the Universe's liquid DNA, the building blocks of all Creation— diluted to the most infinitesimal concentration possible without overtaking the user. So, yeah. I know about *dRops.*

"Th-they're," I stutter, my throat harsh and dry, "*dRops* are flammable?"

"No," Roz says. "Not at all."

"Then I don't . . ." I fumble, barely able to compose myself.

"On their own, *dRops* are harmless. Well . . . you know what I mean. But if they're mixed with *bong water* . . . that's another story."

Panic shoots through my head and chest. I try to control my breathing. "Nobody's figured this out yet? There are plenty of *dRop*heads out there."

"Because," Roz says, "the cocktail has to have direct contact with electricity. And as stupid as pot and *dRop*heads are, even they're not dumb enough to pour water—even bong water—on a live outlet. Besides Cosmic Building Material itself, bong water is the most mysterious substance we know about it. Nobody knows why we get that smell, or what happens on a molecular level. But mixed with *dRops*, you've got the base for a giant flame."

I put my fingers to my eyes, squeeze. Hard. I've been too close to *dRops.* Way too close. "How do you even know this? I never heard of this."

"I was at an ETAI conference last month in Loramey." She shrugs knowingly. "E-Town Arson Investigators. One of the guys ran across a case maybe . . . six months ago. Remember that huge fire up in North Sidwell? Torched an entire fleet of blimps that were commissioned for Astropalooza?"

"Yeah," I say. That *was* a big one. "I thought that was an electrical fire."

"No," Roz says. "It wasn't"

"Then how come . . . ?"

"The last thing we need is for every *dRop*head in E-Town thinking it would be cool to set Eternity ablaze. Plus, the nature of Cosmic Building Material? It eradicates its own trail when set on fire. Don't know why, but it doesn't show up under the celestial light. That's why I couldn't find a source. It literally eats itself."

My phone buzzes. Two more texts. Tarrish says to wrap it up.

"I still don't get what happened here," I say, losing control of how I see the room. Josh? The *dRops*? I'm in a bad way. "Assuming it was Nokasi in some sort of bizarre love triangle, he takes out Lisa Henn, then uses the *dRops* and bong water cocktail to torch the place? There's gotta be a better way."

Roz looks at me with a satisfied smile. "I don't think he planned the fire at all."

Roz explains it like this: Before the show, Nokasi was probably smoking weed at home, accidentally spills bong water on his eye dropper, takes the *dRops* with him. In a jealous stupor, follows Lisa Henn to the show. They're in the club, after hours. Don't know how he got in, but he finds a way. Agitated and zonked on the drug cocktail, Nokasi slaps her around, you can't leave me, I can't live without you, you're mine and all that kinda bullshit, then kills her, intentional or not. Panics.

Reaches into his pocket to do more *dRops*, puts him over the edge. Total drug delirium. But realizing what he's done—and how much trouble he's in—takes the eyedropper and lashes out, smashing it on the floor, against the stage. Blueprints show there was an electrical outlet there, on the step up, with a junction box beneath the stage to handle the various amps and lights. The *dRops*/bong cocktail eats through the wires, starts the blaze,

Nokasi runs like hell.

It makes sense, the way she's laying it out. But I'm still jittery, and I don't know why. . . .

Stop, Hardy. Stop. You know what it is. It's the junction box. The wires. Frankie. You know what you have to do. You just don't want to do it. That's why it's hard to be a private eye and have friends. You never know when you might have to put the screws to them.

And then Tarrish storms in, chest all puffed out. Smiling. "Roz. Hardy. Uniforms confirmed. Gregor Nokasi. He did it. He's our guy."

"Are you sure?" I say as Roz unleashes a self-satisfied smile of her own for being good at her job. "Did you make an arrest?"

Tarrish chuckles. He's much taller than the both of us. "Won't be necessary."

"Why?" I ask, almost afraid to know the answer.

"Because," Tarrish says, then checks his phone, "Gregor Nokasi is dead."

Uniforms found the body, called in detectives. Nokasi was in his living room chair, drug paraphernalia all around. Bongs, *dRops*, tweaks, poppers, pills. Shotgun on the floor, by the chair, Nokasi's fingerprints. Stuck the gun under his chin, blew his brains out.

They found charring on the back of his clothes, confirming he was singed as he ran from the blaze. Chemical composition matches exactly from the club fire.

"Great work," Tarrish says. "Witnesses confirm Lisa Henn was here during the show, another saw Nokasi running from the fire. We've got uniforms reaching out to Boden's people, tell him what happened, tie up some loose ends."

"His life'll be a scandal," I say.

Tarrish waves me off. "Not my problem."

"Sex, drugs, and rock n' roll?"

He nods. "Something like that."

"He'll be okay," says Roz, still with more faith in the system than I have. "With Astropalooza coming up, this'll get lost in the shuffle."

And then panic shoots through me again, because I realize

what I never bothered to confirm, and was here the whole time. Right in front of me. But I was distracted by my own nonsense. My weaknesses. I know what's coming. Oh no no no no no.

"Besides," Roz continues, blinded by sincerity, yet, like me, about to face her worst fangirl fears, as reality seeps into her consciousness, "his real fans'll understand what—"

"Detective!" a junior arson investigator calls from the basement like an asteroid-tipped arrow shot through our chests. "Down here."

Me, Roz, and Tarrish navigate the fallen debris strewn down the stairwell. It took them all night to clear the entrance just to reach the stairs. But now that we're down here, the damage isn't nearly as bad as the rest of the club, although it did take a beating.

In addition to the freezers, refrigerators, and other storage, the basement includes changing rooms for the bands, docks to the loading bays, and an exit into the alley.

We climb over a fallen crossbeam, sidestep a charred door hanging from its final hinge, and enter the back room. There are several fallen beams, blocking the back wall.

"Here," the junior fire inspector says. "You don't have to look for Josh Boden."

There's a gaping hole in my heart. I look at Roz. I can see it in her, too.

"What?" Tarrish says. "What have you—?"

"It's him," the junior says, pointing to Josh, mangled beneath the fallen timber, his guitar case, smashed, lying next to him. His still-boyish face and those curly locks of brown hair reduced to pulp. He suffered massive burns. "Not sure why, but the door leading outside was jammed. No way to reach the alley. He never made it out."

As predicted, media coverage blew up over the case. Stories ran day and night about Josh Boden, the sensitive singer/songwriter with a legion of adoring fans, whose soulful light burned out far too soon, and under tragic circumstances.

He was never a true superstar, as these things go, but his music sold, and he regularly attracted eight to ten thousand fans per show, touring all across Eternity. But the tunes themselves, man . . . they were good. I've heard all kinds of soliloquies about the magic of music. But all I know is that when Josh Boden opened his mouth to let those words come out about love and romance and the gentle heartbreak and joy of what was, what might have been, and what could still be—backed with his rhythm guitar, a piano, bass, drums, and a groovy saxophone—he took me someplace even beyond the realms scouring the Universe.

And now that he's dead—in a murder/suicide love triangle— his seven albums are selling better than ever, while his newest— *The Electric Dream Done Good*—dedicated to his band—shot to the top of the charts. His first number one. For whatever that's worth.

Once the chaos settled down, Tarrish was able to put the case to bed. But Nokasi was in the books for two murders and his own suicide, with techs confirming heat from the blast smelted the door to the back alley, which is how Josh got locked in. It cleared Beatrice of any suspicion. Yet I couldn't let it go.

Frankie the Brush.

The wires they talked about. The junction box. I don't know what, exactly, but he's leaving something out, a piece of the puzzle I don't understand.

So I show up now, at a job site, Frankie installing a home theater for a custom asteroid and comet supplier he does work for up in Pinewood.

"Frankie," I say. He's jotting down notes in his pad, his laser-guided tape measure beaming across what is now a nebula-based relaxation room with maroon-shaded gases and moon-scented incense. It's a big room, would actually make a cool theater.

"Hey," Frankie says. "What's an occasionally semi-nice girl like you doing in a place like this?"

It's misting out, so I'm still wearing my raincoat, fedora tipped down. I raise my head, droplets run off the brim. "The Boden case," I say, getting right to it. "Me and you. We need to have words."

Took me a few days to track down the last of it. But that's the thing about being a private eye. Sometimes the case is over before it ever really begins. Other times? Even when you think it's over, you learn that it hasn't even started.

I was only here once before, about a year ago, when me and Roz dug through a burned-out inter-dimensional travel agency just a few blocks away along Moonbeam Circle. Turns out the owner's younger brother had torched the place to finance a boutique hotel he was gearing to the upper crust galaxy design crowd—and settle an old grudge from back when they were kids. Family. Go figure.

But it's a clear night tonight, the first all week. Eight full moons. I take the three steps, ring the bell, wait a minute. The brownstones blend in along the tree-lined street.

"Oh. Hey," Roz says in her sweats and Josh Boden t-shirt, surprised to see me. Standing at the door, with the porch light on, I can see her eyes are wet and red. She's been crying, drinking wine. A lot. Josh's last album is humming in the background. "Uh . . . what's up?"

"Was in the neighborhood," I say. "Figured I'd see how you're doing, you know, fangirl-wise. I hear him now." His music taps into something far beyond this realm, into a part of me that feels . . . I don't know . . . a part of everything. I pout, smile wistfully. I've lost people close to me, and I've also felt the sting, when I've lost people I barely knew, but for some reason got under my skin anyway. Josh—and maybe it's his music more than him—is in a different category for me. I don't have a name for it. Don't want to give it one, either. "I could use one of whatever you're having. Maybe two."

"Um," she says, hesitating, "yeah, sure. Come on in."

The place is a mess. It's not like Roz to be this way. She likes things neat. Tidy. Everything in order.

She hands me a glass of white. I prefer Scotch, or a good lager. This'll do. I take a healthy swig.

"I needed that," I say, and raise my glass. "To Josh."

She barely ekes out a smile. We klink. "Yeah," she says.

The album drifts into the fourth song, the title track—"My Old New Life and the One I Never Knew"—Josh strumming his guitar, followed by the piano, and a distant saxophone.

"I stopped by the squad," I say. "They said you called in sick again. Third day in a row. You okay?"

Roz squirrels into the corner of the couch, regressing to her younger self. There's a plate of barely touched take-out on the coffee table, dirty clothes lying on the floor. "I just needed a few days. Sometimes it's . . ." A tear rolls down her cheek. I hand her a tissue. She takes it, wipes her face. "Thanks."

"I hear ya," I say. "Actually took a few days myself."

I pick up a glint of suspicion in her eyes, yet also a hopefulness that maybe I feel what she feels, although I doubt it's exactly the same.

"Funny thing," I say, and slug down the rest of my wine. "I went up to Loramey. You put the idea in my head. You had that arson investigator's conference. Made me realize I hadn't been there in years. It's a fun town. Great seafood."

Roz's clutching her glass just a bit tighter now, lamplight catching the side of her face. Her shadow tossed on the wall. Elongated. Distorted.

"I went to the Dartlawn, to get a drink. I love a good hotel bar. Especially the ones that rotate close to meteor showers. It's a break from the dive bars I usually hit. While I was there, I asked the concierge for a flyer from the conference you were at. They had a few left over in the office. Funny coincidence. I was about to chuck it out, when I saw on the 'things to do in Loramey' page that Josh actually had a show the same weekend."

I pause, give Roz a chance to speak. She doesn't. "I checked the venue. Security footage has you there. Strange you didn't mention it."

"I told you," she says, barely above a whisper. "I see lots of shows."

"True, but what you *didn't* say that is that you'd just seen him. But we'll get back to that." I pour another glass, take a drink. "I also went down the roster of attendees. After a dozen calls I took a side trip up to Archknowl on the far side of the Baldamere Mountains. Had a burrito with a guy named Gary Michelsohn. Remember him? He's the colleague who told you about the *dRops*/bong water combo. Thing he also told me about them— same thing he says he told you—is that the only way for them to spark electricity and ignite a fire is if the wires themselves are *already* exposed, either frayed or stripped. But the cocktail can't eat through the outer wire casing. It's why fires hardly ever start this way."

Roz is staring at me, blinking. "My gut told me I was missing something, so I circled back with Frankie the Brush. He confirmed. He used all new equipment, wires fully concealed, up to code."

"He's sketchy," Roz says dismissively. "How do you know he isn't lying?"

"You know . . . I had my doubts. I shouldn't have, but I did. The whole Josh thing had me off my game. But Frankie had photos of the electrical work that were date and time stamped. Needed them for the insurance company, and to guard against any possible lawsuits. Does it for all of his jobs. Standard procedure. He got sued by Emma a while back. The stars in a galaxy she designed only twinkled in alternating patterns. He did the installation right, but she blamed him anyway. Never again."

I can see Roz starting to struggle, her breathing labored, her eyes growing deeper.

"But what finally pulled it together for me? I went to Josh's place. Tarrish let me in. Usual stuff, you know, personal effects. In the corner, by his guitars, was a stack of hand-written lyrics for some new songs, including "Rhyme the Light." The first time he played that song for anyone outside of the band was the night we were there. And then I remembered . . . the day we investigated . . . I sang them out loud, but got the words wrong, because, hey . . . I just heard them the night before. And it was a long night. But you"—I say, and take another sip of wine, dragging it out, leading her to where I want to go—"you corrected me. You had them down pat. You knew them perfectly."

I stand up. Girl time is over. "The only way you could've done that . . . is if you already knew them. Darren, the drummer, said Josh'd been pining over a lost love." I shake my head, feeling so utterly stupid I hadn't seen it before. "*You're* that lost love. Nokasi didn't kill Lisa Henn." Then I let go of two words I most definitely do no want say, and will probably haunt me until my very last breath. "You did."

There's a minute when I'm not sure what Roz is going to do.

You push someone to the edge, corner them, their flight-or-fight response kicks in. Then she puts her wine glass down on top of a magazine. When she does, it shifts. Beneath it, I can see the grip of her sidearm. It's a P853, with enough punch to rip a tiny hole through space/time if you know how to rig it up just right. So I pivot just enough that my coat opens, revealing my own weapon, holstered near my rib. I've also got an expandable, particle-enhanced taser rod in my left zip-boot, butterfly switch-blade in the right.

No longer subverting to her inner teen, Roz leans forward, her grown self taking over. Not a girl, but a woman. She cries—the tears flow. With the base of her hands she wipes them away.

"Josh was my boyfriend," she says, smiling, painfully. Her eyes drift to the side, lost in an old memory. "We were kids, Angela. Young love. But it was sweet and it was real in a way you hardly ever get. He wanted to get married, maybe have a kid or two. He wanted a *life* with me. As much as I wanted it with him. He would've been happy playing coffee shops forever. But the offers rolled in. To make an album, to go on tour. He was on his way up. There was no denying that. So what was I supposed to do? Tell him to forget it? To give it up? I would've been a pariah, and lived my whole life wracked with guilt over what he could've been, the girl who killed a star. What choice did I have? We were only twenty! But he didn't care. He wanted to be with me anyway." She shakes her head. "But I couldn't handle it. So I broke up with him. I made him go. I broke his heart, and with it . . . broke mine."

She cries more, the tears long and heavy, releasing the weight of it all.

"So he goes on tour, becomes Josh Boden. And I got on with things, too. I torched one part of my life, so investigating fires made sense to me somehow. But then about six months ago he reaches out after all these years. Says he's never stopped thinking about me, loves me more than ever. He's ready to give up the road. He doesn't care what anyone thinks. He just needs to wrap up the tour, make sure the band gets paid in full. So, yeah. I saw him in Loramey. And in Perona the month before that and Souverne the month before that. We didn't tell anyone."

"What about Lisa Henn? How does she figure in?"

"He'd been seeing other women before we reconnected. I knew that. But it was over between them. He tried to break it off, many times, but she couldn't let go. She was weak and insecure and in love with a star. You know what that can do to a young woman. Especially with Josh."

I nod, knowing exactly what it can do to a woman who's not careful. Not just to the young ones, either.

"And that beast Nokasi she was with . . ."

"Roz," I say. "Erin. Please. What really happened?"

She's pacing now, past her half-concealed weapon. I'm scanning the apartment, looking for escape routes or items laying around she can use to attack.

"Josh planned to tell Lisa it was over for good. That he was leaving the road to be with me. We were in the club, after the show. She ran up on stage, making a scene, begging. Pleading. Josh was patient, in that gentle way of his, tried calming her down, even as she was slapping him and screaming. He took her arm, just to settle her down. But she pulled away, and tripped over a mic stand. She fell off the stage. Hit her face on the floor, broke her neck. She died instantly."

I hate every bit of this. "So you burned the place down. Why? To cover it up?"

"When Lisa pulled away, Josh accidentally scratched her arm. Defensive wounds. It would have ruined him, even if it proved to be an accident. Our whole lives would have been over, with me as the woman who ended his career, and caused the death of his cute little girlfriend." She wipes her face again. "Who was also pregnant."

My heart is racing, but I keep my eyes focused on hers, quickly checking to see if she's going to try and take me out, take herself out, or both.

"What about the *dRops*? Nokasi?"

"They weren't his. They were hers. When Lisa went down, I checked her pockets, for whatever I could find. She had her phone, and the drugs."

"You had to think to fast," I say, trying to empathize, give her a way out. "You told Josh to run out the back, you'll take care of it." She nods. "You see the *dRops*, smell the bong water on them—because you can't mistake that smell for anything else— remember the story from the conference. You pry open the outlet, strip the wires . . . then set the fire, burning her up in the process. And you always smell like fire, so nobody would pay attention."

Roz's eyelids fall, hold there, then open up again.

"Only . . . you didn't realize Josh was still in there. The damage pinned him down."

Her lip quivers. "I thought he was gone," she says, tears rolling down her face. "Lisa had been yelling at him about Nokasi, how he was an animal, that she was pregnant with his kid, like that was supposed to make Josh jealous. She said Nokasi beat her, gave her that black eye. And that he was going to do it again. He might've, too. He was outside the club, waiting for her."

"But when it went up in flames," I surmise, "he runs like hell."

"I followed him home, and waited. I saw him through the window. He got stoned, sat in his chair, and passed out."

"And then you broke in, and killed him. Made it look like a suicide. If anyone knew how to stage a scene, it would be you. But how'd you know there'd be a gun?"

"I didn't. I didn't know what I was going to do. I made it up as I went along. I only had a few hours. Like you said . . . I had to think fast." Her face explodes into a mulch of red and purple. "I killed him, Angela. I killed my beautiful Josh."

I sigh, to keep my composure. I don't know what to say. And then Roz reaches for her weapon. I do the same. It takes less than two seconds to fire a single round from a holstered position. I hope that's fast enough. Only . . . she turns her gun, grip first, hands it to me. She falls back on the couch.

Her face messy with tears, she's just there. Nothing left. "Tarrish on the way?" she asks.

I don't say a word. I just sit next to her, holding her hand, listening to Josh's voice through the speakers, and the beating of my own heart, waiting for the red lights to arrive.

AS TIME GOES BY
by Patrick Thomas

IT WASN'T EVERY DAY THAT A super villain was released from the Gulag Penitentiary. Marcus McGowan had served his time, the irony of which was not lost on the man called the Tempus Fugitive.

Marcus wasn't a killer, but he had powers. He'd robbed a few banks and jewelry exchanges to finance machines that helped him speed or slow the flow of time. He had the ill fortune of being captured by the Luminary.

Taking a plea deal and returning the money he stole, along with good behavior, got his sentence reduced to three years. But to him, it had been about ten days. He requested solitary confinement and had slowed his time-flow whenever possible, so serving his sentence had been nothing more than a long rest.

None the worse for wear upon release, Marcus walked out into the sunshine and enjoyed his first breath as a free man. By the time he took his second breath, he had company.

Marcus' eyes hurt just from looking at the glowing man. He reached into his jacket pocket and put on a pair of sunglasses, which helped only slightly.

"Hello, Luminary. Come to threaten me? Make sure I don't return to a life of crime?"

In the radiance, the man smiled.

"No lecture. What you do with your life is your decision. I am here to wish you good luck and to point out some things that perhaps you hadn't considered," the world's most powerful hero said.

"How I'll never get away with it, so I shouldn't even bother? That kind of thing?"

The glowing man chuckled. "You know what I've found is the main problem with the Daring who get categorized as villains?

It's not a lack of creativity. Most of you have that. It's a lack of vision. Considering what you can do, there is no reason for you to rob a bank."

"Sure, like money will just fall from the sky."

"Maybe not, but with your abilities, you could have made it rain." The Luminary handed Marcus a lump of coal.

The Tempus Fugitive looked at his hand, then back at the glowing man. "You working for Santa now, trying to tell me I made the naughty list?"

"Your abilities as a mechanical engineer are impressive. It wouldn't be difficult for you to rig a device that would duplicate the heat and pressure miles beneath the Earth's crust."

"Sure, but what'll crushing coal get me?"

"What happens to coal under pressure for a billion years?"

Marcus McGowan's eyebrows raised. His pupils got wide. "Diamonds." He paused a moment to let that sink in. "I could slow the time-flow on the heat and pressure source as I rapid-aged the coal. A billion years would probably take only three years in real time, and if I used a big enough hunk of coal, it would create a diamond worth hundreds of millions. I'd never have to work again. I'd have enough money for three lifetimes. I'm an idiot. I didn't have to become a criminal. I'd still have Sherri."

"You haven't lost your wife," said a black woman with blonde hair standing behind him. "At least . . . not yet."

"Sherri?" Marcus said, shocked that the love of his life—the woman he betrayed with his foolish, near-sighted choices after only two years of marriage—had waited for him despite his life of crime. "I thought you hated me." The Gulag, being an ultramax prison, didn't allow for contact with inmates, including electronic signals or paper because of what the super powered criminals, known in the media as Daring Don'ts, had accomplished with similar opportunities in the past.

"I don't hate you," Sherri said. "But I'm pissed. You didn't need to rob a bank. I was making enough to support us."

"But it wasn't fair. You were working two jobs to support me building my machines."

"Thanks to your time-bending ways, I always got enough

sleep and time to spend time with you. We managed."

"I wanted us to do better than manage. I was an idiot. I'm so sorry, Sherri." Marcus looked at the coal in his hand. "I'll never have to steal again."

"I'm happy to hear that," said the Luminary, who glowed almost a pure white. His light hit the couple, making them feel safe and wonderful. "Perhaps you'll even consider some ways of helping humanity. I'll leave you and your wife to get reacquainted."

The Luminary rose up into the sky and flew away.

"Wow," Sherri said. "He's even more amazing than they say. If you had to get caught by one of the Daring Dos, he's the best one."

"I guess, but it was weird. He came right through my tempus fields like time didn't affect him at all."

The pair walked to the jalopy Sherri had driven. Marcus had always imagined buying her a Benz or Cadillac, but they'd had that car since they first got married.

"I got a motel room nearby," Sherri said. "I figured that after three years in solitary you might be in need of something besides a hot meal." She was wearing a long coat buttoned all the way to the neck, but unbuttoned the top button and flashed him just enough of her bare skin beneath to let him know that the time for talk was over.

Just having powers wasn't the same as having a magic wand. Even magic wands weren't everything they were cracked up to be. It wasn't as simple as Marcus putting out a shingle and offering his time-warping services. As a convicted Daring Don't, his motives were instantly suspect.

Marcus had spent months unsuccessfully making his pitch to investors to fund what he knew was a game-changing device. Sherri was still having to work both her jobs—as a waitress and a cashier—and the largest diamond the human race would likely ever see was still over three years from completion.

Marcus drove slowly, not wanting to break the news to Sherri about his latest failure to woo legitimate investors. He stopped off in a farm town to have a meal. A weather woman on the TV was talking about an early frost. A man at the counter in overalls slammed his fist down on the counter.

"Dammit, that frost will wipe out my grapes."

"It's going to wipe out all of our grapes," said the man next to him.

"I don't see what you two are complaining about," said a third man. "This is only my second year. My grapes get wiped out and my winery is going under."

"Too bad, Chad. We warned you about going up against us. This will hurt us, but there's always next year."

Marcus walked over to the counter. "What if I could offer you gentlemen a way to ensure that your crops survived the night?"

"Night?" said the man who'd slammed his fist into the counter. "They're saying it will be the next two or *three* nights. One night won't be enough."

"There ain't no way to save the grapes, so peddle your snake oil somewhere else," the second man said.

"I was just trying to offer some help," Marcus said, shrugging his shoulders and going back to his table.

The third man sat down across from Marcus.

"I'm Jed. They're jerks, but I'm listening. What can you do?"

"I'm a reformed Don't. I have powers and technology which will allow me to pause the grapes in time—maintaining their integrity—until the frost is gone. I can guarantee your crops will survive."

"Sounds risky to me to get into business with a Don't. How do I know this ain't just one big con?"

"Understandable that you might feel that way," Marcus said. "How's this for a deal—we make out a contract and state that if I can't make the grapes last the next three days, you don't have to pay me a dime."

"How much will that cost me if it works?"

Marcus gave a number.

Jed let out a long, slow whistle. "I don't have anywhere near that amount of money. Almost everything I have is invested in my winery."

Marcus stroked his chin. "I'm willing to wait for the money. How about fifty percent of the profits and half the business to save your crop?"

"After pouring my blood, sweat, and tears—not to mention my life savings—half seems a little steep. I'd almost rather lose it all. How about a ten percent stake in the business, but that means that you do the same thing to protect crops from any frost in the future and I give you twenty-five percent of the net profits from anything made from the crops you save this year."

"Provided you let me record what I'm doing to show other potential customers and you give me a testimonial, you got yourself a deal."

The pair shook hands and wrote up a contract on the back of a placemat.

Jed's grapes were the only ones in the area to survive the frost. Jed's testimonial did the trick, luring in other customers. And not just farmers. Food warehouse distributors called him in the middle of a blackout when all their freezers went down. He got paid plus a bonus of enough restaurant quality food that the couple didn't need groceries for three weeks.

After a few months of doing these nickel and dime jobs, and living off Sherri's wages, he'd saved enough to build ten prototype stasis belts and demonstrated them to customers. When put on an injured person, it paused their personal time flow, allowing them to be brought to an emergency room with less than a second in real-health time passing. The belt could be removed in an operating room.

The military placed a large enough order that he was able to start his own company, Carpe Tempus.

Orders followed from EMT's, high-risk job sites, and even schools.

Everything was coming together. The former bank robber was so happy that his wife had stuck by him—tolerating his former criminal transgressions—that he wanted to do something extraordinary for their fifth anniversary.

Marcus picked up his wife in their twelve-year-old jalopy.

"Where are we going?"

Marcus smiled. "That'd ruin the surprise. With your permission, I'd like to pause your time-flow until I pull in. I want to see the look on your face."

"I told you never again after you froze me to sneak out to rob the Rune Savings and Loan," Sherri said.

"And I haven't, but this is different. I'm asking your permission."

Sherri smiled. "Fine, but if I'm not blown away, you're sleeping on the couch tonight."

"No worries." Marcus paused her time-flow until they arrived at the valet parking and brought Sherri out so she had a view of a holographic sign. He wasn't disappointed as his wife's face lit up.

"Oh, my God. This is Morveux! I thought you had to book reservations three months in advance?"

"Five, actually, but I booked six months ago."

"But you weren't making any money back then."

"But I had you telling me to believe in myself." He smiled at his wife in a way he never had before. "So, I did."

"Can we afford it?"

"Barely. But next month the payments for the stasis belts orders come in. Soon as I cash those checks, you can quit your job."

"I'm down to one. One I can handle. Two? That was tough."

"If you want to keep working, that's great. Whatever you want to do. Maybe you can help me at Carpe Tempus. *If* you don't mind sleeping with the boss."

Sherri gave her husband a soft, passionate kiss. "I'm open to negotiation. Who is he? Hope he's hot."

Marcus laughed then jumped out of the car, ran around to open his wife's door. He offered his hand as she stepped out then tossed the keys to the valet as a man in a tuxedo snuck around the side of the building holding an old-fashioned zippo cigarette lighter, making a face at the rusty, old car.

"Take good care of it," Marcus said to the valet. "Last time I was here, I drove up in a Ferrari. This is what they stuck me with on my way out."

The valet laughed. "No worries, sir. I'll bring it back in the same condition. Maybe better, if you'd like me to drive it through a couple of puddles. Get the dirt off."

"That'd be great."

The couple was shown to a table overlooking the dance floor. Marcus pulled out Sherri's chair, then sat himself. With a flick of his wrist, their waiter deposited napkins in their laps, then handed them menus. "Our special tonight is Kraken Florentine, with a side of quail jellied eggs. Would you like anything to drink?"

"Yes." Marcus ordered a bottle of champagne that he had called ahead to make sure was in his budget.

"Very good choice, sir." The waiter walked away.

"How does it feel to have someone else wait on you for a change?" Marcus said.

"Wonderful. I've always dreamed of coming to a fancy place like this. I can't wait for the band to start. I want to dance."

"So? Did I do okay for our anniversary?"

"You did more than okay. You're going to be lucky if I don't drag you off to one of the restrooms before we leave."

Marcus grinned and reached over and squeezed his wife's hand, but a man in a tuxedo stepped between them, frowning.

"I'll have you know, procreational activities in our lavatories is prohibited." It was the man they'd seen sneaking out around the side of the building for a smoke.

"I'll keep that in mind." Sherri turned her eyes back to her husband.

"While I was on break, someone made a grievous error. I'm the maître d', and I'm afraid you have to leave."

"What are you talking about?" Marcus said. "We have a reservation."

"That may be, but you're simply not the type of people that we allow at Morveux."

"Is this because of our car?" Marcus asked, incredulous. "I assure you we have more than enough to pay for our meal."

"I'm certain you do. And I'm amazed that your hunk of junk actually runs, but that's not the reason. You left out some important information when you made your reservation. Morveux has a strict no Daring Don'ts policy."

"Excuse me?"

"Not very bright for a villain, or you'd have booked under an alias. Sadly, our reservationist didn't do his due diligence and run your name, but after seeing your car, I did. The authorities have been alerted."

"Now wait a minute." Sherri stood, her hands on her waist. "This is our anniversary. You can't do this!"

"I assure you I can. We at Morveux do not discriminate by race, religion, or sexual preference, but it is entirely legal for us to deny service to a Daring Don't for fear that our establishment will be destroyed. Leave immediately or I shall have the authorities drag you out in shackles." He looked down at Sherri's cleavage. "And take your harlot with you."

For an instant, Sherri froze, mouth agape. The people around her were staring. She suddenly felt ashamed and embarrassed. Sherri rushed out, tears trickling down her face.

Marcus leaped to his feet, ready to beat the man senseless, but he had the good sense to speed up his time-flow instead. It took him ten minutes subjective time to get his emotions under control. The cops had been called. If anything happened, it'd violate his parole and everything he'd worked for, the better life he'd promised Sherri, would all be gone.

Taking a deep breath, Marcus returned time-flow to normal, although now he was standing beside the maître d'.

The appearance of having teleported shook the man.

Marcus looked at his nametag. "Jean-Paul Martinez, you've made a grave mistake here. Insulting me is one thing, but insulting my wife is something else altogether. You don't want to do that. Not now, not ever."

The maître d' regained his composure. "Are you threatening me?"

"Not at all. Merely educating."

Marcus rushed after his wife and found her wiping her eyes at the valet stand.

Marcus pulled out a handkerchief. Sherri wiped her eyes, blew her nose, then handed it back.

"I'll cherish it always." Marcus put it into his pants pocket.

"I'm sorry about what happened in there."

"You have nothing to be sorry for. If anyone should apologize, it's me for putting you in this position. I didn't know about the anti-Don't policy, but I should've guessed. I'm so sorry."

The valet arrived with their car. "I'm sorry, sir. Jean-Paul can be a pompous jackass."

"Thanks." Marcus handed the valet a hundred-dollar bill, walked to the passenger side of the car and opened the door for his wife before getting in himself.

"That was a big tip. You didn't do anything foolish, did you?"

"You mean like rob the place? Naw, that moron's not worth it. The valet was nice to us. Since we don't have to tip anybody else, we might as well make his night. I've got a better idea than robbing the place. One day when I'm rich, I'm going to buy Morveux and fire the jerk."

Sherri laughed. "Yeah, that'd be great."

"I'm serious."

"I'd love to see it."

"You know what proved he was an idiot? He couldn't see that you're the most beautiful, kindest, and understanding woman in the world."

"You just don't want to sleep on the couch tonight."

"True. Am I?"

Sherri kissed him on the lips. "No worries."

Flashing lights appeared in the review mirror and a pair of cops slowly approached, one on each side of the car. Marcus considered speeding his time-flow and driving off, but decided against it. They'd just track him down.

"Is there a problem here, folks?" the officer on the driver's side asked.

"No officer. I hadn't known about the management's policy and we were just leaving."

"Thank you for your cooperation, sir."

"Of course." Marcus drove away. He'd half expected them to frisk him, then realized the officers were probably relieved. The average cop wasn't able to deal with the average Daring Don't.

Months flew by fast, even for a man who could manipulate the flow of time. Carpe Tempus became the rarest of things—a company that, as the Luminary challenged Marcus to do—helped people and made a fortune. After three years, the McGowans were billionaires.

When it came time for their eighth anniversary, Marcus again planned something special. He walked down the hall of their corporate headquarters to pick his wife up for their date.

Sherri was in the trophy room. The place was her idea. The Daring Dos kept trophies of their adventures, which inspired Sherri to design their own. Sherri started the room with a single thank you note from someone Marcus' belts saved and it'd grown to the point where rotating panels revealed more panels with more thank you notes and printed emails. A giant screen looped through video thank yous from grateful people and news stories on the crops he and his farming partners grew for disaster and famine relief, taking days instead of months.

Tens of thousands owed their lives to the former Tempus Fugitive's inventions, which had decreased the car accident death rate by almost twenty percent, battlefield fatalities by thirty-five percent, and more people survived battles—caught in the cross-fire of super-powered Daring Dos and Don'ts—than ever before.

Sherri wanted Marcus to see all the good he'd accomplished.

Marcus hugged his wife from behind. "Ready to be swept off your feet?"

Sherri leaned into the embrace. "Sure, if you think you can still manage it."

"I think I can."

The couple walked arm-in-arm out of the building to where he parked the same jalopy they'd had when they were first married. Marcus kept it, claiming that it reminded him where he came from, although it had been modified to have a race car engine, be bulletproof, sport a bomb detector, and was even amphibious.

Some women would've been embarrassed to be seen in such a junker, especially women worth more than some small countries, but Sherri found it charming.

"I'd like to freeze time for you again."

Sherri tilted her head and frowned. "I seem to recall that not working out very well last time."

"Times change. I can practically guarantee tonight will be better."

"Okay."

Marcus drove back across town and restarted time for his wife when they were at the valet stand in front of Morveux.

"Marcus, I hate this place. I don't want to be here."

"I know that, honey. The night we spent here was one of our worst, but tonight may be one of the best. It all boils down to whether or not you trust me."

Sherri grinned and kissed Marcus. "Lead on, Macduff."

Holding hands, they went in only to have Jean-Paul Martinez greet them. It took the snooty maître d' a moment.

"I remember you two."

"Excellent," Marcus said. "Then you must also recall the horrible way you treated my wife. I'm a decent guy and maybe you were having a bad day, so I'm going to give you one chance to apologize to her."

Jean-Paul looked at the video monitors for the parking lot and saw the same jalopy. He scowled as he reached under the counter and pressed a button. "You want me to apologize?"

"Grovel, really. On both knees, but it needs to be sincere."

Sherri tugged at her husband's arm. "Marcus, let's just go."

"Yes, Marcus, listen to the harlot that you were dumb enough to make your wife and go. I've already pressed the alarm so the police will be here any moment. I will never apologize to a criminal and his whore. If you are here when the police arrive, I will press charges."

"Okay. We'll wait." Sherri was nervous, but Marcus gave her the same cocky smile he'd had when he first asked her out, so they stood their ground.

Two uniformed cops arrived less than five minutes later, their hands hovering above their holsters. "We got your alarm. What seems to be the problem?"

"This man is a known Daring Don't and refuses to leave. Please arrest him for criminal trespass."

"Sir, is this true?"

"Yes, but he can't kick me out. I own the place."

The maître d' began to laugh like it was the funniest thing he'd ever heard.

So did Sherri. "You really did it?"

"I did."

"Nonsense," the maître d' said. "How could criminal trash like you buy Morveux?"

"You didn't check my name this time, did you? That's

because the reservationist was told not to tell you. It's Marcus McGowan." The cops shared a nervous look. "I *was* a Don't, but now I own Carpe Tempus. You might have heard of it. It's been in the news. And for the past month I've also been Morveux's owner. Surely you remember receiving the new employee handbook?"

"Of course."

"Did you read it?"

"No."

"Pity. That means you lied when you signed the sworn affidavit confirming you'd read it, which is grounds for dismissal. Morveux has a new tolerance policy. Any Daring Don't who has served his or her debt to society and isn't currently a fugitive is welcome here. By banning me and trying to have me arrested you're in violation of the employee handbook, the penalty for which is immediate termination." Jean-Paul cringed like he was about to be rubbed out. Marcus winked at Sherri. "You're fired. Leave anything that belongs to the restaurant and get out."

"Officers, surely you don't believe a known criminal?"

One of the cops had found an article on his phone with Marcus's picture. "Mr. McGowan is an upstanding member of society whose work has saved many lives around the world from injury and famine. His belts even saved a cop we know who was shot. Thank you for that, sir."

"You're very welcome."

The cop turned the screen toward Jean-Paul. "That's a press release announcing his purchase of Morveux."

Marcus had posted within the last hour so it'd be there to show the cops, but too late to tip off the maître d.

Jean-Paul's face fell.

"Ready to apologize to my wife?"

"Will it get me my job back?"

"No."

"Then not a chance in hell." The former maître d' walked behind the host stand, opened the drawer and took out his wallet and keys.

"Officers, I'm sorry you were called here under false pretenses, so I'll understand if you want to press charges regarding a false alarm. Would you escort this man off our property?"

Before the cops could agree, Jean-Paul stormed out, slamming the door.

The cops, Marcus, and Sherri followed until he reached the sidewalk.

"Oh, officers . . ." Marcus said.

"Stuff it, Don't. I'm off your property. We're done. Mail me my last check."

"You admit you're off my property?"

"Yes, so you can't do anything to me."

"Wrong. Officers, please arrest this man for stealing from Morveux."

"I never took a dime from the restaurant that wasn't mine."

"But you took that tuxedo. I told you to return everything that belonged to the restaurant. Between it and the shoes, the replacement cost is over six thousand dollars, more than enough to qualify as a felony. I will be pressing charges."

One officer took out a pair of handcuffs.

"You've got to be kidding me. I wore this in. You want me to go home naked?"

"I don't care. I just don't want to be robbed. Luckily, you stole in front of these officers and the surveillance cameras."

The officer held the cuffs out toward Jean-Paul.

"You're really arresting me?"

"You committed a crime. I haven't seen such an open and shut case in ages."

"Mr. McGowan, I'm sorry I insulted your wife. Don't do this to me."

"I wasn't the one you needed to apologize to, and that hardly constitutes an apology."

Jean-Paul started to get down on his knees.

"Wait—you're going to kneel on cement, in my suit, and destroy the knees?"

"What you want me to do, strip naked?"

"It would be a start to demonstrate your sincerity."

The former maître d' removed the expensive suit, handing each piece to a police officer. He wasn't exactly naked, but his thong didn't cover much.

Jean-Paul got on his knees with his hands together. "I'm so sorry. Please forgive me."

"I'm not feeling the sincerity," Sherri said. "I believe there was supposed to be groveling."

"I don't need to do this. I know lawyers from the restaurant who did me favors for getting them tables. I'll fight this."

The police officer shrugged. "You can do that, but with the evidence against you, the best lawyer would only get you a plea bargain. Besides, if you can't get them tables now, how many of those highs priced legal-eagles will take your call?"

Jean-Paul rolled his eyes and bowed all the way down so his chest was on the pavement with his arms outstretched in front of him. "I treated you badly. Please forgive me. Was that good enough to drop the charges?"

"Sure," Marcus said, which got Jean-Paul jumping to his feet, smiling. "As long as my wife accepts your apology, I'll be happy to drop all charges."

Jean-Paul turned to Sherri, hope spread across his face, but the look that greeted him chased it away.

"You called me a whore and a harlot. Where do you get off saying that to a woman?"

"I admit I may have misjudged you . . ."

"Misjudged? You shouldn't have been judging me in the first place. Who a woman sleeps with doesn't affect you one way or the other, either as a man or as a snotty maître d'. I do not accept your apology. Go rot in jail. Maybe when you get out you'll be as lucky as my husband and have learned your lesson."

The officers cuffed the mostly naked Jean-Paul and put him in the back of the squad car, taking the suit with them for evidence.

Sherri waved to the police car as it drove away, then turned toward Marcus.

"So, do I get to sleep in our bed tonight?"

"Nope."

"You mean after that I have to sleep on the couch?"

"Nope. After that, you're not getting *any* sleep tonight." Sheri pulled her husband's face in for a long, passionate kiss.

"First, let's get you the dinner you should have had three

years ago . . . after I give you an anniversary gift."

"What could top this?"

"I was going to save it for dessert." Marcus led his wife to their jalopy and popped the trunk. A diamond the size of a basketball greeted them.

"You finished it? That's wonderful! Who are you going to sell it to?"

"We have more money than we'll ever need, so I don't want to sell it. I want to give it to you. You're the only jewel I'll ever need."

"I love you so much," Sherri said.

"I love you even more."

"Anything in that manual about having sex in the bathroom?"

"Totally allowed for the owners."

Sherri's legs betrayed her then, and she collapsed—not because she swooned with lust and desire, but because something was physically wrong. She'd have hit the ground had she not been holding onto Marcus' arm.

Her weakness only got worse from there. A series of doctor visits later, the couple got the worst news of their lives. Sherri had Gerstmann–Sträussler–Scheinker syndrome. Worse, GSS would eat away at her ability to move, and bring about dementia. She had a rapidly progressing form of the disease. The doctors predicted she wouldn't recognize anyone within a year, and die in less than two.

When the best doctors in the world couldn't help, they went to the second best, then cycled through the rest before moving onto the quacks and crazies, and even those who claimed to have healing powers. Nothing worked. Sherri's condition deteriorated.

"I don't want you to die," Marcus said.

"Me neither, but let's enjoy our time together while I still know who you are." Sherri smiled as she pretended her eyes were itchy and she wasn't wiping tears away.

"I'd like your permission to pause time for you."

"Why? Are we going to Morveux?"

Despite everything, Marcus couldn't help but grin. "No. But through our charitable foundation, we've been financing GSS research. There's a good chance they'll have a cure within five years."

"While I, on the other hand, don't have five months before my mind starts to fail."

"Exactly. I've been gearing up to launch a new business venture for Carpe Tempus. Cryo-storage for humans has taken off with Professor Ice turning his cold technology toward stasis, but there's risk of long-term tissue damage. Time status wouldn't have those risks. Sick people will only age a second for every ten years in stasis."

"That's brilliant. You'll make a killing."

"Hopefully the opposite. I've got a hundred stasis pods ready to go."

"When did you do that?"

"Last night while you were sleeping. I put myself in a time bubble for about six months subjective time. No big deal since I don't age when I use my powers like that. We could put you in status and pull you out in five years for the cure, just a half second older."

"Sounds good for me, but what about you? I don't like the idea of you being without me for five years."

"Afraid I'll go back to my criminal ways?"

"No. You only stole to get money for us, and now we're beyond rich. But outside of me, and work, you don't do much else."

"You're my life, my sweet—you're everything I need or ever wanted. But believe it or not, I do have friends and projects to keep me busy. And I designed the stasis pod with a window, so I'd be able to come and see you anytime I want. You'll look like you're sleeping."

"Can I think about it?"

"Of course, but the doctors say we should do it within the month. It'll give us the best chance at a cure."

Twenty-seven days later, Sherri and Marcus got into their old jalopy and headed toward Morveux. Marcus asked his wife's permission to pause time, promising she'd wake up outside the restaurant when they had a cure.

Sherri McGowan was the first person to go into time stasis in a Carpe Tempus pod, but she wasn't the last.

Marcus visited her pod every day. He also cried every day, just not in front of the pod. Time was slowed, but still passed, so Marcus did nothing but smile and look happy when he stood in front of her, not being sure if he'd show up in her mind as a subliminal image.

Carpe Tempus' new temporal stasis facility was a huge success. Plenty of rich people were looking to cheat death themselves, or help loved ones in need. They lined up to throw money at Marcus. Some heirs brought lawsuits against him—people who don't die couldn't leave an inheritance—but he had all his clients' permission to wake them up briefly to testify. Every case was thrown out of court.

The money from the super-rich subsidized pods for the poor. Marcus got richer and won humanitarian awards, but at the end of each day, he was still alone, and mostly friendless, despite what he told his wife. For three years, the first thing he did upon waking and the last before sleeping was to visit Sherri.

Ironically, during that time he happened to be on hand during a bank robbery and ended up stopping it. The press announced his transformation from Daring Don't to Daring Do.

Marcus met regularly with politicians and heads of state, but one day had an appointment with Damien Rails, which troubled him greatly. Rails ran a brute crew. Brutes were big, strong, and bulletproof. Nobody you wanted to mess with if you didn't have to.

Marcus' first reaction was to cancel, but then he remembered how it felt when people had treated him differently because he was a Don't. Maybe the man's crimes were alleged. Perhaps there was a family member he cared about and wanted to put into stasis. A child shouldn't suffer the sins of the father, so he took the meeting.

Rails arrived with four large and well-armed brute bodyguards.

When his assistant showed the men in, Marcus motioned Rails to an extra-large chair in front of the desk.

"What can I do for you? You were vague with my assistant."

"You never know who's listening."

On cue two of Rails' musclebound bodyguards took out

small devices to scan the room.

"The place's clean, boss."

"Excellent. Mr. McGowan, I come to you today with a business proposition. The Otherworldly Science Museum is having an exhibit of the Rhungier weapons a dozen aliens used to conquer and hold New York City and Paris for a month before the Honorees defeated them. With that firepower, my crew could run this town. You help us get them and we'll cut you in for a solid twenty-five percent of the take and leave all your holdings untouched."

"I'm legit now."

"Don't kid a kidder. I know a big time Don't like you misses the action. Me and my boys got the muscle to tear down a building. You don't play ball and things could go badly for you."

The next instant, Damien Rails and associates seemed to magically appear on the street a mile away, in front of a police station. Marcus had left a note in Rail's hand.

It read:

> *Thanks for your offer, but I'm turning you down. And I can do worse than tear down a building, so it would be in your best interest to move on. —MM*

A week later Kevin Pump, a corporate raider, was threatening a hostile takeover of Carpe Tempus, which made Marcus laugh.

"I assure you this is no laughing matter," Pump said. "You only own twenty-six percent of the company. I could get enough shares to vote you out as CEO."

"No, you can't, because my wife also owns twenty-six percent of the company, which gives the two of us controlling interest. And even if you could, it would be an idiotic idea. I do all the inventing myself."

"But Carpe Tempus owns the patents for your inventions."

"True, but have you ever wondered why no one else in the entire world has attempted to create similar technology for a billion-dollar industry?"

"Well, I assumed . . ."

Marcus raised a hand. "Stop right there. No one else has,

because they can't. Without my natural power to control time flow, the technology is worthless. The machines are just hunks of metal and wires. Carpe Tempus has a contract with me stating that if I leave, I'm entitled to take all my power with me. You'd be left with a lot of worthless stock. I'd simply start over again with new inventions."

The door opened. "Sir, we have an issue that requires your attention."

"We're done here. Security will see you out."

As uniformed guards herded the man away, Marcus shut the door. "What's wrong, Mia?"

He had never seen his assistant so pale. "You should sit down."

"What's got you so shook up?"

"It's your wife's pod. It's . . . it's gone."

Marcus sped time around him to give his mind a chance to process the information. Then he sped up Mia's time-flow and they ran downstairs to Sherri's room.

She *was* gone.

"How is this possible?! We have alarms, security, surveillance."

"Video was on a loop. We have no idea when exactly, except the security guard swears Sherri was here when he made his one a.m. rounds. You have trackers in the pods."

Marcus bent and picked up a coin-sized object. "Left behind, which explains why the alarms weren't triggered."

"Was anybody else taken?"

"No, sir. Security's checked and double-checked. All the other guests are accounted for and fine."

"Sherri was likely taken as leverage against me for some shakedown or blackmail."

"Someone from your past?"

"Unlikely. I didn't run with the dark Don'ts."

An idea struck him. Marcus returned Mia to normal time-flow and sped to the parking garage. Kevin Pump was opening his car door.

Marcus grabbed hold of the raider without speeding up his personal time flow. From his perspective, Pump came to awareness face down over a twenty-story drop, screaming.

"None of that, Pump. I have powers, but they have limits. It's *extremely* difficult for me to allow you to be self-aware inside a status field . . . and still prevent gravity from pulling you down. So I suggest you answer me correctly, and quickly. Why'd you take my wife? Think I wouldn't be able to vote her shares if she was missing?"

"I . . . I . . . I have no idea what you're talking about."

"I don't believe you." Marcus let gravity kick in, dropping Pump fifty feet, then went to a fifteenth-floor office and opened the window where Pump had stopped falling. "If I don't hear the truth, I let you go splat."

"I swear on my mother's life!" Pump bellowed, trembling in fear. Even corporate raiders are scared crapless when facing their own mortality. "I did nothing to your wife! I deal with corporate takeovers, not kidnappings. Please! What good's a hundred million going to do me in jail? Or worse, if someone like you makes me disappear. It's not worth it. I didn't do it!"

Marcus cursed because he believed him. Pump's next moment of awareness was back outside his car.

Drained from the exertion, Marcus collapsed back into normal time-flow inside his office. Since going legit, he'd saved a lot of lives, earned a lot of goodwill. He could call in the Luminary or the rest of The Honorees to help. Who would have the best shot of finding her?

His cell phone rang. Less than two dozen people in the world had that number.

"Hello?"

"Hey there, Marcus. Giving us the bum's rush hurt my feelings, so the kid gloves are off. If you'd like to see your wife returned unharmed, I suggest you get what I asked for."

Marcus knew the voice immediately. "Fine, Mr. Rails, but whatever you do, don't tamper with the pod."

"Too late. People normally insist on some sort of proof of life, so I brought out the Missus so she could say hi."

Labored breathing came from the other end of the connection.

"Sherri?"

"Marcus? I'm okay, but I was hoping to be at Morveux, with you to greet me."

"I know, honey. I'm so sorry. I'm going to get something for Mr. Rails and then he'll send you back to me safe. You just relax and know that I love you."

"That's the only thing I'm absolutely sure about. I love you too, Marcus. See you soon."

Rails took back the phone. "Your wife's fine and she'll stay that way as long as I get what I want."

"You'll get it. One request. Please don't put her back in the pod. It needs my power to be done right. If it's done wrong . . ."

"Marcus, you're in no position to tell me anything."

"I didn't tell. I asked. Nicely."

"I want those weapons ready for pick-up outside your headquarters by morning. Once my people are safely away, I'll return your wife."

"Listen carefully to me, Rails. If you so much as hurt one hair on her head . . ."

"McGowan, do what I want and everything'll be fine."

The gangster hung up.

Marcus wished he could pause time for the entire city, but that was beyond his reach. He had briefly teamed up with Dr. Raptor, a genetically-engineered cybernetic dinosaur, who'd designed a machine that even Marcus didn't fully understand. Using his power, it could've paused time for entire cities, allowing for perfect crimes with no one being the wiser.

There was always a catch. It required more power than a dozen nuclear reactors could supply. Dr. Raptor disappeared before he solved the power problem.

Marcus raided the files of the local PD organized crime unit, using up the last of his personal power, so he was forced to return to normal time-flow and take a cab to his old hideout. He'd kept it purely for sentimental reasons and hadn't needed anything there since going legit. Until now.

After stepping on a combination of floorboards, his uniform and equipment rose up from a hidden compartment. For a moment, he considered putting on his Tempus Fugitive uniform, but didn't want Sherri's first sight of him to be of his past, criminal self, so he just took the belt and gauntlets. They stored his temporal energy so he'd never run dry during a job.

He'd lost an hour of real time. Using the files, he found one of Rails' bodyguards, sitting at home, watching TV.

"Where's my wife?"

The brute startled and spun around, reaching for his holster, surprised to find it empty. Marcus disarmed him before he returned to normal time.

"Don't make me ask again."

"I ain't scared of you, rich man. I'm a brute." The big man swung his couch like a bat. Marcus grabbed hold of the gangster's wrist, accelerated the time-flow until his hand turned to dust.

As the criminal screamed and held his stump, Marcus grabbed him by his groin.

"Guess what I'm dusting next if you don't tell me where my wife is?"

The man sang like a canary.

Marcus' sudden appearance at Rails' hide-out startled the three other bodyguards, who pulled their triggers to empty clicks. It was of absolutely no consequence to Marcus that they were aiming for his legs.

Rails laughed. "Cute taking out the bullets, but we're bulletproof. We'll just pound your ass old-school and there's nothing you can do about it."

Marcus held up his right hand and aged the bodyguards to dust so far down the timeline that even the best CSI couldn't identify them as human remains. The right gauntlet glowed then dimmed, its stored power gone.

"Good thing I don't use bullets, then. Take me to my wife."

Rails nodded and lead Marcus to the back of his hideout to a shed, then down a staircase to a mass manufactured bunker hideout.

"Where's Sherri?"

Rails pressed a button and a door slid open.

Marcus rushed in to find his wife under glass. All the color drained from Rails' face.

"I told you not to put her back in the pod!"

"He didn't," chirped a voice Marcus had long forgotten. "I did.

The bitch was annoying me."

Marcus slugged Jean-Paul Martinez' jaw, knocking him down, then opened the pod door. "How long has she been in there?"

Jean-Paul rubbed his jaw. "Half an hour maybe. You shouldn't have done me like that. Rails is going to hurt you. Bad. Real bad."

"No, sir, Mr. McGowan, I'm not," Rails groveled.

The old maître d rolled his eyes. "Your harlot's fine. I put her in myself"

Marcus pulled Sherri's cold and limp body onto the floor, then touched her pulseless neck.

"No!"

Marcus started chest compressions and breathing into her mouth, but no amount of resuscitation would start her heart again. All Marcus could do was cradle her and scream until he was hoarse, tears drenching his face, then hers.

Jean-Paul grinned. Rails tried to sneak out, but wasn't quiet enough. Marcus saw him and the gangster ran.

"I'm so sorry, my love." Marcus tenderly laid his wife on the ground and kissed her lips. "I'll make them pay."

Marcus suddenly appeared in Rails' path. The brute swung his basketball-sized fist, then a section of torn metal wall at Marcus. Both missed. Rails found himself back in the secret room.

"I told you not to put her back in. Without my power, the pod only put her to sleep. Sherri suffocated to death."

"Couldn't happen to a nicer harlot," Jean-Paul said, still grinning.

Marcus turned, a ball of barely controlled fury. "Why aren't you in jail?"

"One of the brutes and I got friendly. He broke out and took me with him. I convinced Rails to get you to steal those weapons so I could turn you in to the cops."

"Snitch!" Rails charged the former maître d, but Marcus froze the brute.

"He's mine. But *you* took my Sherri out of her safe pod. They started human trials on a vaccine. It's working! All we had to do is wait maybe a year or two and Sherri would be cured. We'd be together for the rest of our lives. You destroyed that!"

Marcus waved his left hand and the gauntlet glowed, turning

the lower half of Rails' body to dust. The brute's screams as he bled out, and died, made Jean-Paul finally stop smiling

"What are you doing?! In jail, I looked into you. You never killed anyone before."

"Nobody ever suffocated my wife before."

"It was an accident! Don't kill me!"

"Oh. I'm not going to kill you."

Jean-Paul breathed a sigh of relief. "I can handle jail."

"You're not going to jail, either." Marcus grabbed Jean-Paul's throat and aged him to the far end of what the human body could endure and still live. His remaining gauntlet dimmed and died. Marcus put his belt around the former maître d's waist and placed the now ancient man in the empty pod.

"You're seconds from death, but this belt will allow you to perceive time-flow normally while your body is paralyzed in stasis. You'll feel the pain of your decaying body every second of every minute for the rest of your life until this bunker's power is gone. It's designed to last more than a century. Then, when the energy is finally spent, you'll return to normal time and suffocate, just like Sherri."

"Don't do this! I'm sorry!"

"It's up to my wife. Honey, should I let him go? Oh. No, huh? Sorry Jean-Paul. Looks like you're out of luck."

"Only good harlot," Jean-Pierre wheezed, giggling as only he could, the last words he speak to anyone, "is a dead harlot."

Marcus slammed the pod door, hooked it to the bunker's power, and triggered it with his power. Gently he picked up Sherri's body and walked away, cradling the corpse in his arms.

The terrified and frozen eyes of the former maître d stared after him and straight on into eternity.

THIS MORTAL COIL
by Peter David, Kathleen David, and Sean O'Shea

MY LOVER, WHOM I HAVE NEVER met, is dead.

I do not know her name. I have no idea where I might have met her. Her voice keeps changing every time I hear it, its tone shifting depending on what is being discussed. But she is beautiful and she is mine, and I can feel her moving beneath me as I thrust into her in an environment that keeps shifting around us. Sometimes we are in a bedroom and sometimes on a beach and sometimes in a forest, oftentimes changing while we have sex, because literally anything can happen during that time. She is exquisite and beautiful and everything a woman could ever want to be, and I love her and I hate her. I know I hate her because I can see my hands wrapped around her throat, strangling her fiercely. Her eyes are bulging wide and there is pure terror in them. Does she know that I am about to take her life? What did she say to set me off? What could she have said, because I love her so much, and yet I despise her, the bitch.

She pulls away from me, somehow breaking my grip on her. She staggers and I punch her as hard as I can, in the solar plexus. She gasps, hurtles backward from the impact, and there is a window behind her. Her body slams against it, the glass shattering from the impact and she falls through it. I run to the window and look down, and I have only the briefest glimpse of her spiraling down, down toward the sidewalk. She hits it with a thud and, my God, there is blood just everywhere. People gather around her, screaming, shouting that someone should dial 911. No one does. They are all videoing her. No one is trying to get help for her. They are all racing to be the first person to post the video of her death on line, because that is the world that we live in now.

This is the stuff that dreams are made of.

And as she lies there, unmoving, bleeding profusely, her eyes snap open and she is looking straight up at me. I am now standing by her side, and she speaks in a shattered whisper. "Save me. Help me. Avenge me," she says.

I am screaming when I wake up, but I am making no sounds when I do so. My mouth is open, but all the shrieks that I want to emit are locked in my throat. I do manage to sit up so violently that I knock loose the Dreambucket. That isn't what it's actually called. It has some long, technical name that is typically abbreviated as DMBKT, and that's where Dreambucket came from. It is an elaborate metal grid on my head, carefully fitted to a series of tiny implants that run along the base of my skull. My hair has grown over them so only a close scrutiny would be able to perceive them, and even then the observer might not know exactly what it is that they are looking at.

The techie is standing there, studying the readouts. Her name is Doctor Grace. Once upon a time she might have been beautiful, but somewhere in her life she forgot how to smile and that omission has permanently screwed up her face, turning it into a twisted remnant of something that was once a caring human being. Now all she is concerned about are her readouts. She squints and sees only my reactions as they are charted on the large electronic screens in front of her, either not noticing or not caring about my startled rise from slumber. "Rough outing, Mr. Martini?"

"Yeah. Rough outing," I say. My voice is barely above a rasp that conveys the intensity of my emotion. She doesn't notice. She never notices. Just to mess with her more than anything, because I already know what she's going to say, I ask, "Do you want to know the details?"

For the first time she actually affords me a quick glance, as if to determine whether I am serious or indeed just having fun with her. "Of course not, Mr. Martini. You know better than that. At Dreamwaves, confidentiality is everything."

"You know," I remind her, "you've been my monitor for a year and a half. You can call me 'Marcus.'"

She has gone back to her readings. Either she didn't hear me or she didn't care. Possibly both. "Good day, Mr. Martini. See you tomorrow."

"Right. See you tomorrow."

I ease myself off the sleeping pad and head to the showers to start my day.

Thank you for your interest in Dreamwaves Products. It is obvious from the fact that you contacted us that you are a hard-working, dedicated individual who has no time to engage in the trivial requirements of standard human existence. That your life requires a genuine commitment to 24/7 that is in more than just the figurative sense. You literally have to be available twenty-four hours a day, seven days a week. Not even Dreamwaves can provide you that.

But we can *give you twenty-three and a half.*

The real main purpose of sleep is to allow the brain to rewire itself while slumbering. To reset itself. In terms of the body, thirty minutes is really all that is required. So Dreamwaves will attend to your needs by hiring professional sleepers—what we refer to as Dreamcasters—to slumber for you.

Here's how it works:

The first time you come in for treatment to one of our special facilities, you lie down in a rest chamber and close your eyes. Our instrumentation will bring you to slumber within one to two minutes. You rest for half an hour, and during that time, your cortex is cleansed of everything that is rumbling around in there. The contents are then downloaded into the mind of a Dreamcaster, who sleeps for eight hours while the contents of your dreams play out in his mind. His or her own dreams are subordinated to yours, which is not an easy task. Only one person out of five hundred thousand possesses the mental discipline not to go insane from such a practice, but our people have been thoroughly vetted and trained.

The Dreamcaster's dreaming of your dreams is then downloaded into your mind in the next cycle so that your brain is effectively cleansed and recycled every twenty-four hours. The Dreamcaster will never meet you out of respect for privacy concerns.

If you are interested in becoming a Dreamwaves customer, you will need to undergo a very simple procedure, conducted under local anesthetic, to have three small implants installed in your skull. They will not be noticeable so no one will know that you are a Dreamcasters client if you do not want them to.

Contact 1-800-WEDREAM for further information.

I keep telling myself that it is just a dream. That is standard procedure when faced with a disturbing slumber interaction (the professional term for "dream"), especially when it is a recurring one. The fact that my subject has been having violent thoughts about some woman does not automatically mean that acting upon the visions is going to occur. It is why we have dreams in the first place: to allow the mind to act out the fantasies rattling around in it so that we can go on about our business. You can dream of being an adulterer or a psycho murderer or a pederast or whatever it is, but the odds of you actually undertaking whatever it is you dream about are somewhere between slim and none.

So there is really nothing for me to worry about.

I return to my rundown apartment in my rundown car. I should really buy a new one. I should buy a lot of things. It's not as if I am poor; I am quite well paid. But I continue to fear that the world will eventually collapse or suffer some sort of major economic collapse, so I keep my money firmly squared away and spend only the minimum required to continue to survive.

I don't do much during the day. Being a Dreamcaster is my job. So I spend the day mostly just hanging out in parks or libraries or Starbucks, working on a novel that I'm never going to finish because if I do, I know it's going to stink and no one will be interested in reading it. I have no friends, not really. My parents moved out of New York five years ago to retire in Florida, and since I'm an only child, I have no siblings to talk to. And working for Dreamwaves is not the sort of situation that provides you an opportunity to interact with fellow employees. I don't have a girlfriend because I have no way of meeting any, nor am I especially attractive. I am in my mid-forties and am mostly bald, my hair having started falling out when I was in my late twenties. My weight tends to fluctuate up and down. Since I get little exercise, I don't pay attention to it until I can't fasten my pants, and then I go on a diet to lose it. So it's not as if I have to fight women off with a stick.

Plus there's her. The woman that haunts my mind because she haunts *his* mind. I wish to God that I knew her name. That's all. Just her name.

Be careful what you wish for.

A Greenwich Village woman was murdered last night, thrown out of the window of her five-story apartment and landing in the street. The body of Melissa Kaufman, a twenty-seven year old marketing assistant, was found with bruises around her neck, indicating that she was partly strangled before being hurled out the window, crashing through the glass and hitting the sidewalk. Police have reported no suspects at this time, but are investigating . . .

I stare at Melissa's picture and the rest of the world falls away around me. There is only her face. Her body, which had been moving under me just last evening, is lying dead in a morgue somewhere.

How is it possible? I had the dream last night, but she was only found—what did the news say?—last night, which means that the dream had to have gone through the subject's mind before that. So it was premeditated. That's the only answer. The dreamer thought about what he was going to do. Pictured it so clearly in his mind that he knew exactly what was going to happen. He strangled her and then threw her out the window. This was no crime of passion. This was planned.

What do I do? I'm bound by confidentiality. But that shouldn't matter. I'm not a priest. It's not as if my confidentiality is attached to God or something. I need to go to the police and tell them. Then they will go to Dreamcasters and they will subpoena Dreamcasters' files . . .

And that will be the end of Dreamcasters. Once the police gut their confidentiality, no one is going to want to continue using them.

And they will of course destroy me. They will sue me into nonexistence for violating the agreements that I swore to protect. They will financially annihilate me. I will spend the rest of my life in court. All the money I've saved up? Gone. I'll lose my savings, my crummy car, my lousy studio apartment, all of it. I'll wind up in a refrigerator box in an alleyway somewhere.

But Melissa will be avenged.

Except no, she won't. Because the only evidence thus far is my remembrance of his dreams, and I will wager that that will not be admissible in court. If they can't get any DNA evidence on him, then they won't be able to prosecute. What if he was wearing gloves when he strangled her? Plus he's got to be a rich bastard to be able to afford Dreamwaves, so he's going to be able to hire the best of the best of the best as his attorney. The case, even if there is one, will be tied up for years.

He is going to get away with it. Whoever he is.

With no problem.

So I've got to do it. I've got to find him. I've got to get him to confess and go to the cops and admit what he's done.

My first thought is to hack into Dreamwaves' file somehow. But that's a waste of time. First of all, I'm not a hacker. Second, I don't know any hackers. Third, Dreamwaves has state-of-the-art firewalls. No one short of an FBI guy could even begin to penetrate their files, and once again, I don't know anybody like that. I need to come up with something else.

Over the next couple of days, I keep track of the plans for Melissa Kaufman's funeral. The television news doesn't report it, but Google is definitely on top of that.

The hardest part is going back to work. To download the dreams of the murdering bastard. I cannot begin to imagine what to expect.

There is nothing. A trip to a zoo that segues into an airplane ride in first class, of course, which then lands at the White House, and we're going on a visit through the White House only to have George Washington step out to greet us, and he guides us to an escalator that drops us in the lobby of a hotel and we're checking into a suite.

In other words, it is a typical dream. His mind is clear. Of course it is. He has killed Melissa, his lover, and doesn't give a damn about her. Why should he?

Why should I?

My mind wanders and I think of our own life together, of traveling with her, of making love to her, of living with her forever and ever, all of it something that will never occur. Deep in my soul, I know I have fallen in love with her. Except I've no idea if it is real love, or if she simply represents something that I will never have and so I have become dementedly obsessed with her. Who knows what the human mind is capable of?

Melissa's funeral is scheduled within forty-eight hours. She's Jewish, so that's typical. The specifics of it are easily found and the next morning I am standing in a funeral home in Brooklyn, wearing black jeans, a black polo shirt and black leather jacket. Not exactly a dark suit, but the color enables me to blend in, so that's a positive.

People are speaking softly, still stunned into relative silence. No one is bothering to ask who I am. No one cares. I should be speaking to people, getting them to tell me things that I could use to investigate, but I'm not a cop or experienced detective. I am unsure how to proceed.

Then I notice a woman.

And I know her.

My mind whirls back to other dreams, and her face was there, briefly, passing in and out. I had attached no special importance to her; she was just a passing person in the crowd. But if she was in my subject's dream, then she might well know who he is.

She is standing near the coffin, her fingers briefly brushing against the Star of David that is embroidered on the top of the blue cloth draped over it. She is staring down at it as if she has lost her last friend. She looks as if she wants to cry but is unable to summon the emotional strength. There is a look of steel in her eyes, but the steel is in the process of rusting away. She is not unattractive, in her late twenties or early thirties, I'd guess. If I had a type of woman, she would likely be that type. I sidle up near her and say in a low voice, "How did you know her?"

"Work," she says. "Knew her from work."

"Okay."

Her fingers are trembling slightly. I know what I should do. I should speak to her in vague terms, try to be gentle, sociable, cautious. But I am terrible at doing that because I'm lousy at speaking to people in general. I could completely screw this up if I speak the words that are rattling through my head, but I really can't think of anything else to say.

I drop my voice to barely above a whisper. "You know who killed her, don't you."

Her head snaps around and she stares at me as if seeing me for the first time. She is about to say something but then she pauses, frozen, contemplating her next words with more caution. "Cop?" she finally says.

I shake my head. "No. Not at all."

"Who are you?"

"Interested citizen."

She says nothing, her mouth thinning as she continues to stare at me. Then, before she can actually formulate a response, the rabbi informs us that it is time to take our seats.

She sits nowhere near me.

It is a straightforward funeral, the rabbi not ever having met Melissa Kaufman but nevertheless carrying through with it perfectly well. Melissa's parents are nearby. The father is stone-faced, the mother weeping openly. The father is clearly trying to keep it together for both of them. People get up, one at a time, go to the front, say nice things about her. Perfectly acceptable service.

When it is concluded, the pallbearers come up, several muscular guys, and transport her out of there. I stand alone in my aisle, watching her borne away. I know Jewish men are buried naked with a prayer shawl and wonder if it's the same for Jewish women.

A hand rests on my shoulder. I turn and look and the woman I had been speaking to is right there. Her eyes are gray as she gazes into me as if she were trying to dissect my soul, and then she inclines her head slightly toward the exit. Apparently she has no desire to go with the family to the graveyard. That's fine with me. I follow her out.

There is a bar just up the street. I realize that is not atypical; there are frequently bars or pubs within a block of a funeral home. Perhaps that is just where people want to go after a funeral service. Throw back a few beers or scotches or whatever and drown one's sorrows in the sweet joy of liquor.

She goes in and I follow her, and moments later we are seated at a small table toward the back of the place. She's ordered a margarita. I've ordered a beer. We sit silently until the drinks are in front of us, and then she starts to talk.

Her name is Jane Leeds. She has known Melissa for several years.

"Mr. Montello," she says with absolutely certainty. "Her boss.

My boss. All of our bosses. Hell, he's probably your boss in the end. He's responsible for her death."

"Why?"

Her face darkened. "They were having an affair."

"Really."

She nods.

The drinks come. I sip mine slowly; she throws hers down her throat with such speed that she is on her second before I am halfway through with my first.

"Mr. Montello," I say again, prompting her.

Once more she nods. "Jason Montello. Very rich guy. Two ex-wives, so he swore he was never going to get married anymore. He took up with Melissa."

"Being involved with one's employee is never a good idea."

"I hope . . ." She threw back the rest of her second drink. "I hope he was worth it. I hope he had a good freaking time. I wonder if he ever beat her."

"Beat her?"

"There's a list of people he's beaten the crap out of. But he owns the police so they never do anything to him."

"So you're saying . . ."

"She's dead because of him."

"But why did she take up with him in the first place?"

She leaned forward and scowled. "Melissa was a perfectly sweet girl, but she had a blind eye towards her romantic life. She got involved with Montello for whatever reason. Maybe she was hoping to advance up the ladder. Maybe she really loved him. Who knows what goes through peoples' heads? The point is, she was involved with him and that was a ticking time bomb, and it finally went off. And Melissa paid for it, and the cops are never going to make an arrest."

"I find that hard to believe."

"No, you don't."

That was the truth. I didn't find it hard to believe at all. We live in a world where the richest individuals set the rules. If any of them wind up in jail, it is typically out of their own stupidity. They admit their misdeeds while there is a microphone nearby, or they are so dumb that they are literally caught in the act and even their high-priced lawyers can't get them clear of it. Most evildoers, however, are free to go through their lives doing whatever they wish, and occasionally have to throw sizable amounts of money at people whose lives they've destroyed in order to make them go away.

I need to go to him.

I need to find him.

"Where is he?" I say in a low voice.

She tells me.

I give her my contact info if she wants to get in touch with me and tell me anything else that occurs to her. As I leave, she's ordering another drink.

The Long Island Railroad takes me out to the Hamptons.

Every so often I want to scratch my chest because of the small microphone I have strapped to it. It feeds into a recorder that I have secured in my pocket. It is hardly the most elaborate of listening devices one can come up with, but it's not as if I have the resources of the police behind me. I'm not a cop or a spy or someone with extensive investigative chops. I'm just a guy seeking vengeance. And if I can get him to confess to the killing, I'm not going to bother to take it to the police. Instead I'll go straight to the news media. The *New York Times* or someone like that. The news will take it and run with it and then the cops will have no choice but to bring Montello in, no matter how much money he is throwing at them.

I get off the train, find a cab, and give him the address. He brings me over there briskly while talking incessantly about the chances of the Long Island Ducks baseball team this year. Of all the things I couldn't give a crap about at this moment, they are certainly way up there.

It's a very nice house. House? More of a mansion, like Stately Wayne Manor in the old *Batman* TV series which was, by the way, something I never understood as a child. I always thought that Stately Wayne was the name of Bruce Wayne's father or grandfather or something. Amazing the things we get wrong when we are children.

I am relieved that there isn't some huge gate or something

blocking the way in. While on the train I am envisioning a pair of huge gates, like something out of *King Kong,* but no. I am able to walk straight up to the front door and I push the doorbell. There is a speakerphone nearby and a voice barks out at me. *"Yeah?"*

"Mr. Montello, I need to speak with you."

At first I have no idea if it is even him. It might be a butler or manservant or someone like that. But then I get a heavy sigh over the box. *"I take one goddamned day off a month and this is what I get."*

"It's very urgent."

"Then go call my secretary and set up an appointment with my assistant, but get the hell out of here or I'm calling the police. And I can assure you, they will be here inside of five minutes."

"It's about Melissa Kaufman."

There is the briefest of pauses and when he speaks again, his voice is lower and darker. *"What about her?"*

I decide to go all in. Screw confidentiality. There is no way I'm going to get him to take me seriously unless I'm blunt with him.

"I'm your Dreamcaster."

There is a long pause then, and I am wondering if he has indeed called the police.

And there it is. A police car, cruising right toward the driveway. He called the cops on me. They're going to come up and haul me away, and there is no way that I can tell them why I'm there.

Then, to my utter astonishment, the police car keeps going. It doesn't slow in the slightest. He didn't call them.

The door opens. Montello is standing there.

He is a tall, broadly built man. He could easily strangle her with no problem. His brows are low set, his eyes dark and soulless like a shark's. He stares at me for a moment and then he tells me to come in. Not by speaking, but by gesturing that I should enter. I do so. He swings the door shut behind me. I wait for him to lead me somewhere, a living room or den or some such. He doesn't do so. Instead we just stand there in the main entranceway. It's rather impressive. It has a nautical look to it, as if we are standing on the deck of a yacht. There is actually a large swordfish mounted on the nearby wall. I briefly contemplate ripping it off the wall and stabbing him with it, and then dismiss the idea. This isn't a Michael Bay movie.

He looks me up and down. "What do you know?" he says finally.

My hand is in my pocket and I thumb on the recording device. "I want to ask you about Melissa."

It's as if I haven't spoken. "What do you know?" he says again.

I pause, debating how honest I should be with him. Then I decide, the hell with it, why not be candid? What do I have to lose?

"I know you killed her," I say. "I saw your hands around her throat. I saw you throw her through the window."

He sighs deeply, as if he is slowly deflating. He steps back slightly and something flickers in those soulless eyes. Guilt? A thought of trying to bribe me? Anything is possible with someone like this.

"What you saw isn't necessarily what happened," he reminds me. "You'll have a tough time convincing the police based on that. A man can't be tried and jailed because he thought of killing someone."

"So you did think of it."

"Yes," he says readily. "Recently. Repeatedly. Do you know why?"

I almost shake my head, because of course I don't know why. But he doesn't know what I am and am not aware of. So instead I say nothing. I just study him as if examining a microbe.

He incorrectly assumes I know. He turns away from me and sighs heavily. "You'd think she would have told me. You'd think she'd have cared what I might have to say." He raises his voice and says angrily, "It was my child, too! I should have had a say!"

My mind races. Holy crap. She was pregnant with his child. Except if she had been pregnant when she died, certainly that would have come out in the news cycles.

"She had an abortion," I realize. I say it flatly so it sounds as if I had been aware of it the entire time rather than coming to a conclusion.

"She should never have done that. I have no children. I

would have loved it. Taken it as my own."

"But she didn't want that."

"She claims it was a miscarriage, but I know when she's lying. I know she ended it," says Montello. There is an urgency to his voice, a cold fury that is building as he speaks. "She didn't want to have my child. Because she didn't want to go through the pregnancy. Or she didn't want to be linked forever to me. She was just using me to get whatever she wanted."

"If that was her intention, wouldn't having your child be the ideal way in which she could achieve that?"

"That's not the way her mind works," says Montello.

One would think he is more aware of her mind than I would be, but I do not say that.

He ignores the fact that I don't respond. He is in his own world.

"She shouldn't have done it. She shouldn't have. And she told me about it in a restaurant. Big public place. She figured I wouldn't blow up there. Not in front of so many witnesses. She was right. I managed to rein myself in. But in my mind, I was . . ."

His voice trails off. He had been speaking to himself but now realizes once again that I am standing there. His eyes narrow. "You don't believe me, do you?"

"I don't. It was too vivid. I can tell when a dream is simply an imagining versus a reliving." Which is a lie, but what the hell. "I think you killed her."

"And that's what you're going to tell people, isn't it. You're just going to toss aside confidentiality and all the agreements and let everyone know that you think I killed my lover. You don't care that I'll sue your company into non-existence, do you."

"I have to get justice for Melissa."

"You never even met her!"

Maybe. But I fell in love with her anyway. I can still feel her body pressing against mine. Feel the smoothness of her skin, her breath whispering in my ear. I have never had a woman in my life, and I have invested all of my feelings in her.

"It doesn't matter," I tell him. "I'll do what I have to do and you do what you have to do."

"I'm glad you understand," he says.

He is standing two feet away from me when he pulls the gun out of his jacket and swings it around to point it straight at me.

I never mentioned I took self-defense classes, did I?

I took self-defense classes.

Even as he levels the gun with his right hand, I swing my left hand up and around quickly. I grab his wrist, shoving the gun across his body and inward, and with my other hand I reach for the gun itself, slipping my finger into the trigger.

I pull it.

The blast rips through Montello's chest, his blood spattering on the wall behind him. His eyes widen in shock and he staggers away from me, the gun slipping out of his nerveless fingers.

His knees go out and he sinks to the floor. He offers no further protests of his innocence. He just looks at me dazedly, as if he is unsure of what just happened, and then he falls forward and hits the floor.

I grab a pencil off a nearby table, stick it into the barrel, and lift the weapon off the ground. I bring it into the kitchen and scrub it free of my fingerprints. Then I bring it back into the front hall and lay it down next to him.

Then I get the hell out of there.

I run. I run for blocks and blocks and eventually I wind up back at the train station. I am unaware of how much time has passed. I don't care. My world is shutting down.

He's dead.

Melissa is avenged.

I take the Long Island Railroad back into the city. I am unaware of the passage of time. I keep playing his final moments over and over in my head. Keep thinking of how I could have done things differently. Ultimately, though, it doesn't matter. He was definitely Melissa's killer. Someone who wasn't a murderer wouldn't just take out a gun out of his jacket and attempt to kill someone. He was ready to shoot me because he had already killed Melissa, so it was no challenge to kill a second person. Who knows, maybe I wasn't just the second. Maybe there were others. Who knows how many people he's dispatched in his lifetime?

I may have slain a serial killer.

I go to work to maintain the illusion that I don't know Montello isn't coming in. Doctor Grace looks at me levelly and informs me that my client didn't come by. This annoys her. Our company's policy is that it is harmful to your health and the program to skip days. I don't tell her that he won't be coming by ever again.

Montello's death doesn't hit the news until the next morning. Apparently his office's inability to get in touch with him prompted them to send the police over and they found what I knew they would find.

I sit there, staring at the newly risen sun, thinking about the fact that there is one less person in the world because of me, and then there is a pounding at my door. That's confusing. I am not expecting anyone because I never expect anyone. I cross to the door and open it.

Jane is standing there. She obviously used the phone number I gave her to track down my address. Her mascara is running. She's been crying.

"You did it, didn't you?"

Quickly I usher her into my apartment and close the door behind her. She turns to face me. "You killed him."

I should deny it. There is nothing to connect me to the crime. I even destroyed the recording device in my pocket that documented Montello's last moments on this world.

"Yes," I said. "I killed him."

"How . . . ?" Her voice trembles. "How could you do that?"

"How could I . . . ?" I don't understand her tone. She seems angry. At me. "I had to. For Melissa."

"Melissa never understood him. Not really," she says. "He had no business being with her. She didn't have the brains or the drive to keep up with him."

"But he killed her! You said he killed her—!"

"No, I didn't!" she shouts. She is moving toward me, flexing her hands. "I never said he killed her. I said he was responsible for her *being* killed."

"I don't understand . . ."

"He should have been with *me*! I think just like him! I know everything he's going to do, all the time, because that's how attuned we are!" She comes at me, her fingers reaching for my throat, and she snarls, *"He should have been with me!"*

And that's when I get it.

She lunges and I duck under her thrust. She winds up halfway across my back and I stand up quickly, but her weight causes me to stumble. I fall backwards, the screeching Jane clawing at me, and then I bang into a window. My hands grab the edges of the window to halt my backwards path, but there is nothing to stop Jane and she crashes through. She shrieks as she falls and there is an awful sound as her body slams into the sidewalk below.

I lean against the sides of the window, gasping, staring down at her corpse. People are shouting and pointing up at me and I wonder how in hell I'm going to explain this. How am I going to tell the police that this was no murder victim; this was a crazed woman obsessed with her boss who was furious that he had taken up with a co-worker other than her. That she was the one who had killed Melissa Kaufman.

No one is going to believe me. Plus I'd have to confess that the reason she just tried to kill me was because I had killed Montello.

My life is over. I realize that in a flash. All that is going to follow now is months, years of punishment and torment, and I will end my life rotting away in a cell or perhaps stabbed to death by some convict that I've pissed off in some way. There is absolutely nothing left worth living for.

I leap out the window and plummet.

I hit the ground and just break my leg.

Somewhere in my imagination I hear Jane laughing in hysterics. She finds it funny. I realize that she is right, and I begin to laugh as well. Except there are tears pouring down my face. Perhaps tonight I will dream of Melissa. That would be nice.

SPEEDETH ALL
by Meriah L. Crawford

KEPLER-443b
27 March 2318, UTC 14:27

IT WAS SHORTLY AFTER DAWN ON their thirteenth day on the Bee, as they'd all started calling it. Not just as an abbreviation of the planet's designation, but because it was annoying—and painful, if you didn't watch what you were doing. Long days, vicious heat, nasty bugs, and hidden tunnel systems where the lizards hid. Add to that the lack of water or food, and almost complete absence of cover, and, for a "simple recon mission," it was about as bad as it could get. About the only positive aspect of the place was that the atmosphere was breathable, though no one quite knew why.

Squad Leader Vetter leaned against a red boulder in a small impact crater watching Trine cleaning and repairing their comms unit. The box had taken a hit from a pulsed laser weapon, and it was dead.

Trine had assured Vetter there was nothing that could be done to fix it, short of replacing "almost every single bishtup part," including a lot of parts he didn't have spares for. He'd been removing, cleaning, and repairing parts for the last two hours of his watch, anyway. Vetter didn't need to ask why. She'd have killed for a task, however pointless—but there was little she could do but wait.

Macksin was snoring. Bastard could sleep through anything—was probably the best-rested biped on the dirt—but he seemed to have the mental capacity of a rutabaga. He'd follow orders if you explained them slow enough, but in a firefight, he was next to useless. And most of the time when he *was* awake, he just sat and read through technical specs and manuals, like he'd never set sight on the insides of the machines he'd been trained to maintain. Damn shame, too, because he was an exceptionally well-constructed soldier, and command didn't much mind fraternizing if they didn't see it happening—not during off-world missions. They'd gotten along well, too, at first—until things started to go wrong, and Macksin proved himself to be the least competent mechanic she'd ever seen.

Vetter shook her head. How she'd found herself left with these two—alone in their sector, as far as she could tell—was a mystery. Macksin, at least, should have been the first to go. Some of the squad started calling him a good luck charm after the third time he narrowly missed being killed or maimed. They were dead now. Every last one.

When the war with the lizards started just nine months ago, Vetter's squad and almost two thousand other soldiers—a rough mix of lifers and draftees—were sent to the Bee. The planet supposedly had some very useful minerals but minimal tactical value, though the orders to constantly scan the surface and relay the data to orbit each watch suggested it was far more important than they'd been told. Beyond that, she had little idea what was going on. None of them even knew what had started the war—they only knew it was happening. The better their tech got, the less information command shared. Smart, she supposed, but annoying. Frustrating. And this time, maybe lethal.

It took them almost six months to arrive on the Bee. When they arrived, the soldiers had been deployed on the surface in squads of twelve. The annies had done all kinds of math to select that number for this arena: three watches of ten hours each, accounting for someone to focus on comms, someone to manage nav, one on scout, and a low-level mechanic for the hugos. In the field, of course, it was bullshit. They were all so turned around by the planet's thirty-hour days, massive temp swings, and the aggressive insect life, that they could barely piss straight, let alone function like a trained squad.

Their last transpo was dead, too, as of that morning. All three of their five-ton tracked hugos had been blasted into pieces that were mostly too small to play tag-o with, let alone try to piece back together. Macksin was supposed to be the squad's senior mechanic, but he couldn't change a tire without a manual, a video, and a helper, so there was no chance. Not a single damn chance that they'd reach their evac coordinates on schedule.

Assuming they ever could have.

Vetter re-settled her goggles to protect her eyes, and sprayed the two men with more of the fancy new bug spray they'd been issued, finishing the can on herself. It helped with the flyers and the crawlers, though not so much with the jumpers. *They* wouldn't be out for another few hours, thank god. Not until the temperature reached 43C, or so. Damn near hot enough to fry your brains.

Macksin opened his eyes for a moment as she sprayed, and shifted his goggles, but otherwise neither man reacted. They'd all had their senses dulled by the constant onslaught. The pounding heat.

Next, she deployed the sun screens, knowing they would do little to blunt the force of the heat stabbing down at them from the eternally navy-blue skies. But, it was better than nothing.

There'd been no way to be truly prepared for this planet, since they hadn't known more than the basics about surface conditions until they arrived. The probe they sent ahead was low-tech, and it hadn't reached the Bee until after they'd already left the solar system. But the transit time had at least given the engineers and med ops enough lag to cobble together a kit to keep them alive. She had to give them some credit for that.

She realized she'd been staring at Macksin again. The muscles of his back, straining at his shirt . . .

She shook her head and reminded herself how long it had taken him to recalibrate the nav con on their last hugo—and how much of a tick she'd been about it. She winced. Macksin surely hadn't forgotten about that.

She shifted the sun screens slightly, and focused her attention back on the mission. Thoughts kept poking at her from the dark corners. She pulled up satellite imagery on her pad again and studied it. The orders she'd been given were simple: Go to these coordinates, eliminate any resistance; travel to the next set of coordinates, scanning as you go; set up camp, eliminate any resistance; wait for the order to evac. Minimal hostile presence, they said. Just identify key features, look for traps and weapons caches, upload the data, and get out.

That was before they discovered the tunnel systems. Before they realized there was water underground. And before they learned that the tunnels were filled with booby traps, mines, and a hell of a lot of lizards. And as they'd discovered on their second day on the rock, some of the massive two-plus meter tall lizards were mined themselves, so they exploded after their hearts stopped. None of her squad had gone anywhere near their kills since then. That lesson had cost them Jesson, Paik, and Amaechi.

Vetter overlaid the images with terrain data and started doing the math, again. And then she heard a click and whine, ducking before she realized it came from the comm box.

She gaped at Trine, eyes wide.

Then there was a snap and a pop, and the whine was gone.

"Trine?"

He shook his head. "Residual charge," he said, shrugging. "Dying gasp."

"Is it possible—?"

But he was shaking his head more firmly. "It's chicken sticks," he said.

"Chicken sticks?"

"Battered and fried." He smiled awkwardly. "Sorry, I . . ."

"From the country?" Vetter asked.

"No," he said. "Just used to watch a lot of movies. I like slang. It's . . ." he smirked at her. "It's pretty frazz."

Frazz was slang from her town—her time. He must know, but how? She smiled at him, wishing for a moment that she knew more about him—but glad she didn't know more about the others. The less she knew, the less there was to mourn over.

In the brief pause, Trine focused back on the comm unit.

After a moment, Vetter tipped up her pad again, aligning the map with the imagery, calculating distances and movement rates.

Vetter shifted quickly to the right to scratch at something that might or might not be slithering up her back, and the top of the boulder she'd been leaning on exploded. The cramped, semi-protected circle of rocks they'd been sheltering in was suddenly filled with laser blasts, and the *whumps* of EDs landing nearby.

The only bits of tech they had left, aside from her pad and a scanner, were three kick-ass, high-velocity rifles, and about a thousand rounds of explosive ammo that were far too heavy to carry any significant distance. She rolled to her weapon, hauled it into place, and aimed.

The sights located the targets quickly—five lizards, about three hundred meters away. They had a slight advantage of elevation, but not enough to make a big difference. Rock fragments were kicking up around her as Vetter fired, pausing after each shot to acquire a new target. The rounds had just enough smarts in them to fly true if the targets moved within about a ten-meter range, so diving for cover wasn't much help. Running flat-out could work, but that generally just flushed the lizards into the open so someone else could take them out. She and her squad had decided that was why they saw so few of the lizards: they knew by now that they had little to gain by coming out of the tunnels, and a lot to risk. All they really had to do was wait for the planet to kill the humans—and pop out occasionally to take out the stragglers.

Vetter watched through the sights and confirmed four kills, with one target running. Her magazine was empty, so she looked to her right to see if Trine was sighting on the target. Trine was hunched over the comm unit as if he was ducking—except the top half of his head was gone. Vetter gasped and felt a powerful ache, but she pushed it away. There was no time.

She turned back to her rifle to reload—jumping when a shot was fired from her left and just behind.

Vetter twisted sharply. Macksin? She gaped at him and he looked back at her, scared, as if he'd done something wrong. Vetter turned back and checked her sights, confirming it: the last lizard was down. Dead.

She turned back to Macksin. "Good job. That was fast."

He blushed and looked at Trine. "Could have been faster."

Vetter shook her head, but before she could speak, Macksin said, "Could have been awake, standing guard."

"You were off watch," Vetter said, and ran the scanner across the territory around their position. "You were supposed to be sleeping."

"We're supposed to keep each other safe."

"*I'm* supposed to keep *you* safe."

Macksin shook his head and looked up at the sky, but didn't say anything. He didn't have to. Anyone on this bishtup rock knew whose fault it really was.

And how many of them were left on the ground? Over one hundred and eighty squads had been dropped on the Bee. How many had been retrieved? How many troops still breathed?

Even if they'd had comms, it wasn't a question she could ever ask; it wasn't a question that would ever be answered.

Macksin started opening up a med kit.

Vetter waved him off. "We need to move. Our position is compromised."

Macksin gestured at her head. "You're bleeding."

Vetter swore, with feeling. They'd been warned to dress wounds promptly—both because of foreign bacteria and because the lizards could track blood trails like supercharged bloodhounds. So Vetter let him bandage the wound. At least he was good at that. Better than at repairing hugos, anyway.

"Macksin, why did you put in for mechanic?"

He smiled, just barely. "I put in for medic. Used to be a trauma med tech back home." After a moment, he added, "Only thing I've ever been good at."

"But, why . . . ?"

"My dad is a mechanic. Wanted me to be one, too. Figured the war would train me, somewhere safe, and I'd come home and work for him. He bought the head of the draft board a couple of drinks and slipped him some cash, and here I am."

Vetter sat in silence while Macksin smoothly, gently plucked rock chips from her forehead. "I'm sorry," she said, wincing at the sheer idiocy of it. "Really sorry."

It was heartbreaking, to waste good medic skills. There were always more mechanics—and more kids who loved cars and trucks and shuttles, and who took to the training like fish to batter. But good medics? Rare as hell, and took forever to train.

Macksin shrugged. "At least I can do this. Nice to finally contribute."

Vetter thought she could hear bitterness in his voice, and she felt even worse. *If only I'd known,* Vetter thought. But, what if she had? Would it have mattered? He would still have been their mechanic. *At least . . . at least I could have been less of an arkot about his mechanical skills.*

She winced, and Macksin said, "Sorry, did that hurt?"

"No, no," she said. "Just . . . thinking."

He nodded. "I try not to do that. I guess that's why I sleep so much."

Vetter winced again. "For what it's worth, I'm sorry."

He looked at her and touched the side of her face, gently. "Do over?" he asked, with a slight quirk of his lips.

"Do over," she said, and wished like hell that they could do all of it over.

When Macksin was done, Vetter scanned quickly for any new signs of activity. Nothing. Not surprising: the lizards usually traveled in small groups. But, they could have called for help. She and Macksin had to move.

After they'd packed what they could carry, including all of the water and food they could find in the others' packs, and about fifty rounds of ammo each, Vetter scanned Trine's ident chip with her pad, recording the time and location of his death. She also needed a photo—it was SOP—but she hesitated. All you could see from this angle was his head wound, and the photos were accessible to the next of kin.

She looked at Macksin. "Technically, we're not supposed to move him . . ."

Macksin understood immediately, and stepped forward. "Let me."

"I can . . ."

"No, it's OK. In my work, back home . . . I'm used to stuff like this."

Macksin gently shifted Trine's body and lay him down on the ground, while Vetter scanned the area for movement.

"OK," he said.

When Vetter turned back, Trine's face was visible, and his head wound less so. It was a huge improvement, though still horrible. Still dead.

Vetter snapped the picture and said, "Right, let's get moving. And . . . thanks." Their eyes met for a moment and they nodded to each other, then started pulling on their gear.

When they were ready to move out, Vetter touched Macksin's hand, and he slid his into hers.

"Think we'll make it?" he asked.

Vetter smiled. "I guarantee it. In fact, I'll buy the beer in the next bar we get to, if we don't."

"Deal," he said, squeezing her hand tightly.

Vetter's previous plan had been to wait until a shuttle was nearby and signal. It had seemed like the safest, smartest option, given that they had some rare good cover, and non-transportable ammo. But their position was blown, and she'd seen precisely zero signs of shuttle traffic within the atmo. So, now that they were set, she gestured to Macksin to take point, and they started walking.

She scanned incessantly. The lizards had better stealth tech than any of their equipment could really handle, so they just had to hope for movement. The scanner alarm chirped faintly as she put it on audible, and Macksin's shoulders relaxed just a bit. They might have no more than a split second of warning, but at least she could give him a chance.

If all went well, they'd reach their evac site three days and a couple hours after they were supposed to arrive. Would the squad shuttle wait? No. Not a chance. But, what choice did they have? They just had to keep looking for signs of a shuttle. And they had to keep moving, or the bugs or the lizards, or who knows what else, would get them.

They'd been walking for almost nine hours—trudging, really—trading positions every hour or so to help keep them alert, when they heard the beeping. It was faint but rhythmic—a signal calling for evac. Where was it coming from?

"Shee," Vetter said. "My sense of direction is the worst. Can you locate it?"

Macksin turned his head slowly, finally pointing off to the right. "There."

Vetter led the way, both of them moving more slowly, scanning for an ambush or explosives of some kind. They hadn't found anything like that on the Bee, but that didn't prove anything.

There was no kind of shelter except where they were headed. Was there a squad there? A clutch of lizards?

"Wait," she said. "You wait here." She pointed at a cluster of low rocks. "Hunker down there and provide cover."

"No."

Vetter turned and stared at him. "What?"

"There's no point. If it's lizards, we're dead. Let's . . . let's just go. We need to keep moving, anyway."

"But . . ." Vetter couldn't think of what to say, and that's when she realized how hot and exhausted she was. The stims hid it so well, until all of a sudden you were dragging. And the drugs were mixed in with the food, so you couldn't avoid them. The hardest thing was remembering to sleep, and she'd been due to rest a good eight hours ago.

While they stood, unmoving, a pair of jumpers landed on her chest. She swatted the three-inch-long brown bastards off with just the edge of panic, stomping on them when they hit the ground. The jumpers bit hard, if they had a second on your skin, and they released a toxin that caused swelling and itching that was a good ten times worse than any mosquito she'd ever met.

"Shee. Fine. Come on." At least while they were moving, the jumpers stayed away.

All their caution turned out to be pointless. When they ducked their heads around the boulders into the small, protected site, they found no threat. Just a very big mess.

Macksin groaned softly, and Vetter spun and vomited.

Macksin said, "You want me to . . . Can I . . . ?"

"What?" she said, her voice rough.

"You should rinse your mouth out and drink some water. And I can grab the, uh . . ."

After she rinsed her mouth out, Vetter forced herself to turn and look. Her stomach lurched again when she saw it. The beeping comm box was still clutched in the hands of a woman who had half her torso blown off. It looked like she'd ducked forward to protect the box, but an ED had killed everyone.

Vetter closed her eyes and tried to steady herself. She wasn't exactly a seasoned veteran, but she should have been able to deal with this. It was probably the stims, the exhaustion, the desperation. Still, she couldn't ask Macksin to do it. She shouldn't.

She heard movement and looked, and he was already halfway there, walking through a waking nightmare. Macksin paused and slid the data chip from a broken scanner that lay beside a large headless man. The navigator's dark brown fingers still cradled the scanner, and Vetter shuddered when she saw the distinct pattern of callouses that marked him as a lifer. He had to have been in the force a lot longer than most of the poor bastards who'd been sent to the Bee. Who had he pissed off to get assigned to this damned rock?

Macksin continued forward, toward the woman with the comm box. He groaned again when the woman wouldn't release the box without force. He stepped quickly away once he had it, pressing it and the chip into Vetter's hands as he passed her.

His wake pulled the stench of decomp with it, and she stumbled away, joining him at a safe distance. Both of them took deep breaths and stared at the shimmering rock in the distance.

The comm box buzzed three times, and then: "All squads still on the surface: report, report, report. Last call. Report now."

Vetter fumbled with the box, pressing her code and keying a response. They were supposed to avoid voice transmissions whenever possible, and to be ruthlessly brief in their text messages. Still, she found herself aching to call out to them, tell them what had happened, and summon a rescue. She thought of her mother and how calm and cool she always was, even in the midst of a crisis. It settled her—though she'd found herself wondering, more and more, if her mother had ever had to face anything like *this* while she was in uniform.

A message scrolled onto the screen: "Squad six six eight nine, report. What is your status?"

Vetter keyed in a response, adding a request for evac.

"Squad six six eight nine, upload your data."

She handed the box to Macksin and pulled their data chip out, removing it from its case and wiping the contacts clean. She reached out to insert it into the data slot on the comm box, but Macksin grabbed her hand.

She looked up, surprised, and saw a look of wide-eyed fear on his face.

"No," he said. "You can't. They're not—they aren't coming to get us. If you upload the data, there'll be no need to."

"They wouldn't do that," Vetter said, without even thinking. "They wouldn't just leave us here."

Macksin raised his eyebrows at her.

Vetter opened her mouth to argue, when doubt and fear took hold. "Oh, gods," she said. "Oh, bish."

She put the chip away and keyed in another response: "Chip reader damaged. Chip won't read."

"Is chip damaged?" the screen read.

"No. Can read on pad. Also possess additional squad chip."

Macksin nodded vigorously as he saw her type it in.

"Standby."

The pads and comm boxes had been designed to be 100 percent non-communicative, as a security measure. It was smart, and a pain in the tail, and it might just save them.

"Yow!" Macksin yelped, and spun.

Vetter smacked at the two jumpers on his ass, stomping them, and then whipped around so Macksin could check her back.

"Clear," he said, wincing and rubbing his butt. "Bishtup bugs. Can we walk?"

She bobbed her head and gestured in the direction they'd been heading in before they heard the box. She handed Macksin the scanner, and they continued on as before, except that they had hope.

Both of them walked faster, in spite of the furnace-like heat, though it was probably pointless. The squad shuttle could collect them almost anywhere, assuming they received orders to get them.

"You think they're coming?" Macksin said.

Vetter, still in the lead, shrugged.

Another fifteen minutes in and the comm box bleeped. A message. Vetter leapt to Macksin's side and they read it together: "Standby for pickup. Current coordinates. Six minutes."

They looked at each other, more intently than they probably ever had, and grins spread across their faces. Vetter laughed and Macksin pulled her into a hug, and then a quick, shy kiss.

"This is real, right?" Macksin said, finally. "They're actually coming for us. We're going home."

Vetter nodded and leaned against him, allowing herself to feel safe for just a moment.

And then Macksin smacked at her hip and shuffled her aside, stomping on a jumper. It didn't quite kill the joy, but it brought them down to the dirt.

"Back to back," Vetter said.

They scuffed the ground looking for jumper holes and then pressed against each others' backs so they could keep watch. Given the lack of natural cover, it was the most practical approach. Vetter focused on the scanner again and they waited. Seven minutes in, they heard the squad shuttle's distinctive rumble.

"Where?" Vetter said.

After a moment, Macksin pointed up and to her left. "Coming in steep. Either in a big hurry, or they've been catching fire from the surface."

The comm box bleeped and Macksin pivoted to see it. "Prepare for combat pickup and immediate ascent to orbit for ship departure."

Macksin let out a soft "huh," as the shuttle roared toward them, decelerating hard. "We must have just caught them."

Both of them reseated their goggles and slid dust masks over their mouths.

"Wonder what's really so important about these chips," Vetter said.

He shrugged. "We barely saw anything aside from small groups of lizards. You think there are really minerals here?"

"Scanner didn't report anything. For all I know, they want them because none of the other squads made it."

Macksin grimaced, and he took Vetter's hand and held it,

gently, rubbing his thumb against her knuckles. "Think we'll still be in the same unit?"

"No idea," Vetter sighed.

As the shuttle came into view, they dropped each other's hands, and stowed the scanner and comm box. The shuttle roared up and smacked hard onto the ground, blasting dust into the air, and they both started running. The doors slid open, they barreled in, and the doors boomed shut again.

A voice called out, "Brace! Brace!" and the shuttle lifted off with tremendous force, throwing Macksin and Vetter both to the deck.

Neither bothered trying to fight the forces pressing them down until they reached low orbit. Finally, the voice came over the speakers again: "Come on forward. Shuttle's nearly empty."

They climbed to their feet, walking through the doors and into the pilot's compartment. There were two people in addition to the pilot: a co-pilot and a very ragged-looking mechanic. He nodded at Macksin, who nodded back, but he ignored Vetter.

They settled into two of the three remaining chairs and strapped in. They could see the transport ship in the distance— aimed for home.

The pilot gave them brief instructions, all of which they already knew, and said they'd arrive at the transport in about a half hour.

"Why so long?" Vetter asked.

"They've already begun moving out of the area, toward the Arrowsmith junction. Going to have to burn rubber to catch them."

"Burn rubber?" Vetter asked.

"Hurry," the pilot said.

"Got yer chips handy?" the co-pilot asked. "Command wants them uploaded ASAP."

Vetter moved to pull them out, but stopped as Macksin said, "Why?"

"Hmm?" The co-pilot looked at Macksin.

"Why do they want them now? Why not just upload when we're aboard?"

The co-pilot shrugged. "Because it's command and they asked

for it. And they're called command because they give orders, and then we follow them. Right?"

Vetter and Macksin exchanged a look. She said, "We just would hate for them to leave without us."

The other mechanic snorted and the pilot said, "Look, this isn't a discussion. Pull them out and upload them." When she still hesitated, he added, "They aren't going anywhere without us. I guarantee it."

"How can you be sure?" Vetter asked.

"I'm sure," the pilot said.

The co-pilot released his straps, turned in his seat, and held out his hand. "Give. That's an order."

Vetter sighed and slid the data chips from their cases. "Sure hope you're right."

The co-pilot took the chips and plugged them into high-speed data transfer slots, shaking his head and muttering something about crazy damn troops. In less than five minutes, all 487 exabytes of data had been transferred. The system pinged a confirmation, and the co-pilot removed the chips and passed them back to Vetter.

And less than five minutes after that, the pilot let out a string of curses that even the co-pilot seemed shocked by.

The pilot keyed comms. "Transport, you're moving too fast. We won't catch you."

Silence.

"Transport, please respond."

The ship was visibly pulling away, even as the shuttle increased speed to the point that the vessel was shuddering and an alarm siren began squalling.

"Jack?" The co-pilot said. "What? What's happening? They're not . . . ?" He reached out and keyed in a message.

After a moment, a bleep sounded, and all of them could see the response. "Sorry, shuttle. There's no time. Gods be your tailwind."

"Tailwind?" the pilot said, slamming his fist against the panel. "There's no tailwind in the universe that could catch us up with them now, and they know it."

The co-pilot turned and looked at Vetter. "How did you know? *How*?"

She shrugged and sagged in her seat. "I was hoping I was wrong. I just . . ."

"Are you really that surprised?" Macksin said.

The co-pilot blinked at the question. "Yes! Yes, I'm surprised. Getting us back aboard safely has always been the highest priority." Macksin shook his head. "It wasn't you, it was the shuttle. The fleet loves their hardware."

The co-pilot said, "But what was the bishtup hurry, anyway? They couldn't wait a few more minutes? It doesn't make any sense."

"Yeah, it does," the pilot said. "Sweet Sarah." He tapped a button on the console, and the port side view came on the main screen. It was one of the lizards' ships—a huge one—heading toward them.

As they watched, tiny glowing dots appeared from the side of the alien ship, racing toward the shuttle.

The other mechanic whistled softly and said, "No wonder those arkots ran for it. Gods be-damned cowards."

Macksin reached out and took Vetter's hand.

She turned and looked at him. "I'm sorry," she said.

He squeezed her hand. "At least it's over."

The first missile connected with the shuttle.

They were gone.

MAKE IT DIDN'T HAPPEN
by Glenn Hauman

THE CREEPY OLD PERV HAD BEEN following me around for three days before he finally came up to me outside of school. And he was old. Older than any of the teachers, probably older than that pile of bricks, too.

I don't know why I noticed him at all, really—he stayed a good distance away from the schoolyard, and he never came any closer than two houses away. He just seemed to be lurking. He spent a lot of time fiddling with branches and things like an old guy does instead of feeding pigeons, but he always seemed to be keeping an eye on me. No one else seemed to notice him, and the teachers didn't do anything.

But when I was supposed to be walking home on Thursday, I felt like there was something itching at the back of my neck. I wished I hadn't been wearing a dress, but it was picture day and BitchMom insisted that I wear something nice.

I was sure that I was being watched.

So I took another way home that I knew, one that would take me near the woods. No one had bothered me there since 6th grade, so I was pretty sure I could get away if I had to.

I guessed wrong. He was there waiting, leaning on the big tree at the front of the path.

"Hello, Kelly," he said. Now that I could see him better he didn't look like a pervert, but he was sizing me up as if he was trying to fit a piece of the puzzle into place, like he'd seen me before from a distance, and this was just him wondering what he was going to do with me now that he had seen me up close. Like a stalker meeting his favorite actress for the first time, he seemed unsure as to what to say next.

"Who the hell are you?"

"I'm a friend, I promise." He raised his hands to his chest like I had a gun pointed at him. I wish I had.

"The hell you are. How long have you been following me around, old man?"

He paused and his eyes darted back and forth, like he was trying to figure out the answer and didn't want to tell me the truth. "A while, kind of. Look, I'm just going to reach into my pocket, very slowly, and then I'm going to show you something. I know this will convince you."

"How do you know?"

"I know." His hand pulled out a little piece of shiny metal, about the size of an index card but about as thick as a pencil. He looked at it like he was looking into a mirror, and dragged his finger across it, and tapped it a few times. Then he smiled and turned it around. A picture flashed on the metal like a tiny television. Then I saw her.

"Hey, Kelly-Belly."

She looked like my mom, but with the same little mole over her eyebrow that I have.

"Wow, this is really weird—I'm saying the exact words I remember her telling me. It's just happening. This is just the way I remember it happening. Kelly, this is going to sound crazy, but . . . I'm you. From the future. I'm here with Matt—show her," she said, and the screen's point of view swished around and showed a close-up of the same man in front of me, who waved at the camera, then panned back.

"This is going to sound strange—maybe impossible to believe—but there are two things you have to know right off the bat. One: I'm you, from years in the future. Let me show you— Matt, zoom in here—see, here on my foot? This is the scar that's left from where you dropped Mom's good scissors. Two: Matt has invented a way to travel through time, and he's fit it all into a belt. He's wearing it now."

The future me—if it was truly the future me—continued. "He's come back in time because something very bad is about to happen to you. I don't really want to go into details—if this works, you'll never ever have to deal with it, so I don't want to burden you, but there's a guy who's about to assault you. What you have to do is

take Matt out to the old Ivy Acres barn, and help him find a place
to hide in the loft, so he can stop you from being attacked."

He looked up, and smiled hopefully. "Well?"

"Um," I said, trying to wrap my head around what I was being
told. "Hello."

"Hi. I'm Matt. Pleased to meet you." He paused, then said, "Again."

"Uh-huh. So why were you following me around for so long?"

"Well, I was hoping that I could get in contact with you and
explain everything in a calmer environment."

"Calmer environment?" I snorted. "I didn't tell you what I was
living through growing up?"

"It's only been very recently that you told me anything about
your past at all—shortly after I proved the belt worked safely. But
I was running short of time."

"Run out of time?"

"Yes, we are almost out. You see, the attack is supposed to
happen today. This afternoon."

I sort of zoned out for a moment there, the panic of the situation—a danger I didn't even know existed until five minutes
before, right after I learned that time travel was a *real goddamn
thing*—so I missed some of what he was saying.

"—she couldn't tell me any identifying detail about the man
who attacked her—the man who will attack you. You never knew
who it was, and he was never caught for this. So I have no way
of knowing who it is, let alone having any chance to intervene
before you encounter him. The best that I could do would be to
shadow you and prevent him from causing you harm. I'm here
to protect you."

"And you can stop him? You're some sort of kung fu wizard that
can, like, knock him out, break his jaw? Or you've got a ray gun?"

"No, I'm not. But I think the element of surprise will do the
trick."

"You think?!" This old brainiac didn't look like a weightlifter.

"I suspect strongly," he said. "But we better get going if we
are to make our appointment with what will happen. How do we
get to this barn?"

"This is nuts. Freaking nuts. Why don't I just go home? He

won't attack me there!" Someone else might, but hell … that would just make it another Tuesday.

"Kelly, I'm sorry, I know this is a lot for you to handle. But we have to do this here and now. I have no way of identifying this person, we have no idea who he is, the only things we know is that he will be at the barn in"—he looked at the silver rectangle in his hand, then tapped the center of it— "about twenty minutes. We have to go. Now."

"All right," I said, because what choice did I really have? "Follow me."

It took about ten minutes to walk there. And all the way there, Professor Matt was silent, but he kept trying to steal glances at me. Finally, after the tenth time, I said, "What is it? Why are you looking at me?"

"I'm sorry. It's just very strange to see a younger version of— well, you."

"Uh-huh. What, you're going to tell me we're together in the future? We've been—"

"No, not really. We were together, but we never—well, we—"

"God, spit it out already."

"Look, you have to understand. This is a bit weird for me."

"Yeah, well, it's really fucking strange for *me*, so try to make it less weird, okay?"

"Okay." He sighed. "You came into my life a short while ago, about three months. You were intellectually smitten with me and somewhat romantic, but not intimate. But I was crazy over you. You didn't freak out or think I was crazy when I told you about my theories of time travel, and were supportive of my efforts to build a working system. You even picked out the belt yourself."

That thing? It just looked like a simple black leather belt— wide, with a stainless steel plate for a buckle. I could make out a hinge at the bottom.

Matt went on. "But you were always physically distant, until I proved that the belt worked. Then, you opened up to me and told me that you had been attacked when you were a teenager, and that made you distant and cold towards others. We talked about it, and I told her—you, future you—that now it could be fixed—that I could go back and prevent the attack, so that it never happened. When I told her that, it was like a weight lifted off of her. That was the first and only time we—"

"Ugh. No details, please."

He looked a bit embarrassed. "Right. Anyway, we discussed how to do it, how to go back and find her—you—recorded that message you saw, and off I went."

We walked a bit farther, and something occurred to me. "Wait. You're going to change things. How are you going to get back to me in the future? I'm not going to be the same person! If the attack never happens, we probably never meet."

"I know. I'm surprised you figured that out, your older self never seemed to."

"But then—you're throwing away—"

"Yes. That's how much I care about you. I'm willing to throw away the possibility of a future with you in the hope of making you happy. Hopefully the timeline won't diverge too much and you'll be able to find me at that cocktail party at MIT in thirty years or so. April sixteenth, seven p.m. Here's hoping. She looked so sad when I left, like she knew there was a chance I'd never see her again. Is this the barn?"

"Yes." We'd arrived. The barn was a rickety old thing that was part of an old nursery, but it had closed down a number of years ago. It had been discovered that the gas station next door had a leaky underground tank, which had been contaminating the soil of the nursery and messing up the plants. Some of us came here after school to drink and get high, but the smell of fumes was getting stronger lately so most people stopped coming—no one wanted to light a cigarette in a place they thought they'd make explode with them inside it. There was a fenced-off pump of some sort about 10 yards away that was running, trying to suck the gasoline out of the ground.

"Good. Let's go inside." He opened the door and peered into the darkness. I reached past him and flicked on a light switch past the door, and a dim bulb lit up. He seemed surprised. "There's still power here?"

"Yeah, it's weird. We think it's on the same circuit that they're using on the pump out there."

"Okay. Where's the loft?"

I pointed to the back wall. "Stairs are there."

"All right. You stay down here, and when something goes wrong, I'll come right down." He started up the stairs.

I was surprised that I was scared, but something still didn't seem right—something didn't make sense. I started to call out, "Matt—" but I couldn't hear myself over the sound of splintering wood.

The floor of the loft was breaking, and Matt fell through, landing hard on his shoulder, with more pieces of wood falling on him.

I screamed—I don't know what I screamed—and ran over to him. He wasn't moving. I started to pull boards off of him. He still wasn't moving. I thought he was unconscious, but then I saw the way his neck was bent.

Holy shit. He was dead.

Shit! *Shitshitshit!*

Now what was I going to do? I was still in danger, and the only person who knew how to protect me was dead. The only other person who knew what was going to happen to me.

Wait, no . . . there was one other person, who knew and had the answers for me.

I went to Matt's side, and reached for the belt buckle. The front popped open, and I saw a digital display inside it, with a clock showing what time it was and a few other buttons. I unlatched the belt, tugged and worked the belt off his body, then pulled it around my waist—it was a long belt, I had to wrap it around me twice—and looked at the display. There was a button labeled "Return." I held my breath and pressed the button.

There was a very loud hum, and the world around me instantly sped up like a videotape to incoherent static and strobing blurs. And then it stopped, and I was in some sort of mad scientist lab.

She was there waiting for me. The future me.

"You made it here," she said, with a bit of sadness in her eyes. "Here, have some water." She tossed a plastic bottle to me, and I took the cap off and had a swallow. It tasted a bit chemical, like pool water. "What am I saying? Of course you made it here— this is just what I remember happening."

"Wait, you remember what happened?"

"Every bit of it. And I know Matt's dead."

"Yeah, he died—"

"—breaking his neck in the fall from the loft. I know. I killed him."

"WHAT? What do you mean, you killed him? How?"

"I sent him back there. I told him a story of what was going to happen to me. I lied. The attack, the rape . . . it never happened. None of it. I told him just what he wanted to hear. At least I sent him off happy. He was going back in time, and thought he was going to be a hero. My hero. He didn't know. He couldn't know. But I knew. I murdered him. I had no choice."

My mouth was getting numb. "What do you mean?"

"I see the water is working. It's a little drugged. Don't worry, you'll be fine—it's just keeping you calm and pliant, you're going through quite a shock right now. And it's not going to get a lot easier, but at least you'll know what you have to do."

"But—"

"Shh. Let me talk for a while, I'll explain everything. First, I know that you figured some of this out already, because you remembered me saying on the video that this is what I remembered saying. Which meant that I already knew what was going to happen, which meant that history wasn't going to change after all—but I'd been acting like I'd been assaulted."

Dang, she was right. That's what was nagging at the back of my head.

"No, I don't know why Matt didn't catch it either. He was just goofy and excited, all hopped up knowing that he was going to save me, and probably blinded by lust. But it's okay. It's not your fault. It's mine. Don't argue with me—oh, right now you probably can't anyway, the drugs are working hard now, so you can't talk at all. Don't worry, you'll wake up fine back in the barn, no hangover at all."

I must have looked puzzled. I couldn't feel my face.

"Yes. I'm sending you back. You're going to wake up without that belt—don't worry about how or why—but you'll pull a tarp over him, and you're going to leave him there. There's going to be an electrical short in the barn overnight—probably from a wire that he pulled loose when he fell—and it's all going to burn to the ground. Still too much gas in the soil, saturated the wood. Tomorrow, it'll be nothing but cinders. No one will ever find any human remains." She smiled lopsidedly. "The perfect crime." Maybe it was me that was getting lopsided. My vision was starting to get fuzzy.

"This is a strange feeling for me. In a few minutes, it'll be the first time in decades that I won't know what's coming. I don't know if the police are going to come after me for Matt's disappearance, or whether I'll really be able to get away with it. It's a very odd thing, carrying guilt for so long for something that you haven't even done yet. And then for something you're committing. I thought by now I'd be free of the guilt. But all this time, all the time I was with Matt . . . knowing what I was eventually going to do to him . . . and he was so sweet. And I broke his neck and tossed his corpse onto a funeral pyre. And I never got punished for it. I just punish myself."

Future me started to cry. I dropped the bottle.

"I kept hoping . . . all my life, I've tried to find a way to make it not happen. Make it didn't happen. But a part of me always knew that it was going to end up this way."

I was beginning to slump. Future me came over and held me, so tenderly, so effortlessly, so lovingly. She cried on my head and stroked my hair.

". . . it's okay, baby. It's all right, Kelly-Belly. You've got a long way to go before you get to be me, and there'll be good stuff along the way. You are going to have some wild times, you'll do good things and bad things, but most of all, you'll survive this far."

"But why? Why did you do all this? Why did you kill him? What was the point?"

"Why? Oh, my dear. Does this make us horrible, me sending Matt back in time to die? Maybe. Maybe not. I've thought about this for years, and I still don't know for sure why I did it, or if I could ever hope to stop it."

The last words I remember her saying before I passed out were, "But that's the way I remember it happening."

DUCKBOB: KILLER SERVICE
by Aaron Rosenberg

"DUCKBOB—GET DOWN, MY LOVE!" MARY SHOUTS as she hurdles the couch in an amazing display of beauty and grace—yes, I stop to admire her form, even in the midst of all this chaos—and dives behind it. The couch, ever helpful, rises and solidifies into a small shield wall to protect her.

It always did like her more.

For my part, I duck—yeah, ha ha, never heard that one before, only been ten years since the little gray aliens most people just call Grays abducted and altered me, you think in all that time no one's ever made a "quack" at me before?—as something small, flat, circular, and silvery goes whizzing past right where my neck had been.

"Hey!" I shout, straightening back up and glaring at the room in general. "Was that my *Rockford Files* soundtrack? Do you have any idea how hard it is to come by one of those? That took me weeks of searching, and an entire hour of listening to the vendor's sob story about the death of vinyl!"

A second CD shoots toward me—*The Best of Johnny Mathis*, I think, so I'm a little less upset about that one—and I quickly dive to the ground, thrusting my arms out in push-up position to keep from slamming my bill against the floor. See, Tall, I *do* work out when given the right motivation! A whole bunch more silvery discs follow, racing overhead to imbed themselves in the couch, the wall, and anything else in their path.

Why oh why did I ever think it would be so awesomely cool to buy the seventy-six-disc changer?

"Knock it off, Iris!" I bellow from my forced-exercise pose.

"That is what I am endeavoring to accomplish," her perfectly modulated voice replies from all around me. Which was always creepy to begin with, and is twice as bad now that she's literally trying to kill me.

You just can't find good help these days.

It all started the day before. And, as usual, I didn't really have anyone to blame but myself.

"Check this out!" I told Mary as I returned to bed holding the mail—a handful of bills (it's amazing that you can literally go to the ends of the universe—or its center, anyway, since the Matrix is here at the Galactic Core—and deliberately not leave a forwarding address but somehow they always find you. Especially medical bills—I'm convinced that most physicians' assistants should really moonlight as bounty hunters, if they aren't already. Nobody would escape them! Especially if they've ever gone in for elective surgery), a bunch of ads, two fast-food menus (one for Langnock's Sweet and Sour Stir-fried Mineral Balls, which I order from sometimes as much so I can giggle over the name as because I love the food), a letter from the local Galactic Neighborhood Association (which always has at least one reference to "that glittering pink monstrosity in our midst." Hey, what can I say, I live in a show home.)—and a small box from Tek R Us, delivered by the UPS (Universal Postal Service, what else?). I dropped all the rest at the foot of the bed and clambered back onto the mattress cradling the box like it held my child.

Which, in a way, I guess I did.

"And what does this parcel contain?" Mary asked. She was sitting up with her knees drawn up before her, the sheets pinned between said knees and her absolutely mesmerizing chest, and I swear bed linens have never looked more seductive. Her long hair had come loose from its braid at some point last night—ah, who'm I kidding, I know exactly when and how that had happened!—and was now hanging in tousled strands about her face in that way that you think only top photographers can arrange and make to look perfectly natural.

Six months and counting, and she still takes my breath away every time I look at her. Or hear her voice. Or smell her perfume. Or—yeah, okay, so I'm smitten. At least everybody agrees I've got good taste. Including that one crazy guy in the subway who tries to take a bite out of my shin every time I see him, insisting that he has a marmalade glaze that'd be perfect for me. This is why I prefer not to risk the train on my own. When you look like a walking, talking, man-sized duck (thanks, Grays—you couldn't have decided to modify me to look like Rock Hudson?), you never know when someone's going to see you as a potential victim—or a possible entrée.

"It's my new house system," I explained, slitting the packing tape and parting the flaps like I was cracking open an ancient treasure chest and had to be wary of poison needles. It's a habit I picked up as a kid (back when I was a regular old unmodified person, all original parts, slightly used condition), thanks to my older siblings' penchant for booby-trapping any packages, presents, or unattended backpacks and lunchboxes. Never with anything lethal, but I've got one cousin whose index fingers are now the same length as her pinkies because she got just a little too careless when trying to get that last Fig Newton out of the bottom of her lunch bag. Reaching very carefully into the package, I extracted a small, silvery box about the size of one of those little boxes of tissues that I am convinced were designed to be almost impossible to remove a tissue from without a forceps, a power drill, and a whole lot of lotion. It had a few wires trailing off it, several ports, and a power button. "It's called Iris," I told Mary, showing off my new toy.

"For Interactive Residential Infrastructure Supervisor. Hey, I didn't come up with the name, I just bought the darn thing!"

"And what exactly is Iris expected to do?" Mary wanted to know, arching one of those perfect brows of hers, a tiny frown puckering her ruby-red lips. More than once I've described my girlfriend as "Take Snow White, give her the IQ of an entire think tank and the voice of the world's best sex-phone operator, then make her a Playboy centerfold to boot." I've tried to talk her into wearing the whole animated-movie getup, with the low-cut blue blouse and the high white collar, but so far she's said no. I'm going to try again on my birthday, since I can't think of any present I'd like more. Though I admit, wearing all seven dwarf costumes at once could be a challenge.

"What won't she do?" I countered. "Once I hook her up to the house, she'll be able to control everything—the lights, the heat, the music, the oven. Even the Roomba. I can just tell her what to do and she'll do it, like 'Iris, turn on the living room light,' or 'Iris, clean up the mess in the kitchen,' or 'Iris, run me a bath and cue up "The Flight of the Bumblebees."'" Hey, I like doing aquatic routines—I happen to be really good at them—and I've got a bathtub the size of most people's bedrooms, so why not take advantage of it? I keep telling Tall this counts as exercise, but he claims if it involves cheerful tunes it doesn't count. I think it's actually the rubber cap he objects to, though. That and the sequined outfits.

"I see." Mary's tone sounded slightly disapproving, which made sense since she'd obviously already realized what a tremendous timesaving device Iris would be—and, as a result, what a great way for me to save my energy, too. Mary's not as bad as my best buddy Tall, who's always hounding me to get in better shape (I told him I'd be happy to, but I couldn't figure out how to make a dodecahedron without growing at least two extra limbs), but I know she worries that I'm not active enough. I try to disprove that every chance we get, of course, but she insists I need more regular exercise than that—and something I can do in public. Without getting arrested. Which seriously cuts down on my possible routines.

"C'mon, it'll be neat!" I insisted. She rolled her eyes just a little—a quarter-roll, I'd say; it's the allez-oop that's really hard, but that one's worth major points—but let it go. She knows what a sucker I am for toys and gadgets of all kinds. It's why my bedroom looks like Batman, Willy Wonka, and Iron Man held a makeshift science fair in the middle of it. Almost every surface has some kind of tech doodad, from the lights that only blink when you do (I keep trying to beat them but it never works) to the pencil sharpener that produces pencil shavings in the shape of those paper cutout dolls to the anti-grav ice cream maker (hey, you never know when you're gonna want astronaut ice cream!). Between that and the fact that I'm as lazy as a big orange cat, it shouldn't have been any surprise to her that I'd fallen in love with Iris the second I saw the TV ad. I can still hear it:

"Are you tired of having to get up to turn on the light or

change the TV channel or fix dinner or make sure the kids haven't snuck out after hours? Well, say no more! Now you don't have to do anything if you don't want to—you can let Iris handle it all for you!" Turns out the ads actually got it right for once. Iris can do it all better than I ever could. She can do in a minute what would've taken me an hour or more.

Although it's still been at least five minutes and she hasn't actually succeeded in killing me yet. Considering how many times I've come close to offing myself by accident—how was I to know that thing would explode if held just so and shaken up and hit with a live wire and doused in kerosene, just to name one completely innocent example—she's proving shockingly ineffective at this particular task.

I'm considering writing a strongly worded review about that failing.

Assuming I survive long enough.

"All set!" I'd shouted a few hours after showing Mary the package (no, not that one, get your mind out of the gutter, you! Do you have any idea the last time that was cleaned?). Well, okay, more like eight hours. See, first we'd been in bed, and she had those sheets draped around her, and, well, we might've lost track of time. Then we finally dragged ourselves out of bed to shower and get dressed and get on with the day and, well, maybe a little distraction happened there, too. What can I say, people tell me I'm distracting! Must be the way I talk.

But finally we were up and doing stuff (what did I say? I warned you to behave!) and Mary had some things to take care of for the Grays—filing mental reports on her most recent trip, filling out expense reports (apparently there's like twelve forms for the long-range teleport alone, and even though they're all in her head it still takes some time to make sure she's visualized all the lines being filled in correctly, which just seems excessive to me but those little buggers are huge on bureaucracy, they're basically like wizened old IRS auditors in alien suits, only with a better sense of humor and an even greater love for tapioca pudding)—and I got to work setting Iris up.

"Would it not be wise to consult Ned on this?" Mary suggested when I told her what I was going to do.

"Naw, it's fine, I got this," I assured her. Ned's our bud, and the tech-head in our little quartet. He's a great guy, but after that whole thing on his planet he realized he wanted to spend more time with his fam and who am I to take that away from him? Besides, the instructions for Iris were pretty straightforward. She came with a whole bunch of smaller doohickeys that looked like tiny metal octopi with blinky lights all over them (Best. Christmas. Lights. Ever!), and all you had to do was hook each of those into the relevant house system, like plumbing, wiring, thermostat, and so on. All of those fed back into her base by some sort of convection-based wireless, it said, which just made me think that I was turning my entire house into the world's largest Easy-Bake Oven.

And I'm okay with that. Brownies in every room! Whenever I want!

It did take me a while to connect all of them, but it was sort of fun. Each time I got one in place, it would start blinking faster and faster and then light up completely for a few seconds before going back to a slow, steady blink, telling me that particular system was now connected. It's like when you're screwing something in and you can feel when the screw finally lines up with the threads correctly and there's that burst of satisfaction like "Aha, I've got it now!" Or when you think it'll be all clever and cool to set up a voice-lock on your fridge and cue it to only respond when you sing "Oklahoma!" but you forgot that you had a mild cold when you programmed the stupid thing so your voice is deeper and raspier than usual and now every time you want a snack you've got to pretend you're Harvey Fierstein.

The good news is, I lost about four pounds before I figured that one out. Tall keeps threatening to hack the darn thing and set it to some song I don't know so that he can put me on an enforced diet (even before the Grays converted me to a man-duck I liked to eat, and afterward, well, it wasn't like I was too concerned about my looks). Every time he's suggested that I've pointed out that my fridge is fireproof, cold-proof, laser-proof, and radiation-proof according to its warranty ("Keeps your food

nice and cold, and can double as a nuclear bunker if needed!"),
but the voice-lock makes no such claims, and he shuts right up.
The only reason I haven't attacked it with a fire axe already is that
when I'm starving I don't feel strong enough to play DuckBob the
Barbarian, but I've been careful not to tell him that.

Anyway, by evening I'd finally gotten Iris set up completely.
Everything in the house was now wired into it—except for one
room. Even I'm not crazy enough to try hooking an automated,
semi-aware system directly into the Matrix that protects the entire
cosmos from extradimensional invaders (though there're some
who'd claim that was exactly what the Grays had done when
they'd plugged me into the darn thing as its "human" operator). Who knew what'd happen to it when I gave a command?
And whether that'd interfere with the wireless interface Ned had
rigged for that I wore on my head twenty-four seven? I could
just picture shouting, "Iris, make me some popcorn!" and the
Matrix translating that to "disconnect all safety parameters and
go full-on extinction event." No thanks. I didn't even hook the
TV out there into Iris. I figured I could handle changing channels
the old-fashioned way—by remote—in order to avoid putting the
entire universe at risk.

I should really get a medal for being so selfless and all.

But everything else was now connected, and I was proud as
punch (which I've never understood, unless it means "proud as
when I punch someone and they go down with the first blow,"
which never happens to me because I've got this old Tennis Elbow
thing and can't really put my full weight into it and I also have this
fear of commitment so I tend to hold back a little and that's all it
is, I swear) as I stood there in the living room and shouted, "Iris,
turn on the TV!" and the TV turned on behind me. "Iris, change
the channel to *House Hunting*!" and one of my current favorite
shows came on. It was an episode I'd seen before, they're stalking
this sturdy little cabin up in the mountains somewhere, the darn
thing is crafty, too, and keeps going to ground in snowbanks then
ambushing them as they go past, they're down two team members
already and they've only managed to crack one window on it but
that's what makes it such compelling television!

Now for the *piece de resistance.*

"Iris," I called out, "start the popcorn and bring me a beer and Mary a G & T!" We heard the popcorn popper whirl to life in the kitchen, and the fridge open, and the sound of stuff being poured and mixed, and a minute later a servitron—another recent acquisition, basically a small hoverboard with claws on these extensible metal arms, it's like a Frisbee mixed with a serving tray and one of those Claw games—came flying into the room, bearing a bowl of freshly popped popcorn, a pint of beer, and a mixed drink. "Ta-da!" I proclaimed. I was as proud as if my kid had taken First at the Science Fair after waking up that morning and wailing that he'd only just remembered it was today and he hadn't even started his project yet and the only two things he knew how to make were pipe bombs and potato clocks.

True story—I did take first for that, and then my project disappeared, along with my notes. But there was a weird rash of vegetation-based explosions all around the world after that. And there had been those two guys in sunglasses and suits at the science fair, who'd seemed really taken with my project. Looking back now, I know they weren't MiB—wrong suit, Tall and his cronies all wore what he once admitted was UltraBlack, designed to actually yank the color from everything around it and then throttle the color into submission—but probably some other three-letter government agency.

So I not only won the science fair, I also helped keep the world safe for democracy! How's that for a big win? I should've gotten a medal for that one, too!

Admittedly, Iris hadn't buttered the popcorn the way I like it—with two whole sticks of butter per bowl, to really get that caked-on, slide-down-your-throat flavor—and Mary's drink wasn't exactly right—apparently Iris thought "G & T" meant "goat cheese and tea," which Mary claimed was "bracing." Still, Iris was an adaptable device, so once I explained those things to her she said, "I have noted these instructions, DuckBob, and have added those recipes to my catalogue. Thank you."

Pretty nifty, right?

And everything was great—right up until this morning, when Iris decided to kill me.

"I have something I wish to discuss with you, my dear," Mary had started off with.

That's rarely a good sign. In my experience, when people just want to chat, they chat. When they want to share a joke, they tell the joke. When they want to compliment you on your amazing fashion sense and applaud your bold choice in wearing striped pants, a paisley shirt, a checked tie, and a herringbone vest— well, they apparently keep that to themselves.

But nobody ever says "I want to talk to you about something" and follows it with anything you really want to hear.

Naturally I immediately racked my brain for what this could be about. I was pretty sure she wasn't breaking up with me, not after this morning, and earlier this morning, and last night, and earlier last night, and yesterday afternoon, and before noon, and . . . hey, I may not be all musclebound and stuff but I've got stamina! Plus I'm pretty sure ducks rate a close second to dolphins when it comes to amorous intent, if you know what I mean.

So with that one blessedly off the table, I turned to smaller stuff. Leaving the toilet seat up? Naw, I'd been good about that one ever since I was a kid, on account of one sister and her penchant for swirlies when angered. I still shudder when I even hear the word "whirlpool," and just seeing one of those toilet cakes is enough to make me gag.

Snoring? Yeah, I definitely do that, but Mary knew that going in. Hey, I've got the bill of a duck, people! Not exactly designed for stealthy breathing! She says it isn't so bad, though, especially now. You know those machines people use? Yeah, they don't work for me, wrong construction, no lips and all that. But I found a makeshift solution. I modified a kazoo with a rubber band to hold it in place, and now at least when I do snore it's all musical!

I'm trying to figure out how to train myself to play "Only in your Dreams."

Eating with my mouth open? Again, no control there, sorry. Though straws and long-handled spoons have cut down on the mess a lot. And not tossing an entire box of crackers into my bill at once.

Not separating the reds and other bright colors in the wash?

I only did that once! Okay, maybe twice. Three times, max. But hey, I like tie-dye!

I still hadn't come up with anything when Mary took a deep breath—which immediately made me forget everything I'd been thinking up to that point, including my name and what day of the week it was—to continue.

"Iris—" I called out quickly. I figured if I got us breakfast that'd at least buy me some time.

But Mary knew better than to let me get another word in edgewise. "I believe it is time that I made the acquaintance of your maternal progenitor," she declared calmly but with that glint in her eye that said she was pretty well set on this.

Maternal progenitor? It took my brain a second to translate that one—I blame that deep breath, still—but then I got it. She wanted to meet my mother. "Just kill me now," I muttered, slumping at the mere thought of that titanic encounter.

And then, from overhead, came a voice I was about to dread even more than Mary's suggestion: "Order acknowledged," Iris confirmed.

And that's when one of my favorite driving CDs tried to take my head off.

"Iris, cut it out!" I yell from my place on the floor.

"Understood," she replies, and I hear the unmistakable sound of a drawer opening. Specifically, a kitchen drawer.

"Oh, come on!" I groan, lifting my head from my hands to shout up at the ceiling. "Really? Stop being so damn literal!"

"You ordered me to cut it out," she answers as servitrons come zooming at me with knives in their claws. "I must obey."

"Yeah?" I holler as I bound to my feet and dodge and swerve to avoid the darn things buzzing me with their blades. I think they're just trying to get even for all the times I ordered them to bring me "one semi-moist towelette" or "exactly one point two ounces of water, chilled to exactly fifty-eight degrees."

Yes, I get bored easily.

Still, I don't think that's a good enough reason to try dissecting me! Especially while I'm still alive!

And besides, those are dairy knives they're waving around.

Everybody knows that in a kosher household, poultry falls in the meat category!

"Stop trying to kill me!" I yell out. But if I thought the servitrons were just gonna stop their little kamikaze-surgery runs on the spot, well—ah, who'm I kidding? I know by now that it's never that easy.

"I am sorry," Iris informs me as calmly as if she's warning me that dinner might be a few minutes late—though admittedly, growing up, my mom didn't issue that kind of statement without first donning protective gear and preferably secluding herself in the bunker out back by the woodpile. We took our meals seriously in my house. "You have issued the command multiple times, in several variations. That makes it an imperative, which requires command-level access to countermand."

"Command level?" I grab a heavy book from the coffee table—one of Mary's, mine are mostly graphic novels—and belt the nearest servitron, sending it sailing backward and the knives flying from its claws. "I am your master and I command you! Isn't that enough?"

"Command-level access is strictly by direct manual input," Iris explains even as her servitrons line up for another go and more CDs pelt me and try to herd me into a corner. "This is to prevent unauthorized overrides."

"Manual input? Fine, you want manual input, you got manual input!" I shout. I leap over the coffee table, startling the servitrons enough that I'm able to bat two of them aside with the book, and charge through the gap. They all turn on me, of course, but I'm already past them and making a beeline for the door to the Matrix room. Because of course the house's main generator sits in an alcove off there, and that's where I'd plugged Iris in.

This is going to be fun—on the same level of "fun" as watching your own root canal in real-time, without anesthetic, as performed by an old blind man with palsy and a small blowtorch instead of a scalpel.

This is what I get for trying to make my life easier.

"Be careful, my love!" Mary calls out as I start my mad dash.

"Trying!" I call back. She seems to be staying put, which is definitely the smart thing to do. Iris is only trying to kill me, after all, but if Mary goes for the base unit Iris could interpret that as a direct threat, and I vaguely recall seeing something in the manual about a defensive mode. And that's the last thing I need, my house getting defensive. It's already murderous—now just add "condescending" and "high-maintenance" and it would fit in with most of my ex-girlfriends.

I'm almost out of the room when something slams into my right ankle hard enough to leave a bruise and to knock me sideways. "Hey, watch it!" I yelp automatically, before glancing down and realizing what happened.

I've been attacked, of course.

By my Roomba.

"Aw, not you too, buddy!" I moan as it reverses and comes at me again. Yep, it's under Iris's control. I can practically see its little red sensors narrowing with murderous glee.

Fortunately, I've had this little unit for a while now. I know its particular weaknesses. So I grab up a bunch of magazines and fling them in its "face"—then follow that by sweeping some cookie crumbs from the coffee table onto the floor and shoving the ottoman in its path.

It stops, unsure whether to continue attacking me or pick up the crumbs. It opts for the former, but first it has to stop and reroute around the ottoman, then pick its way carefully through the magazines.

By which point I've climbed atop the coffee table and leaped off it, on the other side of this particular mess. The Roomba whines like a penned puppy watching its master go, but there's nothing it can do—evidently Iris was able to override some of its programming to get it to try killing me, but not enough to make it ignore the obstacles it was hardwired to go around instead of over or through.

It's good to know I can still outthink a mindless cleaning device when I have to. Probably best not to expect a medal for that one, though.

It's a relief to step into the huge, football-stadium-like space that is the Matrix room, since nothing is actively trying to kill me here.

I mean, the servitrons are still pursuing me, sure, but none of the furniture or systems in here are linked up, so at least I don't have to worry about them. Then I step into the little alcove that holds the generator—

—and nearly keel over.

"What the hell?" I shout, and watch as my words puff out of my mouth in big gouts of frost. I'm shivering, and I can already feel my fingers and the tip of my bill going numb. It has to be subzero in here! I've been in meat lockers (don't ask—trust me, getting trapped in one of those with a hot date is a lot less fun than *Penthouse Letters* makes it sound, especially once you start worrying about frostbite and also learn that the whole "sticking to freezing metal" thing is real) that felt practically tropical compared to this! Taking a single step is like trying to march uphill through an instant blizzard when you were just caught out wearing only your swim trunks and a smile. (So I misread the forecast by a bit. At least it turns out webbed feet make excellent snowshoes.) But I've never been good at knowing when to quit—ask any of my former bosses—so I clamp my bill shut, narrow my eyes, and forge ahead.

"I know what you're up to!" I shout. "Trying to freeze me out! I should change your name from Iris to Clara—Crazily Literal Aggressive Residence App!" Another step. I can see the Iris base unit right where I left it, on the floor maybe two feet from the generator. It's all lit up, like the base of a holographic Christmas tree that's warming up before it starts projecting for real. But those lights look anything but warm to me. If it's possible for a bunch of little digital lights to glitter angrily, that's what these are doing.

"I am attempting to carry out your commands," Iris points out. "You requested that I kill you. I must obey."

"Your snark sensor is offline," I argue, managing another step. My feet are turning blue, and I'd bet under all these feathers my skin is doing the same. Good thing I'm always wearing the equivalent of a down jacket! Still, I'm pretty sure I can feel my eyeballs starting to freeze, and each breath is like downing a bucket of knives. I can't keep going much longer.

But it looks like I won't have to. I fall to my knees in front of the base unit, wincing and trying to ignore what sounds an awful lot like glass shattering. At least I'm now so numb I can't feel the pain. I grab up the unit and fumble for the little control panel on its back, but my fingers are so cold I can't get the thing to open. Why the heck did they design it like that? "Hey, let's include a panel for super-critical manual overrides, like if everything else has gone to hell and this is the only way to fix it—but let's make the whole panel about the size of a doll's cell phone and lock the lid down nice and tight so you'd really have to pry it open with a small crowbar in order to even get at the miniscule little keyboard that only a stunted fairy could hope to use."

And the really obnoxious part is, I bet whoever designed that part got a nice bonus, too, for keeping the whole thing so "sleek and unobtrusive." Next time just have a big red "Hit In Case of Murderous Rampage" button right on the top, please. That's going in my customer survey, you'd better believe it!

Except that the way my vision is starting to swim and black spots are starting to encroach on the edges, and my lungs are starting to ache and my heart's beginning to pound hollowly in my chest, I might not be around long enough to complete another survey.

So, you know, mixed blessing there.

I still have the unit in my hands, but I can't feel it there. And it's starting to look all hazy, and my head is starting to get real heavy. I mean, it's always heavy, but I'm having trouble keeping it up (my head, I mean. Will you quit?). I just want to lay down and take a quick nap, maybe a short siesta, possibly a little hibernation too, then I'll take care of this thing once and for all.

"Don't fall asleep, DuckBob!" I hear my wise inner voice say. "If you do, you won't ever wake up again!"

Only, that wise inner voice?

Sounds an awful lot like Mary. Which it never does—it's usually John Wayne or Al Pacino. Or, if I'm being totally honest, Pee Wee Herman. Not this time, though. This time it really sounds exactly like Mary.

And, judging by the lack of echo, it's possibly coming from somewhere outside my own head.

Which makes more sense, actually, because even my wise inner voice has always been a bit of a dumbass.

Then someone's shaking me. Someone whose perfume I know better than my own deodorant, though that's in part because I recently bought Infinitely Adaptable Antiperspirant—the scent changes to suit your mood! "Wake up, my love!" she urges. "Quickly!"

Between her voice and her obvious concern and her shaking me, I manage to stagger back to my feet. Then together we lurch out of the generator room, the base unit still clutched to my chest. The Matrix room feels like a sauna after that, and we both collapse gratefully onto the couch there and just lie there gasping for air and feeling our bodies start to warm back up from the outside in. I want to crawl into an oven and stay there until I'm nice and broiled—mmm, crispy duck!—but every minute we wait gives Iris more time to plan her next attack.

"Okay," I say after I've regained the power of speech and the feeling to my extremities. "Thanks. Now, how do we shut this thing off once and for all?" I wave the base unit at her.

But Mary shakes her head. "I do not know," she states. "You are the one who handled the setup. I have not read the manual. Can we simply deactivate it?"

I want to say yes but I'm pretty sure the answer's no, just like when Ma used to ask me if I'd been behaving. "I think," I answer slowly, my brain still a little on the frozen side, "that if I just pull the plug it'll short out. Which'd be fine except all of its little remote units'll fry too, and those could take all the house systems with them." Just like I said—never easy. "We need a way to cut her cord without killing the rest of the house."

Mary eyes me, that one eyebrow arching up again. "And do you have any idea how to go about this?" she asks, her lips curling up in a small, sweet smile. She knows me so well!

"I might," I admit. "It's dangerous. And stupid. And probably really dangerous and really stupid, if I stop and think about it too much. Which is why I'm not gonna." I heave myself to my feet. "Instead I'm just gonna do this." And, cupping my hands to my bill, I shout as loud as I can,

"Iris! I order you to terminate yourself immediately!"

Then, just to make sure that takes priority, I repeat: "Terminate, terminate, terminate!"

There's a pause, and I get worried. Can she act to protect herself from something like that too? Does she have some kind of "thou shalt not off thyself?" programming in place? Though you'd think that, if she did, "Thou shalt not off thy master, nor any other flesh-and-blood types in the near vicinity unless they're crazed killers about to murder people with a rusty pickaxe or a large chainsaw" would have been right up there, too. This is what I get for only skimming the manual and looking at the pictures. I keep arguing that manuals should be in the form of comic books. Those I'd read all the way through and probably be able to quote chapter and verse, too. Variant covers might be a bit much, though.

Finally, Iris responds. "Order acknowledged," she states, and I swear I can hear a hint of self-pity in her perfect voice. "Commencing self-termination in three, two, one . . ." And the device in my hand flashes once, then goes dark.

And all the house systems flicker and shudder and fall silent for just a second, then return.

"I think that did the trick," I tell Mary, collapsing back onto the couch with a heavy sigh. "I'll double-check soon as I can use my legs again, but it doesn't look like she shorted anything else out in her death throes. More like she did some kind of internal purge or something, then shut down." Just to be on the safe side, though, I set the base unit carefully off to one side.

"Then everything is back to normal, yes?" Mary asks, wrapping her arms around my neck. "This is very good. And it means we may return to our previously interrupted conversation."

I look longingly at the now dark and cold base unit, but Iris is done for, and no amount of wishing for a sudden, life-threatening distraction is going to bring her back.

And I can't even order a drink to drown my sorrows.

Iris clearly had terrible timing—that's going in my review!

As soon as I can figure out where she hid the colored pencils.

I think next time I'm just getting an old-fashioned British butler and calling it quits.

ABOUT THE AUTHORS

RUSS COLCHAMIRO is the author of the rollicking space adventure, *Crossline*, the hilarious sci-fi backpacking comedy series *Finders Keepers, Genius de Milo*, and *Astropalooza*, and is editor of the new anthology *Love, Murder & Mayhem*, all with Crazy 8 Press. Russ lives in New Jersey with his wife, two children, and crazy dog, Simon, who may in fact be an alien himself. Russ has also contributed to several other anthologies, including *Tales of the Crimson Keep, Pangaea, Altered States of the Union*, and *TV Gods 2*. He is now at work on a top-secret project and a *Finders Keepers* spin-off.

For more on *Astropalooza* and Russ's other tales, you can visit www.russcolchamiro.com, follow him on Twitter @AuthorDudeRuss, and 'like' his Facebook author page www.facebook.com/RussColchamiroAuthor.

MERIAH LYSISTRATA CRAWFORD is an associate professor at Virginia Commonwealth University, as well as a private investigator, writer, and editor. She has published short stories in several genres, a novella, essays, a variety of scholarly work, two poems, and co-edited the anthology *Trust and Treachery: Tales of Power and Intrigue*. Meriah has an MFA from the University of Southern Maine's Stonecoast MFA program, and a PhD from the Indiana University of Pennsylvania's Literature and Criticism program. Her work as a PI, spanning over fourteen years, has included investigations of shootings, murders, burglary, insurance fraud, backgrounds, counterfeit merchandise, patent infringement, and missing persons.

Writing under the pen name PAIGE DANIELS, Tina Closser is the author of the Non-Compliance trilogy: *The Sector, The Transition*, and *Equilibrium*, all through Krisell Ink. They are fast-paced science fiction/cyberpunk tales with elements of humor and romance and a strong heroine that explore different themes such as family, government control, and how one seemingly insignificant person can make a difference. Feel free to contact her at: http://www.goodreads.com/PaigeDaniels, www.facebook.com/paigedanielsauthor, and www.twitter.com/TClosser.

PETER DAVID is a prolific author whose career, and continued popularity, spans nearly two decades. He has worked in every conceivable media and acquired followings in all of them. He has written more a hundred novels, including numerous appearances on the *New York Times* Bestsellers lists. He is the co-creator and author of the bestselling *Star Trek: New Frontier* series for Pocket Books. His comic book resume includes an award-winning—some would say "legendary"—twelve-year run on Marvel's *The Incredible Hulk*. Peter is also the co-creator, with popular science fiction icon Bill Mumy (of *Lost in Space* and *Babylon 5* fame) of the Cable Ace Award-nominated science fiction series *Space Cases*, which ran for two seasons on Nickelodeon. He lives in New York with his wife, Kathleen, and their daughter, Caroline.

MARY FAN is the author of several sci-fi/fantasy books about intrepid heroines, most recently *Starswept*, a YA sci-fi romance about classical music and telepathic aliens. She is also the author of the Jane Colt space opera/cyberpunk trilogy, the Firedragon YA dystopia/fantasy novellas, and the Fated Stars YA high fantasy novellas. In addition, she is the co-editor of the Brave New Girls sci-fi anthologies about girls in science and engineering, proceeds of which are donated to the Society of Women Engineers scholarship fund. Chevonne and Sherlock also appear in *Brave New Girls: Stories of Girls Who Science and Scheme* and the standalone novella *The Adventure of the Silicon Beeches*. Find Mary online at www.MaryFan.com.

MICHAEL JAN FRIEDMAN is the author of 76 books, nearly half of which are set somewhere in the wilds of the *Star Trek* universe.

He has also written for television, radio, and comic books. His novelization of *Batman & Robin* was, for a time, the #1 bestseller in Poland (really). You can follow Mike on Twitter @FriedmanMJ; on Facebook (Michael Jan Friedman), or on his website, Michael-JanFriedman.net.

ROBERT GREENBERGER is a writer and editor. He has worked for Starlog Press (where he created *Comics Scene*, the first nationally distributed magazine to focus on comic books, comic strips, and animation), DC Comics, Marvel Comics, *Weekly World News*, *Famous Monsters of Filmland*, ComicMix.com, and is a founding member of Crazy 8 Press. His dozens of books, short stories, and essays include *Hellboy II: The Golden Army*, for which he won the IAMTW's Scribe Award, and *The Further Adventures of Sherlock Holmes: Murder at Sorrow's Crown*, co-written with Steven Savile. He is a member of the Science Fiction Writers of America and the International Association of Media Tie-In Writers, and holds a Master of Science in Education from the University of Bridgeport and a Master of Arts in Creative Writing & Literature for Educators from Fairleigh Dickinson University. He can found at bobgreenberger.com and @bobgreenberger.

GLENN HAUMAN is uniquely qualified to be in this book, as his love life is mayhem and he's soon to be murdered.

He also writes, edits, colors comics, designs websites, designs books, performs marriages, reaches things on high shelves, changes lightbulbs, bats right, sings baritenor, snores loud, draws to inside straights, drinks too much DMD, and stays up way too late at night. Having come to the grisly realization that the *New York Observer* called him a "young Turk of publishing" two decades ago, he now patiently awaits the sweet embrace of death. He is looking ahead to being killed by many contributors to this book with a candlestick, knife, lead pipe, revolver, rope, and wrench.

You can find out more at Glennhauman.com or by looking at his Wikipedia page. No, really, someone wrote up an entry for him. He can't believe it either.

PAUL KUPPERBERG is the author of the mystery novel *The Same Old Story* and short story collection, *In My Shorts: Hitler's Bellhop and Other Stories* (Crazy 8 Press), and more than two dozen other books of fiction and non-fiction for all ages, including the humor book *Jew-Jitsu: The Hebrew Hands of Fury* (soon to be re-released by Crazy 8 Press), and the GLAAD Media Award nominated YA novel *Kevin* (Grosset & Dunlap), featuring the first gay character in the Archie Comics universe. He has also contributed to anthologies from Pocket Books, Titan, Ace, HarperCollins, Warner, Bantam, DAWS, and Moonstone and has written more than 1,000 comic books and newspaper comic strips for DC Comics, Archie Comics, Charlton Neo Comics (http://morttodd.com/charlton.html), and others. You can follow him at PaulKupperberg.com and on Facebook and Twitter.

KARISSA LAUREL lives in North Carolina with her kid, her husband, the occasional in-law, and a very hairy husky named Bonnie. Some of her favorite things are coffee, chocolate, and super heroes. She can quote *The Princess Bride* verbatim. On weekends you can find her at flea markets hunting for rusty things to re-use and re-purpose. She is the also the author of The Norse Chronicles, an adult urban fantasy series based on Norse mythology; and The Stormbourne Chronicles, a young adult fantasy series.

Born and raised in Southern Delaware, KELLY MEDING discovered Freddy Krueger at a very young age, which forged a lifelong obsession with horror, science fiction, and all things paranormal. She writes the Dreg City urban fantasy series, as well as the Metawars original superhero series. As Kelly Meade she writes the Cornerstone Run trilogy. You can find Kelly on Twitter (@KellyMeding), Pinterest (http://pinterest.com/kellymeding/), her website (http://www.kellymeding.com/), blog Organized Chaos (http://chaostitan.blogspot.com/), and on Facebook.

AARON ROSENBERG is the author of the best-selling DuckBob SF comedy series, the *Dread Remora* space-opera series, and, with David Niall Wilson, the O.C.L.T. occult thriller series. His tie-in work contains novels for *Star Trek*, *Warhammer*, *World of*

WarCraft, Stargate: Atlantis, Shadowrun, Exalted, and *Eureka*. He has written short stories (such as the Sidewise-nominated "Let No Man Put Asunder"), children's books (including the award-winning *Bandslam: The Junior Novel* and the #1 best-selling *42: The Jackie Robinson Story*), educational books, and roleplaying games (including the Origins Award-winning *Gamemastering Secrets*). He is a founding member of Crazy 8 Press. You can follow him online at gryphonrose.com, on Facebook at facebook.com/gryphonrose, and on Twitter @gryphonrose.

HILDY SILVERMAN is the publisher of *Space and Time*, a fifty-year-old magazine featuring fantasy, horror, and science fiction (spaceandtimemagazine.com). She is also the author of several works of short fiction, including "The Darren" (2009, *Witch Way to the Mall?*, Friesner, ed), "Sappy Meals" (2010, *Fangs for the Mammaries*, Friesner, ed), "The Bionic Mermaid Returns" (2014, *With Great Power*, French, ed.), "The Great Chasm" (co-authored w/David Silverman, 2016, *Altered States of the Union*, Hauman, ed.), and "A Scandal in the Bloodline" (2017, *Baker Street Irregulars*, Ventrella & Maberry, eds.). In 2013, she was a finalist for the WSFA Small Press Award for her story, "The Six Million Dollar Mermaid" (*Mermaids 13*, French, ed). In the "real" world, she is a Marketing and PR Specialist at Sivantos, Inc.

LOIS SPANGLER is a Mexican-American ex-pat currently living in the antipodes. Some of her stage works have been performed in New York City, and her short fiction has appeared in *ReDeus: Native Lands* and will be appearing in works produced by Tiny Owl Workshop. When she's not at her day job or tooling around doing narrative design research, she's likely trading stabs and cuts with friends using centuries-old sword manuals, and occasionally translating bits of those manuals for folks to use.

PATRICK THOMAS is the award-winning author of the beloved Murphy's Lore series and the darkly hilarious Dear Cthulhu advice empire, which includes the collections *What Would Cthulhu Do?*, *Cthulhu Knows Best, Have A Dark Day*, and *Good Advice For Bad People*. His more than thirty-five books include *Exile & Entrance*;

a slew of urban fantasies that include *By Darkness Cursed*, *Fairy With A Gun*, *Fairy Rides The Lightning*, *Dead To Rites*, *Rites of Passage*, *Lore & Dysorder*; the steampunk themed *As The Gears Turn* and the science-fantasy space adventures *Constellation Prize* and *Startenders*. He co-writes the Mystic Investigators paranormal mystery series and The Assassins' Ball, a traditional mystery, with John L. French. A number of his books were part of the props department of the *CSI* television show and one was even thrown at a suspect. His Soul For Hire story "Act of Contrition," included in *Greatest Hits*, has been made into a short film by Top Men Productions. Drop by www.patthomas.net to learn more.

www.ingramcontent.com/pod-product-compliance
Lightning Source LLC
Chambersburg PA
CBHW070840250626
47159CB00003B/868